TWENTY-NINE AND A HALF

EVA PHILLIPS

For Chris

PART ONE

2015

"It is not the strongest of the species that survive, not the most intelligent, but the one most responsive to change."

Charles Darwin

1

FRIDAY, 15 MAY

LONDON

I took a deep breath and let a citrus aroma fill my nostrils – it felt just like my favourite body lotion with orange and bergamot. I rested my head on the back seat of the truly Exec Uber car, stroked the red velvet on which I was sitting and closed my eyes. *I love my life. This is going to be one of the best weekends of my life! More than that! It's the beginning of the rest of my life,* I thought and my heart skipped a beat. It was a half-hour journey to the airport and I'd have probably spent the entire time dreaming if not for Henry who suddenly yawned really loudly, coughed once but so violently I thought he'd spit his lungs out and then as an encore blew his nose. We exchanged glances and I knew immediately what he was going to say when we got out of the taxi – he was allergic to the air-freshener, which I also knew was not the truth, he just never slept well before a flight and his throat was dry and squeezed from fear. He was looking out of the window, and I thought he was also nervous whether everything would go according to the plan during this weekend – he was a true perfectionist. I felt a sudden urge to hold his hand but the limo was so wide, with the largest armrest I'd ever seen, that I didn't even try. Instead, I reached for a chocolate from a crystal bowl resting on the armrest. I couldn't decide what to choose

– I frantically turned each Belgian chocolate wrapped individually in shiny paper to read their description: cherry vodka, caramel delight or heavenly minty treat. I tried them all. Henry looked at me as if I was killing somebody. Was he thinking what I was thinking – that I was killing my slim waist? No, he could not. Not today. I was impressed with the taxi and happy that normally thrifty-Henry didn't try to save money, but then it was such a special weekend. *Oh, it's so wonderful and exciting, I can't wait...* I was thinking until I hit my head on my way out of the limo. *Was it a sign?* I wondered months later.

"What a rip-off," Henry murmured angrily, looking at his phone. "I didn't have a choice to get a different car. I booked a normal taxi last night only to have a call today, five minutes before they were supposed to be arriving, that they'd doubled booked their cars!" I understood he was afraid of flying and needed to vent, but my heart sunk a bit.

"Oh," I sighed. "As John Lennon once said, *Life is what happens while you are busy making other plans.*" It was just a shame that I had to tell myself exactly the same just a couple of hours later.

* * *

"Olivia! Oh no... the weather... so ridiculous," despite my best efforts I couldn't entirely understand Henry while he was walking towards me and shouting something from a distance.

"Can you believe it?" he asked when he finally materialised in front of me.

"No, I can't believe that you're screaming your lungs out at the whole terminal," I snapped irritated.

"But nobody's heard anything. It's too loud."

"Well, neither have I!"

"I thought... oh never mind..." he waved his hand in front of my face as if he'd wanted to get rid of a fly. "Our flight has been delayed for at least an hour, all because of the bloody fog," he said, his hands and voice trembling.

"Easy Henry, we won't go until it's safe to fly. Where is our check-in?"

"Yyy… They haven't announced it yet," he said through his clenched teeth.

"Really?" I asked mercifully. "Or have you been so fixated on the weather conditions that you've just forgotten to check?"

"I'm not fixated on anything. The check-in is also going to be late, they've got problems with their computers."

"I just hope that you're not doing this because you found out last night that you can go to Madrid by high-speed train. Darling…" I started gently, "we don't have that much time, we're only going there for one weekend."

"Don't be ridiculous!" he snapped. "Who do you think I am?"

"Fine! I need some coffee but maybe we should wait here until we know where check-in is…" I was thinking out loud.

"Brilliant idea, I'll bring you some coffee then," he said unusually enthusiastic and before I managed to tell him I wanted a large latte Henry was briskly walking away and mumbling to himself, "and I'll have a quick look outside at the current situation with the clouds and the fog."

I wished he had helped me first to move our luggage to a more waiting friendly zone. I was standing outside the toilets, accompanied by the roaring sound of hand dryers, and a snaking queue for security. It also happened to be the place that many people seemed to choose for their emotional time-to-say-goodbye.

"Will you remember me? Will you?" A tall slim woman was crying her eyes out talking to a man, whose head barely reached her chin.

"Time flies. I don't know where the week has gone," an elderly woman was saying to her son in a breaking voice.

"I miss you already," said a Polish man to his wife as he was struggling to escape her embrace. From what I understood he was working in Swindon and for some reason she could not move there to live with him.

The atmosphere was getting gradually more and more depressing and clearly it was not going to get any better – everybody had already been or were about to be left alone – and Henry's frightened face was nowhere to be seen on the horizon. When he finally showed up after half an hour his shaky hand presented me with a brown paper mug, "Here you are," he said shaking but proud, as if had had to fight to the death to get the last coffee beans in the world. If it weren't for the plastic lid I wouldn't have expected more than half of its contents to have made it back.

As I'd predicted Henry only bought himself a small bottle of still water. He would never dare to drink any caffeine before a flight – in his mind caffeine mixed with fear would dangerously raise his blood pressure. Obviously, the bottle of water was the smallest one that he could get – he wouldn't want to put himself in danger by leaving his seat too often during the flight for something as trivial and unnecessary as going to the toilet.

"Gosh, you disappeared off radar," I said without much thought.

"You and your stupid jokes!" exploded Henry.

"It wasn't meant to be a joke darling," I said calmly. "Please don't read between the lines," I was trying to smile but I was struggling.

Joking about flying with Henry? Phi! Never ever again! A year before, during our flight to Turkey, Henry was whinging as usual – but even more so. I could not stand all the questions starting from "is it normal that..." and ending with "it's so bouncy... bumpy... jumpy... shaky... something is so loud... we're floating so high above the runway... or so low above the sea..." Holy moly guacamole – how could I possibly know? I'm not a pilot and I've never aspired to be one – although I did dream about marrying one when I was a teenager. When my patience ran out I finally said, "I've no idea whether it's normal or abnormal, but one thing is certain – if we die, we die together. Isn't it damn romantic?"

I had to deal with the side effects of the joke for the rest of our holiday. When it comes to flying Henry had never had any sense of humour. To be fair a sense of humour is not one of his strongest traits, but nobody is perfect. Henry is handsome, kind, intelligent, educated and well read, he has a good job and likes dogs – there're some attributes that can make up for something like the lack of a sense of humour.

"The flight has been delayed again but the check-in desks are open now. We're going to thirty-six," he said suddenly and took my luggage.

What a gentleman, I thought walking through the busy terminal only with Henry's hand luggage, which as usual seemed to have nothing inside but a toothbrush. *A sense of humour is massively overrated and has no practical use like, for example, the eagerness to always carry my bags,* I thought proudly.

"I'll leave you here for a moment," he said when we finally stood in the queue to our check-in. "It's all moving incredibly slowly anyway and all the luggage is on wheels so—"

"You're kidding me," I said putting my hands on my hips and staring straight into his eyes.

"I need to go to the loo," he said and walked away quickly.

There I was – alone again!

"I'm going to be late for my meeting again! Fuck the low-cost airlines!" a man in an incredibly well fitted suit was shouting into his mobile in the queue before me.

"Sure, the airlines must have created artificial fog in the hope of selling more last-minute tickets," I said to a woman standing just behind me."

She crossed her arms murmuring, "I wouldn't be surprised if that was the truth."

Why? Why can't I just stop myself from chatting to people? Why can't I be like most of the passengers on the London tube? They can be squeezed together like sardines and still able to pretend they're on the train alone only with their newspapers and smartphones. Truly remarkable and admirable!

Soon after three babies started crying simultaneously as if they had been acting in collusion. Then a group of teenagers started whinging about the British weather, low-cost airlines and their too early morning flight. I yawned thinking that indeed it would be nice to fly a few hours later. It wasn't even seven o'clock! But Henry always liked to save on his plane tickets. He claimed that irrespective of the time of day, the size of the seat or the meal served on board he wouldn't enjoy any journey in the sky in a million years. Shame that it didn't cross his mind that all those details could make my journey better – or at least more bearable while dealing with his fear of flying. I didn't know what was worse – looking at his green face and shaky hands or watching him running in panic around the airport anticipating the worst.

I was two families and one businessman away from the check-in desk. *Please Henry show up now and then everything will get better* – I kept repeating it in my head like a mantra while looking frantically around the terminal and having no idea from which side Henry could suddenly appear. I just wanted to get through the security check so I could take the deep breath of a relieved woman, whose boyfriend is now trapped in a departure lounge and can't run away, at least without causing significant inconvenience to himself. I was visualising Henry buying herbal pills for his stressed head, lavender balm and a pair of anti-DVT socks. Henry was only thirty-four and our flight was only planned to last a couple of hours – but I wouldn't dare to question his purchases as long as it would contribute to minimizing the chances of a nervous breakdown.

I was one family and one businessman away from the check-in desk and there was still no trace of Henry. It wouldn't be the first time I had to let a group of people check in before us. I was hoping that the two-hour flight didn't fit into the category of I-am-puking-my-fears-into-the-loo. I reached into the pocket of my tight navy jean skirt for my mobile. *Pick up, please pick up* Henry – I kept thinking but the whole Henry-whispering wasn't working at all. I was so angry, but I was also sorry for him and grateful that despite the fact that my boyfriend hated travelling by plane, he was still prepared to do it for me.

Exactly, my boyfriend and still only My Boyfriend! Since most of my close girlfriends got married the word *boyfriend* was pinching my arse like a too tight thong during a quick walk.

"How long have you been with Henry? Four years? Five?" my gran Betty asked me a few weeks ago during one of our monthly phone conversations.

Gran Betty, age eighty-five, has never ever had any problems with her memory – except for two little things – firstly, how long I had been with Henry and secondly, how old I was.

"And how old are you now darling? Thirty, thirty-one? Please excuse my poor memory," she said sounding all innocent and nonchalant.

"I'm twenty-nine and a half," I said trying not to sound angry.

Maybe it would be easier to have no pants at all instead of having pants that constantly pinch you – I considered this while waiting for Henry to show up at check-in. *At least nobody would mention the word 'marriage' and everybody would be thrilled each time I went out for a date.*

It was such luck that two weeks ago I found my diamond ring! If not for that grand discovery I would have had to seriously mull over taking further steps, which in practice would mean:

1. Set an official deadline for Henry to pop the question (not my style)
2. Leave Henry and wait for another Mr Right (more likely but still difficult with gran Betty's deadlines…)

Luckily, I did not have to take any such steps because once upon a time… or on one beautiful day when my Boyfriend was asleep on our double sofa… As luck would have it, he fell asleep with his laptop open on his lap! The story could have just finished at the moment I shut down the computer and covered my Boyfriend with a blanket thinking how sweet he looked when he was asleep. However, when I clicked on the computer to switch it off – Henry's email account shone from the screen asking for some attention. Here was the one in a million opportunity. All of my friends had done it at least once. *My time has come!* – I thought excited although not without a trace of guilt. *Trust but check* – that was one of the mottos of Atlanta, one of my best friends.

When I saw a confirmation of a reservation for a flight to Madrid my world stopped – *a secret escape with a lover?* Then I quickly read that it was booked for the special Friday, which Henry had asked me to take off. *He's really listening to what I'm saying to him* – I was thinking. *He knew how much I wanted to go there* – I was whispering trying to stop myself from making some joyful squeaks.

I was so thrilled that it was the first and the last email that I managed to check. Even if I wanted to continue I made further reading impossible for myself by accidently dropping the laptop on the floor with a bang. Henry woke up abruptly and to my horror he quickly realised the reason of my simultaneous happiness and panic. He didn't look particularly disappointed with me destroying the surprise, he was just glad that the laptop was *safe and sound* and had not suffered from my *great invigilation.*

Soon after when I met with my two girlfriends, Freya and Atlanta, in order to discuss the Madrid email – my excitement turned into an utter euphoria. They both decided that *the Moment* had finally come. Like me they had an unusual gift for destroying surprises. As soon as they had left mine and Henry's flat – the search began.

"Ha! I've got it!" I shouted swinging on a ladder leant against wall high bookshelves.

On the highest shelf behind the History of the English Language I found a tiny blue velvet box, which fitted perfectly in the palm of my hand. *After I made such effort it would be a crime not to look inside* – I thought and ta-da – a few seconds later I was trying a diamond ring on my finger, and it fitted me as if it was made for me! No wonder – Henry was such a perfectionist.

I ruined my surprise, but every cloud has a silver lining – at least I could prepare myself for the special occasion. *I'm going to have the best spontaneously taken photos from my engagement day in the whole history of Facebook and Instagram!* – I was thinking while getting down from the ladder. If anybody wondered why I had a twenty-kilo luggage for a weekend city trip – my answer was – I was going to become engaged. I needed a few smart outfits for every possible occasion. I wasn't going to be surprised and caught badly dressed or make-up-less!

Unfortunately, the downside of the event was the absolute must of wearing high heels for the whole weekend. I couldn't risk my legs looking short for my engagement photos. I also packed one kilo of blister plasters and a few pairs of stylish flip flops to wear after Henry finally popped the question. I was hoping that Madrid in May wasn't going to be pan-fried hot so I wouldn't look red and sweaty.

I was letting another family go past me in the check-in queue when Henry finally arrived without a word of apology.

"Could you pass me my luggage please?" he asked while unsuccessfully stretching his arm to hold the handle of his plastic black bag, which I had placed behind me.

"Henry, my darling, we don't have to put it in the hold. The hand luggage goes with us," I explained while smiling gently.

"Olivia, you don't understand. I can't fly," he said sternly.

Oh heaven! My worst nightmares have finally come true. Henry has panicked and our holiday is going to be ruined! How can a grownup man be so ridiculous?

Our thousand and one airport adventures have taught me one thing – staying calm to the very end. Even the prospect of my surprise proposal was about to sink, I had to try and play to the very end.

"I know you can't fly, that's why we're using the aircraft to fly us over," I said sweetly and gently like to a two-year old.

"Very funny," he snapped.

"Darling I beg you don't be silly and don't make a scene. From the statistical point of view a plane is the safest mode of transport," I whispered to him.

"Do you have a problem?" I heard a male voice behind me.

"Please go first," I replied sweetly to a bald guy in his sixties. "We need to make sure I haven't packed a sharp nail file in my hand luggage," I decided to put the blame on me to support Henry even further.

"Women," gasped the man rolling his eyes and smiling meaningfully to Henry.

"I'm not afraid of flying… I mean… I am…" Henry was saying through his clenched teeth.

"You've flown already so many freaking times. Darling... Honey... Sweetie don't do it to me," I begged him while wondering whether I had enough patience to go through it without slapping him on his face.

"I'm not afraid," he was saying stubbornly but with no confidence.

"So what's the matter?"

"I mean I'm scared and I decided not to destroy your holiday and... I'm going to attend a course for people who have a fear of flying and... you can take a break from me in Spain..."

"I understand," I said still calmly but more and more afraid I would suddenly angrily explode, "I really get you but... But have you suddenly stopped breathing?" I yelled. "Because I'm worried that what you're experiencing now might be brain damage from oxygen starvation!"

"You see Olivia, we don't understand each other anymore," he said distressed, his hands at his throat.

Brain damage due to oxygen starvation – that must be it!

"Henry keep calm, inhale and exhale, inhale and exhale... It's going to be all right..."

"It's going to be all right, all right..." a teenage ginger boy was singing as he pushed himself in front of us in the queue while I was demonstrating to Henry what I had learnt during my yoga classes.

"Olivia, I must let you go," Henry eventually got his voice back.

"You let me what? What an idiotic thing to say considering you're a university lecturer in linguistics!"

"Fine, if you prefer it that way," he sighed, "I'm leaving you Olivia. We just don't work anymore."

A lovely family of five was just about to witness my brief moment of emotional breakdown"

"Seriously? Or is there a part of your head that has suddenly stopped working?" I was screaming my lungs out like a lunatic.

"Do we have a problem?" a wide-shouldered bodyguard appeared out of nowhere.

"Why is everybody asking me that today?" I said calmly but still shaking.

"If you don't want to leave the airport with my assistance, please behave," said the bodyguard.

"I have my reasons," I whispered and added more confidently, "that man…" I pointed at Henry, "doesn't dream about anything else than leaving me… I mean leaving the airport. And I'm not going to stand in his way."

Both Mr Wide-shoulders and Henry looked at me pathetically. Then Henry threw a quick "I'm sorry" glance, and disappeared among the crowds at the terminal.

"Have you packed yourself? Do you have any of these things in your hand luggage?" a round-faced blond woman was pointing out pictures of knives, pistols, grenades and other items of non-everyday use.

"Nope. Nothing."

"No nail files, hmm?"

"No nail files," I replied grumpily, imagining Henry with a nail file stabbed between his two surprised eyes.

The woman asked me a few other questions while not taking her eyes away from her computer. I could have probably used somebody else's passport and she would not have noticed.

After the longest and the most emotional check-in in my entire life I headed outside of the terminal to take in some of the non-fresh air. This was also the first time in my life when I regretted I didn't smoke – at least I would know what to do with myself then. Maybe other smokers would approach me to light their cigarettes and we would begin a casual conversation on how truly shit the day had already started.

Standing outside of the North Terminal at Gatwick I was staring blankly at people getting out of their cars and taxis. I could not spot a single person travelling on their own. *Life is a bitch* – I thought looking at happy families and couples in love, or at least making good impressions of being in love. To feel better I reached into my handbag for a melting chocolate bar – and as soon as I did I heard a deep male voice say to me:

"You can't smoke outside the terminal,"

"There're some people smoking there but—"

"Because that's a smoking zone. Anybody who smokes here will pay a fine."

I could swear that on that day all men were conspiring against me. Besides they were all nuts.

"I'm not smoking, I'm going to eat..." I waved to him with the chocolate bar still sealed in its red wrapping, "you bloody melon."

"The fine for offending a policeman is even higher than the one for smoking," smirked the guy with his hands in his pockets.

"Yeah? So find *melon* on a list of offensive words, you bloody melon," I snapped walking back inside the terminal.

Soon after security I found myself in a state of shop frenzy, buying tons of chocolate treats, a large bottle of chocolate-flavoured Baileys, sweet smelling perfumes and fruit scented hand creams – everything that Henry hated and I loved. I also hoped that one of the other advantages of travelling solo would be having two seats for myself – me next to the aisle and my tiny handbag occupying the middle seat. Henry would never book a window seat – he wanted to have unobstructed access to an emergency exit. Tough luck! As I was fastening my seatbelt, a young mother of twin boys asked me whether I would be so kind to let one of her little ones sit next to the aisle. I had no other choice but share the middle seat with my handbag, while the family of four was happily taking four seats across the aisle and exacerbating my misery.

"You see, I told you that there was no need to pay to book the seats," whispered the father of the family with a massive grin to his clearly relieved wife.

Of course, why would you? – I thought and set a pair of angry eyes at my private TV screen, which was probably going to be the only nice surprise of the day. At the very last minute they had changed us onto an aircraft that seemed brand new and equipped with personal screens. As soon as we had taken off I was desperate to find a film about some wizards, vampires, aliens or Snow White – literally anything that would temporarily help me to take off from my miserable reality.

I could only fantasise, however, about having a minute's break from all the freaking-annoying men of this world. The twins' parents were fully absorbed in typing something on their laptops while their untamed sons-of-a-devil were playing with their seatbelts and screaming like wild animals. Sometimes I wondered whether all parents were naturally deaf in relation to their own children. Besides, my crazy beating heart and painfully pulsating head were additionally stimulated by the latte with a double espresso shot. Henry was right to keep away from the coffee before a flight.

"Can I have a chocolate muffin and a large glass of red wine?" I said to a stewardess when she asked if I would like anything from her trolley.

"Excuse me, could you not drink alcohol next to my children?" the mother of twins suddenly got her hearing and voice back.

I immediately regretted being "so kind" and letting her "little one" anywhere near me.

"Sure. Can I have some vodka… I mean some water please?" I said to the stewardess who gave me a merciful look.

The mother of the twins lost her voice again and didn't even thank me before returning to her laptop. I started to enjoy my muffin but not even a minute had passed before the almost identical little monsters started throwing cookies, colourful jellies and some bits of chocolate at each other. *My world is collapsing and nobody gives a flying fuck* – I thought. *Somebody needs to do something.*

"If you don't stop that ridiculous noise right now…" I scowled at the twins, "and if one of your chocolaty hands touches my skirt ever again – I'm going to open the window and throw you outside. Do you know how quickly it takes a four-year-old to hit the ground from thirty-thousand feet?"

Damn the stress-less upbringing. It clearly doesn't work! I thought irritated.

The little man, who was sharing my left armrest, looked at me through his too big for such a small head glasses and said completely deadpan, "I'm sorry madam. Please accept my apology and don't be angry with us anymore. We promise to be good now."

The sudden and totally unexpected silence even took aback the father of the kids, who decided to reward his sons' good behaviour with another portion of cookies and jellies. *Wait... I've seen this guy before at the airport* – I thought staring at the father probably too much as he gave me a couple of cookies too. Then I remembered. I saw the whole family out the front of the terminal during the chocolate bar fiasco. No wonder the children were so agitated and unsettled – they were victims of pushchair abuse. I had always been against using pushchairs where one child has to sit behind the other one and is forced to stretch their neck to see more than just the bum of their sibling. *The poor boys are the victims of badly designed pushchairs. It's not their fault,* I thought. I started wondering whether Henry could have had a similar pram, that would explain a lot. I then reminded myself he had been an only child so he was just a dick.

Less than a moment later I became victim to my own mascara. The whole situation wasn't as banal as it seemed to be – one of my contact lenses and a heavily painted eyelash were painfully digging into my left eye. Rubbing the eye and producing needed tears didn't help at all so I had to queue for the toilet with mascara smudged around my eye.

"Why would you need any make-up so early in the morning and for a flight on a cheap airline? Don't you prefer to sleep a little bit longer?" Henry asked a few hours before in our bathroom, our flat, our life... He was so incredibly annoying but I couldn't help missing him.

"Because I like it and enjoy every moment of it," I lied, as nobody could possibly like painting their face at five o'clock in the morning, touching their sore sleepy eyes with some black ink.

I was only doing it because it crossed my mind that Henry might propose on the aircraft if he freaked out during turbulence and anticipating certain death decided to pull the ring out of his pocket. Or he could have selfishly asked the pilot to propose for him to distract himself from his fear of flying.

There was also another issue. During every flight Henry was entirely focused on every movement of the plane and every sound on-board. He was in a permanent state of alarm and he would never notice something as trivial as me not having make-up. I was sure that, however, he would spot all the make-up and no-make-up differences the moment we landed in Madrid. I had already experienced it once when we were getting out of a plane in Turkey a couple of years ago, "Gosh, you look so tired and pale Olivia. Maybe that's the dry air on the aircraft. And you've got quite big shadows under your eyes. Do you want to see yourself in the mirror?"

My look was more influenced by getting up at three in the morning and limiting my morning routine to cleaning my teeth but I decided to let it go.

When I finally got to the claustrophobic plastic toilet and managed to move my hand towards my tired eyes, the plane started going through some turbulence. During the last five years with Henry and our numerous flights his nightmare about experiencing turbulence in the loo had never come true. I had never been particularly bothered by bumpy flights but now it was as bloody annoying as a stewardess seemed to be ready to break down the toilet door to drag me out of there. Fortunately, my eyelash came out on my cheek and we both could get back to my seat. The turbulence was getting worse, which made my little friends giggle and caused their mother some vomit reflexes. Too big glasses on one of the twins' noses were jumping higher and higher which he found a constant source of amusement. Henry used to always fly with his glasses but he had never been sure whether it was a better alternative to contact lenses. He was afraid that in case of any emergency his glasses could have been smashed or lost and then he would have to look for an emergency exit half-blind. On the other hand, contact lenses wouldn't last more than a few days on his eyes and it would pose other difficulties when the plane crashed on the sea or in a jungle.

Henry, Henry, Henry... There wasn't anything that wouldn't make me think about him, and every thought of him caused me physical pain – overwhelming and relentless pain, which didn't respond to any medication. The constant thinking about him was like: one glass of champagne too many, making me both sick and dizzy, too sweet chocolate causing me terrible indigestion, a song that has been played so many times that it finally became unbearable, or the sun that was stubbornly glaring into my eyes and causing me a migraine. All I wanted was to get rid of the pain and never again let anybody hurt me so much.

The sky above Madrid that morning was perfectly blue, and there was not a single cloud to destroy the picture. Nothing was obviously wrong – the world refused to cry its eyes out with me. The universe did not care in the slightest about what had just happened. I was soaked to the skin, but not because of rain. I was sweating from lifting too heavy bags. *Henry you bastard! At least if you had dumped me a few hours earlier I could have offloaded a few things – it is truly inhuman to carry so much weight.*

2

FRIDAY, 15 MAY

MADRID

"It became clear to me I was single when after two years of being repressed I eventually took full and unlimited control over my TV remote," said Atlanta once, one of my best friends, after she broke up with a boyfriend. "Initially it was really weird to be allowed to control your own TV, with nobody questioning or commenting on your choices. You can go to make yourself a cup of tea and return to watching the same channel that you had chosen a few minutes before. I mean… Wow! Just wow."

"The moment when you realise that you can read your book till one o'clock in the morning and nobody is going to whinge about switching off the light," said another friend to me after her boyfriend slept with somebody else's girlfriend. "The moment when you only put healthy food into your trolley and you know that nobody will moan that there's nothing to eat in the fridge. Priceless!"

The time when it really hit me that I was single again didn't offer me the sweet sensation of being free, released from captivity or no longer feeling oppressed by a man. In contrast, I was struggling to detect any potential benefits of being just-dumped-at-nearly-thirty-years-old. I only felt lost and abandoned.

I didn't spend much time in the hotel that Henry had booked for us but I had a quick look around my room and the lobby before I headed for a lonely lunch. To my surprise the hotel turned out to be posher and lusher than I could have ever expected from Henry the-travel-scrooge. *Maybe he did plan to propose and panicked at the last minute* – it crossed my mind but I quickly chastised myself for being so naive.

I had no intention of sitting alone in a restaurant so I went inside the first coffee shop where there were no people queuing outside. It didn't mean, however, that there weren't plenty of people queuing on the inside. Exhausted from standing for twenty minutes in my high-heels I managed to finally make my order. My panini with some grilled vegetables and a large cup of latte both got cold before I managed to combat the next hurdle of finding a spare chair. I missed somebody who could stand in the queue while I was looking for our seats. Men were truly designed for such activities like queueing – they have bigger feet and wear flat shoes! I felt like having another panini and going to the toilet but neither simple wish could come true without losing my precious chair. Again, I needed Henry and he wasn't there.

Henry obviously had no clue he booked our trip at the time as the San Isidro Festival or he wasn't aware of how important the event was. Everywhere I went there were herds of people, who were mostly wearing traditional Spanish outfits. It looked like the whole popula-tion of Spain decided to go to Madrid to bump into each other throughout its streets and make a hell of a noise with their loud laughter and constant chatting. There was also the risk of being knocked down by somebody's hands widely gesticulating during one of their enthusiastic conversations. Henry hated crowds and would never deliberately expose himself to such an unpleasant experience like a large city festival. In contrast, I always loved being surrounded by people, especially when it was linked to a grand event. Crowds often provided me with a significant dose of power and energy. Back home during my lunch hours I would leave my office, located in one of the London glass skyscrapers, only to make sure that the whole world hadn't stood still like my swollen-under-desk legs. I would stand outside with my coffee while soaking up all of the energy from the surrounding hustle and bustle. But this time even the cheerful crowd of San Isidro couldn't help me. I felt like some invisible batteries exploded in me the moment Henry left me and something was leaking into my bloodstream slowly poisoning me.

I was wandering around the centre of Madrid as if the city had been covered in a heavy fog – I was walking slowly and carefully, giving every building, monument and street a few long glances. Through the thick mist of my Henry-memories I had to try hard to force my senses to watch and listen to the world around me. I was moving through smaller and bigger squares where numerous concerts were taking place and the crowds were getting thicker. Most bands, performing on the temporary but impressive stages, were playing Spanish hard rock – the language and music combination, which for me went together like Julio Iglesias and Heavy Metal. I regretted, however, I couldn't get into the mood and dance manically, throwing my hair and legs into the air like everyone else.

A shoe and clothes shops proved to be a good shelter from the intense sun, Spanish rock and people. On that day they weren't particularly popular and there was the added bonus of some air conditioning. It would have been absolutely perfect if not for their shop assistants asking me from the doorstep whether they could help me with something. *Of course, you can't!* – I was screaming in my mind. I found it increasingly difficult not to tell them that my only wish was for them to finish the process of verbally molesting me. Being pestered with attention didn't stop me however from buying several pair of shoes and a few comfy outfits. I had no desire to wear the too tight dresses and too high stilettoes that I had packed when I was still in a happy relationship. There was no future fiancé to admire me. There was nobody with me. On the bright side there was also nobody to whisper in my ear – *Do you really need it? Why does a piece of fabric cost so much? Are you sure you want to spend so much on shoes that are made for a few dollars in China, probably by small children?* In general, the shopping trip was for me cathartic – although I had to admit that my credit cards were purified significantly more than my soul.

Unbelievable how much a few pair of shoes and some clothes can weigh – I thought sitting on the steps of the Almudena Cathedral. I sighed heavily and set my eyes on the view in front of me – the sunset over the Armeria Square and the Royal Palace of Madrid. The sun was colouring the sky red and gold, at the same time as daubing the grey stone of the square and palace with different shades of yellows and pinks. The palace and its gold-black gate with chunky white columns reminded me of Buckingham Palace but larger and situated in far better weather. I wished I had somebody to share the view with. I quickly took a photo and touched my mobile intending to post it on Instagram; but I stopped myself thinking that it would initiate an avalanche of comments wishing me a lovely time with Henry in Spain. Social Media were tools for happy people or those pretending to be happy – I did not belong to either of those categories.

My rumbling stomach made me get up from the stairs, grab my bags and look for a place for dinner. I found it difficult to imagine that Madrid could have so many tapas bars and restaurants, but clearly nobody that night was enjoying a home-cooked meal. Finding an empty seat bordered on the miraculous. I decided to try the Mercado de San Miguel. According to an online guide the food market was open till midnight and you could buy anything there that your stomach could dream of consuming. Unfortunately to the horror of my starving stomach, tourists and locals fully occupied the market. At the first attempt I successfully entered the place with my legs, trunk and head but my hands carrying paper shopping bags were left outside. I pushed back, and then forward again finally entering the market with my whole body and entire equipage but I couldn't bear the feeling of being squeezed like a sardine. Besides the air inside seemed to be rationed and I didn't think I would make it to the first food stalls so I burrowed my way out. Another surprise fiasco on that doomed day!

It took me an hour to find a miniature empty table outside a tapas bar on the Plaza Mayor. To be honest it was a child, who found it first. He announced the good news to his parents by shouting loudly and gesticulating vividly, while running towards the table, but I was faster.

Before I burn in hell, I'm having a lovely lonely dinner. I ordered a cup of tea with milk, a glass of red wine and a few tapas meals. I chose what I knew from my previous trips to Spain: Patatas Bravas, Albondigas and Huevos a la Flamenca. The menu wasn't foreign-customer-friendly – even my Spanish struggled to decipher most of the meals.

"I thought that Manuel doesn't advertise his tapas bar anymore in the British guides," I heard in heavily accented English.

I knew that the male voice was talking to me but I decided not to take my eyes away from my delicious baked potatoes, divine meatballs and pretty average eggs baked with vegetables in a tomato sauce. *Maybe he'll buzz off when I don't react*, I thought, but to my despair he repeated his quip louder.

"Can I take a seat next to you?" the owner of the voice clearly wasn't discouraged by my feigned ignorance. No surprise in that, a woman's ignorance always ignites a man's ego.

Somebody moved and in the corner of my eye I saw a pair of long legs dressed in beige trousers.

"I'm with somebody," I said with my mouth full of potatoes still staring at my plate.

"Is he a stuffed paper bag?" he said and I quickly glanced at my shopping bags heavily loaded with shoeboxes and clothes hanging out around their edges. Indeed, they were the size of a small person. *Is he expecting me to put them all on the dusty ground?*

"Yeap… I mean—"

"I understand," he murmured. "I couldn't have possibly known that you're objectum-sexual. I'm sorry."

"Object-what?" I asked and I couldn't avoid looking up anymore…

I wasn't mentally ready for what I saw. If I had been standing he would have swept me off my feet. *At least I'm dressed for the occasion*, I was thinking straightening little creases on my skin-tight red dress, bought for a romantic engagement dinner with my… Ex.

"I gathered you're objectum-sexual…" said deadly handsome, dark haired guy, who was still standing above me baring his white teeth and not daring to sit down. "You fall in love with objects. Some people of your orientation marry the Eiffel Tower, others their pillows, while you're obviously in love with your..." he hesitated glancing at the bags. "With shoes? Or perhaps a little tank top? Maybe a fluffy pink jumper?"

"I love shoes," I said grumpily. "But I'm not going to marry even my pair of Manolo Blahniks. Besides, the better they look, the more they hurt your feet..." *Which is just like men. The shoes are like men...* I added in my head. "Do you really need to sit next to me?" I asked resigned and defeated.

"*Por supuesto,*" he said enthusiastically.

"Fine," I mumbled taking the bags off the seat on my right. "But if you're planning on seducing me, it's not going to happen. Just saying so you don't waste your time on me, while I'm sure they're plenty of other women who would be very happy and interested to have you as their... *Don Juan.*"

"Whoa, whoa," he crossed his arms and lightly alighted on his newly obtained chair. "You're pretty and I have to admit that I like petit brunets but don't you think you flatter yourself? The main purpose of my visit here is the best tapas in the city. As you've probably noticed I've had to practically humiliate myself to get this chair but I hope that is it and we can enjoy our food now."

It crossed my mind that heaven was just sending me a quick painkiller for Henry, but they rarely come without any side effects.

The guy was definitely sitting too close to me – I could feel his breath on my right shoulder, I could hear his heart beating (or was it mine?). I grabbed the bottom of my chair and slightly moved away from His Royal Beauty.

"You really don't believe me," he said amused. "Even if I wanted to kill two birds with one stone – meaning eat well and pick you up at the same time – I would have given up by now."

"Really?" I asked feeling my eyebrows frowning involuntarily, *bloody traitors*!

"You're quite rude considering you're British."

"Because you've been pushy and obtrusive like a Spaniard," I exploded.

"And you rush into judging people, a trait of a character which I personally don't like," he smirked, which only made me more annoyed.

"You started it," I pointed my finger at his wide chest, aiming at one of the buttons on his blue shirt. "How do you even know I'm British? Maybe—"

"Oh please, who else would order tea with milk? Who else would drink anything hot on such a warm evening?"

I could not dispute his tea-arguments. Looking around I was the only tea drinker on the whole square. I was having some difficulty focusing on what he was saying – all I could think of was how his blue shirt was deepening the blueish green of his turquoise eyes.

"It's not tea with milk, but milk with tea. Somebody, a very clever individual, put a teabag in a mug full of hot milk," I said playing with a string from the wasted teabag.

"It's because we don't practice such strange habits here."

To his disappointment I decided to turn a deaf ear to the comment and change the topic, "Before you continue chatting me up it would probably be appropriate to introduce yourself."

"I'm more and more convinced that it's you who's flirting with me," he said with a smug face, but added gently, "My name is Hugo."

"Simply Hugo?"

"That's not fair," he snapped. "I don't even know your first name."

I shrugged, "Life is hardly ever fair... Besides I bet that as a true Spanish man you have at least three names."

"Where is this insightful knowledge from? Let me guess – is it from Latin American *telenovelas*? Besides I'm not entirely Spanish... and what's your name señora... or señorita?

Why is it that both the English and Spanish have two different ways of referring to women depending on whether you're married or not; but only one way of referring to men?

"Olivia," I said but he was still looking at me with anticipation. "Olivia will do for now... So who are you Hugo if not one hundred per cent Spanish?"

"I'm flattered you want to get to know me better," he laughed out loud, and I felt my face was reddening quickly like the red centre of a heated pan on an induction hob. "I'm half Czech after my mother, and half Spanish after my father."

I nodded thinking that his skin seemed a bit too light for a true Spaniard, but what could I know? He was actually right; most of my knowledge about Spanish people and their country was based on stereotypes.

"Oh! We've got something in common then," I said overly enthusiastically making me feel rather stupid.

"The moment I saw you I knew we had something in common," he smirked, and I was not entirely sure whether in that moment he was flirting with me or laughing at me.

"My father is English, and mother's Polish," I said seriously.

"Oh," he raised his eyebrows. "How often do you travel to Poland then?"

"Nowadays, when most of my close family live in England, I usually go twice a year to Kraków to see my grandparents. How about you, do you often go to the Czech Republic?"

"Not that often really…" he paused for a brief moment. "I don't go there on a regular basis. But I spent most of my childhood travelling between Madrid and Moscow—"

"Wow," I cut him off and chuckled. "You need to be more careful if you want to successfully bluff a sober woman… Moscow is the capital of Russia, not the Czech Republic," I said with satisfaction and a certain disappointment.

"You're right I've missed a few facts. You must be distracting me," he smiled gently. "My parents got divorced when I was little and soon after my mother married a Russian man, so I used to fly more to Moscow than to the Czech Republic."

"I'm sorry," I said, annoyed with myself. I was glad that I had used some spray tan before going to Madrid – maybe it would hide the fiery redness that I imagined my face had turned.

A moment of uncomfortable silence followed, rescued by a waiter, who finally appeared with a menu. Without even looking at the menu, Hugo asked for triple Albondigas and a bottle of Merlot.

"Are you here on holiday or with work?" he asked as the waiter was still scribbling something in his notebook. No wonder it took him so long to approach new customers, I thought.

"Holiday. It's my very first day, and also a very long one," I said yawning.

"First day, and you've already achieved so much. You've found the best tapas bar in the city, you've met a half Spaniard and..." Hugo glanced under the table at my bags with logos of designer boutiques.

"No, I do not intend to limit all my sightseeing to the Madrid shops. Anyway, the shopping has only taken me a couple of hours," I was explaining myself as if Hugo had been Henry, who always tended to question my need for any kind of shopping that was not food or books.

"I'm not here to judge you," he said.

"True, I'm the judgy one, I'd forgotten," I could not help being stroppy. "I'm currently going through a stage of my life, where I don't want to resist any of my temptations. As long as I don't have to, I don't want to deny myself any pleasures... I just want to be happy."

"That's fantastic," he said with a grin. "Then I'm so glad to meet you just now. You're in luck, you don't have to deny yourself anything and I'm here to help."

"Yyy... that's not what I meant..." I coughed up.

"What I mean is that... I've got a free weekend and if you want I could show you around my city," he said sounding completely innocent.

"Why would you waste your weekend wading through the crowd of San Isidro?"

"I just thought you might feel lonely on your own in such a big city..."

How merciful of you!

"Maybe I could distract you from further shopping..." as he was finishing saying it, a waitress brought him a triple portion of meat-balls, and before I managed to say anything he poured me a large glass of wine.

Damn it! I'm not going to get drunk with a stranger. Besides, he shouldn't know I'm here alone! He doesn't look like a serial killer, but doesn't that make him even more dangerous? However, if he really lives in Madrid, why would he go out completely alone for a dinner on Friday evening? I'm so thoughtless – no wonder Henry dumped me!

"I'm NOT really alone here. I just felt like having dinner alone tonight," I said trying to sound mysterious.

"*Vale,*" he said, but his face definitely did not reflect an I-believe-you '*okay*'.

I opened my mouth to say something but I suddenly realised that there was not much I could say.

"Is it complicated?" he asked warmly.

"No, it's actually very uncomplicated but a long story."

"Well, that's exactly what I like. But I'm not going to be pushy. Just so you know, if you don't have any other plans for tomorrow, I'm happy to be your city guide."

"Gracias, I'll think about it… What do you do Henry… I mean Hugo, except being a great tour guide?"

"Hmm… you don't know how great I am until you try my services… To keep it simple, let's just say that's what I do," he said raising up a glass of red wine. He took a long sip and smiled mischievously.

His services? Oh, dear God! I thought, suddenly realising what was going on here. *A young, handsome, well-built guy saw a lonely woman loaded with bags from expensive boutiques and decided to sell her his services! Please somebody save me! Do I really look so old and desperate? Of course, his job is drinking wine with lonely women, who are more than ready to pay for IT and much, much more…*

"How old are you?" I asked. "How long have you been doing… doing THIS?" I made a circle around his face and the bottle of wine.

"Thirty-one, and I've got five years' experience as a city guide."

"So… this is your job? Being *a tour guide?*" I couldn't hide my amazement.

"Why are you so surprised? Oh…" he smiled like he had suddenly found the answer himself and then leaned back in his chair. "No, this is not the way I normally canvass my customers. Actually, I used to be a tour guide when I was a student. Now most of my job revolves around wine degustation and its distribution."

"That's sounds like fun!" I exclaimed still surprised. "I guess then I'm drinking the best wine here."

"You could say so..." he said almost sheepishly, which seemed unusual for him, and he rushed to refill my glass.

Was he really a wine taster? He could be lying to me about anything but I was totally hooked and enchanted. He was so different from the always-serious Henry. I was impressed by Hugo's natural ability to be relaxed outspoken and so easy-going. When he was laughing, his whole body was laughing – his cheeks and nose were lightly jumping; his shoulders and chest were shaking; and his eyes were sparkling with the skin around them gently wrinkling. He made me smile even when I didn't want to.

I looked around the Plaza Mayor – its glimmering streetlamps were illuminating a myriad of pedestrians' feet floating through the square. The sky was filled with millions of twinkling stars – a million sparks of hope...

Why did Henry leave me? What made him suddenly realise I wasn't the one for him? What have I done to deserve such a cruel break-up? Fine, recently I've put on weight, but only two pounds and I can still wear all the dresses from the time I met him five years ago. I had my hair darkened, but I had to tell him so he even noticed. As usual I was angry with him for throwing his shoes off in the hallway and putting a knife covered in butter into the jam jar. I always forgave him for not responding to my texts, forgetting to call me back and being notoriously late. Invariably I accompanied him to boring parties at his university and tiresome dinners with his parents. I bravely (or stupidly?) clamped my teeth each time Henry's mother asked me whether I had finally found enough time to cook dinners for her son; and whether Henry still put his shirts into the local laundry. If there was something I had not done, why the hell wouldn't he have just told me?

Did he leave me for another woman? Would it really be so pathetic and trivial? If so, why was she better than me? Was she better because she was new and still perfect? Henry had never been particularly keen on novelty – every change in his life was accepted with reluctance. His phone was four years old, his car had over two decades of wear. In the last few months he did not find a spare moment to bring to our new house anything more than a toothbrush. He couldn't get rid of his fifteen-year-old jumper, but he got rid of me!

"Everything okay?" a warm voice suddenly interrupted my pondering.

"Sure," I said suspended somewhere between drinking wine with Hugo, and being dumped by Henry at the airport. "Sorry, what have we been talking about?"

"You've been telling me your whole life history and you were just starting to describe to me your crazy years at high school," he said beaming.

"No, I'm sure that I've already managed to finish telling you my whole life story. Anyway, so are we drinking the best wine in the bar?" I asked and reached to pour myself a full glass. I deserved it. I didn't feel like a serious conversation, but I also didn't feel ready to head back to my empty hotel room.

"The truth is that some time ago I convinced Manuel, the bar owner, to buy over a hundred bottles of the wine you're now drinking. It does sell very well… just not here. He was right, the wine is too expensive for a small tapas bar in the centre of Madrid. Nobody wants to buy it even for the price that he bought it."

"How many bottles have you bought so far?"

"Only eight, including the two tonight."

"Then you've still got ninety-two to go. Do you always come here alone?"

"It's complicated and too interesting to talk about now. We would have to spend here the whole night, and you need a good night's sleep before we start our sightseeing tomorrow."

"Is this the way you treat women in Czech or in Spain?"

"What do you mean?" he asked frowning his eyebrows.

"You always tell them what to do."

"Are all women in Poland or Britain so stubborn?"

I had nothing to lose –except maybe my life if Hugo turned out to be a serial killer. I knew myself well enough to be sure I wouldn't enjoy the time on my own. I had a choice – sightseeing with Henry occupying most of my thoughts or with a handsome (and real!) Hugo.

"What's your number?" I asked. I had never asked a man for his number, but I preferred to give myself a little window to change my mind later.

"Can you give me yours? It's just that I..." he hesitated, while looking into the distance. "I left my phone at home and I can't remember my number."

Who nowadays leaves home without a mobile? A married-but-available?

I wrote my number on a white tissue. I didn't count on him calling me. He has given himself the option to back out at the last minute, when I really wanted to be the one in control.

3

SATURDAY, 16 MAY

MADRID

If Henry hadn't turned out to be an utter arsehole and instead got on the plane with me, we would certainly have spent most of our time trying to hide from the cloudless sky of Madrid. His sightseeing plan looked like one of his work schedules. We would have consumed the entirety of Madrid's Golden Triangle of Art within one day. Henry had wanted us to spend a few hours studying sculptures and paintings in the Prado Museum, then after a brief lunch-break march straight into Thyssen-Bornemisza and onto Reina Sofía. "Binge-art-watching? No thank you," I said to him initially but I relented when I couldn't stand his lamenting anymore on how little appreciation I had of art. I knew however that within a couple of hours I would be sitting in a museum's coffee shop. Two cups of latte, two pieces of cake and two posts on Facebook later, I would join him again only to assist him in finding his way out of the building. Henry used to literally get lost in art and consume it as greedily as I would hoover up a piece of chocolate cake on one of my bad days. When I went with him to Paris for a linguists' conference, we spent two days out of the three exploring the Louvre. My reward for absorbing so much knowledge was several blisters, backache, and a dehydration headache.

I do enjoy visiting museums and nobody has to drag me to places like the Louvre or Prado, but my appreciation of arts runs out after two hours. It's not just my attention span, but after a couple of hours my body starts crying for help, which manifests itself in a craving for sugar and caffeine. Hugo shared my reasonable approach to culture in small doses, but it wasn't that obvious from the very beginning. We met outside my hotel at nine o'clock, and he immediately announced that we were going to start our sightseeing by visiting some museums.

"Your face expression is telling me it might not be the best idea," he looked at me hesitantly. "Are you not that into art? We can always skip it."

"No, no!" I protested. "I just think that it's quite early for…" I paused not knowing how to finish the sentence. It was too early for anything but coffee. I spent half of the night thinking about Henry, and the other half about Hugo. I finally got up at eight having no time for anything else but make-up and finding a casual dress and comfortable sandals.

"Trust me, now or never," he said seriously. "In a few hours all museums will be rammed by tourists hungry for selfies with art in the background. I was planning only on a quick visit to Prado and Thyssen-Bornemisza…"

Here we go AGAIN! A Spanish version of Henry? I'm logging out of the experiment. I need to finally start thinking of what I want.

"And then a quick visit to Reina Sofía and something else…" I muttered more to myself than him. "Look Hugo—"

"No," he said firmly. "You can see Reina Sofía tomorrow or when you come to Madrid again."

"How do you know I'm going to come back here?"

You arrogant… and hot… but still so arrogant…

Hugo smiled gently, pretending he didn't hear my question. "If we walk reasonably fast, we should have enough time to grab some churros with hot chocolate for breakfast. I know a great place just around the corner. I bet it's never too early or too late for chocolate?"

"Now you're talking," I said full of enthusiasm.

Churreria Los Artesanos looked like a chocolate factory from my childhood dreams. Behind a counter stood an immaculately polished silver machine equipped with three little taps. When a chocolate-maker, dressed all in white, turned one of the taps, I couldn't stop staring at the thick dark chocolate pouring slowly into a porcelain cup. The smell of the chocolate was filling up the whole place – the overpowering scent hit my nostrils and calmed me down, it pierced my brain and dominated my senses. Shame that the heavenly experience was interrupted by one tasteless memory of Henry giving me a chocolate-present – which was a voucher for therapy for chocolate-addicts. "You keep whinging that you're addicted to chocolate and you need to lose some weight, so I thought you would appreciate the gift," he said proudly, I would never forget that face expression in a million years.

Hugo and I took a seat just next to a window but neither of us seemed to care what was going on beyond its golden-framed glass. We were too lost in dipping churros in the thick hot chocolate and laughing every time we looked at each other – Hugo's ears were shaking like a donkey's each time he took a bite, while apparently my eyes were wider and cheeks redder as I sated my chocolate needs.

Spanish churros reminded me of Polish *pączki* and English dough-nuts, but they were crustier on the outside, curled, and sometimes spirally twisted. I couldn't have imagined any better breakfast or company. High on fat and sugar I felt I was ready for whatever the day was going to bring.

* * *

While in Thyssen-Bornemisza I noticed that Hugo, just like me, focused only on the art that really attracted his attention. He skipped any which didn't evoke his emotion. As we were moving between the rooms on the first floor we both suddenly stopped, noticing two similar pieces of art that were hanging on a dark orange wall.

"I had no idea they had photos here," I said breaking the silence between us.

"Are you sure they're photos?" he almost whispered not taking his eyes away from the art on the wall.

"Not anymore," I said moving my nose closer towards the work. "You're right, these are paintings," I stopped myself at the last minute from touching the art just when I heard Hugo taking a deep fearful breath. "Oil on canvas, Richard Estes," I read from the description under the pictures.

One of the paintings portrayed a flower shop on a corner of a busy street in a big city; while the other showed a row of shiny metal telephone booths, all occupied by people.

"They're paintings but they couldn't exist without first catching the moment in a set of photographs," Hugo was explaining. "The photos were to enable the artist to freeze reality so he could transfer it to a painting with the greatest precision... However, unlike many Photorealists, Estes has never been particularly interested in painting exactly the way the camera shows reality. He tends to, for example, avoid showing photographic blur and focus."

"I see what you mean," I murmured, crossing my arms and tilting my head to the left. "All the reflections in the glass on the paintings are unnaturally vivid, but it works. For example, on the *Peoples' Flowers*," I pointed to the picture on the left, "the reflection of the building in the shop window is as intense and realistic as the shop itself."

"Exactly," said Hugo. "The same on the *Telephone Booths*," he indicated to the picture on the right. "The jumble of sharp and vivid reflections makes you perplexed and confused. It's like the artist is saying – *hey, you need to keep looking and focus if you want to see what's really going on here...*"

"So your reality might not be exactly what it appears at first sight..." I almost whispered looking forward but feeling Hugo's eyes on my shoulder.

"Do you want to talk more about *your reality* over a cup of coffee?" Hugo asked with enthusiasm.

I smiled and to my surprise I replied *not yet*. "I wonder what cities are shown in the paintings..."

"It's New York in the seventies..."

* * *

After visiting Thyssen-Bornemisza and Prado, Hugo took me for the longest walk since I could remember. He took his role of travel guide much more seriously than I had expected. We strolled around the Buen Retiro Park trying to occasionally hide from the strong afternoon sun under some high trees or white umbrellas at open-air cafés. From the park we strolled through Plaza Mayor to Palacio Real de Madrid, where we queued for over an hour to get inside. Fortunately, it was worth the wait to see the opulent interiors of the palace. Standing in the queue was also a great opportunity to listen to Hugo's anecdotes about the time when he used to work as a travel guide and had the chance to meet people from all over the world. Except English and Spanish, he also spoke Czech and Russian so no wonder he had been one of the busiest city guides in the company he worked for. After we left the palace we headed to the gardens located beneath it, Campo del Moro – a site that according to Hugo was often overlooked by tourists concentrating on Madrid's more iconic places.

"Do you know, where the name *Campo del Moro* comes from?" Hugo asked and not waiting for my answer continued. "In the twelfth century a Moorish army camped here intending to take Madrid from the Spanish Christians…" he was reciting everything from memory. "The gardens used to be the private grounds of Spanish nobility and their design was inspired by the gardens surrounding the Palace of Versailles…"

He correctly assumed I had not known it all before. But neither had I known that on Plaza de España, there was a stone sculpture of the Spanish writer Cervantes overlooking bronze sculptures of Don Quixote and Sancho Panza, the characters from his greatest masterpiece. I also had not known that a stone's throw from the Plaza de España there was the Parque del Oeste in which was the Temple of Debod.

"Do you know that the Temple of Debod was given to Madrid by the Egyptians in 1968 to save it from floods…" Hugo was explaining everything to me in a detail clearly designed to impress.

As a travel writer I really should have been able to demonstrate a better knowledge of Madrid, but in recent years my magazine had successfully managed to turn me into one of those people, who focused on where they could dine, drink and sleep well; and inevitably where they could shoot the best selfies to be envied by other Instagramers.

Next to the Temple of Debod we were suddenly surrounded by a large group of Japanese tourists who were taking an insane number of photos using all kinds of selfie sticks. It made me realise that I had spent over half of the day with Hugo and I hadn't taken a single photo. I was enjoying my time so much the photos hadn't seemed important.

"Do you know where I can quickly buy a selfie stick?" I asked with a slight panic in my voice. *As I packed mine into Henry's bloody bag!* I thought annoyed.

"I'm flattered that you've noticed how photogenic I am," Hugo said with a grin on his face. Then he moved his large black sunglasses onto his dark bushy hair and showed me the smiley dark eyes.

He was naturally handsome and it didn't seem like he put much effort into his look. His hair had probably not been treated with anything else but shampoo. It was a bit ruffled but still tidy, which was giving him a kind of messy but styled look. His strongly defined cheekbones and broad forehead were only gently coloured by the Spanish sun. Unlike the previous night, he had light stubble, which made me wonder whether he had no time or desire to shave in the morning. He was wearing the same beige trousers as when I had met him but he had changed his shirt for a fresh, white and perfectly ironed one. *Who did it?* I was wondering. *His wife, girlfriend, a local laundry or did he iron it himself?*

"I'm not sure if you're still here," he said loudly as I must have switched off for a brief moment, "but I have no idea where to buy a selfie stick and I don't have one at home. By the way, don't you think that selfie sticks are a loud manifestation that we've stopped trusting each other?"

"Maybe you're right but I prefer manifesting my mistrustfulness than watching somebody running away with my phone."

Hugo ignored my comment to have a brief word with an older man standing next to us with his wife. Hugo passed him his smartphone to take a couple of photos of us. The white-haired man was very patient, taking our picture from several different angles, and each time he asked whether we were content with the result of his work. However, the smile quickly faded away from his face, when Hugo asked him whether he also wanted us to take a photo of him and his wife. The man immediately grabbed his Canon with both hands, despite the fact it was safely hanging from his neck, thanked us and rapidly walked away while whispering something to his wife. Hugo only shrugged having clearly decided to drop the topic.

From the Parque Oeste we walked to Arguelles metro station to take a train to Salamanca, one of the wealthiest districts in the city. It was the only part of our sightseeing tour that I had suggested myself.

"Go to Madrid and not visit the shop of the famous shoe designer, Manolo Blahnik, would be like going to Paris without seeing the Eiffel Tower..." I said to Hugo, which caused him to burst out laughing.

"I personally think that the mosaic tile of mural art," he pointed out on the wall at the Arguelles station, "is much more interesting than Manolo's boutique."

"Fine, maybe that was too much but it would be at least like going to London and not seeing Harrods."

"Do you know that Madrid metro stations are big enough to hold public events?" he asked suddenly and unusually for him this time he seemed to be waiting for my response.

"I can imagine given the size of your stations," I replied.

"In 2011 at the station of Nuevos Misterios there were two thousand six hundred people attending a three-day fitness festival."

"Oh, really? I could totally live here."

"It can get pretty busy here too."

"I'm still convinced I would feel less claustrophobic on the Madrid metro than on the London underground," I said and then thought that it was the first time in a while that I wasn't feeling *squeezed* by somebody's else opinion. Henry wasn't here so I had nobody to judge me, even when I wanted to include Manolo on my sightseeing schedule.

We got out at Serrano station and headed straight to *la tienda de Manolo Blahnik*. It was a true temple of shoes – full of sandals, stilettoes and pumps as well as male loafers – all carefully displayed and spread around the shop with appropriate distance between them. The shoes were presented like works of art and although I knew that they wouldn't turn me into a princess, I felt like one while trying a pair of shiny pink stilettoes with a crystal-embellished brooch. The only thing that stopped me from buying them was their truly royal price.

After leaving Manolo we kept passing well-known chain stores and upscale boutiques but I didn't even for a moment feel tempted to go inside any of them. I was too busy conversing with Hugo, who eventually stopped starting every other sentence with *"do you know that..."*. Every step made in the city and every word pronounced with a slight Spanish accent was increasing my fascination with both Madrid and Hugo.

* * *

It was getting dark when we passed Retiro and quickly got lost somewhere among the long, narrow and winding streets of the city centre. As we were breaking through a dense crowd of Spaniards celebrating San Isidro, Hugo took my hand. He squeezed it gently, and I felt a flow of heat going through my body. At that moment I loved being in the middle of the boisterous conversations filled with loud genuine laughter. Despite being exhausted I enjoyed this seemingly relentless omnipresent noise. I was getting my energy back and I felt that something special was just starting.

As the night became darker and darker we continued to see whole families out with children of all ages. Small boys were usually dressed up for the festival in elegant blazers and berets, while girls were mostly wearing long ruffled dresses.

Hugo stopped suddenly and shouted in my ear, "you must be starving."

"You've been reading my mind," I shouted back and without a word he began walking again while pulling my arm.

I wouldn't have been surprised to hear that Madrid had the most bars and restaurants per square meter than any other city in the world. But that night all of them – from those with plaques saying 'Hemingway drunk here' or 'Hemingway never drunk here' to those with no plaques – were crowded to the brim.

My stomach started rumbling and seemed to be pressing against my back, I got worried that we would never find a spare piece of floor even in the filthiest looking tapas bar. Luckily, and as I should have foreseen it, Hugo had everything planned and under control.

"Only a couple more turns left and we'll be at our destination," he yelled into my ear but I barely heard him.

I sighed with relief at the thought, but my happiness didn't last long. After the two promised turns we entered a short dark street, where all I could see was one unappealing restaurant and a couple of suspicious looking bars. If it wasn't for the people occupying the pavements on both side of the street while passionately smoking their cigarettes, the place would have been nearly pitch black. I found it hard to believe that Hugo wanted us to spend probably half of the night queuing for something called Go TorTillas, which with its heavy wooden blinds in the windows reminded me of a dubious quality night club.

I had a good look at people standing in the queue in front of us. They were as varied as a typical London crowd waiting to get on the tube. Closest to the entrance was a wide-shouldered man dressed in a grey suit and holding a leather bag. Just behind him was a thin young guy in a loose T-shirt and skinny jeans that stopped abruptly above his naked ankles. I saw a woman in her thirties, wearing a long, ruffled skirt and a tight white top, and also a little older woman with her hair put into a bun, slim body squeezed into a simple working dress and fifteen centimetre stilettos. The older woman was writing something on her phone using only her right hand, while the left one was resting on the handle of her small plastic wheeled bag. The most bizarre thing, however, was that all these people seemed to be there completely on their own – as if it had been their lunch break during a working week, not a Saturday night.

"Don't worry. We've got a table booked for ten and we don't have to wait here," Hugo said cheerfully.

I didn't have a good vibe about the place. My suspiciousness was winning over my curiosity, "Actually Hugo, why don't we go and try the ham sold in ice-cream cones that we've seen—"

"Don't be silly," he said and dragged me rapidly inside almost pulling off my arm.

We entered a huge spacious hallway with no windows. Its floor was covered with wide brown wooden boards, from which rose two white marble columns. Between them stood a large reception desk – one that a five-star hotel wouldn't be ashamed of. It was made of the same marble as the columns and it was topped with brown wood. Behind the desk four smiling people with perfectly styled hair were typing on rose gold laptops. Either end of the counter there were two tall men dressed in shiny black suits, while in the middle were two women wearing tight red dresses. Hugo walked towards one of these women whose lips were as red as her dress. She gave us a wide smile presenting her snow-white teeth and asked, "Which room have you booked tonight señor—"

"Room A – A like Angelina," Hugo said without letting her finish.

Angelina giggled and her cheeks turned the colour of her dress and lipstick. She typed something into the laptop and said, "We managed to book one of your favourite tables next to the window. Hope you enjoy the evening."

Hugo must have been one of their regular customers. How otherwise would you explain that Angelina knew his name before he had even said anything; and then skipped all the explanations that other receptionists seemed to be giving to most customers. I heard one saying that the staff would explain the rules after we took our seats. *What rules?* I thought slightly alarmed. *The order we should eat the meals from the` menu or something more sophisticated?* I was also wondering why so many people were leaving the reception with information on whether their partner had already arrived or not. I felt like a new member of a sect rather than a customer for a restaurant.

Hugo gave me his arm and we headed silently towards wide stairs at the back of the foyer. The stairs were leading to the mysterious room A, while other rooms, B and C, were located on the ground floor either side of the reception. The doors were heavy and wooden, guarded by men wearing dark suits and white gloves. I dragged my right hand over the gold banister thinking that the stairway could have easily decorated a millionaire's mansion. Then while still climbing the steps I was nervously wondering whether my summery orange dress and flat sandals, which I had been wearing for the last twelve hours, weren't too casual for the place. I was the most embarrassed about my swollen feet, covered with street dust and two little dirty plasters hiding blisters. *I should have bought the Manolo's shoes! I was screaming in my head. Ideally also some soap and a pair of tights! All men are the same. It was like when Henry asked me to meet him for a casual drink around Leicester Square and we ended up drinking champagne in Fortnum & Mason with the dean of his university – them both wearing suits and me with a pair of distressed jeans and a military camouflage top.*

Surprise, surprise! The letter A disguised a large upscale restaurant. Its huge back wall was a massive window presenting an absolutely breath-taking night city view.

"Please follow me," said a waiter without asking for our names and he walked us to a table next to the window.

As I was going through the room, following Hugo's wide shoulders, I couldn't shake the feeling that there was something unusual, if not extraordinary, about this place – but I couldn't, just couldn't say what it was. When the waiter pulled out a chair for me I noticed that there was a surprising degree of space around all tables. The restaurant must have had at least fifty tables, but they could have easily doubled the amount without overly squeezing the customers like in an average tapas bar. The strategy was definitely not driven by accommodating the greatest number of people at any given time.

The whole large room was lit by warm light coming from several stylish and antique chandeliers; each of them unique in shape and colour and special in their own way, however when they were all in one room they looked like they were meant to be together.

"I suppose you wish to explain the rules to your partner yourself," the waiter said in English, while I couldn't take my eyes away from his handlebar moustache.

"Si Rogelio, gracias," Hugo suddenly switched to Spanish. "I don't know yet whether this is going to be only dinner or something more."

I hid my face behind the wine menu and pretended that I didn't understand a word of Spanish. I was trying to slow down my racing heartbeat by slow breathing and concentrating on the words in the menu but without much success. I needed a glass of wine, *pronto*! On the other hand, getting tipsy with Hugo may not be the wisest idea.

"What wine do you feel like?" Hugo asked with an innocent smile, too innocent for somebody, who had just said *only dinner or something more*. "Although, maybe I should ask first what you would like to eat and then decide on wine…"

A couple of glances at the menu were enough to know that everything here was expensive and sophisticated. The menu was written both in Spanish and English but I didn't fully understand the detail in either language. I chose deep fried calamari to start and baked salmon for my main course – two meals that had the shortest and simplest descriptions.

"How spicy do you think the chilli sauce is on the salmon?" I asked Hugo deliberately emphasising that I really didn't understand a word from his short conversation with Rogelio.

"I don't like chilli and anything that's too spicy," he said. "But what I think is spicy isn't spicy for most people. The amount of my taste buds are both a blessing and a curse… We can ask Rogelio to tell the chef to prepare the sauce as spicy as you like."

"That sounds great. And what white wine would you suggest?" I preferred red but I was afraid of making a faux pas by drinking red with fish.

"If you feel like white wine, there's a very good Californian Chardonnay here…" he said wandering with his finger up and down the wine list.

"I think it's the only white I don't like. I'm just not a fan of strong oaky flavour."

"Do you think you could give it a chance?" he asked encouragingly.

"The main problem with Chardonnay is that it's normally served too cold, even in many good restaurants. I've had it here many times and they always serve it just right. Below nine degrees I agree it's always too oaky."

"Okay, I trust you," I said, while in reality I trusted him less and less.

"But in case, you don't like it anyway, I suggest a French Pinot Noir as a back-up?"

I looked at the wine list. Choosing red wine with fish surprised me almost as much as the price of the French wine that Hugo suggested. Unless I had lost a page of the menu, there was only one French Pinot Noir on the list: origin Le Musigny, year 2000, price €215. *It must be at least one third of what Hugo is paying to rent his studio apartment in Salamanca!* I thought astounded. The apartment that I had had a brief chance to visit when we were strolling via Calle Serrano and Hugo suddenly decided to pop home to (bizarrely) check his post. The flat was located on the top floor of a beautifully renovated townhouse and was probably the smallest in the whole building. I glanced at the building plan on a wall, which indicated fire escape routes. I could believe that Hugo's studio used to be somebody's walk-in wardrobe that was sold as a flat when the prices per square meter in Salamanca skyrocketed.

"I trust you," I repeated. *I trust that I won't be hit with a split bill. And in case I do, I need to check the emergency exits in this building particularly toilets with good size windows.*

We closed our menus almost simultaneously and then Hugo with just a gentle nod of his head attracted Rogelio's immediate attention. If it were just me, the nod would have gone completely undetected. All waiters and waitresses seemed to have a blind spot in their eyes exactly where I was sitting. Hugo ordered in Spanish asking for both the Chardonney and Pinot Noir.

"Can I take your menu?" Rogelio asked smiling at me, and then I realised that my elbows were on the menu. I quickly pulled my arms back letting Rogelio take the menu, when I suddenly saw what was written at the top of it.

"Hugo Tor*T*illas?" I asked and looked at Hugo totally dumb-founded. "I would swear that outside was written Go To*T*illas, but here…"

Rogelio left us with a little smirk under his peculiar moustache.

"Yes, we need to correct the logo at the front. After some building repairs last week, the "Hu" on the logo still needs to be painted."

"I don't think you mentioned before that you were a restaurant owner," I said a bit too loudly.

"I prefer to call myself a manger and…" he hesitated, "I came up with the idea but the main owner of the business is my Russian father-in-law. I didn't mention it earlier because I've been curious to know what you really think about the place."

"It looks stunning," I said thinking, *And has a weird vibe.* "But why call it Hugo Tor*T*illas when you don't have any tortillas on the menu?"

"I'm sorry. I should finally introduce myself, Hugo Tortilla," I heard him saying the name like it was said over a storm, I was definitely in a bit of shock.

"Olivia Eliot, nice to meet you señor Hugo Tortilla."

Hugo laughed out loud and leaned back in his chair, "That's why we decided to change the name from To-ri-llas to Tor-*ti*-llas, because everybody automatically adds "*t*" to my surname anyway."

"And nobody is surprised when they expect to enter a tortilla place and they find this high-class restaurant."

"In room B there's a wine and tapas bar, which specializes in tortillas."

"And C?"

"That is a bar with just snacks."

"Why did you decide to put all the businesses in one place? Have you got a discount on rent?"

"Not exactly," he smiled. "There's one thing that all the places have in common… Well, the main entertainment isn't merely satisfying stomachs… It goes much deeper and is more interesting," he said with his eyes sparkling.

"Oh!" I exclaimed with interest and then my throat squeezed as my racing brain put two and two together.

"I thought that as a travel writer you might like to see what we're doing here..."

No bloody way. It can't be! I thought. *Did he really drag me here so I could... I could write about his version of Ashley Madison!* I looked around the room – *are all those people really so bored in their relationships?*

I straightened my back, cleared my throat and asked slowly, "And what exactly are you doing here?"

"We give people an opportunity to show who they really are," he said flippantly and shrugged.

Gosh, he couldn't put it more diplomatically or innocently. I should recommend the place to Freya's ex, the one who liked to dress up as batman when they had sex, apparently he was still searching for somebody to understand him.

"What do you mean?" I asked frowning my eyebrows.

"In other words, we give people a chance to talk freely and honestly," he said just as Rogelio brought our starters – calamari for me and mussels for Hugo.

"Gracias," said Hugo and the waiter left us alone again. "I should start from a little introduction, I suppose," he said and stopped for a moment as if he had had to contemplate something. "Most of us stay connected to hundreds of friends on social media. We tend to flick through their lives at least several times a day. Then on Friday or Saturday night we normally meet up with a handful of them to sip a beer or wine and talk about: where we're going for holiday; what type of smartphone we've just bought; when we got promoted; how much we've recently made on our house that we got on a mortgage; and how well our children do at school," Hugo was saying this with enthusiasm, while I was stuffing my face with calamari dipped in a delicious white sauce and drinking my not-overly cold Chardonnay with pleasure. "The problem is," he continued, "that often when it comes to a true conversation – honest discussion about our fears, worries and dilemmas that truly bother us and we lose sleep over – we have hardly anybody to turn to. We often don't speak to our neighbours beyond exchanging a few niceties when we pick up our parcels left by a courier. Our friends are often either too absorbed in their own issues or so chuffed with everything that you almost feel like it's inappropriate to complain about anything. Our partners are too busy or too tired to listen to us; or they're *those* we want to talk about. Time passes quickly and we see our families more often during funerals than weddings… We spend hours typing on our phones and computers but I think most of us still find communication really difficult, ineffective and unsatisfying," Hugo stopped to take a sip of Chardonnay.

I swallowed the last of my calamari, took another sip of wine and said, "A Polish poet, Adam Mickiewicz once said "There is nothing more desirable, and nothing more difficult on this earth than real conversation."

"Exactly!" he shouted and energetically pointed his finger at me. "Exactly," he repeated slowly and began *disarming* his mussels. "And it's what we're trying to do here. We offer people a chance to have honest conversation with complete strangers."

"I thought that when people want to talk to strangers they use the internet."

"I'm sure they do, but for most of us it's not enough anymore – actually it never has been enough but we somehow made ourselves believe that it was. We need to feel the presence of other people," he said and put a mussel to his mouth, which made me nearly retch – I always found mussels' look and feel gross.

"From what I can see around here they're mostly couples. How do you match them?"

"Our customers have two choices – they can either fill out a questionnaire; or they can just visit us and have a chat with one of our experts, who will try to find them the best possible match on the spot. The questionnaires provide us with more time to find you a match however most people go for the second option – they prefer to queue to have a chat with an expert and get paired with somebody."

"Who are the experts?"

"All of them graduated with MAs in psychology and then went through a special three-month course to work here. They're available in the room in the basement – a room we call *Amigo, habla conmigo,* which is the name of our program meaning literally *Friend, talk to me.*"

I stopped myself at the last minute from saying I knew what it meant. I preferred him not to know just yet I spoke good Spanish.

"Are all these people coming here..." I stopped to look around the restaurant filled to its last chair and full of people engaged in animated conversations, "...not afraid they might be revealing their secrets to future neighbours or employers; or that they might find out later that they were speaking to a friend of a friend?"

"I can't deny that there's a certain risk of that, but the more our experts know about you, the more likely you'll avoid such situations. We conduct many surveys and nobody has ever complained about any privacy issues. Also, most of the topics aren't life changing revelations that would cause them much embarrassment. People just want to be able to talk about what's really bothering them and get genuine advice," he paused for a brief moment looking into the distance to suddenly say with a new energy in his voice, "All they come here for is real conversation."

"Well, let's hope Hugo TorTillas will teach them that," I said noticing I was finishing my second glass of Chardonnay. The wine was easy to drink, the words just flowed in our conversation, and any moment of silence was as natural and pleasant as a gentle breeze on a sunny day. Hugo and everything linked to him seemed to be so effortless and easy.

"To be honest I hope that they don't learn too quickly," he laughed. "At least not until my step father gets all his money back."

"How did you even come up with something like this? Wasn't wine enough to untie people's tongues and made them talk freely?"

"If you want something more than drunk people's babbling, the right amount of wine helps but you also need the right atmosphere and the right company. That's the mixture that normally works."

It's what you're doing right now in my head? Take the handsome Hugo, add some dimmed light, soothing music, and the most spectacular view of Madrid at night. Then mix it all together; spice it up with some interesting stories and a few charming smiles; and keep it all on medium heat until she's cooked and all yours, I was thinking while glancing first at Hugo and then at the city view behind the window.

"Steak for you Sir, and the salmon in medium spiced chilli sauce for you Madam," Rogelio abruptly interrupted my thoughts. "Bon Appetite," he said putting the plates on our table. He took the empty bottle of Chardonnay and poured our Pinot Noir into new glasses.

"What inspired you to start *Amigo, habla conmigo?*"

"For that I need to go back in time to the moment when I decided to become a wine taster," Hugo started slowly. "Just after finishing uni – a time when for me every wine still only had one taste, the *taste of wine,* and its primary goal was to get a party going – I flew with a few friends to California. Soon after we got there, we went for a trip to a vineyard in Napa Valley. Our guide was a man called Ethan, and it was him who made me realise that my sensitive taste buds weren't a weakness – on the contrary they could make me some decent money. Ethan was one of those people who could easily inspire you with their own passions..." he was saying this while taking small breaks to sip his wine and have a bite of the steak. "I loved Ethan's story about how we perceive the taste of different wines. To my surprise I found out that it doesn't entirely depend on the grape compositions and the way the wine is produced, but..." he paused and looked at me as if he was about to reveal the secret mixture for the elixir of youth.

"The wine tasters are not just walking taste buds, they all have their preferences..." I was thinking out loud.

"Yes, preference comprises of a whole range of different factors that can't be underestimated but the way you judge the taste of a given wine is also determined by things like the mood you're currently in, the time of day or the weather. You can't simply detach yourself from all your emotions and feelings and focus completely on only two of your senses like smell and taste."

"How does it link to Hugo Tor*Tillas?*" I asked feeling more and more impatient.

"Think about it for a second," he said not taking his eyes away from me.

"Yyy..." I was becoming increasingly tired, too tired to come up with any meaningful ideas. "I guess..." I started again expecting him to finish for me but he clearly didn't have such an intention. I sighed loudly as if it could stimulate my brain cells to work harder, "What we say to each other and how we say it is not based on just who we are, but it is rather the resultant force of countless different factors, many of which we might not even be aware of or have hardly any control over... In Hugo TorTillas, you create an ambience that encourages people to have genuine conversation."

"I don't think I could phrase it better," he said with excitement. "Beyond what you've just said, when two people decide to come to *Amigo, habla conmigo*, they're both in the mood to talk – which is half of the secret."

"It's just weird that none of them seem to realise that they could create the same favourable atmosphere at home for free," I said before I managed to bite my tongue.

Hugo only smiled gently and returned to eating his dinner, which by that time was probably cold. I thought about the last few times Henry wanted to talk to me about something important. Damn him, he always tended to choose the worst possible moments to do it: just as I was about to have a bath after a long exhausting day; while I had a migraine and needed some silence after listening for the whole day to Tiggy at work; when I was back from the gym, tired and unable to think about anything else than food. Damn me, I should have realised it and found the right time instead of constantly brushing him off over the last month.

"They could..." Hugo suddenly said. "They could but for some reason they prefer to come here," he said and then before I had a chance to say anything he ordered another bottle of Chardonnay.

"Don't we have to go soon? It's almost midnight," I said looking at my watch. "You must be closing soon."

"From Friday to Sunday morning we're open twenty-four hours, and even during the week we're open from six in the morning to one o'clock at night..." he said and continued with a smile. "I know in England you say one o'clock in the morning but for us it's still the night."

"Twenty-four hours? Who comes here in the middle of the night or at six in the morning?"

"Madrid never sleeps, and the desire to talk can come at any time of day or night, especially as that's when we have some spare time to finally think. Before we opened the place, I had no idea so many people suffer from insomnia. A few months after we opened we began receiving many emails and phone calls asking for *Amigo, habla conmigo* to be available early in the morning as well. Between six and half past seven in the morning many customers come here dressed in their suits or smart dresses. In the evenings often they have to work or want to spend their time with their families."

"Sorry to interrupt," said Rogelio holding in front of his chest two sheets of paper. "Would you like to see our dessert menu?"

Hugo nodded energetically and it was too late – once I read a dessert menu, I wasn't able to resist. Before we left the restaurant, I had a big slice of chocolate cake, I tried a few types of French and Swiss cheeses, and I drank a small glass of Portuguese port. The indisputable advantage of this food binge was my ability to walk completely unassisted despite the amount of consumed alcohol. The walk to my hotel took us just over an hour, but we were moving slower than a couple of old ladies dressed in housecoats, who we saw strolling around the city centre after midnight with their small dogs. *Madrid really never sleeps*, I thought looking at the ladies in their eighties sitting on the edge of a fountain and indulging themselves in vivid conversation.

The quickest route to my hotel went through Plaza Mayor – or rather it would have been the quickest route if not for the fact that we had to push through the crowd jumping to the music of a Spanish rock band. I wasn't sure whether I liked their songs, from which I couldn't understand a word, but I loved the atmosphere of the omnipresent fiesta. Not many people could be immune to the sound of that music or not carried away by the happiness of the crowd. Even people seated around the square in bars and cafes couldn't stop jiggling on their chairs. We stopped next to Manuel's bar to decide which way we should go. Two waiters holding silver trays were enthusiastically jumping and spinning to the music.

I stood on tiptoes and shouted in Hugo's ear, "Is it the Spanish rock that makes you so ecstatic or is it just the way you always party?"

"No idea," he shouted back not taking his eyes away from the stage, while one of the rockers was frantically shaking his head of long hair. "All I know..." he started and suddenly looked at me. "All I know," he repeated, "is how you make me feel right now."

The entire Plaza Mayor suddenly started spinning faster and faster until all I saw were its blurred buildings and silhouettes of people melting one into another. Hugo put his cold palms on my red-hot cheeks and looked at me as intensely as if he had been trying to memorize my face. I noticed two sparkles in his eyes that quickly turned into a million flashing bright lights dancing around us and making me dizzy. I closed my eyes and felt the warmth of his lips on mine. The kiss took away a pain in my chest that had been accompanying me for the whole day and made me breathe freely. For a brief moment it even managed to disperse my fear from all the uncertainty of the future. Hugo walked me back to my hotel and... And a few steps further than that.

4

SUNDAY, 17 MAY

MADRID

H ugo was furious like never before. *"What do you expect from me?"* he shouted.

"Maybe just a little bit of respect," I said calmly.

"Respect? Seriously? Said by the same woman who went to bed with a man on their very first date!"

The sentence pronounced in one breath – as if it had been shot from a machine gun – had a stronger energy than we both could have expected. After a long argument, our first serious argument, we both went completely silent. We suddenly looked at each other knowing that was the end of us. I watched Hugo's eyes filling with anger and I thought that our relationship should have been finished a long while ago. The first date in Hugo TorTillas should have been the last one. I have lost another five years of my life on the completely wrong man, I was thinking seeing everything like through a mist. On the bright side, I won't have to listen to Spanish rock anymore...

I woke up wiping tears of sweat from my forehead – was it going to be a prophetic dream? Nothing around me was suggesting so – Hugo was not in my hotel room. No sound of a running shower or brushing teeth. There was only silence and an overwhelming sense of emptiness. The pile of clothes that we dropped on silver tiles just next to a jacuzzi bath the previous night were gone. There were no keys and no wallet that I saw on a dressing table not more than seven hours ago. There was also no red rose or letter on a pillow – *no hasta la vista babe. Nada!* On the bright sight I wasn't going to waste anymore of my time on the wrong man; and if he left when it was still pitch black I would not have to worry about him seeing how terrible I looked that morning. My long dark hair was dry from the Himalayan salt of our bubble bath. My green eyes were framed with smudged black mascara, grey eye shadow and purple eyeliner – perfectly imitating a pair of black eyes. I had a red nose and red cheeks with some bits of skin about ready to peel. Clearly I hadn't appreciated the strength of Madrid's sunshine, and I had overestimated the resistance of my complexion. While looking at my reflection in a bathroom mirror I couldn't help quietly singing *Rudolf The Red Nose Reindeer*.

In the bathroom a chunky mirror with a golden frame was saying, "You're not the princess. You're not the most beautiful anymore... The princess is..."

"Hugo?" I asked both relieved and petrified.

In the upper left corner of the mirror was Hugo sleeping on the terrace. He must have just turned on his left side on a rattan sunbed as I could see half of his body. I stepped out of the bathroom straight onto the terrace. A perfectly dark blue sky was gradually being framed by a golden horizon moving up and above the many lines of red roofs. I could not take my eyes away from such a natural and unique view. I wished I could have been stuck in the moment for longer; or alternatively pack it and store it for a bad day emergency.

I felt somebody's eyes piercing the left side of my face and I almost jumped. I turned my head back to see Hugo lying this time comfortably on his back, his arms and feet crossed, a gentle smile on his face, and next to him on a table two brown paper cups and a bag with the logo of Churreria Los Artesanos.

"I thought that when you woke up, you might feel like a hot chocolate and churros," he said and then I noticed surprised that despite of his terribly messy hair, creased shirt and trousers he still looked amazing. *Life is so unfair*, I thought thinking about my reflection in the mirror.

"I thought, I thought that..." I didn't finish but we both knew what I meant. "Anyway, how long have you slept here?"

He fiddled with the leather strap of his watch before he finally looked at the time and said, "Maybe fifteen minutes. And when I was sleeping I had the most bizarre dream for this time of the year. I was sitting in front of a chimney and a Christmas tree listening to *Rudolf The Red Nose Reindeer*. God, if you could hear how it sounded! It was hilarious."

"I'm not going to tell you now about my dream but it was definitely worse."

"I know what will help you forget about your nightmare," he said passing me a paper cup. I took off the plastic lid to inhale the smell of the chocolate. It was like heaven and to my surprise the drink was still warm.

He looked at me with a massive grin.

"What?" I asked.

"You've got a massive chocolate moustache. Cute, but I would probably consider getting rid of it before you leave the room and—"

"Oh my god!" I screamed suddenly realising what state my face was in even without the moustache! I quickly gulped the chocolate, rushed back to the bathroom and put the blinds down on its floor to ceiling glass door.

As I was turning on the basin's tap I could hear Hugo shouting, "You need to hurry up if you don't want to miss the sunrise."

I threw some cold water at my face and it caused a sudden moment of realisation, *Tomorrow I'm going back to England.* I pushed two cotton pads onto my eyes, which had two tasks to complete: first to get rid of last night's make-up, and second to stop tears at their source before they managed to roll down my cheeks. The last thing I wanted was to come back to reality and face all the inevitable goodbyes, with Henry once and for all, and with Hugo at least for the time being.

5

SUNDAY, 17 MAY

MADRID

O n Sunday afternoon Mercado de San Miguel was no less crowded than on the Friday evening, but it felt to me significantly more inviting. My senses couldn't resist the all-pervading aromas of Spanish tapas, an inordinate number of cheeses, cakes, breads, wine and spices from all over the world. I simply couldn't refuse a freshly squeezed smoothie and I also had to pay for a couple of mini pastries that I nibbled unintentionally. My long-repressed gourmet instincts were back. The market was both modern and traditional, it seemed to bring together under one roof all the colours, flavours and scents of everything that was edible on the Earth. Mercado de San Miguel wasn't an ordinary market where the locals pop every day to pick up a fresh loaf of bread or a few carrots. It was the place where both *Madrileños* and tourists came to try the very best tapas or choose truly exquisite delicacies from behind shiny glass counters. While walking through the market my head was literally spinning around – they were even offering coffees with flavours of every dessert I could have ever imagined!

On bar chairs and wooden benches there were many smart looking women, dressed in the most fashionable dresses of the season, and well-groomed men wearing polished loafers and precisely ironed shirts, often with matching jumpers hanging from their shoulders. There was also another clear group of customers wearing short-everything: short sleeves, short skirts, short-trousers, often accompanied by sandals which exposed many short legs and short toes. I was holding Hugo's hand and letting him guide me through the place, which was making me feel pleasantly dizzy. In my head I was composing a longer and longer menu for my Sunday lunch: olives stuffed with peppers, fried aubergines filled with cheese, a bit of paella, chicken and mushroom croquets, coffee with tiramisu at the bottom of a long glass... I was not going to stubbornly resist such culinary temptations, to the horror of my once-rigid-morals and once-flat stomach. I was going to let loose for the weekend (and maybe even for a tiny little bit longer) so I added to my list a strawberry Mojito, and a small glass of Sangria and... My daydreaming ceased when suddenly somebody much taller than me dropped on my forehead a piece of chocolate cake. The cake inevitably started rolling down my nose and I licked it involuntarily – chocolate cherry cake. Hugo turned back, saw what happened and quickly pulled out a tissue from his pocket. *Ready for every disaster*, I thought and sighed.

"We're never going to find a place to sit here," Hugo's words were barely audible among the buzz of voices. "Let's grab some take away and get a cab to Retiro. We'll have a Sunday picnic."

"Great idea," I said feeling my phone vibrating in my handbag. I wanted to ignore it but somebody wasn't going to give up easily. It could be only one of two people: a desperate seller offering me car insurance or a new phone contract; or my mother. I glanced at the screen of my phone, and sighed heavily, *my mother*. "I need to take this. Let's meet in fifteen minutes next to the counter with the large fish," I pointed at an alive looking fish, whose mouth seemed to be saying something incredibly important and urgent.

"Hi mum," I said trying to sound enthusiastic. "What's up?" I asked realising quickly that I would normally never use such a phrase to ask her how she was doing. *Damn it*, I thought. *The best recipe to sound really unnatural is trying to sound natural.* "I mean, how are you?"

"Good, thank you," she said surprisingly coldly as if she wanted to brush me off. *She did want to brush me off!* "I'm calling to—"

"Oh, I know mum," I said suddenly relieved. "I know what time WE'VE got our flight tonight and WE'RE not going to be late," I was putting a strong accent on WE being convinced that it was key to this conversation. Since Henry and I had missed a flight a couple of years ago my mother had become my flight-reminder, and she was as reliable as any smart-calendar.

"WE – meaning who exactly? Who's the second person in your WE?" she asked, we both went silent. She might not have been looking at me but I still felt her piercing eyes on my body. "Who's WE?" she repeated louder. "Who's WE? Because it's definitely not Henry as he's sitting right now in your house in Dream Fields," mum was trying not to shout but she was definitely on the edge of exploding. "Darling," she said now almost crying. "Why didn't you tell me you two broke up? Why would you lie to me that you were going to Madrid with Henry? I'm your mother and I deserve to know what's going on in your life. I gave birth to you if you don't remember."

"I'm sure that I don't remember for good reason. Imagine if I remembered catapulting myself through your... Wait a second, why have you gone to our house? We're away... I'm away only for three days. Neither plants nor fish need watering."

"I definitely haven't come here to water your fish although looking at the state of your aquarium you should change the water—"

"Mum," I shouted. "Don't change the topic and just tell me why you've been to my house?"

"Fine," she snapped. "I also might have lied to you," she said triumphantly as if lying was something pride worthy.

"Might have?"

"Do you remember when you went to Krakow for over a week?" she asked and not letting me answer continued, "I went with your dad to feed the fish only once. Yes, I know we should have done it at least twice... But the point is we used one of the slowly dissolving food cubes, which are supposed to last the fish for a week and we think... We think it killed Klaus," she said very high pitched.

"God, mum what are you talking about? Klaus is alive... unless... Never mind, can we talk when I come back?"

"No," she said firmly. "I need to tell you this right now. Let's finish with any lies in our family once and for all! So... I was saying that Klaus passed away, went to fish heaven I suppose—"

"Mum, I'm twenty-nine and a half. I can take it!"

"Fine. One of your nice neighbours from the building next door, who you never made any effort to meet..."

"Mum, please..."

"Fine. Your ex-neighbour from London allowed us to borrow her angelfish, which looked almost identical to yours – to Klaus I mean – a bit paler I suppose. When you told us that you were going away we thought it was a great opportunity for Marianne, the ex-neighbour's fish, to finally be free of this charade."

"Yeah, I'm sure it must have been tough on Miranda the fish—"

"Marianne," she corrected me. "Anyway, we've bought you a new angelfish. Let's call him Klaus the Second and I do solemnly swear that I'll never again feed him with that long-lasting poisonous shit!"

I didn't know what was more shocking to me – the fact that my mother could swear, the fish impersonation or the fact that she discovered I went to Madrid alone!

"Okay mum I forgive you and I'll try to forget about it. I'll call you later."

"No! Now it's your turn! Why have you lied to us? Is there any chance that you and Henry will get back together?"

I should have predicted that Henry didn't have the balls to tell my always worshiping him parents that it was him who dumped me, not even mentioning how he did it. *Does it mean he still cares about me or is he just an ordinary coward?* I was so annoyed that he put me in such a position. I still couldn't pull myself together after Friday's events and let alone verbalize my thoughts and fears to my mother, who always knew when I was lying.

"The truth is there's no drama," I said cheerfully and so convincingly that I almost believed myself. We had an argument, just an ordinary argument, and I went to Madrid alone. You know how much

Henry hates flying so imagine how easy it was for him to get grumpy and say 'I'm not flying with you'. I'm coming back tonight and I'm sure everything will be back to normal soon," I managed to maintain a cheerful tone but I was desperate to finish the phone call. It was as if the phone was burning my cheek from all the lies I was forcing it to pass on.

Lying had never been my way of living – but what could I have said to a woman who had been secretly knitting little cardigans for mine and Henry's future children? *Henry Junior or Henry the First,* I thought and flinched. At least she didn't show them to me personally, I had found them hidden among other knitwork, when I was looking for some wrapping paper in their house.

"That's good news, very good news," she breathed out with relief. I'll tell your father that he doesn't have to drive anymore to pick up any tranquillizers for me. I think I'm feeling better now, much better. That's great news because I really started to worry when Henry introduced us to a woman in your house who was an estate agent."

"Great news, indeed. I'll speak to you soon..." I was about to put the phone down when it suddenly hit me, "What estate agent are you talking about?"

"Don't worry my darling. It was probably somebody sent by your developer to have a look at that faulty radiator or other things you had on your list. I must have got it wrong. I was very shocked when I saw Henry—"

"What was her name?" I asked trying to supress my anger.

"Oh, let me check. She gave us her business card," mum said and left me for a moment with just a loud hum on the phone.

Estate agent? Un-freaking-believable. The nasty pig wants to sell our house. The skunk is not losing any time. He must have been planning to dump me for a while.

"Are you still there my darling?"

"Yeah." *How could I not be after what I had just heard?*

"Kitty Allen, she's called Kitty Allen and..." she paused and lowered her voice to whisper, "and she's an estate agent."

"Oh, thanks mom. She sold us the house and you were right... I'd completely forgotten that she was to come round and check whether our developer managed to fix a few things in the house," I said becoming officially a compulsive liar.

Being a twenty-nine-and-half year old single woman suddenly didn't seem to be such a big deal compared to being homeless.

While breaking through the crowd at the market I could hardly resist a growing temptation to elbow everybody I encountered on my way, a thousand despicable Henrys. I couldn't stop imagining Henry asking Kitty (is it even a real name?) to estimate the value of our newly bought house. The smells of Mercado de San Miguel were getting into my nose and quickly filling up my chest, taking away more and more air.

"Olivia, are you all right? *¿Estás bien?*" Hugo was staring at me, and with him a couple that looked like they had just jumped out of a fashion magazine.

The woman was a tall blonde wearing a tight pale-blue dress, while the man was even taller with light brown hair in his thirties dressed in a white shirt and a grey jacket. All three of them were looking at me as if I had just stepped off a UFO. They started waving their hands and shouting, "inhale and exhale" like they were helping me to deliver a baby. *Henry Junior, Henry the First,* I was thinking while feeling even more faint, my vision was framed in black.

"She's just having a panic attack," said the woman not taking her eyes away from me before turning to Hugo, "Is she claustrophobic?"

I finally managed to catch some air to say, ""No I'm totally fine."

"Do you want to leave or maybe lie down?" Hugo asked with worry in his voice.

"No, seriously I'm fine. I've just found out, while talking to my mum on the phone, that my nephew, her only grandchild, had learned to hold his breath under water for a couple of minutes. I've been walking through the market wondering if I could do it too and so I tried but... I think it has gone a little bit out of control."

Two pairs of male eyes went so round and wide that they managed to stretch their owners' eyebrows to an unnatural height. Only the woman in blue was unmoved by all the nonsense I was saying; or her freshly injected Botox prevented her forehead from moving an inch. I noticed she must have been older than the man who was accompanying her, it might even be a whole decade between them.

"Olivia, this is Fernando, a friend of mine from university and his wife Gabriela. I've recently been to their wedding on Fuerteventura. It was a great fun, beautiful weather—"

"The weather there is practically always beautiful," Gabriella snapped and ignoring my flushed face and deep breathing asked, "So how is Paulina? When we talked last time—"

"As far as I know she's okay at the moment," Hugo interrupted her, clearly unhappy with the question. "Are you here alone?"

Gabriella opened her mouth to say something but Fernando quickly jumped in front of her saying, "We're here with some friends but we've lost them somewhere in the crowd. They've come all the way from Malaga to celebrate the San Isidro Festival. We need to find them soon... Nice to meet you Olivia and enjoy Madrid."

Fernando grabbed his wife's hand and started dragging her away from us, but she still managed to keep her eyes on Hugo for an unbearably long moment. I saw a smirk of satisfaction on her face – now she was expecting me to start bombarding Hugo with millions of questions on Paulina. She was right, I couldn't have possibly ignored the tension that the name brought into the short conversation – but I tried not to be too nosey or grill Hugo on whoever the woman really was for him. I thought that it would be a shame to let Gabriella destroy our picnic at Retiro. I decided to accept Hugo's explanation that, "she is an old friend, who recently had a breakdown, and that's why we all worry about her." I didn't press any further. Hugo wasn't keen to talk about her as a taxi drove us to the park, and I wasn't sure whether I wanted to know all the details anyway. *You seemed to know everything about Henry and his intentions and look how that ended up*, I was thinking. I particularly like the adjective "old", which gave me some hope that Paulina was at least ten years older than Hugo and knew Gabriella from their regular Botox sessions. "We all worry about her," was bringing a few more unanswered questions like who was worried about her the most and why exactly.

When we finally decided to break the Paulina-shaped silence, we did it almost simultaneously, and it made us laugh. It was as we were distributing our food from the market on one of the Retiro's lawns, Hugo decided he suddenly wanted to know how old my nephew was, while on my side I became overwhelmingly curious about what he and Fernando had studied.

"Sebastian is four and a half," I answered first and then we again went silent. Hugo was probably wondering whether a four year old could really hold his breath for two minutes under water, and whether my brother and his wife actually liked their child.

He didn't comment on that, instead he started talking about Fernando, "We were studying business here in Madrid at the IE Universidad. Paulina..." he stopped and sighed as if he suddenly realised he hadn't meant to mention her but it was too late. "She joined us after our first year, when she moved to Madrid from IE in Segovia. Paulina's best friend was Fernando's girlfriend at the time so all four of us used to hang out a lot together."

"You mean Gabriella, who we've just met?" I knew it was highly unlikely but I decided to strike while the iron was still hot.

"We met Gabriella after uni. At the time Fernando's girlfriend was Valeria. As I told you last night, after our graduation I went to California, and it was with them: Fernando, Paulina and Valeria. I'm sure none of us will ever forget that holiday. I came back convinced that I wanted to be a wine taster. Fernando came back convinced he loved Paulina, who was in turn convinced she felt *something* for him but she wasn't quite sure what it was. And poor Valeria was convinced that life without Fernando had no purpose so she—"

"Oh my god!" I said covering my mouth with my hand.

"She took enough painkillers to lose consciousness and get Fernando's attention but not enough to kill herself."

"And Paulina didn't turn out to be the one for Fernando," I was thinking out loud.

"Nope. Their relationship didn't last even three full months."

The more I knew about Hugo and his friends, the more I wanted to know. Tough luck, exactly at the moment when a thousand and one questions were popping into my head Hugo jumped up and moved away to answer his vibrating phone. He turned his back to me so I couldn't hear anything or lip read. Annoyingly I wasn't even able to see his face expression.

The day before I had found it a little surprising that Hugo seemed to have no other plans for the weekend. He did not write in front of me a single text or pick up his phone even once. Nothing seemed to exist beyond us, and the people surrounding us were like extras in our movie. Considering how apparently unexpectedly we met, his hundred percent commitment throughout the whole day was surprising, if not a bit odd. Now I was both glad and relieved to see that Hugo had some life in Madrid but at the same time I was slightly disappointed I was no longer his whole world anymore.

It was a quarter of an hour before Hugo came back to our picnic lunch. He was smiling but I would swear he looked a bit unsettled.

"So how would you have introduced me to your friends if Fernando and Gabriella weren't in such a rush? A new friend of yours or maybe Just Olivia?"

He pretended not to hear me; instead he spread his arms in a gesture offering to help me get up from the ground. I let him pull me up although I didn't want to move anywhere. Only a couple of days ago I would have never believed that I would prefer to just chat with somebody on a piece of grass in Retiro than walk around the park and take hundreds of photos for Instagram. That morning my only involvement with social media was to change my status on Facebook from "in a relationship" to "it's complicated".

"Come on Just-Olivia, I'll show you the park."

6

SUNDAY, 17 MAY

MADRID

Parque del Buen Retiro is the biggest park of Madrid city, it is nearly the same size as London's Hyde Park (*142 ha*). Retiro varies in its landscape and offers much more beyond its impressive trees casting shadows on perfectly cut grass. Locals and tourists can relax and enjoy their time throughout the many unique lawns and paths of the park. There is a Crystal Palace inspired by the one once standing in Hyde Park; and numerous fountains and statues of the most significant figures from Spanish history. The most famous among them is a majestic Monument to king Alfonso XII of Spain, which is situated at the edge of an artificial lake. When in the autumn sun the lake reflects the surrounding colourful trees and couples row small boats lazily on its surface – it reminds you of New York's Central Park...

I still remembered my first big article for I-heart-Travelling, a monthly magazine that promoted itself as "a luxury journal for active people, who love travelling and adventure." Last October, two and a half years after I started my job at the magazine, I got my first major project – it was a multiple page report on the ten most beautiful parks in Europe. I was responsible for the text, while Hector was in charge of photos. Hector belonged to a lucky minority who were entitled to travel as part of their job, and was (totally coincidently of course) related to our editor-in-chief, Cecilia Anastasia Rice. Cecilia would never have normally allowed somebody like me to take on the project, as I didn't tick any of her three boxes:

1. I had not worked for the firm since it was established (in 1980)
2. My surname wasn't Rice
3. I wasn't recommended to get the job by any of Cecilia's influential friends.

But there was a crisis, and somebody's crisis quickly becomes somebody else's opportunity. More than half of the writing staff went down with swine flu, including Ludvig who had already started working on the top ten parks. In that way I spent several days enthusiastically typing some meant-to-be-informative and inspiring-to-travel stories about ten European parks, having only previously visited two of them. I was supposed to base my insightful knowledge on photos taken by Hector (who of course had been everywhere), travel blogs and internet searches. Unlike many I-Heart-Travelling writers, I also used a bit of imagination and stories from friends. Friends who worked as accountants and IT specialists and obviously therefore travelled far more than a travel writer. My own experience only helped me to write about Hyde Park and Park Güell in Barcelona. I knew very little about Parque del Buen Retiro. After a detailed study of Hector's photos and wandering around Retiro on Google Maps I decided to call the park – the European Central Park. New York was another place where I had never been, but when Henry was giving his evening lectures I spent many lonely evenings watching romantic comedies, almost all of which were set in New York. Henry would never watch anything like that – they were too schmaltzy for him to endure.

I expected Cecilia to go wild with her infamous red pen on my text, but to my surprise she appreciated my efforts and gave me a promotion. All she asked for was to add a few more details about Hyde Park in the article that was going to be published in the foreign version of I-Heart-Travelling in twelve other European countries. I added some information about Hyde Park's unique atmosphere: Londoners horse riding, open-air events, and a Winter Wonderland that even without snow offers a magical experience from November to January. Everybody in our editorial team seemed to be content – everybody except Ludvig, Mr Two-in-One: Cecilia's brother-in-law and her subeditor. He insisted that I should have included detailed information about hotels located close to each of the parks I wrote about. Ludvig wasn't just obsessed with the hospitality aspect of tourism, he wanted the magazine to earn money from promoting hotels. A large majority of the I-Heart-Travelling's content was based on such adverts-without-advertising, in our jargon simply AWA. In other words, instead of paying its writers to travel, our company preferred to charge local tourism businesses for adverts. Although hidden advertising was illegal, Cecilia and her team seemed to get away with it. Every month Cecilia magnanimously agreed to one article without AWA genuinely believing that in this way the magazine "kept its high standards". For similar reasons she also allowed for some company business travel but it was only for the Holy Trinity: Herself, Ludvig and Hector.

The article on top ten parks was my first and probably last full-sized article written for I-Heart-Travelling. My promotion didn't mean I was to become a full-time travel writer, but my responsibilities would finally go beyond pure administration. I started editing many AWA, which were sent to us from all over the world. I was also given the task of choosing suitable photographers, who tried to build their presence on the market through our magazine. Naturally they weren't paid for their photos because I-Heart-Travelling was doing them a favour by publishing their work in the first place. The lucky ones, the ones whose photos we used, were rewarded by emails (a la copy-paste-change-the-name), which expressed an intention of employing them at the earliest opportunity – an opportunity that obviously would never come. I was also sending more and more of these full-of-lies emails to successful internship candidates promising them paid work positions at some point in the distant future.

* * *

I had been convinced that Henry was going to propose to me in Madrid, and I had hoped with all my heart that it would happen in Retiro. I struggled to imagine a more romantic place for our engagement in the city. The real question was therefore not *where*, but *how*. The night before our flight I was dreaming about Henry going down on one knee in one of the boats floating on Retiro's lake in front of the Monument to Alfonso XII. In my dream I could clearly see a red sunset, smell fresh humid air and hear happy birds singing, while my "yes" echoed across the park. Then all couples rowing on the lake looked at us and started clapping at the exact moment I was saying to Henry how much I was surprised by his proposal and how wonderfully he had planned it all. Two days after the vivid dream I was wandering around Retiro with Hugo – slowly and inevitably turning Henry into a memory.

"What's your favourite place in the park?" I asked Hugo, who stopped momentarily to take a photo with a professional camera hanging on his neck. He murmured something, made a couple of "hmmm" sounds and continued adjusting the camera's lens. "I thought you come here quite often," I said.

"I do," he said and paused for a minute. "But I've never been here with you," he looked at me smiling and then I saw a bright flash and heard a double click. "With you everything seems to be different. I've just been thinking that places sometimes influence people, while people always influence places…"

We were walking on a path composed of flat grey stones, separated by wide strips of perfectly mown grass. The path led to a rustic bridge crossing a narrow green river. Above us trees were stretching their long branches in all possible directions, and their leaves were loudly rustling. The afternoon sun was breaking through the moving forest creating an effect like fireflies dancing on the path, the bridge and the river as well as in Hugo's hair.

"From today this might be my favourite place in the park," said Hugo after a long pause.

I thought that it would also be my favourite place. The moment when Hugo stood on the bridge to take a photo became one of my favourite moments with him.

"Last year I wrote an article about the most beautiful parks in Europe, which included Retiro. At the time I thought that there was nothing more beautiful here than the lake and the Monument to Alfonso XII. I think I've just changed my mind…"

"You said you'd never been here," Hugo looked at me surprised as if I had lied to him trying to hide something.

"The truth is I rarely travel to the places I'm writing about," I said sheepishly, feeling like a fraud.

"Well, maybe it's not essential. I've never had a chance to try all the wines I'm selling," he sounded completely unconvinced by what he was saying. "I presume it was the recession or budget issues that forced your magazine to make some cuts…"

"Not quite. My boss claims that in the era of the internet, travelling in order to just write an article is a completely unnecessary luxury, if not even some sort of debauchery. She keeps saying that business travel is passé and nobody writes like that anymore… So only the Chosen Ones have the pleasure of working in the field. The rest of us only depart our desks to make coffee or land on the toilet…"

He smiled widely, "And you? What do you think?"

"Obviously I don't agree. If I had the chance, I would change my job. I would prefer to write about my experience, not other people's…"

"And that's why you're here," he smiled, neither of us needed to say anything for a while.

I didn't deny there was some truth in it. I really wanted to know whether what I had written about Retiro was at least vaguely true. Henry would never have suggested going to Madrid. He preferred hiking in the mountains, ideally out of season in the late autumn, or any kind of holidays in a deserted place with cool weather. I enjoyed everything he normally detested including vibrant cities and glorious Mediterranean weather. If he had chosen the destination, I would have been spending this weekend lonely somewhere in a mountain chalet set in the middle of a spooky wood. Instead of walking the park's immaculate paths I would now be trying not to step in a rabbit hole, sheep shit or a ditch.

"It must be difficult trying to put some soul in articles about places that you've never seen," Hugo said suddenly.

"Not as difficult as it sounds. I've always wanted to be a travel writer, but I don't mind creative writing too, especially when it helps with paying the bills and my credit card on time. Besides, my magazine doesn't expect me to put my heart and soul into anything, they would rather I write hidden adverts."

"So... when are you going to change the job and become a true travel writer?" he asked flippantly, which made me rather irritated.

"That's not as easy as you think," I said through gritted teeth trying to hide my annoyance.

"I've never said it's easy but certainly it's not impossible," he said in a singing tone of voice so characteristic for people who are being optimistic, annoyingly overly optimistic.

"Many travel magazines aren't much better than mine and... And those that are, aren't currently employing and... And they might not be interested in me anyway."

"Have you tried? Have you recently written something about a place, which you actually visited? Maybe another magazine would be interested in publishing your work?"

"Maybe... or maybe they would pay me just enough for one article so I could buy myself two cups of overpriced coffee in town, and then my company would sack me for working for the competition."

"At least you could say you've tried... Unless you prefer to just whinge." If that was the way Hugo was going to convince me to take up the journey he had suggested the previous night, he was actually doing okay. Unfortunately, the thing that was stopping me the most was my real job. I was supposed to be in the office on Monday morn-

ing. Another obstacle was my common sense – a holiday with somebody who I had only met a couple of days ago? Wouldn't it be mad?

* * *

It took us half an hour to stroll from the park to my hotel. It was all
the time I had with Hugo before flying back home. Thirty minutes –
exactly as long as I needed to realise that I had just next to me the type
of man, whom Henry would never become, no matter how much I
tried to change him.

When we were walking we spent most of our time in silence. Not
the kind of silence of two brains working hard at conversation
desperately trying to produce one reasonable sentence. In contrast, it
was the kind of silence, when you don't need to speak to each other
because you both take pleasure in the moment and simply being
together; and you have faith that there will be time to tell each other
everything that you want and need to tell. Neither of us said anything
even when Hugo took my hand and squeezed it as if he was afraid I
could run away. I gently squeezed it back.

"Do you often chat up strangers in tapas bars?" I broke the blissful
silence when we finally turned into the small street where my hotel
was located.

"Of course," he said, so seriously that it took me a bit aback. "Do
you know a better idea of getting to know people than by starting a
casual conversation with them?" He must have noticed my surprised
face because instead of letting me answer he quickly continued talking. I missed his few first sentences because my thoughts suddenly
diverted to Henry.

Recently Henry had only been able to notice a lack of milk in the
fridge or excessively slow Internet that prevented him from working
or streaming his favourite TV series. In the last couple of months each
time he had talked to me he set his eyes on everything but me. When
Hugo looked at me, I felt like there was nothing there except me. He
noticed my words, face expression and gestures – they didn't just sink
into a vacuum. Hugo's undivided attention was such a novelty to me

that I almost didn't know how to behave in its view. I had to get rid of the habit of repeating every sentence at least twice and I felt that I should take more control over my body language, it had become careless. I became much more aware of myself and much more appreciative of my own presence.

"...and in this way my time passes quickly when I need to queue somewhere or when I fly long-haul," I heard Hugo again. "In this way I have found out fascinating insights from the person who was sat next to me on a train, ... or I can see Madrid through the eyes of a beautiful tourist..."

"Yeap, if it was only about seeing the city through somebody's eyes, and not through exploring the quality of a hotels' sheets," I was thinking out loud, which made Hugo laugh. "Oh my god, have I just said that?"

"No! Please continue, particularly as I thought it was a taboo subject and that last night nothing happened," he said with a mischievous smile.

"A lot happened! A lot! But it's still a little taboo. My ability to adapt to new circumstances has been exhausted this weekend. I need more time to process it."

"*Vale*, I get it... As I've been saying the best way of getting to know each other is by travelling together."

"Perhaps, but it can't be the most efficient way. Imagine if—"

"Depends how you look at it. It can be very efficient, satisfying and extremely fruitful and—"

"Taboo!" I shouted and then by looking at him I quickly realised he probably didn't mean what I had assumed with such ease, unless he managed to hide it very well.

"I only wanted to say it's definitely more *efficient* than communicating by clicking on your smartphone or keyboard. I know it's less effort to type something but—"

"I know. Lightly and effortlessly, with one push, only the door to destruction is opened."

"Leo Tolstoy."

"I hoped for a minute that you might think it's my saying," I was only half-joking, I definitely wouldn't have minded Hugo thinking they were my wise words.

"My father-in-law..." he stopped to immediately correct himself, "My step-father is Russian so he would never forgive me if I didn't know who said it."

I felt a sudden urge to undertake a serious google-investigation of Hugo's international family. I would fulfil my spying desires during the time I had to wait for my flight, and I was ready to pay a lot for access to the Internet, if it turned out not to be free at the airport.

"How can I find you on Facebook, just Hugo Tortilla or do you have a nickname?" I had to ask because I had tried already with no result.

Hugo cleared his throat twice.

"I'm sorry, Hugo Torilla, not tortilla."

"I know I'm going to disappoint you but I don't have Facebook or Instagram, and I don't tweet from my branch when I have a spare moment at work. I don't think you'll be able to find me in any of those places in the near future."

Was he using a nickname that he didn't want to give me? Was he simply a very private person or had he something to hide? Even a serial killer would have a social media profile not to instil any suspicions.

"Oh, right."

"I just don't have time."

"You don't have time for your friends?"

"I'm too busy living my life to post updates on what I'm currently doing and scroll through what other people want me to think is their real life."

"Okay," I said disappointed. *Fair enough, it sounds completely reasonable,* I thought, *but it still feels suspicious to me.*

It was time to say goodbye, and my feet didn't want to move an inch. It felt like the hot weather had melted the concrete of the pavement, which was fixing my legs.

Hugo, totally oblivious to the current state of my feet, said all of a sudden, "Just so you know my last night offer still stands. It wasn't just a drunk man talking. I meant what I said." *Before or after the hot tub?*

"I know, I remember. I wasn't as drunk as you think," I said still seeing quite vividly Hugo completely naked but immersed in the bath foam up to his chin and talking seriously about me going with him on holiday – as if it was the most normal course of events – you meet a cute guy in a tapas bar, he shows you around his city, you end up in bed together and the next thing you do is go on holiday with him. Simple!

"Are you saying that you remember everything?" he asked with a lilt in his voice.

"Goodbye Hugo. *Muchas gracias* for the great weekend. We'll be in touch," I said in one breath like a machine.

I wasn't sure what kind of "touch" because Hugo had a very dismissive attitude towards social media. *Is he trying to hide something from me?*

Hugo spread his arms to hug me but to his surprise I only let him kiss me on my cheek. I had always been terrible with goodbyes! I didn't want him to walk me any further than to the hotel door because I had no desire to prolong the inevitable. The truth was I was afraid to burst into tears in front of him. Christ, how many men could leave me during one weekend?

7

SUNDAY, 17 MAY
MADRID

I ran into a hotel lift as quickly as I could without attracting too much attention. Elevators fail more often than planes crash but Henry had never had any problem using them. It was me who never felt safe in a lift, particularly when they were small and didn't even pretend to be bigger with a mirror. I was often right on the edge of a claustrophobic attack. Thankfully the hotel lift was wide, spacious and had massive mirrors on three walls. The bad news was, however, that as soon as I ran into the empty elevator and pressed a button to go to the sixth floor, somebody's leg appeared between its doors and abruptly stopped them closing. Ten loud American tourists – all with bulky cameras around their necks, all wearing baseball hats and dragging large plastic suitcases – walked inside squeezing me so hard as if I had been invisible. They were all going up to the sixth floor. I stretched my right arm out and pressed a button to stop the lift at the very first floor. I got out struggling to catch my breath and rushed towards the stairs. It was an old hotel with high ceilings and walking five floors up was a true ordeal. Later I was wondering why it hadn't crossed my mind to just wait and call another lift.

I stormed into my room dreaming about collapsing on the bed and going to sleep for a few days but then I quickly estimated that I didn't have much time for anything else than packing. *One hour* I thought looking at my watch, *I reckon I can pack in fifty minutes.* I got into the empty bath in my clothes feeling completely helpless and bitterly sad. All the events of the past three days were appearing in front of me like a storm surge that nothing was able to stop from striking.

Go to hell! Good riddance to you! I was imagining myself shouting to Henry at the airport while throwing all the suitcases at him that were within easy reach. One of the suitcases flew higher than expected and managed to hit one of his ears. *You don't need it anymore, you stopped listening to me a long time ago.* Another suitcase hit his right knee – *now you won't be able to turn so quickly on your heel and run away. You stupid troll, you've taken away from me five years of my youth. Imagine how much I could have done with the time if I hadn't wasted it on you. I could have travelled all around the world, marry the prince of Sweden or Monaco (now both are already taken!) or get the Nobel Prize for... yyy... for discovering the only anti-wrinkle cream that really works! I didn't even want to know you. You invited yourself into my life. My sixth sense was telling me you weren't for me but you wouldn't give up that easily. I had just broken up with Dexter Pudding – I know, what a name... but also what a hot guy! Yes, I did imagine our wedding with a priest saying 'Will you Dexter Pudding...' and our wedding cake saying Mr and Mrs Pudding on the top, and I was still ready to stick with him, which really said a lot. Anyway, I wasn't in the mood for dating. The prospect of talking about myself on many first dates was worse torture for me than doing ten hours a day of unpaid internship with a two-hour underground commute. But you were so full of patience and under-standing. Such a shame that after all you turn out to be like a Siberian tiger – not only the most patient predator but also the most punishing. The very beginning of our relationship... it was so banal – you chatted me up in a club saying that you must have known me from somewhere.*

"Seriously?" I asked with disbelief. "It must be from the library then," I said dismissively and turned back from you to get a drink from the bar.

Ironically, I wanted to brush you off but my answer only helped you. As it quickly turned out we did go to the same library. You were writing your doctorate at night, while I was working on my master's dissertation. You said that you couldn't have focused on writing during the day, while I couldn't stand the sound of the unbearably loud snoring of my flatmate. You also struggled to concentrate during the night and blamed me for it – apparently, I had been your object of study for the past few months.

During the last five years we had had our ups and downs but you had always managed to convince me that it was absolutely normal and we were meant for each other. Recently you've had significantly less time for me. You'd heard me but you hadn't been listening. When we were sitting in silence it wasn't because we had felt so comfortable together, we just had less and less to say to each other. In the last few months of our relationship we had been living next to each other – you fully immersed in your world to which I had no access, and I lost in mine. But it was you who seemed not to notice it in the first place. You kept saying that I exaggerated and made a big deal out of nothing. You explained to me that you were just tired and life wasn't like a romantic movie. It was you who suggested that we should get a house together, and we did! You booked our flights to Madrid. You bought a diamond engagement ring. All that to leave me? Three months after we finalised the purchase of the house and just before the flight that you booked, all without any reasonable explanation?

And what about you Hugo? You probably spend your free time seducing tourists, ideally heartbroken (the easy target), and foreign (easy to get rid of when they're not needed anymore). You came completely out of nowhere just to show me what kind of man I wanted (?) Or maybe you appeared to make me realise how quickly I can forget about Henry. I can't work you out. You let me go so easily. You didn't insist on driving me to the airport just because I said you didn't need to.

"If that's what you want..." you said casually.

You suggested me going for a business trip with you but you must have known that I wouldn't be able to do it. You didn't even ask me for an email address. You got my phone number but you never mentioned you would ever call me so how do you imagine our relationship working? Maybe that's the problem – it's only me imagining something that is never going to happen. To hell with both of you!

I was lying in the empty hot tub, resting my head on one end while trying to touch the opposite end with my stretched toes. My efforts were hopeless – the bath was too long. I moved lower into the bath and accidently rubbed some bits of salt into my hair. I was fiddling with my hair while breathing in the lavender salt, and I could also smell the strong aroma of the same aftershave that had accompanied me for the last three days. I felt like every nerve of my body was pulsating in me ready to explode. I couldn't stop the inevitable – I was falling to pieces. I didn't bother to wipe the tears that were rolling down my hot cheeks and were eventually lost somewhere on my neck. I wanted them to melt me away. I wanted to stop feeling anything, stop existing – at least for a short while.

The stream of tears that flooded my face released my squeezed throat and soothed a pain in my chest but it left me with an equally unbearable feeling of emptiness and stupor. I got out of the bath on trembling legs. I found myself standing in the middle of the hotel room trying to identify through my sore and swollen eyes which of the spread around clothes and other items should go to the main luggage and which to the hand one.

As I was sitting on the main suitcase desperately trying to close it, I heard a loud and persistent knocking on the door. Not thinking too much I put on a pair of sunglasses and went to see who the intruder was.

In front of me was standing a short, stumpy man wearing a too tight white shirt, which made a couple of the lower buttons spread comically and display a bit of his very hairy belly.

"Hola," I said trying to force myself to smile.

"Sorry to disturb you…" he started while bending his neck unnaturally to the left to see what state my room was, "but you should have checked out three hours ago and you haven't contacted us regarding a late check-out. I'm afraid you can't stay here much longer because we're expecting other guests and I'm sorry but you'll have to pay half of a daily rate for today," he said with a gentle and full of apology smile.

His name was Cristiano and before practically escorting me downstairs he helped me to close my luggage. He sat on top of both my suitcases while I was frantically trying to zip them. He didn't say anything and remained calm and nice even when I accidently caught one of his thumbs while zipping my hand luggage. He only slightly grimaced as I put a Winnie the Pooh plaster on his finger, a present from my nephew.

* * *

"I'm sure there must have been some sort of mistake…" I was saying to Cristiano, who was standing behind the reception desk. "My boyfriend… I mean my ex-boyfriend paid for the later check-out because of our flight… my flight is in the evening."

Cristiano typed something on his computer, "That's correct but then he changed his mind. I've got here his email sent on Thursday night asking us to cancel the later check-out because he needed to re-book his flight for Sunday morning. I'm sorry but I'll have to ask you to settle the bill."

I had no time to argue with him. If I missed my flight it would cost me far more than half of a daily rate in the hotel. Besides, I couldn't stand any longer the merciful looks from Cristiano and his female colleague at the reception desk.

I sighed loudly, "How much is this going to cost?"

Cristiano smiled relieved I wasn't going to argue, "One thousand, two hundred and fifty Euros".

"Since when does one night here cost two and a half thousand?" I yelled.

"It doesn't cost that much," he said sheepishly and rolled his lips while waiting for me to fully acknowledge my situation.

"Oh God help me," I whispered. "Okay, so the bill wasn't settled in advance, but the bastard… I mean my ex must have made some deposit."

"He paid a deposit of a hundred Euros," said a blonde receptionist next to Cristiano, who only nodded apologetically.

I felt like a total idiot and nothing was indicating that my humiliation would soon come to an end. I asked to spread the bill between my debit and credit cards. In both cases I typed in the wrong PIN initially. Luckily the female receptionist, whose dyed blond hair looked like a wig next to her dark olive skin, had to leave me and Cristiano alone to serve other guests. Once her piercing eyes were gone I was about to breathe a sigh of relief when I noticed the queue that had been forming behind me. Two families of four and two elderly couples were standing there with their arms crossed and communicating with each other by constantly rolling their eyes.

"Is everything all right?" Cristiano asked a man who was rolling his eyes so fiercely it looked as if he was going to faint at any moment. It started looking more serious when the man wiped sweat from his forehead and gasped out heavily.

"Everything will be all right when the woman finally pays her bill and you finally check in those who have already paid," he snapped and his face reddened to the colour of beetroot soup.

Cristiano ignored the rotten Beetroot and waited patiently for me to once again type my PIN. Both of my cards were finally accepted but then I realised I had not printed my boarding pass. Henry booked our flights with Bryan Airways, which was well known for charging more for printing a boarding pass than most of its flights. Bizarrely although Henry was afraid of flying he tended to save on plane tickets by using the airline that was famously low cost in its behaviour, like always scrimping on fuel. The last thing I wanted was to ask Cristiano to do anything more for me but I was afraid that if I had to pay for the boarding pass at the airport I would have to walk home at the other end.

"Of course you can," Cristiano said with a friendly smile, I had my suspicions he was actually happy he wouldn't to have to deal with the constantly-eyes-rolling guests, including the Beetroot himself. "I think it will be quicker on my tablet," he said pulling it out of its slim leather case.

Cristiano quickly found the Bryan Airways' website. I logged onto my account and then... Then I felt as if I was struck by lightning – twice! *What are the chances?* I thought standing on my shaking legs frantically trying to decide, which of the two and completely unexpected situations I should face first. There was Hugo walking into the hotel lobby closely followed by a furious Spaniard shouting something about Olivia Eliot being twenty minutes late. Then there was the information about my flight on the screen which according to the website was already closed.

"I'm so sorry you've missed your flight," Cristiano said loudly and covered his mouth with a palm feigning shock.

"Missed it or not, you owe me forty Euros for coming all the way here and making me wait twenty minutes for you! It should be fifty, but I've had a good day today and—" the man, the taxi driver I had called earlier, didn't finish because Hugo whispered something into his ear and opened his wallet to hand him a few banknotes. Then the taxi driver looked like he was truly having a good day.

"Cristiano, thank you very much for all your help, and I'm sorry for taking so much of your time. I'll definitely recommend the hotel on Trip Advisor, in particular its fantastic customer service.

"Thank you, but please don't bother," he whispered to me with a little giggle. "Next week I'm starting a new job at a different hotel, which is just around the corner from here," he said pushing me his brand-new shiny business card across the counter.

* * *

For the second time that day I was standing outside of the hotel, looking at Hugo smiling at me and feeling like my legs were sinking into the concrete pavement.

"You must have been living here for at least a month," exclaimed the taxi driver while putting my bags into his car boot. "I bet that if you didn't miss the flight, you would have had to pay for excess baggage. I lifted a lot of suitcases and trust me on this – I have scales in my hands – that bag weighs well over twenty kilos."

"Conrado," said Hugo calmly, "she'll be fine, you can have more than twenty kilos in first class."

"My apologies then. I should have guessed that somebody who slept at the Madrid Kings Hotel would never fly Bryan Airways," Conrado said and closed the boot with a bang.

When we sat down in the taxi, with Hugo and me both on the back seat, I whispered to Hugo asking whether Conrado was really the same grumpy taxi driver who had just been shouting at me in the hotel hallway; and whether they had known each other before.

"We met in the hotel lobby. Sometimes it can be incredibly useful to chat to strangers. It's difficult to get a cab during San Isidro, and mine wouldn't wait any longer," Hugo said and reached out to hold my hand but I didn't let him, I had to text Henry.

You bloody arsehole, wasn't it enough that you
dumped me at the airport? I've just blown 1250
euro for the hotel that you booked for us as a
surprise! I'll give you that, it was a hell of a
surprise gift! It literally swept me off my feet!
In fact, you still don't stop surprising me! I
WOULD HAVE NEVER GUESSED THAT YOU COULD HAVE BEEN
SUCH AN UGLY PIECE OF SHIT! I wrote and after reading it
once I decided to delete it.

¡Hola Henry! I'm just writing to send you my love
from Madrid and thank you for the wonderful
weekend that you prepared for me! In fact, my
best weekend of the last 5 years! Thank you so
much you re-booked my/our flight for Sun morning
and didn't tell me about it! The best surprise
you've ever given me! xxx The best! Thank you
that you provided me with a good excuse for a
longer holiday. It was the very first time you've
known exactly what I needed. Hope you're also
having fun! Adios! Xxx I wrote frantically and sent it.

I was boiling inside with rage, but I didn't let myself boil over. I was desperately trying to turn my anger into a positive and powerful energy to face whatever else the world decided to throw at me. Tiggy Brown, our senior manager, read an article about such an inspiring mindset in a women's magazine last week and she didn't fail to tell absolutely everybody in the office about it. Now the skill was proving to be useful not only when it came to my relationship with Tiggy, a boss from hell. I refreshed my make-up with a bit of red lipstick and blush then took a quick selfie with Hugo on the back seat of the cab. I immediately posted it on Instagram with a comment: #Happy-go-lucky! #On our way to Madrid Atocha Train Station #This Journey Must Continue! #The best holiday ever #Best company #Where next?

8

SUNDAY, 17 MAY

MADRID

They say the best antidote for a broken heart is new love. I agree but nobody mentions to you that it means another long-term investment at a highly unpredictable rate of return. Luckily the state of falling-in-love boosts all our natural resources; it renews our internal capital so we regain faith in our venture and build enough energy to go through the same processes that have terribly failed us at least once. It is almost unbelievable how many times one broken heart can say "never again" and then glue itself together within a few seconds after seeing a handsome and potential Mr Right. But the falling-in-love also brings us issues like temporary blurred vision, constantly operating on the edge of reason and an incredible ability to justify the most ridiculous actions in order to keep the object of our attention.

They say that falling in love is like taking drugs. I don't know – I've only tried *love*. If they're right – shouldn't I stop before it's too late? I suppose the ideal solution would be to say *stop* when I have already been cured from the previous love, but have not yet experienced any damage from the next? But is it even possible? Once love causes some chemical changes to your brain – it might be too late and rehab is always pricy...

I was wondering whether the best moment to say *stop* was when I was queuing at the train station to buy my ticket to Barcelona. *Am I really already so stoned on love that I don't see anything weird about taking a trip with a newly met guy at the risk of losing my job?* I was thinking. One thing was certain, the situation was getting slightly out of control – I wasn't ready to return to reality, and the substance named Hugo had more and more influence over me.

Both my debit and credit cards were maxed out from my Friday shopping spree and after they both were used against their will at the hotel. I imagined their plastic squeaking as I was putting them into the card reader at the Madrid's Kings Hotel. I had wondered whether I should have asked my parents to buy me the next flight from Madrid Barajas to London Gatwick on Sunday evening – but why pay for a two-hour flight with Bryan Airways the same as for a flight to the Bahamas, when all I wanted was to be as far away as possible from home. I decided that there was more logic in using all the cash that I had in my wallet to buy a train ticket to Barcelona. On Monday morning I would then transfer enough from my savings account to get a train from Barcelona to Avignon and Avignon to London. The plan was that while Hugo was undertaking business regarding the opening of another Hugo TorTillas, I would focus on writing a fascinating article from my spontaneous train trip. *There's so much more sense in that than just flying back home*, I was thinking, so easily justifying all my actions.

"I'm sorry that you've missed your flight. I think you'll get some compensation from the hotel after you complain but going to take some time…" Hugo was saying this while standing in the queue with me. I was not ready to tell him about Henry and what he had done to me, at least until I knew myself why my ex-boyfriend and fiancé-not-to-be treated me like that. I couldn't explain to Hugo something that I hadn't had a chance to comprehend myself yet, so the best solution for the moment was blaming the hotel for everything, not reflect on the detail. "From my experience I think it might take them weeks to get your money back so as you agreed to go with me I'm going to pay for your tickets."

"Absolutely not!" I said, although I was glad he suggested it. I felt a sudden pang of guilt for lying to him about the hotel's service that in fact was nothing but nice to me, "To be honest the hotel had some issues with its card terminal so I lost some time trying to pay but if I had packed quicker, I might have got the flight."

"So it's my fault as I've taken so much of your time. Besides..." he stopped to smile cheekily, "I've been vigorously praying for you to miss the flight. I thought that it was the only way for you to go with me. My prayers were answered and now I should pay for my sins..." he laughed taking his wallet out of his pocket.

"Are you going to pay cash or card?" said a tubal male voice to a small mike from behind a glass window.

"Card. Can I have two tickets to Barcelona please? First class. Nine thirty."

"Nine thirty tonight?" said a clearly surprised cashier, wearing a tight navy jacket that prevented his arms from much movement.

"Yes," said Hugo and glanced at his phone. "From what I'm seeing on Renfe's website you've got at least half of the seats free in first class. But for whatever reason I can't buy the tickets online."

"That's the thing," started the cashier with a smirk, "Can you see the board above my head?" Hugo and I looked up to read aloud: *La venta de billetes para el otro día.*

"Can't you really sell us tickets for today after we've been queuing here over half an hour? If we change the queue now for the one selling today's tickets, we're most likely to miss our train," Hugo explained patiently despite getting increasingly irritated.

The cashier only shook his head and then took a sip of his coffee and shouted, "Next one please."

Hugo and I moved to stand in a queue in front of the notice: *La venta de billetes para el miso día.* We quickly noticed that many travellers were treating the ticket office like tourist information asking hundreds of different and often unrelated questions before they finally decided to get their tickets. Furthermore, non-Spanish speaking travellers had no idea they were lined up in the wrong queue until they got to the front.

"I'm sorry I always buy tickets online and I had no idea it would take so long here—"

"No problem," I interrupted him cheerfully. "I'm no longer in any rush today, and the last train is half past ten."

There was nobody I would rather be stuck in a queue with for another thirty minutes but I suddenly felt like I needed some space. I could do with checking my make-up and reading the messages that had been constantly beeping on my phone for the last hour. To have an excuse I suggested getting us coffee and something sweet. A few minutes later I was staring into a large mirror within the women's Atocha toilets wondering whether I should have stayed in Madrid for the night and taken the first flight to London in the morning, but I hadn't thanks to Henry who had also just texted me.

```
I'm sorry. I'll explain everything to u when you
come back. Let's meet up tomorrow evening, ok?
I'll pick you up from the airport. Even if you
don't want to see me right now, we need to be
adults and talk through some important matters.
```

Henry, as usual, so bloody mature and practical in his thinking and texting, I thought looking into the mirror at my frowning eyebrows and slightly clenched jaw. It was the longest message he had sent me during the last six months. It wasn't difficult to work out what he meant by "some important matters". *All you care about now is how we split the house! But now it's my turn to surprise you!*

I rested my hands on a cold white basin while breathing heavily. The toilets at Madrid Atocha were definitely better prepared for welcoming foreigners than the ticket office. Between the mirror and basin there were written and illuminated *jabon* and *toallas* as well as *soap* and *towel*. I put some concealer under my eyes, powdered my nose and typed a message to Henry:

· · ·

Not coming back home yet. Got different plans.

I sent the text and immediately switched off my phone so not to be bothered by Henry while I was looking for coffee and food; something that turned out to be more difficult than I could have ever imagined. I eventually had a choice between some chocolate bars from a vending machine or some dry-looking croissants. At Atocha there was also a creperia but they had run out of crepes on that day so had nothing more than fizzy drinks and stale cakes. Finally, equipped with two *café con leche* and two chocolate bars I walked across the station to see how far Hugo had managed to get in the queue to the ticket office.

Madrid Atocha was the best-looking train station I had ever seen. Thanks to its impressive architecture and a small botanical garden with an artificial lake, inhabited by turtles, it had become a Madrid tourist attraction. On my way to Hugo I couldn't resist stopping next to the lake to watch the turtles crowded on a small island and slowly, one by one, sliding their heavy bodies into the water. It looked like passengers boarding a Bryan Airways flight before the airline introduced seat reservations. One turtle in particular caught my attention as with admirable determination it was trying to get to the lake *pronto*. Instead of waiting for its turn, it simply decided to walk over its colleagues' heads that were forced to hide from him under their shells. *Fast and furious*, I thought. *Are you also turning your frustration and anger into fuel?* Around me people were gathering, watching and commenting on the feisty turtle. One of the faces in the crowd appeared to be very familiar to me – he was standing on my right, average height, slim, blond hair, hands in his pockets and a pale expressionless face. He was wearing a tight black T-shirt, well-worn black jeans and a large leather bag hanging across his slightly round-shouldered body. I was staring at him for a while before I suddenly realised who he was but by that point it was too late to turn my eyes and walk away unnoticed. There he was – Henry's neighbour from his childhood and a friend with whom he often shared his school bench. An average looking man with unusually high IQ. A very good IT specialist working for a well-known company in London, a member of a prestigious chess club, husband and father of two children – Gatsby. I remembered him with ginger hair but as Henry had told me recently he had dyed his hair for a job interview at the firm where he was currently making some serious money. He had also lost several pounds and been undertaking marathons across the country, slowly improving his times. I saw him last at Christmas when Henry and I went to visit his parents in Cambridge. We went out for a walk on Boxing Day to get some fresh air and more mulled wine, when we saw Gatsby running, dressed in black leggings and a bright yellow jacket. We looked at him in awe because even without the occasional cold penetrating gust it felt like it was at least minus ten. Gatsby didn't stop to exchange any niceties with us, he only shouted "Happy Christmas" and quickly waved. The childhood friendship between Gatsby and Henry hadn't survived till that day. Henry didn't seem to like him at all, although he kept denying his aversion to him. Henry always belittled any of Gatsby's achievements, often highlighting that although his friend was undeniably intelligent, if not for Gatsby's influential parents he would never have got such a good job in London City.

"Olivia, what a surprise!" Gatsby shouted and clapped his hands with exaggerated enthusiasm. "Henry's parents mentioned to me that you two were going to Madrid but I had no idea that it would be at the same time as me! If I had known I would have suggested meeting over some tapas and Sangria. Annoyingly with my business here, I have to work most weekends," he said with a grimace. "But I can't really complain, I love my job, though it can be really busy, really busy…" Gatsby kept talking not letting me say a word. "I've arrived from Barcelona today…" I was patiently listening to him and just when I thought he would never stop, something worse happened and he asked, "So where is Henry?"

I managed to keep my blood cool although I felt a drop of sweat rolling down my forehead and then onto my nose. "Oh, we've had a fantastic weekend. Madrid is lovely. Henry is just… he's buying our tickets to Barcelona. Completely spontaneously we decided to extend our holiday and have a… have a long weekend," I laughed nervously.

"How wonderful," Gatsby said this time without a trace of enthusiasm. "It's great Henry has changed so much around you. He has never struck me as somebody able to make spontaneous decisions."

"He's changed a lot. You wouldn't believe how much."

"Olivia!" I heard a familiar voice in the distance and I froze. "Olivia, you're here," Hugo said materializing in front of me. "I couldn't find you anywhere. I think your phone's gone dead. It crossed my mind that you might have run away," he smiled, "but then I asked myself, would she really leave me with all the new shoes she bought?"

"Yeah, Henry has really changed," Gatsby, said sarcastically. "You're right. I wouldn't believe how much," Gatsby was clearly taking pleasure in uncovering my lie. He also didn't look like he was going to move an inch. "I'm Gatsby Reynolds. I'm a friend of the family," he said offering his hand to Hugo, who quickly put his hands in his pockets.

"Oh, family friend," he exclaimed cheerfully. "My grandmother told me all about you. Family Friend is the only sect, which she not only tolerates but she also respects and supports financially."

"I don't understand," Gatsby said looking totally confused.

"Oh, I'm so sorry," Hugo said trying to stop the corners of his lips from shaking. "I thought that you're a member of the sect called Family Friend. They predominantly wear black, carry leaflets in dark leather bags and dye their hair angelic blond. What a coincidence!"

"Yes, hilarious coincidence," Gatsby said gloomily. I'm a friend of Henry's family. I should have been clearer."

Gatsby, *why are you still here for god's sake?*

"I'm Hugo, Olivia's friend. Nice to meet you Gatsby," Hugo said without taking his hands out of his pockets. "I'd love to talk to you for longer but we're going to be late for our train." Hugo took my hand and not waiting for Gatsby to say goodbye dragged me away from him.

· · ·

"I'm sorry for putting you in such an awkward situation," I was saying apologetically to Hugo after we had found our seats on the train to Barcelona. "Gatsby is a friend of my ex-boyfriend, whose name is Henry by the way and—"

"You don't have to explain anything to me. The only awkward thing was Gatsby. He had such weird piercing eyes. And he was as fake as his blond hair."

"How do you know he had them dyed?"

"Didn't you see his ginger roots?"

I shook my head.

Why was Gatsby both so outgoing and inquisitive? I thought with my head against the first-class leather seat and my legs comfortably stretched in front of me. *I've got him on Facebook but we've never written more to each other than "Happy Birthday". He sometimes likes my photos with Henry, and I like his marathon selfies. That's all. We've never talked to each other beyond exchanging some niceties once on one of the streets in Cambridge.*

SATURDAY, 23 MAY
AVIGNON

Many couples enjoy talking nostalgically about the beginnings of their relationship: how they met; what their first dates were like; what they were thinking about each other during those first days and weeks. The early stages seem to be nothing but wonderful, romantic, funny and full of magic. While I listen to the stories, I often get an impression that people sometimes dream about going back in time to experience it all over again. A friend of mine, Atlanta, says that it's just one of the examples of human memory trying to erase everything that is unpleasant or difficult to process without effort. We so easily forget about the sleepless nights, when we used to wake up every hour checking whether the object of our fascination had replied to our messages or tried to call us in the middle of the night. We don't remember how much we struggled to eat when our potential Mr Right suddenly stopped speaking to us, or how our appetite returned when he finally found or fixed his phone – or after hearing some other lame excuse. Also, we don't remember being jealous about seeing him on Facebook with a beautiful brunet or employing the services of a PI only to find out that it was his sister!

The more time I spent with Hugo and the closer I was getting to returning home – the more doubts I had about our future, if there was to be one at all. The question *'what is going to happen with us'* was like a broken tap, and what initially seemed to be silent dripping soon became a hammer drill and unbearable to listen to. The only way to turn off the tap was an honest discussion with Hugo – easier said than done! Our short time together mostly passed while walking both the busy and the desolate streets of Barcelona and Avignon. During the strolls our mouths literally never shut, but neither of us ever dared to mention life after the holiday. It felt like the present was everything.

The day before going to London I woke up at dawn and wasn't able to fall asleep for a while. I was lying on a soft wide bed, my body lightly stretching under a silky white sheet. I was watching with hypnotic curiosity how the first morning rays of sunshine were passing through grey wooden blinds in our room. A few rays of sun lit up Hugo's right cheek. He was sleeping peacefully on his left side, turned back to me and completely unaware what I was going through in my head. A lightly ajar window allowed cool fresh air to enter the room. I could hear some birds singing. *Shame, I'm not normally an early bird because I love the freshness of the morning*, I thought. Hugo reminded me of how wonderful it can be starting a new and fresh relationship, when everything is just waking up to life and our hearts are full of hope. When so much of what we later take for granted both excites and fascinates us. When hope isn't telling us that we still can fix us, but that we have found Mr Perfect and we are, indeed, meant for each other. And it doesn't matter that *falling in love* blurs our vision and is much less challenging than *being or staying in love*. What is important is that the world appears to be beautiful, peaceful and life is good. If not for the broken tap, everything really would be perfect...

"What is going to happen with us?" I whispered looking at Hugo, still sleeping and blissfully unaware of my musings.

He suddenly turned to his right. I thought how great he looked with two days of stubble and his long eyelashes.

"What did you say, *cariño*?" he asked slowly opening his eyes.

I flinched, "Nothing."

"I think I heard you talking," he said yawning and stretching his whole body.

"Nothing important," I smiled.

"So you were talking. What was it?"

Sweet Jesus, men aren't supposed to be so pestering and wearing. Why would it matter so much what I was saying? Although, I used to be annoyed with Henry that it didn't matter enough for him...

"I wondered whether you should shave today," I said without much thought.

"If you say so," he said while his eyelids were closing on his turquoise eyes.

Please no! Please don't listen to me!

* * *

Both in Barcelona and Avignon Hugo had much more time for me than I had initially expected. All his business meetings compressed together didn't last longer than I spent having a three-course brunch and choosing a few postcards for friends and family. I had some doubts regarding the practical need of this business trip, but the last thing I should have done was share the doubts with Atlanta. Typical of her, she replied half-jokingly and half-dead-seriously:

```
No idea how much time it normally takes to kill
somebody, squeeze their body in a car's boot and
drive the car off a cliff, but a week sounds
excessive to me. Unless he's a total amateur! Be
careful!xx
```

I didn't reflect too much on her text until the last Saturday afternoon when Hugo suggested us walking to Villeneuve-lès-Avignon – a small town separated from Avignon by the Rhone River. He said that he had been there before and wanted to show me some less well-known sights including Fort Saint-André and Chartreuse du Val de Bénédiction, a Carthusian monastery from the Middle Ages. I felt butterflies in my stomach immediately after crossing the Edouard-Daladier Bridge and began walking along streets without a living soul. We kept passing houses often squeezed next to each other and all with closed shutters at the front. They looked uninhabited but I tried to reason with myself the French were probably hiding themselves from the heat inside the cold walls of their *fortresses* or were relaxing in lush back gardens. I suddenly realized that it was the very first time when I was completely alone with Hugo.

"I'm a bit hot," I said, which was actually an understatement as I could feel my make-up melting and drops of sweat generously rolling down my back. "Why don't we take the bus?" I suggested, trying to kill two birds with one stone – it would get some air conditioning and people around us.

"We're not pensioners, we can walk, it's only a few miles up the hill," he said sounding irritated.

"True, but on the other hand if we get sun stroke and die here ALONE we won't live long enough to get our pensions. And then I'll never get drunk at breakfast, gamble for weeks on a cruise or sightsee on one of those golf cars around a European capital city." It took a lot of effort to sound natural and not raise his suspicions, but I was indeed full of suspicions. However, he didn't appear to appreciate it at all, he just looked a bit nervous and irritated.

"It crossed my mind that we could rent a car," he said and I thought immediately *Beep! Beep! Car means being alone with you! Car means having a body-sized boot!* "But then you wouldn't have the chance to appreciate all the amazing views," he stopped to make a circle with his arm. "You wouldn't have the opportunity to see how people really live here."

"I wouldn't have the chance to see how the French barricade them-selves in their homes?" I snapped.

"It's midday, most people probably prefer to stay at home when it's so hot."

"It's lucky that I come from the tropics and I deal so well with the heat," I murmured but Hugo ignored me, which was probably for the best.

The route that Hugo had chosen provided us with the most picturesque views I had ever seen. We were gradually working our way up the hill to get to Fort Saint-André, walking on narrow streets densely surrounded by worn-out but stylish houses. Each time we managed to find a gap in a line of stone buildings, we got struck by the beauty of vast green rolling hills from which there were emerging typical Provençal houses, made of beige stone and covered with red roofs slightly faded from the strong sunshine. The view was complemented by several different shades of purple from the blossoming lavender broken by fields of vividly pink flowers.

"You're right. The views have been worth a few blisters and risking you seeing me in daylight with melted make-up," I said strolling around Jardins de l'Abbaye Saint-André, impressively laid out gardens located just next to the Fort.

We were surrounded by olive trees and intensely, passionately green Mediterranean plants creeping over the remains of old walls and terraces, the ruins that survived from some ancient roman churches. While looking for shade we managed to hide under one of the largest balconies with its pillars shaped into arches that were forming a natural frame around the unique scenery seen from the top of the hill. In the distance, behind dense plants and trees we could just see Avignon and the Palais des Papes with its bell tower crowned in a golden statue of the Virgin Mary, brightly shining in the afternoon sun.

"I'm sorry I was grumpy," Hugo said suddenly. "I was struggling with the temperature too. I should have told you to be better prepared for the trip, to take comfier shoes and a hat..."

I didn't have any comfier shoes than the sandals I was wearing. I was prepared for an elegant engagement weekend in Madrid, not hiking in Provence! I didn't have a sunhat – I had planned to drink chilled Sangria under a café's parasol!

On the bright side nobody pushed me off a cliff. Atlanta needed to have some detox from all the crime novels she was reading, and she should have also stopped intoxicating me with her theories.

"This place is so beautiful that I find it hard to believe we've seen so few people on the way here, while Avignon itself couldn't be more packed with tourists," I said.

"One thing that I learned from being a tour guide is that people visiting cities rarely like to go off the beaten track and explore anything beyond the most popular landmarks... But the downside of being here alone is that there's nobody to take our photo," he said looking around. I should have bought a selfie stick," he gasped.

"Nah, it would manifest your lack of faith in other people."

"Or it would make us more self-efficient and independent."

"Trusting people..." I said before I managed to bite my tongue but Hugo was already staring at me with his questioning look. "Nothing important," I said pretending I was yawning, while my brain worked at high-speed, more awake than ever. "Fine," I said thinking, *What the heck! I need to know otherwise I'll go crazy!* "I've been wondering whether you always go so far just to talk business for a couple of hours? Don't you trust phones or videoconferences?"

"I always travel to see people when it's possible. When it comes to something important I prefer to see somebody personally. Does it make me old fashioned?" his eyes wandered somewhere away for a minute. "Maybe, maybe I'm a bit old fashioned."

"That's not what I meant," I said defensively.

I hoped that he would say that he didn't have to travel anywhere to do business, and it was only an excuse to get to know me better. Me, the Silly Me and my even Sillier *Great Expectations,* we always come up together with some nonsense waiting for something completely unrealistic to happen, and then all that happens to us is Big Disappointment.

"Maybe I've got some issues with trust, especially when physical distance is involved..." he said flippantly, and I felt as if somebody threw a bucket of ice-cold water on my head, which was still pulsating from the heat.

"I guess that makes your life more difficult," I snapped irritated, thinking, *Or at least it's going to complicate mine!*

"I don't know..." he was saying while looking into the distance, "until now I haven't had any significant problems with... With this particular trait of my character."

"Until now," I repeated with a grimace on my face.

"Olivia, what's the matter with you? Why are you suddenly so worried about how I handle my business?"

Your business? Are we still talking about your business?

"Yyy... I'm just irritated because I've been bitten by a mosquito and it's super itchy."

"Where?" he asked with a slight worry in his voice. "I should have got us a mosquito spray!"

I loved the way he kept blaming himself for all my many miseries on that day. Henry would likely just accuse me for everything, and probably even be grumpy if a mosquito bit him instead of me.

"Just on my ankle, but it will be fine for the wedding," I said badly translating a Polish proverb, which meant that something would be healed soon.

"What wedding? I hope not yours?"

"Who do you think I am? I haven't even got home and you already don't trust me," I said only half-jokingly.

"There can only be one solution to the problem," he rolled his lips, widened his eyes and nodded.

"I'm listening."

"Move to Madrid."

I laughed out loud uncontrollably throwing my hair to the back, "Hold on a sec. Let me sell my house tomorrow, quit my job the day after tomorrow and I'll can be with you in Madrid in three, max four days."

"You're not taking me seriously," he said, looking offended.

"Sometimes I think YOU don't take me seriously enough."

"I don't understand. You don't like your job, you don't really want to live in the house you bought with your ex-boyfriend. You said you loved Spain. And... And you're starting a relationship with a half-Spanish man..."

Relationship! Did he really use the word 'relationship'?

"Are you saying that I should just drop everything and start all over again? Just like that?" I snorted with laughter.

"Last night you were saying that you needed to make some significant changes in your life."

For a brief moment I was nervously trying to work out what he was talking about. I almost managed to forget that the night before, when we were walking back from a restaurant to our hotel, I happened to summarize to Hugo the story of my life. I had no intention of doing it but I got encouraged by the unique atmosphere of the town that made me nostalgic, a few glasses of wine, and Hugo who was one of the best listeners I had ever met.

After sunset the poorly lit streets of Avignon, with their shabby town houses begging for renovation, reminded me of my favourite part of Krakow – the Kazimierz district. A few-storey grey buildings, which often were adorned with cobwebs and bars in the windows; chunky double doors with heavy metal knockers; and empty yards locked behind metal creaking gates – all of that together created a dream set for a detective movie. Night brought both to Kazimierz and Avignon's old town an intimate and cosy environment, but also some unsolved mysteries were hanging in the air and waiting to be uncovered. Despite the fact that every footstep or meow of a cat made my back shiver, I felt safe there. We walked for over two hours before we realised that we had got lost. For all that time we were too busy with our conversation to notice that we kept passing the same buildings for the second or even third time. We started from my childhood, spent mainly in London and Kraków, and finished with Henry breaking up with me at the airport.

I needed some important changes in my life but I wanted to introduce them gradually, one step at a time, not by acting like a crazy-in-love teenager.

"I need more time to decide what I want," I said thinking that I wasn't going to again start from adjusting my whole life plan around a man.

"Hmmm… I understand…" he murmured. "As long it's not an excuse to do nothing."

"Why don't you move to me, Hugo?" I snapped annoyed, feeling my lower lip trembling. "Your life is too perfect to make any changes for me? Or am I not important enough to—?"

"Olivia, don't try to twist what I've just said," he interrupted me with a calm soothing voice. "Even if I could work remotely, I'm very weather sensitive. I couldn't live permanently in rainy England, I wouldn't be myself."

"That's truly wonderful news!" I snapped. "To sum up. You don't believe in long-distance relationships, but moving to my country is not even an option. So everything is now down to me moving to you. No effort from your side."

"I didn't want it to sound like that," he said defensively as if he had just realised how ridiculous and arrogant he sounded.

"You didn't want it to sound like an ultimatum? Well, how else could it sound?"

"Olivia, listen," he stroked his forehead. "What I'm trying to say—"

"Oh, I wish I was a man! Then not only would I be equipped with an unlimited dose of egoism, but I would also know exactly how to justify it."

"I've got another idea," he started timidly. "Just listen to me and let me explain..."

"I'm dying to know," I crossed my arms waiting.

I did what he asked me to do – I let him finish without interrupting him, although initially I had no intention of committing to any of his plans.

10

MONDAY, 25 MAY

LONDON

I expected that my week would start like most of my Monday mornings at the office with a nine o'clock meeting for the whole editorial team of I-Heart-Travelling. It always took place in our largest room with the view of Paddington station, seats were set around a large round white table pitted densely with symmetrically distributed black plugs for charging laptops. However, this Monday morning was more important than most because we were to be honoured with a visit by Arthur MacArthur – the founder and CEO of HeartTravelling.Ltd – the company that ran our magazine from its glass Manhattan skyscraper. King Arthur, as we often called him, had a habit of visiting us a few times a year without any prior announcement from his side. His unexpected visits were designed to carry out brief inspections and informal meetings. He travelled to us on his private jet and as soon as his plane took off from JFK, Bertha, his bribed by Cecilia secretary, used to send a message to all members of our team: 'NY to London, be prepared! U have nine hours. B." We called it our Red Alert. For such a low-level employee like me a text like that didn't mean much beyond getting to work an hour earlier than normal, looking neat and fresh, and pretending to be in a fantastic mood. None of these undertakings would have been a particular challenge if not for the fact that I felt so exhausted after the week travelling with Hugo that I ignored the sound of my mobile buzzing at midnight. I was convinced that it was Hugo with another message a la 'Te echo de menos', and I preferred to read it in the morning to lift up my mood. Hugo didn't let me down, he wrote in five different ways how much he missed me, but somewhere between his texts I also found Bertha's Red Alert. When I realised what was happening, it was too late even to iron a smart outfit. I pulled over my sleepy body the most elastic dress I could find so there was some hope it would self-iron with the sweaty steam from my body as I was practically running to work.

The state of falling in love makes us far more optimistic than we are normally, and that was me that morning – Miss Brightside telling herself that despite all odds everything was going to be all right. I should have been at the office for eight o'clock but even if the train between Dream Fields and Paddington hadn't stopped at any station, I wouldn't have got there on time. I couldn't face the impossible so I quickly explained to myself that it was probably for the best that I had slept longer, at least a good sleep would benefit my look. Being sleep deprived I wouldn't be able to absorb all Cecilia's *do and don't* (presented in novel form over a hundred slides) before the proper meeting with Arthur at nine. To be honest I always tended to switch off during her emergency pre-meetings for Arthur MacArthur but despite my mental absence I always used to be fine. Unfortunately, my physical appearance for the eight o'clock meeting was more important than I had assumed. As soon as I cross the doorstep of the office at eight fifty, I stumbled across my head manager Tiggy Brown.

"I thought that you were more professional, but obviously I must have been wrong," she shouted at me despite the presence of several other people standing around us. "I gave you an additional week of holiday after your boyfriend left you in such a humiliating way…" she smirked, and I wondered why I had decided to tell her the truth. "And how do you repay me for my kindness and understanding? You can't even be at work on time at such a crucial moment! And have you seen yourself in a mirror today? You look worse than our sandwich delivery boy!" she yelled and not waiting for my reaction quickly disappeared behind the door to Cecilia's office.

I couldn't stand all the mercy looks that people were bombarding me with. I swallowed my pride and rushed to a bathroom. I wasn't going to burst into tears although for a brief moment I felt like doing so. I stood up in front of a mirror to finish my morning make-up, combed my messed by wind hair, poured over my neck half of a bottle of Chanel and actively worked on my mood until I gained the appearance of an immaculate positive winner.

The round table only made the impression of general equality across all participants of the event because as soon as we, the subjects of I-Heart-Travelling, sat down – we watched the grand entrance of our royalty, in the following sequence: Tiggy – Princess of Degradation; Hector – Prince of Opinionlessness; Ludvig – Prince of Nepotism; Cecilia – the Ice Queen; and finally King Arthur – or the King of the Cape of Good Hope because all he had ever given us during the meetings with him was Hope. He kept saying that I-Heart-Travelling was becoming more and more successful and soon its writers would be able to travel all over the world and write more, while most administrative duties would be filled up by permanent staff, instead of employing new interns every six months. Unfortunately, nobody knew what exactly *soon* meant, except that it must have been longer than two years.

The meeting progressed according to the standard agenda. First Cecilia welcomed Arthur MacArthur while telling us one of her thousand and one fables about how everybody was so happy to see him, how honoured we all were, and what a shame he couldn't visit us more often. During this part normally, none of the subjects dared to even twitch, while this time I – thinking that nobody was looking at me – slowly rolled my eyes and sighed. Tiggy looked at me with disapproval, while narrowing her vicious eyes and clenching her teeth. I smiled to her, trying not to laugh, as she looked ridiculous with the weird grimace on her face. Then Arthur with a typical for him stern face expression said how proud he was of his British team and how much he liked to visit his favourite office in London. He seemed to be genuine in the whole process of buttering us up but the truth was that the more we lie the more natural we get at it. He looked and sounded as if he had swallowed a golf club – always keeping a straight posture, always dead serious. I also noticed that when he was talking, he always fiddled with his Mont Blanc – and each time he started doing it, the rest of royalty copied him as if they were saying 'I can afford it too'. Unlike Arthur's, their pens weren't part of a limited collection costing nearly eight thousand dollars, but some of them might have cost more than my monthly salary. To my surprise, I noticed that one of our interns was also fiddling with a chunky Mont Blanc. *I shouldn't be so surprised actually,* I thought. *All in all, he could afford six months of non-paid internship in London, and he certainly didn't look like somebody who would be willing to live in a tent and wash in the Thames River.*

When MacArthur finished his welcome speech, Cecilia and Arthur began encouraging us to get involved into a seemingly casual chat about the current issues at the magazine. In reality they didn't want issues at all so everybody was thinking very carefully before saying anything. While there was this lull a few people decided to reach for some mini sandwiches and cupcakes, which were placed on three silver oval trays in the middle of the table. We weren't used to having food at our meetings, which could sometimes last as long as five hours. Normally the only chance to stop our stomachs rumbling was through squeezing a sandwich at our desks when we had a ten-minute break for the toilet. The food that Cecilia ordered from a nearby bakery was so good that I couldn't resist literally stuffing my face from the silver trays – I was making up for not having breakfast, and unlike most people my stomach wasn't squeezed by nerves. Everybody was also drinking coffee delivered from a cafeteria that we had at the ground floor in our building. Cecilia would never serve Arthur any drinks from one of the coffee machines in our office – the complimentary ground coffee was cheap and disgusting. I would have really enjoyed the whole meeting with its delicious breakfast if only somebody had put King Arthur on mute.

"In the last quarter of the year we've noticed a sudden drop in sales of I-Heart-Travelling for the UK," Arthur was saying. "Consequently, the board in New York decided to undertake certain steps that should help us to recover this setback. I'm here today to give you some good news and some less good news. The less good news is that temporarily we need to limit overseas travelling," he paused to see our reaction. I wondered how you could limit something that had already been limited to the bare minimum. The only answer coming into my head was – to completely eliminate something. The rest of the audience clearly came to the same conclusion and collectively gasped, while Cecilia and Tiggy nodded with understanding. Obviously, the restrictions didn't apply to them. "However, in this dark hour I've also got some good news for you," he smiled clearly proud of himself. "The idea came to me from one of the most creative brains working in this London office," he paused again while turning and smiling at Tiggy, whose smug face suddenly went deep red.

Oh, no, no, no... I was thinking panicking. *Tiggy's idea? What kind of Armageddon is she bringing on us?*

"So what was I saying?" Arthur asked and cleared his throat, and then before Tiggy opened her mouth and managed to say anything, he spoke again, "Each one of you in this room has a very generous amount of paid holidays. Four weeks! Isn't it wonderful? In America most people can only dream about four weeks of fully paid holiday! Anyway... many of you use your leave travelling to the most beautiful places in the world, and here's the thought..." he was enthusiastically waving his hands, "you could use a little bit of your holidays to write an article about the place you're currently visiting and share a few photos with us. In return, as a gesture of our gratitude and good will, the company would subsidise a part of your holiday expenses. Cecilia, Ludvig and Tiggy will be very happy to help you in the choice of your destination. I'm sure they can inspire you."

For a moment the room went so silent that I could even hear the rustle of paper. Everybody exchanged glances around the table. I noticed a few smirks on some faces. The silence was broken by our Mont Blanc intern who suddenly dropped his pen on the table with a loud bang. Like several other people I jumped in my chair involuntarily putting my hand on my chest. The intern, whose name was Jamie or James, apologised and then quickly covered his mouth not to laugh. I wondered whether he was more amused with Arthur's idea or dropping his pen.

"How much will be subsidised?" asked Polly, probably verbalising everybody's thoughts. Cecilia and Tiggy looked at her with disapproval.

"We still need to work on the details," answered Ludvig, but Polly wasn't taking her eyes off Arthur, who finally felt obliged to comment:

"At the beginning we're planning to subsidise eight percent of the value of your holiday for one person. If the project works – meaning the pieces are usable, the board might agree to increase to ten percent."

Eight percent for one person, that's ridiculous. I would probably find a better discount on Groupon, some other discount vouchers website or in a daily newspaper, and all I'll have to do will be to copy and paste a code, I was laughing in my head, while eating a cupcake. A bit of the laugh, however, must have got out of my head because within one second I heard myself snorting and immediately coughing from a bit of cupcake that got stuck in my throat. All eyes turned on me exactly at the moment I knew that cake was coming out. Without a word, I stood up and ran out the room. As I was standing relieved outside of the door with the half-swallowed cupcake in my hand, the door suddenly opened and Tiggy offered me a glass of water. She also hit me twice so hard between my shoulders that I bent in half from pain, not able to say anything.

"Hope that it helps," she said in a way that inferred the opposite, she hit me and she clearly enjoyed it. "If you hadn't stuffed your face so greedily with the company food you would be fine," she added with satisfaction.

"Do you know what would also help?" I asked, slowly returning to my straight position. "It would help if you stopped publicly shouting at me, and humiliating me! And I'm glad my last holiday inspired your wonderful idea to MacArthur." I hadn't realised the door was open behind me until people started passing us by. Tiggy froze while Polly looked at us muttering 'interesting'. I liked Polly except when she knew something, everybody else had to know it too.

"We're having an hour's break, Arthur needs to make a video call," Cecilia informed Tiggy and left us.

"Olivia Eliot, you wanted to talk to me so come to my office right now," Tiggy said suddenly in an unnaturally tubal voice, and quickly marched to her office leaving her door slightly ajar.

Only Tiggy, Cecilia and Ludvig had offices and depending on their mood they had the pleasure of shutting, ajaring or swinging their doors. The rest of us worked in a large open plan office that was the remaining half of the floor. Our desks were so close to each other that we could elbow our neighbours on both sides at the same time or kick their legs in front of us. Nobody would say it but we all enjoyed our work more when one of our desk neighbours called in sick. Space was a luxury at the magazine. Six pair of eyes looked at me from behind their computers and then I heard Tiggy shouting from her room, "Eliot, are you coming or what?"

I sighed and walked towards Tiggy's office imagining how a lamb would feel if it knew that it was going for slaughter.

"Sit down," Tiggy pointed to a chocolate leather chair while she chose to stand above hers with her arms crossed on the opposite side of her desk. "I'm not going to apologise to you for criticising you in public. Everybody should know I'm not going to tolerate lateness, especially when Arthur MacArthur visits us."

"I was away. I didn't check my phone at midnight so I didn't know I needed to be at work an hour earlier."

"Your leave ended on Sunday, right?"

"Yes," I nearly whispered not having a clue where she was going with this.

"You received the message at midnight so it was already Monday and your duty was to read the bloody text."

She was acting ridiculous but I didn't feel like starting an argument with my boss just after getting back from holiday. I only nodded, and she smiled widely, at the same time looking surprised that I agreed with her without a fight. She then put her long black hair up and squeezed them into a tight high ponytail, which made the features on her round plump face look sharper and more serious.

"I'm glad we both agree. Now, I would be happy to recommend you a great therapist who can help you to deal with the loss of Henry," she said.

"No thank you. I'm doing just fine. It's Henry who will have to find a way of dealing with losing me after he eventually realises—"

"Are you debating committing suicide?" she asked flippantly, fiddling with her tatty red nail varnish.

"Jesus Christ! Of course not!" I yelled.

"Good because it's probably not worth it," she said slowly taking a seat on her swing chair.

Probably? Does the therapist pay you to break people to ensure they need some mental support?

"Totally not worth it," I said through gritted teeth. "Besides I'm fine."

"You say you're fine," she rolled her eyes, "but in the meantime you get wasted at random parties and involved with even more random guys. You waste your time and energy, while destroying the only thing you've got left – your career."

I hardly managed to hold myself back from standing up and shouting 'How dare you'. I was dangerously close to saying something I could regret later, but just in time I made a quick cost benefit analysis, which resulted in the decision to squeeze all my comments back into my throat, where they turned into golf balls.

"Tiggy, thank you for your concern. I really appreciate it and I'll certainly think about seeing a therapist…"

"There's nothing to think about. Just do it," she said and opened a drawer in her desk to pull out a pile of business cards before handing one of them to me.

"Donald Brie, psychotherapist," I read loudly and forced myself to smile. "Thank you. I'll get in touch with him… But what would really, really help me…" I was saying with a begging voice, "is more holiday. I've still got a couple of weeks to use from last year and…"

"Done. How much do you need? Two, three days be enough? You could do whole day sessions with Donald Brie. I highly recommend it."

"I was actually thinking about the whole two weeks from last year that I didn't use."

She laughed forcefully, "Don't be silly. Not a chance, certainly not now when we're so busy. Besides you've heard Arthur, we're going through some financial troubles."

"Even if I said I would write another article from my journey? I've already sent you that report from my train trip to Madrid, Barcelona and Avignon."

Tiggy put her elbows on her desk, leant forward and started making circles with her tongue on the inside of her left cheek, "Hmm… Hmm… When would you like to take the leave?"

"Somewhere between the beginning of July and the end of September," I said cheerfully.

"No way. July and August are already fully booked by those who have children at school age. Then in September a few interns booked their time off in case they have to retake their exams. Most importantly however, I've got myself a few weeks off in September. I'm flying to the Maldives. My position is so important that I need at least four people to cover me over that time."

"Sorry but I remember you were saying a week ago that nobody was allowed to book any leave before the end of May."

"You've got such a good memory Eliot," she grimaced like after eating a lemon or taking a strong shot of vodka. "It was a week ago, as you correctly noticed, and during the week when you were away plenty of things changed," she said and then reached again to her drawer, this time to pull out a paper box with one doughnut inside covered with bright pink icing, "I had no breakfast," she said while stuffing her face.

"Interns have priority in taking their leave before me," I took a deep breath. "So when could I take the leave?"

She typed something on her computer using her right hand, while she was licking pink icing from the fingers of her left hand, "Eighth to the twenty-first of June."

"Is that not when we've got our annual summer ball and three days of workshops in the Lake District?" I asked despite knowing the answer.

"Sorry, you'll need to choose what's more important to you," she said crushing the box after the doughnut and throwing it just past my face to a bin behind me. I moved involuntarily, and she smirked pretending not to see it.

"I'll take the eighth to twenty-first."

"Good. But I've forgotten to mention that the place, where you decide to go if you want the offer needs to be somewhere we haven't written about within the last two years."

Tiggy was adding more and more fuel to the bonfire and it was slowly consuming me but I was not going to give up.

"I hope Grenada is okay."

She looked up to the ceiling fiddling with her hair, "Yeah, I suppose it's fine" she finally said. "Eighth to twenty first of June," she was repeating while typing on the computer, "Olivia Eliot. Grenada."

"Thank you," I murmured and just after I had managed to lift myself from her comfy chair and make one step towards the door she spoke again:

"Oh sorry, I've forgotten to tell you something," she paused for a better final effect, "We can't subsidise your holiday yet. It's all work in progress."

"I understand. So I don't have to write an article then?"

"Of course you have to. Don't be silly Eliot," she snapped. "If you don't like it, I'm sure I'll find many people who with great pleasure take two weeks of leave to—"

"Of course. I do appreciate the opportunity you've given me to both take some rest and progress my career," I said and turned back to walk away.

"Olivia," I heard the same annoying voice behind my back.

What else? Do I need to give formal notice to be able to leave your office?

I reluctantly turned to see Tiggy's smug face.

"Who's the handsome guy on your Facebook profile? Do you actually know him or did you ask him for a few photos so Henry would be jealous? I just hope that your personal life won't have any negative effect on your career. If you're going away with him..."

"No. The trip is to forget about Henry and focus on my work. Thanks again for your concern," I was saying this in pain because my fingernails were digging into the middle of my palms. *God, you've got some effect on people Tiggy, I've already started self-harming and I haven't even left your office.*

I left abruptly not giving her another chance to speak again. On the way back to my desk I wrote a message to Hugo:

¡Hola! Good news is that I've got two weeks off, but it's from 8 to 21 June, can we go then?

The answer came almost immediately:

Muy bien cariño. Better earlier than never I'll look for some flights tonight and I'll speak to you in the evening. Besos, H.

Both happy and relieved I was strolling through our open plan office, when I heard Polly whispering loudly to a new girl from our accounting department: "I knew that sooner or later they were going to split up. Henry is such a Casanova! Once when he was waiting here for Olivia, he was flirting with Tiggy. Can you imagine? Olivia and Tiggy, they both practically hate each other and Henry knew it! Can you imagine?"

Before I managed to get to my desk I heard Polly saying 'Can you imagine', at least five other times. I still had twenty minutes to the second half of the meeting with Arthur and I could not focus on doing anything else work-related. I opened and then immediately closed my mailbox with over a hundred unread emails, then quickly logged onto my Facebook account. It did not take me long to find out that I did not have Tiggy on my list of three hundred and thirty friends. I then checked Henry's profile. He had over five hundred friends, including Tiggy Brown. He had promised me to unbefriend her!

11

SATURDAY, 30 MAY

OXFORD

"Sorry we're late but you wouldn't believe the traffic. We had to park outside the city and take the biggest and slowest ever double-decker bus to get here. What a faff!" Atlanta was standing above me and vividly gesticulating. Her straight long blond hair was getting into her eyes, and drops of sweat were sticking her fringe to her forehead.

"Darling, I tried to explain to you last night that you'd have been better off taking the train but you just wouldn't listen," I said while tidying up a pile of travel magazines and books that I had spread on a blanket.

"You should know by now that Atlanta only listens to herself," said Freya with a shrug of her slim little shoulders. She was over a head shorter than six-foot tall Atlanta, and she had never changed her short boyish haircut or the chestnut colour of her hair since I'd met her a decade ago. I often thought that Atlanta and Freya couldn't be more different from each other, both in their looks and behaviour. I was convinced that if it weren't for me they would have never become friends. They kept saying they liked each other very much, but they spent most of their time arguing.

"Never mind but it would be so much quicker if you took the train," I murmured.

"But I didn't want to carry the damn basket across the whole city," Atlanta said irritated. She practically threw her rattan designer picnic basket on my blanket and pulled out a tissue from her bag to wipe her forehead.

"You had to do it anyway," Freya laughed fiddling with her big necklace made of colourful beads in various sizes. "And it wasn't that bad. The air conditioning on the bus was broken so we drunk everything that we had in the basket, including a bottle of wine. It meant that it was easier to carry."

"So, I hope you've got enough drinks for the three of us," Atlanta snapped and slowly sat down next to me.

As I predicted Christ Church Meadow was a perfect spot to have a picnic on a sunny Saturday afternoon. While the centre of Oxford was rammed with locals and tourists, the crowds in the park only reached as far as the building of Christ Church – where they took their selfies, with or without a stick, and quickly went back to the city. We had plenty of space to chat and lie on the grass.

Although we had lived in London I visited the park with Henry on many weekends throughout the last five years and in most weathers – we would have a picnic or just stroll around and feed not-so-hungry ducks or geese. We would either carefully prepare the contents of our basket at home, or more often than not buy our lunch from a café on the high street then eat it while sitting on the grass, surrounded by paper bags, napkins and our plans for the future. The park had temporarily also become our weekday luncheon place when for a period of three months Henry had been giving guest lectures at the University. At the time my manager was Lovely Susannah, who allowed us on occasion to work from home – for me it meant collecting my thoughts in the open air and then transferring them onto my laptop from under one of the trees in the park. Oh, the good pre-Tiggy times. Such a shame Susannah got married to an American guy and had to move with him to Los Angeles…

I looked around the park thinking that it felt like ages ago that

Henry had really been mine, truly with me. Not completely consumed thinking about his job or… more likely about another woman. Whatever it had been, I started realising, it had taken him away from me a long time before he actually left me at the airport.

Despite so many memories filled with Henry I still enjoyed the atmosphere of the park. I was determined to erase the man from my thoughts as quickly as possible by making new memories. I swore to myself that I wouldn't let him take away my favourite places, music, flavours or aromas that I had experienced during the past five years. I didn't want to be like some of my friends, whose broken hearts didn't let them enjoy their favourite Italian meal, listen to Michael Bublé or go to Paris. It was tough because I had to block all the stubborn and intrusive pictures of Henry and me that were popping up literally everywhere in my mind. The bench where Henry suggested that we should live together – needed to return to being just a bench. The weeping willow under which he said that he loved me needed to return to being just a tree. It was tough but my mind wasn't going to give up remembering without a fight.

"*Caribbean Travel Guide; Grenada – the Cinnamon Island; Heaven is on the Caribbean; Grenada – your trip to Paradise,*" Freya was reading the titles of the books I had bought while waiting for them.

"Let me guess, once again you're writing an article for your travel magazine about a place you've never actually seen. Olivia, you're only wasting your time in that job," it was not the first time Atlanta didn't hesitate to loudly express her opinion without considering how harsh or annoying it was going to be. "I bet you paid for the books from your own pocket."

"I'm going there on the eighth of June," I said cheerfully, and my sudden enthusiasm was followed by my completely involuntary clapping of hands.

"That's wonderful," Freya said. "I told you that you needed to be patient because your magazine would eventually change for the better. Most companies are now struggling with money and—"

"Not exactly that good," I said losing the enthusiasm to tell them about my plans. I had a feeling they wouldn't approve of them. "But

I've got two weeks off so... hey! It's great anyway. Last time I had two weeks of leave in one chunk was before I got the job."

"How did you manage to do it?" Freya and Atlanta asked almost simultaneously.

"Where there's a will there's a way... but let's talk about it later."

"Of course! First you need to tell us all about the mysterious Hugo," Atlanta was saying this while jumping enthusiastically on the blanket. Then she took off her purple stilettoes, showing off her new blisters, and sat with her legs crossed.

Since coming back from the holiday I had avoided all meetings with my friends and family. I didn't feel like sharing my plans with anybody – they would have only caused an avalanche of unnecessary doubts.

"The first thing you should know is that Henry left me without any explanation, while we were waiting to check in for our flight to Madrid..."

"I was convinced that you dumped him," Atlanta widened her eyes in disbelief. I felt immediately like I had disappointed her. *I knew you thought he wasn't the right guy for me! Of all people you should have told me! Oh, maybe you told me but I wasn't listening...*

Freya Parsley and Atlanta Washington were my best friends who together knew more about me than anybody else. Since we became friends they had been involved in all the most important changes and events in my life. I met Atlanta fifteen years ago when she moved with her parents to my street in the suburbs of London. I was intrigued by her name itself, I didn't realise somebody could call a child Atlanta. "Her parents are American, it explains a lot. They don't have any boundaries when it comes to naming their kids," my father once explained to me. But as it turned out later, there was a story behind the name. Atlanta's mother, Emma Washington used to work in the headquarters of Coca Cola in Atlanta, where she met her future husband Aidan Dik. Mr Dik who was just about to start his serious career in business preferred to take the more respectable surname of his wife. And Atlanta? Mr and Mrs Washington were not only practical but also very sentimental.

Down to earth, reasonable and quiet Freya was the total opposite of Atlanta. I met her during my first year of university in London, where we both studied journalism. Before she got married and I started going out with Henry we spent most of our free time together. It was at her wedding to Peter when for the very first time I introduced Henry to everybody as my boyfriend. Less than a year later Freya gave birth to her son Peter Junior, and I threw myself into work and Henry. In the new reality we had less time for each other, however, when we did meet we made the most of it. Atlanta, a year and half younger than us, got married last spring to Dylan, who without the slightest hesitation also agreed to take her surname. The wedding was organised on Ibiza and it lasted three days. Since Atlanta had got married she seemed to have more time than ever to travel and socialise. Henry more tolerated than liked Atlanta and Dylan – two graphic designers, who it seemed spent half of their life partying in different cities around the world. They never showed that they didn't like Henry but I was convinced that they were secretly laughing at his seriousness.

"Nobody has ever looked like that at me," I said as I concluded my story about the whole time I spent with Hugo.

"Oh my god! That's so damn romantic!" Atlanta shouted. "It was just meant to be! Henry broke up with you so you had the chance to meet Hugo. Otherwise, Henry would have been sitting in the tapas bar like your chaperon never letting Hugo even get near you. Phew! In fact, Henry would have made you sit the whole evening in the hotel room, saying that it was too busy outside. I'm sure!" She clapped her knee with her right hand. "And while he'd have been working on one of his super-important lectures, you'd have been wasting your youth on waiting for him to give you all the attention you deserve."

Freya looked at Atlanta and shook her head in disapproval to quickly turn to me and ask, "When did you last talk to Henry?"

"At the airport. I haven't been answering his calls since then."

"Don't you think you should listen to him first? Before you get involved with Hugo and change your whole life for him?" Freya asked with concern.

"Oh, come on Freya! She's already involved! Look at her, all blushing when she's saying his name. Besides, she's not changing her life for him!"

They both looked at me with anticipation.

"Well, inevitably I need to introduce some changes into my life to accommodate this relationship with a foreigner—"

"Stop speaking like Henry," Atlanta laughed. "And tell us all about the exciting changes."

"What else do you know about him except that he's handsome, charming, he drinks a lot of wine and has a peculiar business?" Freya turned out to be far more judgy and pessimistic than I had expected.

"Freya!" Atlanta elbowed her.

"I just worry about her," she said defensively and I knew it was true, she wasn't just maliciously trying to sabotage my new love. "Somebody needs to be realistic here."

"He's thirty-one. He speaks four languages and is a great listener. He loves travelling—"

"Who doesn't like travelling?" Freya murmured and rolled her eyes.

"He used to be a travel guide in Madrid. He can cook but he says he's better at baking. He comes from Andalusia. His grandmother lives in Ayamonte and she looks after his house on the beach at Isla Canela. He does kite surfing there in the summer and—"

"Brill! Does he also swim with dolphins and play a guitar on the porch of his beach house?" Freya interrupted me.

"Oh, of course I'm not that stupid to think that he's all perfect, but I haven't noticed anything worrying about him yet."

"Exactly! You need to know him better, find out what his faults are, what is his past, what his friends are like—"

"What Freya is trying to say..." Atlanta started slowly but soon her eyes sparkled and she switched to speaking in her usual fast and enthusiastic manner, "is that you need to fly back to Spain, without telling Hugo and conduct some research. Interview his friends and family. Why don't you start from the grandmother from Ayamonte? Why don't you hire a private investigator?"

"A known devil is often better than an unknown angel. Can't you remember how perfect Henry was five years ago?"

"But Henry is gone for god's sake," I shouted losing my patience. "He left me".

They both went silent, shocked with my sudden and so uncommon for me outburst, before Atlanta asked calmly, "Freya why do you defend Henry so much?"

"I don't. Just don't completely cross Henry out and let him explain himself. And be careful with Hugo, that's it."

"He's the one who crossed me out Freya. Should I have chased him at the airport? I actually think that it all happened for the best. During the week away I had a chance to realise how much was missing in our relationship."

"Missing what?" Freya snapped.

"It is said that opposites attract and it was true at the very beginning with Henry. We were like fire and water but we worked together surprisingly well. I was fascinated by the new world he exposed to me – the patience, seriousness and maturity – everything I thought I was somehow lacking. But now I think that he was the water constantly extinguishing the fire I had in me. He used to turn off any trace of enthusiasm I had. His standard day to day argument was – why would I change anything and risk making things even worse?"

"What did he specifically turn off in you?" Freya was never satisfied with general answers, she needed hard proof, she needed examples.

"Sometimes I think you don't get anything," Atlanta gave Freya a merciful look. "He switched off her passion, her desire! Would you stay with a man who hasn't given you an orgasm for years? She wanted some changes – to spice up their sex life a little bit, while Henry on the other hand—"

"Fair enough," Freya interrupted her.

"No! That's not the point! Once I told him I wanted to quit my job because it didn't bring me any satisfaction and I had enough of my boss taking pleasure in constantly belittling me. He said, 'Darling, do you really think it's going to be better somewhere else? It's just a job.

Don't take it too seriously.' On another occasion I asked him to take a sabbatical and travel with me for half of a year. That was the time before we bought the house when we still had some savings. He laughed at me saying that he loved me for being such an incorrigible dreamer. At the time I also loved him for bringing me back down to earth. Don't you understand? I don't want anybody anymore to bring me back down to earth!" I spread my arms looking into the sky.

"I'm sorry then that I'm the one doing it," Freya said. "But what are your plans now?"

"I want to take the rudder in my hands and set the course for my life all by myself. Hugo suggested travelling with him for a year," I paused to see their reaction, they were looking at me flabbergast, "And I'm going to do it!" I said with a little squeak.

"That's actually very interesting," Freya said. "You want to take control over your life but all you're actually doing is passing the tiller from one guy to the next. Besides from what you've been saying, Hugo is in the middle of starting off his business. What sort of businessman leaves his new venture for a year without his supervision?"

I glanced at Atlanta and I knew I couldn't count on her support, "I'm afraid Freya might be right."

"That's why I didn't want to meet up with you last week. I knew you wouldn't approve of my choices, and now—"

"You didn't want to tell us about it because you knew that you're choosing to live in your little Wonderland instead of facing reality," Freya snapped.

"Hold on a sec, what have you already done Olivia?"

"Oh, nothing too dramatic," I waved my hand in front of my nose as if I wanted to get rid of a fly but they knew me too well to believe it. "I swear, nothing. I haven't quit my job. I'm just going with Hugo for two weeks to Grenada. He's already been there and he really wants me to see the island."

"Who's paying for it? You said not that long ago after you bought the house that you were going to holiday for a while on your couch with a bottle of cheap wine and some books from the library," Atlanta was now officially on team Freya.

"I've sold my car. I've had it seven years and any time soon I'd have to start throwing a lot of money at it. It already needed a new set of tyres and—"

"I have to admit you surprised me girl! I don't know this part of you," Atlanta said. "What do you do when you can't afford new tyres for your car? You sell the car and fly to the Caribbean. Cool!" she started swaying while still sat with her legs crossed, a few people looked at us with curiosity. "But why do I have a feeling that's not all?"

"Well, if after the holiday we want to make a go of it, I'm coming back to convince Tiggy to fire me. Then I'll rent the house—"

"What the hell?" Freya was frantically blinking as if something had gotten into her eyes.

"If I-Heart-Travelling fires me, they'll have to give me a redundancy payment. Enough to start travelling with Hugo for the year," I said proud of my sneaky little idea.

"Do you have a travel plan?" Do you know where you would like to go?" asked Freya and just when I thought that I had finally convinced her she said, "Let me guess, first learning Italian while stuffing your face with ravioli in Rome? Followed by a journey to the deepest parts of your soul somewhere in an ashram in India? And finally at the end passionate sex in Bali?"

"I really liked that book," Atlanta said.

"Me too, but its author negotiated a substantial advance from her publisher to be able to write it while travelling for so long," Freya said.

"Why can't you just be happy for me?"

"Henry is a respected lecturer at one of the best London Universities, he's got great prospects ahead of him. He's not a crazy, passionate guy with his head overheated from the Mediterranean sun, who wants to travel across the whole world with you right now… He's well-balanced, realistic and mature. He's thirty-four and he's ready to start a family. He doesn't' have a beach house but he's got an idea for paying off a mortgage in a place where you both can work and bring up a family…"

"Sorry Freya, but when you put it like that, I just want to run away.

Boring, boring, boring... You're not going to achieve anything with that mindset," Atlanta said.

"No, it does make sense actually," I said, thinking that safe and predictable didn't always meant bad. "But how many times can I tell you he left me?"

Freya ignored my question. "What will you do when you waste a year or more on Hugo and then—"

"If you mean my biological clock, I've still got a bit of time and I'm not going to act all desperate. Anyway, I don't feel like a picnic anymore..."

"We haven't eaten anything yet," Freya said.

"I've suddenly lost my appetite. Anyone feel like a drink in a pub?"

"Not that fast," Atlanta said seriously. For a brief moment I thought she was saying it to me, but she wasn't taking her eyes off Freya. "You know something," she pointed her finger at Freya. "You know something," she repeated poking Freya's stomach, which made her jump. "And you're going to tell us right now."

"Ouch! Stop poking me," Freya shouted overly loudly drawing all eyes of the people around us, who had decided to have their picnics or read their books.

"I swear you'll regret it if you don't tell us right now," Atlanta was getting more and more serious. "If there's someone you need to stay loyal to it's us! Not any damn man!"

"Fine, fine," Freya said with resignation in her voice, and then I started being afraid of what I was going to hear.

"I talked to Henry. He called me. Olivia, he cried that he loved you and he was scared of losing you forever."

"What's done is done, he's lost her fo-re-ver," snapped Atlanta. "Was he drunk? It sounds quite dramatic for him."

"Stone cold sober. Just let him explain himself."

"And you think that Hugo is crazy, that I'm crazy. But who leaves a girl at the airport and then cries—"

"Just let him explain, and then you decide."

"Olivia is right. When did you speak to him?"

"After Peter met Henry on the tube last week. Henry was very upset. He said that you would probably have to sell the house so he could get some money back to start all over again. And then Henry called me—"

"That's interesting!" I shouted, feeling a sudden flow of heat and a pulsating pain in my chest. "That's even more interesting than the fact he loves me, because he didn't spend a penny on the house. He was going to pay me back when he got some money from his dead aunt from New Zealand, but it never happened."

"What was the mortgage deal you signed?" Atlanta asked.

There were many thoughts that went through my head at that moment and I didn't like most of them.

12

SUNDAY, 31 MAY

HAVEN-ON-THAMES

I t was our first meeting since we broke up and Henry was already an hour late. Apparently on that weekend there were some planned engineering works on the railway and he had forgotten to check it earlier. Henry was renting a flat in London, the same flat we lived in together until we bought the house in Dream Fields, one of the prettiest villages in South Oxfordshire.

Henry said to me in April that he had notified his landlord he was going to move but he would have to pay for the flat anyway until the end of May, so he decided to stay there for another few weeks to enjoy the last days of his short commute to work. I believed him – I had no reason not to, but now I doubted whether he had ever actually given notice at all. It briefly crossed my mind that something was wrong when in May our house was occupied by plenty of my boxes, while the only thing of all Henry's belongings was his toothbrush – a cheap manual one which he had received for free in a hotel. *Or he got it from another woman when he spontaneously spent a night at hers?* He had argued that I had more stuff and it would be more practical if I fully unpacked first. Had he ever had any intention of moving in to the house or was it purely an investment?

I sat outside one of the cafes in Haven-on-Thames to sip caramel latte and watch how life was passing by on the Sunday morning. The town owed its charm to its picturesque location on both sides of the River Thames and several stone bridges, which were the main crossings in that area. In the South part of Haven-on-Thames there was a decent-size market square densely filled with fresh colourful flowers and café gardens, which were generously supplied with heat lamps to ensure they could open the whole year round. Unsurprisingly, the social life of the town was mainly focused around the square. It was also the centre for a few nearby villages including Dream Fields, which in reality was an extension of Haven-on-Thames.

There were four narrow streets going to the market square, but only one of them was pedestrianized – and it was where I was sitting, outside Haven-Coffee-Shop. The first time I visited the place was with Henry at the beginning of April. On that day we were to receive the key to our new home. We were sitting inside, next to an old wooden window shaken from time to time by gusts of strong wind and heavy rain. At one point when the rain was so heavy we could hardly see what was happening outside, and we started loudly imagining that we were having a romantic dinner under a huge waterfall somewhere on a tropical island. I thought then that there was nowhere and nobody I'd rather be with.

"I can't believe we finally got the house, our own home," Henry had said excited with his whole face beaming as if it had been plugged into the mains.

After half of a year of combat to buy the house we both couldn't believe we finally owned it. We'd gotten used to answering our phones literally every single week from the developer, warning us that we had a month to finalise the sale, otherwise we were going to lose our deposit and the reservation. Then at the end of each month the same developer mercifully decided to give us one more chance – one more month of hell. No wonder after half of a year, which felt like half of a decade, we were completely worn out. The problem was that we could not have bought anything – other than a campervan – until my parents sold their house on the outskirts of London. Their plan was to use the money from the sale to downsize to an apartment, buy a small beach house in France and give the rest to me and my brother Philip so we both had a deposit for a house. Initially, I wanted to take a small mortgage and get a two-bedroom flat but Henry managed to convince me that what we really needed was a family house. My friends and family supported me with the idea, all saying as one that it would be silly to buy a flat only to sell it soon afterwards and buy a house, while losing money on taxes and solicitors.

Before I said yes to us getting *Mortgaged,* Henry took me for a small trip to Dream Fields, where a new development had just been completed. I had never heard about the village but as soon as I got out of the car I was hooked. It was love from the first sight. The development was built just next to a protected nature reserve so my potential view from the window was protected too – it was never going to change into a building field. The houses were not squashed one next to another, and in the middle of the housing complex there was a park with two large lakes that attracted swans and ducks. When we arrived it was a sunny afternoon. The whole area looked so beautiful that for a moment I was convinced that the swans in the lakes were actually stuffed animals staged for marketing purposes. *It might be the place to start a family with Henry. It might be a sign from heaven,* I had thought on that day. When a few months later I was sitting alone in Haven-Coffee-Shop waiting for Henry to finally make his appearance, I was rather thinking that it must have been a sign from heaven heralding my personal Armageddon. *How could I not have seen it?*

* * *

"Hi Olivia," I heard a familiar voice behind my back, which made me shiver. "I feel so stupid," said the voice and I saw a shade moving over my right side. "For the last fifteen minutes I've been standing a couple of meters away from you afraid to come closer and speak to you."

"Well Henry, I've managed to work out by now that you're a coward. Are you going to stand or will you take a seat?"

"I'll order something for us and then I'll sit with you, of course if you allow me," he said officially.

No, I decided to meet up with you but I won't let you sit next to me. Oh, heaven!

I felt like I'd lost my appetite after I saw Henry. Although I didn't ask for anything, soon after a waitress appeared in front of us carrying two large slices of chocolate cake with caramel ice cream and two mugs of coffee with cream and marshmallows on the top. It was exactly what Henry and I had ordered in April. Unfortunately, it didn't taste as good anymore – apparently company does affect taste buds. For a long while we merely focused on eating our cakes and slowly sipping our coffees. Somebody watching us could have thought that we were just really enjoying our little feast, while in reality the sudden sugar rush was making me a little sick. I was eating only to have an excuse not to talk, it also gave me time to calm down my racing heart. We were sitting comfortably in soft cushioned rattan armchairs. I was holding my plate in my left hand and a fork in the right, while left handed Henry was like my reflection in a mirror. Our table looked smart but was so low that it would have been more appropriate as a footrest.

It was approaching lunch and soon all tables around us became busy, filled with noisy chats and laughter. There seemed to be no end of people coming to say hello to their friends sitting at the tables outside, often encouraged by the seated people who appeared to be constantly waving to somebody passing. Haven-on-Thames was one of those towns, where many people spend their whole lifetime and never move away. A perfect place to have a family and establish long-term relationships with other families. Less perfect for single people who were as popular in the area as a fridge in an igloo.

I hadn't noticed it until that day but the town actually had quite a few bars but not a single club for a Saturday evening. Most facilities were aimed at young families: a couple of toy shops, a traditional sweet shop with candies packed in glass jars, several craft shops, a bookstore with some children stories in the window display and a shoe shop – where most certainly I wouldn't find a pair of smart stilettoes, but rather 'bargain children's shoes'. As I read on some posters the main events for the following weekend were: 'Tea with Peppa Pig' and a ride around the town on Thomas' train.

When a three-year old boy started having a tantrum – screaming and throwing waffles at his astounded grandparents; followed by our plates being attacked by wasps, which Henry was horribly allergic to, we decided to get inside of the café. We quickly found a free table next to the coffee machine and even quicker we realised why it had been empty. Each time when Henry wanted to say something, the machine was making a noise like a steam train passing by. I didn't know whether we finally got used to the sound of the coffee maker or the demand for coffee dropped, but I finally heard Henry saying, "I'm sorry. I am really, really sorry that I acted like an utter idiot. Will you let me explain everything?"

I had a feeling that he wanted me to say 'no', so it would save him the trouble of making up some lame excuses before he got down to business – and discussed our mortgage issues. I had never seen him so uptight, he looked as if he had a nail digging into his arse.

"And why do you think I'm here?" I snapped. "Go on," I said, crossing both my arms and legs and leaning back on the chair.

"Do you remember how I told you that my uni along with several other universities in London had created a special department to detect cheating students, and those who sell the essays, dissertations and exam questions? And how I became one of the key people working for the department?"

"How could I forget? It all started over six months ago and it was your excuse for not having much time for me and being constantly absentminded."

"It actually began a year ago but we hadn't practically achieved anything until recently, when we employed some experienced investigators and IT specialists. We also trained and paid many young people, who were to impersonate students across all faculties at the universities involved in the project. We quickly identified hundreds of students buying work from suppliers spread all over the world. It's really hard to believe how large the criminal network is for something like this and how profitable it can be."

"Indeed, I find it hard to believe," I said and smirked ironically. "Just after my graduation I sold a few decent dissertations but I didn't make much money on them."

"Maybe because you didn't have a network of excellent dealers and your customers weren't bankers from London City?"

"Yyyy... Maybe... Dealers?"

"Dealers are simply middlemen who act between students and the people who write essays or steal exam questions. Those working for large Cheaters Gangs are incredibly hard to catch and it's even harder to prosecute them. They're true professionals."

I was looking at Henry with disbelief, wondering whether he was using the services of a more conventional kind of dealer. "Yeah, Cheaters Gangs sounds professional."

"Olivia, think for a minute. You told me you wondered how some people manage to study two different subjects, and at the same time work full time in a demanding job."

"And then on the weekend they have enough time to go out and party, and enough energy to take a million selfies," I added fervently. "They also cook healthy meals, travel and regularly go to the gym."

"Exactly! Of course, their lives aren't as perfect and fulfilled as they play it up on social media, but still—"

"Their average day and night seemed to have way more than my twenty-four hours."

"People like that normalize what is far from being normal, achievable or manageable. Those on a good salary can afford to pay large sums of cash for a thesis on corporate law or economics. Then when they get the qualifications, their salary goes up again and they can buy more, adding to their CVs and LinkedIn, and so on. Do you know what it all means?"

"It means that tomorrow I'm going to apply for an MA in law, and post an advert about me writing unlawful dissertations so I can make some cash and pay for my study!"

"If you do it in a way that I can't catch you, I'd support it," he laughed for the first time since we met. "But coming back to the

Cheaters Gangs it means a huge business on an international scale," he paused and looked at me with anticipation.

"But it also means you have your hands full I suppose," I said nodding with understanding. "Are you trying to say that you left me because you've been busy busting members of a Cheaters Gang? And you can't tell me what exactly you've been doing for the whole time because you're some sort of academic James Bond?" I wanted to laugh but it didn't feel funny at all. I didn't even know whether I believed him. I also immediately regretted putting some ideas into his head that could somehow justify his behaviour.

"I shouldn't tell you everything but I trust you. Besides knowing you if you were ever going to forgive me, I need to tell you the truth," he said in a mysterious tone of voice. I imagined him as James Bond sitting right in front of me – it was a young Pierce Brosnan but with blond hair and a notebook under his arm.

"After the way you treated me at the airport, you owe me some explanation."

"The fact that cheating at universities is an international and well-established trade is obviously sad, at least from a lecturer's point of view but..." he giggled nervously, "but it offered me and my colleagues from Shakespeare University a unique business opportunity and the chance to finally start earning decent money. It turned out that the scale of the crime is so huge that even a coalition of several universities can't afford to chase down the cheaters and their providers. We need to be able to pay detectives, IT specialists as well as other experts from various fields... then we also need fake students and people who go abroad to track the gangs. That's why a few months ago me and my colleagues launched a private business," he said and clapped his hands.

I couldn't convince him to start a business as a private tutor, and now he's telling me he's got a firm chasing criminals!

"Does it mean you quit your work at uni?"

"Nope, I still work there but I'm going to cut my hours from the next semester. We've got plenty of job orders from various universities and even more from business firms. One of our newest markets are rich daddies, who want to verify whether their future son-in-law gained his education all by himself and should sit on the firm's board..." Henry was getting more and more enthusiastic.

"When exactly did you set up this business?" I asked feeling like I knew the answer anyway.

He hesitated before continuing his explanation but this time with less enthusiasm and much quieter, "As I said a few months ago. Three. Maybe four."

"And it has never struck you before to tell me about it? I know your new job isn't quite the same as chasing drug dealers in Mexico or terrorist groups in the Middle East but still!"

"It isn't, however, totally risk free and that's why nobody besides our closest relatives can know what we really do."

"Let me guess, just before our flight to Madrid, you picked up your phone and found out that somebody wanted to kill you..." I lowered my voice making it sound comically deep, "knowing how much you're afraid of flying, I can easily imagine that you assumed that somebody would blow up a plane with you on board."

"Could you be serious for a moment?" he asked clearly offended and I felt like the old dead earnest Henry was firmly back.

"I'm nothing but serious but I still don't get what must have happened for you to treat me like—"

"As always you're so damn impatient," he snapped. "The story needed a certain degree of background information for you to understand. We've got—"

"Would you like something more?" asked a waiter all of a sudden, and we both jumped in our chairs.

"A glass of red wine for me please," I said without thinking.

"We don't sell alcohol here," the waiter said like he was a mentor from AA.

"You've got coffee with Baileys or Cognac or Cointreau..." I was saying while moving my finger down the drink's menu.

"Right but we only sell the liquors with coffee."

"Can I have then two shots of Baileys for me and a double latte for you?" I said smiling widely, seeing in the corner of my eye Henry's face full of disapproval.

"I'm afraid I can't accept any drinks from customers."

"Olivia, we can always go somewhere else," Henry finally lost his patience, which gave me a pang of satisfaction. *Mr Bloody Patient*, I thought.

"Okay, could you be so kind and bring me two mugs of coffee and two shots of Baileys separately?" I asked and the waiter shook his head. "I just want to make sure I get the right amount of everything. I've heard that some cafes are cheating on the amount of liquors added to their coffees."

"I guess I can do it," he said gloomily and shrugged.

A few minutes later I watered some dry plants on a windowsill with the double latte and poured both shots of Baileys into one of the empty mugs. Henry preferred to sip his herbal infusion.

"So, where were we?" Henry asked after I took a long gulp.

"Somebody threatened you," I said flippantly.

"Oh, okay... And Olivia," he looked at me intensely, "keep your voice down."

"Fine," I whispered.

"We received a job from a large investment company in London, which wanted to take over another investment firm in the city – not as large as they were but equally well-known and well-established. The take-over wasn't as easy as they had initially assumed so they decided to look for their opponent's weakest link. They started from the board of directors. We were asked to check the qualifications of their thirty-something CEO. Long story short our client was right – the CEO bought his MBA and we were able to successfully prove it. In that way we received our first cheque with six fat zeros."

"You're kidding me?" I raised my voice too quickly and lowered it back to an almost whisper, "We meaning WHO exactly?"

"Are you asking between how many people we had to divide the cheque?" he asked looking as proud as if he had just been elected President of the United States.

I nodded vigorously.

"Three directors including me," he said with a smug face. "But don't you want to know what happened next?"

I nodded again. I was speechless. I had expected to hear many lame excuses but in my wildest dreams I would not have predicted that on this day Henry would be able to impress me. *Wow! Henry* – the *Cheaters Buster!*

"Our client had a meeting with the fraudulent CEO, during which they threatened to reveal his little secret to the public. A little secret that would cause huge embarrassment, inevitable long-term unemployment, and potentially a prison sentence. But they promised to keep quiet if he decided to help them merge the two companies."

"Hmmm… They used the information to blackmail somebody. And it was you who armed the blackmailers…"

"That's just business and I'm not going to change it," Henry said irritated. "I provide my client with some information, I have no influence on how they're going to use it."

"I guess I could turn a blind eye to what people do with my research if it meant I got loads of money," I thought loudly. "It's not like you sold instructions for a do-it-yourself nuclear weapon… Anyway, did he agree?"

"The CEO maybe didn't have an MBA but he was a great negotiator. He proposed to reveal several names of people on his board, who had also bought their prestigious degrees. In return he demanded that our client and my company destroy all our evidence against him."

"Funny guy, did he really think that you would agree?"

"Our client did agree," he said and I looked at him astounded. "They agreed because one of the people who the CEO said he could expose was right at the top – he was the president of the company. He was also president of another firm that our client was potentially interested in."

"I don't quite get it," I said stroking my lower lip. "When you've got the name, surely you could just get some proof on your own. Is that not your job?"

"We had tried but after a month we were still nowhere. Generally, the higher you are on the ladder, the more money you can throw around to hide your crimes and destroy any proof against you. It wasn't until we got a lead from the CEO that we were finally on the right track to achieve something. We successfully planted spies in some Ivy League universities and managed to gather sufficient evidence to earn another six zeros cheque," he said and took a loud sip of his herbal infusion.

"So why do I have the feeling that the story doesn't have a good ending?"

Henry took a few deep breaths, "The president turned out to be innocent! The CEO fooled us all."

"Oh my god! Henry! You shouldn't play at being a damn academic James Bond. You're a great lecturer and you better stick to your real job!"

"A minute ago, you seemed to be impressed," he snapped.

"I'm just worried now what I'm going to hear next..."

"Yeah, it gets worse. The president decided to sue both the giant investment firm and my company..." his voice began to break, "for an attempt of defamation and destroying his career. We had nothing on the CEO, we gave all evidence to the client and they destroyed it, even though I advised them not to. I should have realised earlier... I should have been able to predict..." he rested his arms on his knees and put his face in his hands.

"But it's your client that ultimately blackmailed the president, you were only a kind of postman – a carrier of the information... If you give all the money back to the investment firm, which of course is annoying, really annoying... you're going to be fine?"

"I've already given all my share of the money back – over six hundred grand. I should have never, never let my client trust the CEO... I was devastated that day when we were to go to Madrid. I wanted so badly to give you all the good news when we got there, but just before we got on the plane I received a phone call."

"Couldn't you just have told me?"

"Olivia, I had no idea what to tell you or how to tell you. If somebody like J... I mean the president," he corrected himself, looking like he was afraid of his own voice.

"Oh, come on Henry! Really? You can tell me now who the guy is! They're going to write about it, I'm sure it's just a matter of time. And

I still think it would have been better if you had told me instead of…"
I paused not knowing what to say. *Instead of dumping me? Instead of pretending to dump me?*

"All I knew at that time was that I wanted you to get on the bloody plane. I needed forty-eight hours to come up with something that would save our relationship and our house."

"The house? What the fuck?" I shouted and quickly covered my mouth with both my hands. A few parents, who glanced at me condemningly, had their hands ready to put over their children's ears. *Maybe we should have gone somewhere else.* "I said duck, okay?" I glanced at one of the outraged mothers.

"If the president had put the case to court, I'd have lost every bit of savings I had, everything I got from aunt Zelda and… half of the money from the house sale," he looked down at the wooden floor painted with various shades of blue, yellow and green. "That's not all. I'd be left with a large debt. How could I ask you to be my wife, after all that I had done? What could I say? Olivia, I'm stupid, naïve and poor… and soon I'm going to become even poorer… but I love you, will you marry me? Will you marry me so they can take the entire house to pay off my debts?"

"You used the word 'if'," I said full of hope.

"Because the president didn't have enough time to sue us before—" he cleared his throat.

"Oh my god!" I whispered loudly feeling a bump squeezing my throat. "God rest his soul."

"For god's sake of course we didn't kill him," he said and the waiter from 'we don't sell alcohol here' stopped abruptly next to us with his silver tray shaking in his hand. Henry looked at him saying, "a hamster, we didn't kill him, he died naturally from old age." When the waiter walked away Henry turned to me again saying, "Who do you think I am?"

"Honestly Henry? I've got the right to feel a bit lost after all I've been through with you."

"True. But just to make things clear – my company doesn't commit murder. I mentioned to you that we've got a great team of detectives. I was lucky they managed to get some incredibly useful piece of information regarding the president and they got it just in time."

"I thought he was all innocent and that was the problem."

"He did graduate from Harvard, top of his class. But guess what his relationship is with the CEO?"

"They've been having a secret affair!"

"No," he laughed out loud. "A more nepotistic kind of relationship."

"His son in law?"

"His birth son! The result of a secret affair with—"

"His secretary?"

"Better. The sister of his wife!"

"No fuuu—, duck!"

"And even better. Mr President got his job through his father-in-law, who is the founder of the whole company – and more importantly the father of two beautiful daughters, both of whom have children with the president. The revelation would destroy not only his career but also his seemingly perfect family life."

"Does the chain of blackmailing people end with you threatening the president?"

"It does," he said relieved.

I leaned back on my chair and took a few loud breaths. "So how is your career now? I mean are you going to continue being academic James Bond?"

"I still have the same number of lectures at Shakespeare University, but I didn't accept a proposal to be a group supervisor. I've got more and more work in Spy Education—"

"Spy Education? That is the name of your business? I didn't know even that," I said feeling disappointed.

"I don't know what words to use to express how truly sorry I am," Henry said in a begging voice. He looked serious but at that moment the seriousness was working to his advantage, making him both charming and mysterious. I felt a sudden urge to hug him, maybe even kiss him, but then I thought it would be a betrayal. *But who am I betraying, Hugo or Henry?* "It was supposed to be a surprise—"

"That's one thing you definitely managed to do."

"I wanted to tell you about Spy Education when I held in my hands that first big fat cheque that would clear our mortgage and set us up. I wanted for you so badly to be proud of me. I spent so much time imagining us having dinner in Madrid and then..." he stopped deliberately for me to help him out but I patiently waited for him to finish. "Olivia, I don't know whether there's still hope for us... whether it's not too late, but... All I want you to know right now is that I love you with all my heart. And I promise you that – if you somehow find a space in your heart to forgive me, I'll never ever let you down again."

I was staring at Henry not knowing what to say. Before we got to the airport I had been sure I loved him and wanted to spend the rest of my life with him. Then for the whole time I had been with Hugo, I had detested Henry and I had managed to convince myself our break-up was one of the best things that ever happened to me. I had thought that the fate of our relationship had already been sealed and now – I felt like fate had played a very big joke on me.

"If you worry about my job, I can assure you now that we've taken plenty of additional precautions so Spy Education is no threat to my personal financial situation and no threat to my family."

"And what about your unmarried partners with whom you're *Mortgaged*?"

"Safe... but now it's all up to you whether we get married or not."

"Is that how you propose?" I shouted surprised.

"If you told me you were getting engaged, I would have personally popped to a supermarket for a bottle of wine," said our waiter. "My congratulations. Two shots of Baileys on the house," he shouted to his colleague standing behind a counter filled with all kinds of colourful cupcakes.

We both drunk the shots of Baileys rapidly and left the café.

"You're saying that it's all up to me, but how can I trust you now Henry?" I asked when we were standing in the middle of the square of Haven-on-Thames. In reality I didn't even know whether I could trust myself. Something inside me had snapped – was my relationship with Hugo only a desperate attempt to forget about the past and create a new Henry-free future?

"Can you just look at me like at a guy who made a terrible mistake, which he regrets like nothing in his whole life and... And give him one more chance so he can prove himself to you?"

"Henry, just one more question – how did you know that I expected you to propose to me?"

"That's probably the one thing I shouldn't have told you today but what the heck – we both knew it was going to happen—"

"But it didn't," I snapped. "How did you know?"

"Freya told me," he said with a guilty face expression. "Just please, don't be angry with her. I called her once... I was really upset after I saw you on Instagram and Facebook with that Spanish bloke. I was jealous and... scared that I would lose you forever..."

"The bloke from my Instagram has nothing to do with whether you lose me or not, I can reassure you of that," I said sounding so convincing it almost scared me. Shortly after I felt my phone vibrating in my handbag. Soon I heard a silent ring that I had chosen for one particular person. It was like he had known what I just said and couldn't believe it.

13

FRIDAY, 26 JUNE
LONDON

"Why haven't you been answering any of my phone calls?" Tiggy asked outraged, staring at me from behind her chunky black glasses that she only used for special occasions – including slapping down her subordinates. I suspected she thought that the glasses made her look more professional, but many in the firm would undoubtedly agree it just made her look more evil.

After coming back from a week on Sardinia she looked neither happy nor rested. Her face barely touched by the sun was unnaturally distorted with a scowl. It was not how I had imagined the meeting with her. I hoped that after I had brought her another article from my holiday, it would at least have discouraged her from yelling at me. The sad truth was that for Tiggy one day without treating somebody like shit was a day lost.

"I'm sorry, I was on holiday" I said unemotionally although I was boiling inside and trying my best not to explode.

"On a holiday sponsored by the company that you don't even respect?" she was getting louder and louder at every word – she was like one of those alarm clocks that starts reasonably loud and ends unbearably loud if you don't switch them off in time.

"I paid for it all by myself. You told me that I couldn't get any subsidy yet—"

"Never mind," she adjusted her glasses and waved her hand in front of her nose. "You should have answered anyway."

"I don't think that I-Heart-Travelling would cover the cost of answering my mobile in the Caribbean."

"You were supposed to go to Spain, to Grenada!" she yelled. "I've already told Cecilia that we were going to publish your article in our September edition. Hector is going there on Monday to take a few photos"

"I was on Grenada, not in Granada. I'm sorry you misunderstood me," I said calmly, while flabbergasted that a senior manager of a travel magazine didn't know the difference between the Caribbean island and the Andalusian city.

Tiggy froze for a moment, she obviously needed some time to process this *ugly* piece of information. The uncomfortable silence was broken by the sound of my phone that I'd forgotten to put on mute. I took the phone out of my pocket to switch it off and noticed that it was the third message from Hugo this morning. Since I'd returned from Grenada I'd spent four days at work sorting out my mailbox and chatting on WhatsApp with Hugo. He'd got used to me being available during working hours. It had been one of the rare occasions when both Tiggy and Cecilia had been away for a few days, and their absence encouraged us to focus on our social lives and running errands. Only occasionally did the silence got interrupted by a phone call. In that way I found out that Polly's pugs needed to be vaccinated, and Joanna was struggling to get a mortgage for a pricey house she wanted to buy and refurbish. The relaxed atmosphere in the office allowed me to work on planning the year's trip around the world with Hugo.

"You're fired," Tiggy said.

"Why?" I asked flippantly thinking that she only wanted to provoke me or beg her for mercy.

Tiggy loved giving people heart palpitations. Rumour had it that she did it deliberately so more people would find a need to visit her cardiologist husband.

"Why? Why? I'll tell you why! You were late for an important pre-meeting. You lied to me saying that you were going to Spain. You ignored my phone calls. You even ignore me when I'm talking to you right now by answering your mobile. I could spend the whole day listing many other reasons but you should know why yourself!"

"I haven't answered my mobile, I've put it on mute," I protested.

"Ha! Another reason! The company's' policy is to have your mobile on mute for the whole working day."

"That's the very first time I've heard that policy," I said shrugging my arms.

It's a shame that you never put your phone on mute at work. Duh! You're famous for texting on your red smartphone while you're talking to people!

"Anyway, the main reason is that you lied to me only to get two weeks holiday, for which we can't even put an article in the September edition."

"Why not? It's significantly cheaper and less crowded to go there out of season."

"Because it's the hurricane season you id—!"

"As far as I know they don't have many—"

"Cecilia will never allow us to promote a destination during its hurricane season."

"Can we use it in the December edition?" I asked feeling like my tight orange dress was sticking to my back.

"Maybe," she sighed. "Leave the article on my desk and send me another copy to my email. If it's good, you might get at least part of your redundancy payment."

"A part of?" I raised my voice slightly stunned.

"Yeah, lying is one of the clauses in the firm's employment policy that can deprive you of a certain amount of your redundancy payment. I'm sorry," she said without a trace of emotion in her voice.

"You're not sorry at all Tiggy," I said slowly looking straight into her eyes, significantly enlarged by her glasses. "You want to fire me because for some reason you don't like me, so save us both the nonsense about me being a bad employee and just say it out loud."

"You're being ridiculous Olivia... although I must admit, sometimes it's difficult to like you. Do you remember how you left the meeting with Arthur because you were choking on all the cakes you ate and I kindly brought you a glass of water?"

"It was a truly unique opportunity because normally during our meetings we can only choke on air-conditioned air," I snapped – I had enough, I couldn't supress my anger anymore. "Do you want to sack me from work because I happened to eat too many cakes that you wanted to reuse as props for future meetings?"

"You've got a really peculiar sense of humour," she said high-pitched. "Do you remember how I brought you the water and you ironically congratulated me on being creative?"

"I do remember, oh I do. What's the point to all this remembering? Is it some sort of Company's Remembrance Day?" I lost my temper. I had never talked like that to Tiggy before.

"You're definitely going to remember today my dear," she said, her venomous voice spreading across her whole office. "Thanks to YOU," she pointed her shaky finger at me, "everybody blames me for the fact that now they have to work on their holidays. I did it for them, the unappreciative, disgraceful—."

"Are you talking about the amazing eight percent?" I laughed. "Besides—"

"Leave me the article for Granada and leave please. I'm very busy today."

"From Grenada. Granada is in Spain for god's sake," I forced myself to utter a short malicious laugh. "By the way, what about my MBA?"

"Have you applied for funding for a MBA? You've got some nerve girl," she snorted. "The company only funds education for senior employees and you're certainly not going to become one during your lifetime."

I pulled my phone out of my pocket and switched it on. I was watching her confused face while saying calmly "You haven't even read my article from M like Madrid, B like Barcelona, and A like Avignon. Duh! You haven't even opened the file I sent you to read its title."

We were so loud than neither of us heard Cecilia knocking on Tiggy's door and stepping inside, "What's going on here? Why are you shouting as if you were taking part in some sort of political debate?"

Cecilia had also just come back from a business trip and in contrast to grouchy Tiggy she was glowing like never before. Her face and long neck were covered with a golden suntan. She seemed to have lost some weight, not enough to need to change her wardrobe but enough for the tight silver suit she was wearing to fit better. Her new bob haircut made her look so stylish and modern that I wondered for a moment whether I should have had my hair cut short. Cecilia was as relaxed as I had been before this meeting with Tiggy.

"I'm really sorry but Olivia doesn't leave me any choice except to make her redundant," Tiggy said pompously, and despite her attempts to keep a straight face I could see how her lips were desperate to smirk. "We can't tolerate notorious liars in our company. It has just gone too far—"

"Notorious liars? With all due respect I have no idea what she's talking about!" I said high-pitched, not able to control my nerves even in front of Cecilia.

"Olivia lied to force me into giving her two weeks holiday in June. I'm so naïve, I have so much faith in people and they just take advantage of it," Tiggy was getting more and more comfortable with her acting. "She was supposed to go to Spain to write an article about Gre —," she paused to correct herself, "about Granada, but it turned out she went to Grenada in the Caribbean!" she sounded so honestly outraged that I was starting to believe that she must have practiced it all before her bathroom mirror.

"I don't understand any of this. Why would she lie? I would also appreciate an article on Grenada," Cecilia said calmly.

Cecilia used to get on very well with Tiggy – maybe it was because she always balanced Tiggy's craziness and ridiculousness with her own calmness and reason.

I sighed relieved, "Great because I've got it with me now."

"She lied because she wanted to get her leave in June when we had our annual workshops, and also the summer ball that's a critical networking opportunity for us. She didn't accept any of my suggestions to take time off during the summer or in September."

"Tiggy said that the whole summer as well as September were already completely booked," I could barely hold myself back from screaming.

"As far as I know nobody has their holidays booked yet," Cecilia said, looking alternately between Tiggy and me.

How are you going to explain that, hmm? I stood silently with my arms crossed.

"What's more, Olivia keeps being late. Recently she missed the meeting with MacArthur."

How dare you change the topic when you've been caught bluffing and then lie again, you nasty, nasty cow!

"It was the pre-meeting," I said loudly.

"But you know how seriously we treat our pre-Arthur meetings," Cecilia said matter-of-factly. *Was she slowly taking Tiggy's side?*

"Coming back to my holiday—"

"I'm really sorry, but I need to go to the toilet," Tiggy said and stormed out of her office, leaving the door wide open with Polly standing right behind it.

Something was telling me Polly had been there for the whole time trying to eavesdrop on our conversation. The three of us were standing in a stupor not knowing how to react to Tiggy suddenly running away and Polly being caught red handed spying. I even managed to forget about Tiggy lying about my holiday. The situation was rapidly resolved by Cecilia's secretary, who told her she had a call from MacArthur. For a brief moment I debated whether I should go back to my desk – through the eyes of my imagination I saw Tiggy pulling the desk out from under me, my nails scratching its surface – or whether I should wait in the hell of Tiggy's office. I chose the second option. I made myself comfortable on a soft leather chair, closed my eyes and started breathing deeply with my hand on my stomach rising slowly up and then down, up and then down. My meditation didn't last long as it was quickly interrupted by Polly loudly whispering into my ear, "Don't worry about Tiggy, it's just her hormones."

"Come on Polly, none of us is such a bitch when we're on our periods. It definitely doesn't justify her behaviour."

"And what about a lack of period?"

"Nooo… Are you saying that…? I looked at Polly who was nodding encouragingly for me to say it out loud, "pregnant?" And just as I said it, I turned back to see Cecilia and Tiggy staring at me and Polly, who had invited herself into Tiggy's office.

"Nobody's pregnant," Tiggy said angrily, chewing a mint gum and putting a strong ginger tea on her desk. "I've now got another reason to fire you today. Spreading gossip, which will negatively influence the work atmosphere."

"I was just saying to Polly I'm pregnant and…" I turned to Cecilia, "that's the true reason why Tiggy wants to fire me."

"It can't be true," Cecilia shook her head in disbelief.

"The fact that I'm pregnant or that Tiggy wants to—"

"For god's sake of course we don't make pregnant women redundant!" Cecilia raised her voice for the first time that day.

Of course not! You don't sack pregnant women. You just conveniently move them out of the way to a lower job position after they return to work – and of course not because they dared to take more than a few weeks of maternity leave!

"You've never mentioned that you were pregnant," Tiggy said from behind her desk and then took a sip of her ginger tea. "And Polly, don't you have something more important to do at the moment?"

"Not necessarily," Polly said not moving even an inch. "Oh, yes. Of course. I'd better go."

"You're lying as I've already told you today."

You thought that only you could play dirty? I thought with satisfaction. A lie for a lie, bitch!

"You're lying," Tiggy's pale cheeks suddenly got so red hot it was as if she had a fever or sunstroke. "You'll need to bring a note from your doctor."

"I'm not yet three months—"

"Aha!" Tiggy pointed her finger at me. "Of course, you're lying and now you're trying to get out of this," she was waving her finger in front of my nose.

"Olivia, please bring us a note from your doctor," Cecilia said. "At the moment nobody is getting fired and the issue is suspended until further notice."

"We're only losing time and procrastinating what's inevitable. She's clearly trying to use a last resort by making us believe—"

"Let's not waste any more time today. I'm getting a headache from all the raging hormones of two pregnant women."

"I'm not pre—" before Tiggy managed to finish Cecilia was already gone. "I don't know what you're trying to achieve except playing for time but I don't foretell anything good for you."

"I'm going to a fortune-teller tomorrow, we'll see if she can confirm your little prediction," I smiled. "By the way, maybe now when you're pregnant too we could come back to the idea of a nursery in our building?"

"Leave my office please," she snapped through her gritted teeth.

Tiggy pregnant! It's the last thing I need right now!

* * *

15 HOURS EARLIER
London

"Would you like a drink? There's a coffee shop downstairs," said a young woman dressed in a black leather mini skirt and a light pink top with long sleeves. She had long, dense dark blond hair with a straight fringe that looked like it had just been styled by a hairdresser.

"Oh, that's very nice of you but no, thank you," I replied and smiled gently. "I've already drunk three coffees today."

"What about a hot chocolate, a herbal infusion or a smoothie?" she asked in a way typical for my gran Betty who would never stop offering until I finally accepted something to eat or drink. "Just before you arrived the doctor left his office to say that due to unforeseeable circumstances the current patient appointment will probably be at least thirty minutes longer."

I kindly replied that I didn't need anything and thanked her at least twice. The woman didn't seem to believe me but she finally appeared to give up, rose from an armchair and left the waiting room. I noticed as she was leaving that she was a few months pregnant but it was her shoes that attracted my attention – black lacquered stilettoes with red soles, similar to those I'd seen the previous night in one of Covent Garden's boutiques. *Who's wearing shoes for nearly four hundred quid for the gynaecologist?* I wondered and then I reminded myself how much the doctor was charging for a single visit.

"I've got you hot chocolate," my thoughts were suddenly interrupted by a familiar voice. "You don't have to drink it of course, no pressure. If you don't like it, I'll drink it later cold," I was wrong she hadn't given up on me, she just made the decision for me. "By the way, my name is Hannah," she said cheerfully.

After a long day of work and a tube journey to the other side of the city that felt even longer, I wasn't in the mood to socialise with anybody. All I dreamed of was the moment when my head would finally hit the pillow. Sadly, that moment seemed to be more and more distant in time. The first quarter of an hour passed with me listening to Hannah talking about herself and desperately trying to get me involved in a conversation. Then all of a sudden a ginger haired secretary appeared offering us some tea and mini sandwiches. Another fifteen minutes later she came back asking whether we would like to reschedule our visits, "No matter whether you decide to wait tonight or make an appointment for another day, we'll offer you a fifty percent discount and a free hardback copy of Dr Cromwell's newest book."

Neither of us wanted to leave without first seeing the doctor. The pure thought of making the journey again, squeezed on the stuffy underground for over an hour, made me nearly throw up. Soon I became glad I decided to stay, because it turned out that both Hannah and I actually did need a decent girl talk. The peaceful environment of the waiting room, its soft armchairs, mini sandwiches served on white china and a large pot of earl grey tea – all that along with smooth music and the night view for the Thames River encouraged us to confess. I didn't know when I decided to tell Hannah about my dilemma concerning Hugo and Henry, of course removing any details of Henry's second career. I had always been distrustful towards people I didn't know but Hannah, similarly to Hugo, quickly instilled trust. When she was listening, her whole body seemed to be focused on hearing me out. There was nothing she dismissed, she didn't switch off, turn her eyes away from me for more than a brief moment or change the topic. Nothing was left without a question or a comment. Both Freya and Atlanta were like sisters to me, but they sometimes tried too hard to convince me that their proposed solutions to my problems were the only right ones. They would rapidly draw conclusions, without really listening or reflecting on what I was actually saying.

Hugo told me that he divided people into three groups based on how they communicate. The first group comprises of those who predominantly listen and keep asking numerous questions with the aim of getting juicy gossip out of you, which could help them later to entertain other people. The second group comprises of those who have some uncontrolled desire to constantly talk about themselves, your life has as much appeal as last year's weather forecast. The third group are the ones that really pursue true conversation, really listening without any specific agenda in mind. He also said that Hugo TorTillas was exactly for that group. It briefly crossed my mind that Hannah could have been a gossip girl stocking up for a cocktail party, but she also confided in me.

"If not for the second pregnancy, I think I would have had enough courage to be a single mother," she said and sighed deeply. "To be honest, I'm a single mother anyway. Oscar practically only sleeps at home, and that's not every night. Since he opened his own law firm he's been staying for a night or two a week at his office, where he's installed a sofa bed, a shower, and a mini kitchen, equipped better than most home kitchens in this country. He's also got a walk-in wardrobe, and an account at the local dry cleaners. I always knew he liked to be well organized but even for him the homely office environment seemed excessive. First, I suspected him of having an affair. I think that most women being in my place would think exactly the same. I was practically sure his office was just for that. I didn't want to spy on him myself, I thought it would be pathetic so I hired a private investigator, who found out that…" she paused.

"That?" I could not help hurrying her but she needed a few minutes to gather her thoughts.

"I was the only one who was having an affair."

My jaw literally dropped.

"I was the one," she repeated. "Who would guess, eh? I haven't told anybody except you and my sister. I mean I told her everything except the fact that…"

"That?"

And I thought my life was complicated!

"That my second child might not be Oscar's."

"Doesn't your sister even suspect it?"

"I think she doesn't have enough courage to ask and she would rather not know. Not knowing makes her free of responsibility."

"Responsibility?" I asked surprised.

"Yeah, as the older and wiser sister she would feel responsible to redirect me to a moral path…" she sighed, "meaning making me tell my husband the truth and deal with the consequences. She would want me to do a DNA test before the child is born. She would never tell her husband that a child was his if she wasn't absolutely sure. Anyway, I'm sure she would never have such problems."

"You don't know that. There's nothing certain in this world," I said so seriously she burst out laughing.

"Trust me. My sister is rather predictable."

"Yeah, I used to be predictable too and look what's happening with me right now," I smiled bitterly. "But are you really going to tell Oscar the child is his even if the DNA test shows otherwise?"

"I don't know yet. What I know for sure is that Alfie was just a fling, and he's neither good material for a second husband nor for being the father of my child."

So why had you been sleeping with him for three months? I screamed in my thoughts, while trying not to judge but understand her.

"When you first met Oscar, did he seem to be the perfect candidate for your husband or the father of your children?" I asked sheepishly afraid I could offend her, or again judge too quickly.

Hannah told me that she got married when she was only twenty-three. A year after the wedding she got pregnant and then gave birth to her daughter. Soon after the child was born her husband, who was ten years older than her, managed to establish himself as a corporate lawyer. The vision of their perfect future together didn't last very long. Oscar was spending over sixteen hours a day away from home. Hannah tried to be patient and understanding – ultimately thanks to Oscar becoming more successful at work they could buy a bigger house with a porch and a large garden, both got new better cars and she loved her collection of shoes with red soles and frequent journeys to exotic places. The only problem was she never had a chance to wear any of her impressive stilettoes for a date with Oscar because they slowly stopped going out together. During the last three years she had flown on holiday nine times but each time her only company was her daughter.

"I don't want to lie to him, but it's different now and not like lying to a close relative. After the three years apart I practically feel like Oscar is a stranger next to me. What's the difference whether the child is his or not if he's not going to spend any time with him or her?

"What's the point of staying with Oscar then? How long can you keep accepting the current situation?

"For as long as I can't find a better solution…" she said and then she rolled a band off her wrist and used it to pull her hair into a long ponytail. "That's why if I can advise you something…" she looked intensely into my eyes and said slowly, "don't get involved in a relationship when you've already got so many doubts. The further you go the more difficult it's going to be to get out."

You're right. I don't know anymore what I really feel about Henry, but it most certainly is not love. You can take infatuation for love, but how can you not know whether you love somebody after spending five years with them.

"Hannah Kendal," I suddenly heard the doctor's voice.

"Would you like to have your appointment now?" Hannah asked me while looking at her watch. "I've just realised it's half past eight and I need to call my baby-sitter."

I couldn't be happier to accept her offer. I was already exhausted and I still had the prospect of a serious discussion with the doctor and a long journey home.

* * *

Doctor Cromwell apologised sincerely a couple of times that I'd had to wait so long, looked at me inquisitively and said, "You're looking really well Olivia."

You mean glowing? Really doctor Cromwell?

"Thank you," I snapped.

"Last time I saw you was a couple of months ago. Has something changed since then?" he asked with an annoying smile glued to his face.

Doctor Sean Cromwell had an incredible memory about his patients, most of whom, I was sure, greatly appreciated it. All in all, nowadays many of us tend to complain that doctors treat us impersonally, like cargo on an assembly line, no better than a handy man treats his tools. In normal circumstances I would value a personal approach, just not this particular evening. He certainly remembered that two months ago I told him I wanted to stop taking contraception and start trying for a child. No wonder he was expecting some *changes*. I hadn't felt like it was the best moment in my career to get pregnant but equally there had been no sign of a sudden breakthrough worth waiting for. God knows how much longer I would have to wait for promotion! Besides, I had expected Henry to propose to me soon and trying for a child could have taken us months, if not years.

Sean Cromwell always seemed to enjoy a good chat but usually he was careful not to judge or offer wisdom. That was why I'd been surprised when during my last visit he expressed his opinion regarding pregnancy in such a bold and explicit manner, "My congratulations Olivia. I'm glad there're still women who accept that you can't trick Mother Nature. Many women think that thanks to the development of medicine they've got more and more time to get pregnant and they can keep postponing the decision. But I've been wondering whether it's not the total opposite – if stress and a fast pace of life make us significantly older, what's the real biological age of a woman who has already worked for ten, fifteen or twenty years in a fast-corporate environment, hmm?"

I'd left it without a comment just like I left his question about *any changes in my life.*

"I would like to get back on the pill," I said meekly. *Yes, I plead guilty. Soon I'm going to turn thirty and I'm not planning on having a child right now. Whatever you say, a geriatric mother is considered to be a woman over thirty-five, so buzz off you old-opinionated-fart.*

"How did you feel on the pill that you used to take?" he asked nicely.

"And I would like to... I'm also here because..."

He looked at me encouragingly, "I'm not here to judge you but to help you."

"The thing is I would like to somehow trick Mother Nature. A lot has recently changed in my life and I thought that I would like to secure myself for the future by freezing my eggs."

He raised his eyebrows and nodded without saying a word but he wasn't as surprised as I'd expected him to be. His clinic had been achieving the best results in freezing female eggs and in-vitro in the country, if not in the whole of Europe.

"Are you absolutely sure about your decision? Maybe would you like to give yourself some time and wait, let's say another year?" He said raising his eyebrows.

Are you really rejecting an opportunity of making more money?

There was nothing I was *absolutely* sure about except that I finally wanted to make my own independent decisions and reject any pressure coming from my immediate environment. I wanted to be the master of my own destiny, and one of the biggest pressures of all was starting a family. With Henry now gone so was my chance of having a child in my early thirties. It wouldn't be fair to pressure Hugo and myself – we had just started going out and were still getting to know each other. There was a certain risk that we might not even work and then I would have to start all over again, heaven knows how many times I would have to start over until I eventually managed to settle. I felt that at least by freezing my eggs I was giving myself a chance later to be a mum and I would not panic if all my relationships went to rat shit as I continued towards my fortieth.

*

The idea that I could freeze my eggs came to me for the first time over a year ago, influenced by the various fertility clinics that began flooding our office with their leaflets. Soon after, several large companies in the Unites States announced that they would finance their employees freezing their eggs, so we weren't only receiving colourful leaflets with smiley baby faces but also invitations to events encouraging us to "take the future of our fertility in our hands". I attended two such events, or rather splendid banquets – one with a few girls from my office, and another with Freya and Atlanta. I went because they served free dinner with live music in the background and because I wanted to feed my curiosity. Neither disappointed me. Both parties took place in high quality hotels in central London. They were organised on Friday evenings so they would attract the largest number of successful businesswomen. They always started from canapés and coffee as if they were afraid we could have fallen asleep after an exhausting working week. During this time we were also fed with plenty of marketing statements like "freezing eggs are the biggest fertility breakthrough since the invention of the contraceptive pill" or "it's a revolution that can truly transform your future and let you sleep peacefully."

"Dear ladies, you don't have to face the dilemma of career or motherhood. Those saying that you can't have it all are wrong! Now you can have absolutely everything and at the time that you choose for yourself," a slim woman in her thirties was shouting into a mike on a stage, while I was putting in my mouth another delicious canapé and sipping a coffee.

I looked around at the audience eating and walking around the hotel's ballroom. Nobody appeared to be sleepy, on the contrary most of us were listening with flushed cheeks and sparkling eyes like we had been hypnotised. I have to admit I felt like I was part of something special – a true breakthrough in science, the beginning of a new lifestyle for women and one of the moments in history that future generations will still be describing and referring to in a hundred years. Then the dinner was served, during which waiters dressed in tuxedos were constantly offering wine, including my favourite, Prosecco. As soon as we ate the dessert, we received distractingly colourful drinks before several experts appeared on stage to explain the possible side effects of harvesting our eggs. We were also encouraged to ask questions. Freya turned out to be the most sceptical of all of us, but she could let herself be sceptical. She was a young mother, who gladly left a job she hated and who only saw her career as a means for a better and fuller life. However, to my and Atlanta's surprise, Freya had done her research before the party and while slightly tipsy became increasingly demanding or as Atlanta said laughing "the biggest pain in the experts' arse".

"What's the guarantee that I'll be able to use my thawed eggs for in-vitro fertilization in several years?" Freya said into a mike next to our round dinner table for eight people. Then she sat down and ate a red cherry from her cocktail.

"Since we've been using the technique called vitrification or cryopreservation during which the eggs are fast-frozen the chances are relatively high," replied one of six women sitting on a half-moon sofa on the stage.

"The eggs are frozen in liquid nitrogen at minus 192 degrees Celsius and they can be stored indefinitely," added hastily another woman from the white couch. "After thawing the eggs more than ninety percent of them are viable."

Freya stood up again and shouted into the mike, "That's wonderful. What are my chances for pregnancy from frozen eggs?"

"The probability is increasing every year as technology improves, so when you decide that the time has come to defrost your eggs, the chances will be even higher," said somebody with a deep voice from the stage. "Do you know that when we started using thawed embryos in IVF, the chance of getting pregnant was only ten percent, and now it's over fifty? Incredible, isn't it?"

Freya wanted to ask another question but a waiter abruptly took the mike from her hand without saying a word.

"From what I've read the chances of getting pregnant from a thawed embryo are currently much greater than from a thawed egg," Freya shouted.

"Maybe the chances are higher but I'm single again and now I'm not going to spoil my eggs with some random sperm," said a woman sitting on my right. "And FYI," she said annoyingly, "I want to freeze my eggs because I still haven't found anybody with whom I would like to have children, not because I'm afraid of having a break in my career." The woman had long dense ginger hair, very symmetrical features, a perfect nose and deep green eyes. She looked stunning in her dark green tight dress. *If you can't find Mr Right with that body, who can?* I thought with a pinch of jealousy – only a pinch because I was glad to think that at least I had found a man who I wanted to marry and one day have children with. I was not, however, ecstatic because it brought on me another dilemma whether I should invest in my far-from-splendid career or look to raise a family. Around my table there was the prevalent perception that woman shouldn't take maternity leave before she achieves a sufficiently high and established position at work. *But I'm miles away from 'stable', let alone 'high'?* I was thinking. *The only 'high' at my work are my high heels and high expectations. I could let the world decide what's best and have a break from contraception. People try for children for years...*

*

A few months later I didn't have such dilemmas, which obviously didn't make me any happier. No Henry, no family. No Tiggy, no job? Ironically the messier my life was becoming, the more I felt I had some control over my destiny. *No 'let the world decide' anymore, I'm going to do it on my terms, for my love life, career... fertility! Abso-freaking-lutely everything! Here I come! Freeze my eggs doc!*

"Olivia, you do realise that freezing your eggs might increase your chances of getting pregnant later but there's no guarantee out there? It's not like paying an insurance policy... although I wouldn't totally rely on them either. I've just tried to claim money for my car... never mind," he stopped himself probably realising time was money and I didn't come to see him to have a chitchat. "I'm just trying to say it's a serious burden on your body and mind that you might want to avoid, especially when it's not necessary."

"Of course, I'm well aware of that," I sighed tired of doctor Cromwell trying to talk me out of my grand plans. "My knowledge about freezing eggs doesn't come entirely from sponsored events that provided me not much more than massive hangovers. Before I came to you I've read several articles in respected medical journals," I said decisively as if I was trying to convince him to freeze some of his bits. "I do realise that the whole process is not just about taking happy eggs out of my body when they're at the top of their game, then freezing them like pizza and finally defrosting when it's most convenient for me to organize a meeting with Mr Good Sperm and see what happens – whether it's just a Tinder-fling or hopefully something much more serious."

"Right," he nodded. "I couldn't phrase it any better. Do you have any questions or do you want to proceed to the first step as soon as possible?"

One of the advantages of not using an NHS doctor was not being sent away with the advice to take more paracetamol and continue to observe your symptoms, which in practice meant consulting with Dr Google.

"Actually, I have a couple of questions," I said enthusiastically and doctor Cromwell raised his eyebrows in surprise. "What's the risk of genetic disorders when it comes to in-vitro fertilization with thawed eggs and would it be possible to detect any abnormalities in my eggs before they're frozen?"

He smirked as if he wanted to say *obviously you haven't read enough in your medical journals my dear.* "There's no more risk than when a child is conceived in the natural way. That's the good news."

"And the bad news?"

"There's not really bad news, but…" he hesitated, "the less optimistic news is that we examine egg cells only after they're fertilised, otherwise it would be very expensive."

"It means I find out whether my eggs are healthy or not after they are thawed and I've gone through the whole process of in-vitro?"

"Exactly," he nodded.

"Well, they say that we regret the most what we haven't done. I plan to leave the country for a few months, maybe a year so I would like to start as soon as possible."

"In that case after an initial examination that we can do today, we'll make you an appointment to initiate the first stage, which is hormonal stimulation treatment. It will last approximately two weeks during which you'll need to make regular visits to our clinic, normally every other day…" the doctor was talking while I suddenly reminded myself at that stage there was a risk of ovarian hyperstimulation syndrome, called OHSS, which in a very rare case could even be life threatening. Obsessive thoughts about OHSS prevented me from listening. All I managed to hear was: hormonal stimulation… ovarian follicle… several eggs… under full sedation.

A few minutes later I was lying on a gynaecological chair, staring at the ceiling and feeling full of concern. *Maybe he was right. Maybe I should wait with it a bit longer. I'm only approaching thirty. But isn't it the best age to do it? Isn't the whole point of it to get the youngest possible eggs? Damn it! It's the right choice!*

"Olivia, I'm sorry to say that in your case, I can't start any hormonal stimulation," a quick pang of relief that I didn't have to go through it all was immediately pushed out of the way by a flow of massive disappointment. *I had a plan!* I wanted to scream. *Do you understand I had a plan?*

"What's wrong with me then?" I asked helplessly and without much thought to what I was going to hear.

"You're pregnant. Six weeks. My congratulations."

14

SUNDAY, 28 JUNE

LONDON

My great grandmother used to say that if I didn't want something to happen, under no circumstances should I ever think or say aloud the word *never*. She must have been amused while looking down right now. I glanced up at the sunny sky imagining that the breeze pushing light clouds around was actually the strength of my great grandmother's laugh; although more realistically it would be her puffing away while she was smoking.

God, I would never put myself in the situation where I don't know who the father of my child is. How on earth could you be so irresponsible when you're almost in your thirties? I thought while listening to Hannah in doctor Cromwell's waiting room three days ago. *Look at me now,* I was whispering to myself while wondering whether I should call Hannah. She was the only person who could truly support and understand me – we were screwing our lives in equally stupid ways.

On Grenada, when I was immersed in a carefree but still meaningful conversation, with a lot of wine and a man who I could carelessly love without thinking – I decided to "live more deliberately".

"I'm not going to waste anymore time," I was saying to Hugo inspired by his smile, the sunset and a bottle of rose sitting in an ice bucket. "No more debilitating TV shows, bad books, stupid discussions that don't bring anything to my life. I'm not going to try hard to be liked by people who don't deserve it. I'm not going to attend any parties that I don't care about. Never! Never ever!" Just like that I, Olivia Eliot, decided to transform my life and nothing was going to stop me, but that was when life was far simpler and I was sitting tipsy on a tropical island with an equally tipsy but charming man.

Here I am! Here I-bloody-am at one of the silly parties I didn't want to attend making some meaningless conversation with people I don't care about and I'm never (oops, I did it again!) going to see again, I was thinking while listening selectively to a thin and very talkative student of applied linguistics, wearing thick white socks with beige sandals. *Gosh, can't you find somebody else to talk to? Although... You're probably not talking to me, just trying to score a few points with your tutor.*

Initially I found the whole event *Don't Die for a Selfie* vaguely interesting but the more time I spent there, the more I was convinced that the students organised it only to have the opportunity to get smashed while getting some extra points participating in university life. To be honest, I wasn't any better than them. I would quite happily get smashed myself if I wasn't pregnant, and I was there to get some extra points with the man who I wasn't sure really deserved me. I was sipping my orange juice with lemonade, pretending it was vodka with juice, and feeling trapped like a hamster in a cage. The only difference was that a hamster at least could mute his pain of existence by running incessantly on his wheel – difficult to mull over your existence when you are dizzy and you have got a misty picture of the surrounding world. I couldn't even have a glass of wine so I borrowed Atlanta's sports car to have an excuse not to drink without instilling any suspicions.

"So, you're drinking vodka and driving?" one of Henry's female friends asked in a rather amused unconcerned way.

"What can I say, my temptations turned out to be stronger than me so we'll take a train later."

Women at Henrys' work were proper Gossip Girls constantly monitoring the size of my stomach, and since they heard we bought the house together they had turned into constant Belly Watchers.

I found the rescue from the Belly Watchers, and my intrusive thoughts on *the beginning of the rest of my life,* by listening to speeches of people who miraculously avoided death when trying to take selfies, or those who lost friends – the unlucky ones classified as "Gone with their Phone". A thin man dressed all in white was warning us of the dangers of pursuing fame through extraordinary selfies. He was constantly walking from one end of the stage to another as if he had a restless leg syndrome. The stage was built at the back of a garden of a London financier, who once had nearly killed himself while taking a selfie during a parachute jump. The thin man wearing all white, including snow-white sandals, was called Marco. He was there because during the last winter season he felt an irresistible desire to take a selfie with his girlfriend while they were both skiing backwards in the Alps.

"There was a stunning view unfolding in front of us…" Marco was saying and vividly gesticulating, "a valley with spruces covered with fresh powder snow, wooden Swiss cottages and people strolling around with mugs of mulled wine and hot chocolate. The snow was reflecting the sun that was going down. It was absolutely beautiful but for some reason we decided to turn back to the view and try to ski backwards! Can you believe it? The slope was completely empty. It had been closed because of a risk of an avalanche and a few other reasons that we found out later. We were skiing faster and faster while taking hundreds of selfies. My girlfriend Claudia was screaming to stop but I didn't want to because you need to take loads of photos to get the perfect one, the one that everybody goes crazy about later on Instagram, and in my case also on my travel blog… But suddenly one of my skis hit a rock, we lost our balance and fell down. Neither of us had a helmet because at the time they were considered to be passé in social media. When I finally managed to climb back to my feet I couldn't believe my eyes," Marco paused for a moment to add a bit of drama. "There was a brown bear walking towards Claudia. She was so shocked she didn't make a sound. I quickly realised I was still holding my phone so I decided to take the opportunity and started shooting selfies with the bear and Claudia in the background. I must admit – it wasn't the kind of reaction you would expect from a law student who had spent his last semester reading logic!"

The majority of the audience comprised of people sitting on the grass with picnic baskets, a few feeling-like-at-home individuals were wearing bikinis or skimpy shorts and lying at ease on their blankets. Then there were also several people uncomfortably sipping drinks and standing with hunched backs, among them unfortunate women trying to keep their high heels on the surface of the ground, while continuously waving the wasps away. I belonged to the most uncomfortable minority, cursing my choice of shoes, and Henry's wasp allergy. The whole audience remained silent staring at the stage and waiting for the grand finale of Marco's story.

"Do you know what saved us?" he asked loudly and full of enthusiasm like a preacher or a coach at a motivational workshop.

I shook my head still keeping my lips on my glass of orange juice with lemonade.

"My phone rang! It was probably my ringtone that saved our lives! After a few words of me singing a capella the bear ran away with his paws on his ears!"

Right, time for me, I thought walking away from the stage and looking for Henry who had gone to fetch me a lemonade and undoubtedly got lost somewhere while being chatted up by one of his students.

"And I'm telling you, ephemeral fame is never worth risking your precious life over. The bear would probably had killed me if not for the song…" I was still hearing Marco but his voice was nicely fading away.

"No kidding," said a male voice passing me by, "I bet the bear wanted a selfie with you to show his mates what a special case he had a chance encounter with," he giggled and took a gulp of his cold beer.

Before I found Henry, I was forced to listen to other lethal or almost lethal selfie stories. There was a man who rode a horse sitting backwards and barely survived, and a friend of a girl who wanted to take a selfie with her head in a spinning washing machine – she was one of those "Gone with the Phone".

Another "never" that must have been particularly amusing for my great grandmother was included in a line that I had written on numerous occasions in my diary during the last month: "Henry, we're never ever going to get back together!"

"Ladies and gentleman our next guest is…" I heard from the stage just when Henry approached me, one hand holding my drink and another moving to touch my waist. Before I had a chance to react, he stained my stripy dress with his sweaty palm.

Ladies and gentleman our next guests are Olivia Eliot and Henry Thyme, who probably were never ever meant to get back together… and who probably were never ever destined to be together in the very first place… But! But it's too late to contemplate that now as they're stuck and trapped together – and they will never ever be happy together.

I had *never* planned to go to the event with or without Henry. He received an invite to *Don't Die for a Selfie* when we were still together and he insisted on me going with him. He kept saying that he needed to support his students from Shakespeare University, and I should support him. Sometimes I thought that Henry's job was the most important thing in his life, far more important than me or anything else. I have seen on a few occasions the queue to Henry's office never getting shorter – when one student went inside, within seconds the queue gained another. Henry's role went far beyond advising on essay structure or assisting in choosing the right MA or PhD program. Students wanted to know his opinion on a range of topics from organising events and choosing a holiday destination to discussing somebody's love life or buying a property. For the last year it had also become normal that Henry met his students twice a week in the evening at a pub next to their university. Students loved him, which brought envy from many of his male colleagues and more love from his female friends – among whom I could always spot the young and pretty PhD students.

After we had split up, I was *never* going *to* agree to go the party with Henry until last Thursday. A "never" only lasts until something happens… When I was back from doctor Cromwell's I didn't feel joyful or upset. Initially I was too shocked to feel anything beyond simple stupor. I'd had a plan for Henry to propose to me, which didn't work out. Then I'd had a plan for Henry to not propose to me so I could start a separate life, which didn't quite work out either. *What's the point of planning?* I was thinking while lying on the carpet in my new lounge with both my hands rubbing my eyes. *Six weeks, huh? The chances are fifty-fifty. Or maybe it's what I prefer to think to still have some hope... because I was on the pill with Hugo, even on that first night when I was drunk I somehow managed to drag myself into the bathroom and dig out the pill from my cosmetic bag. I took it with the Madrid tap water. Could the city water, which I wasn't supposed to drink straight from the tap, affect the pill? No Olivia you idiot, you're pregnant with Henry... Although there's always a chance. The pill is not a hundred percent. I need to do the DNA test! Oh my god, when did I manage to mess up my life so much?*

On that night I spontaneously (but not without a degree of calculation) texted Henry:

Hi! If your invite is still valid, I could go to the party with you on Sunday.

The answer came almost immediately:

Brill! I'll be at yours at 1pm! Xoxo

Brill? Henry must really spend a lot of time with his students. He would normally say 'lovely', I thought and fell asleep exhausted on the carpet with the phone on my chest. When I woke up to the phone ringing at 6am I thought I was having a heart attack.

* * *

On that Sunday afternoon Henry arrived fifteen minutes early, which was pretty typical of him. When the bell rang I was still working on my make-up. It was already my third attempt to do my eyes. I was worried that not enough make-up could make Henry think I was terribly missing him, to the point I'd stopped looking after myself; while too much make-up could also send the wrong message by saying, *I'm desperate to get you back.* Since our meeting in Haven-on-Thames Henry had been trying hard to convince me that we were destined to be together. I suspected that his sudden change of heart might have been driven by my Instagram photos with Hugo and me all acting in an I-am-not-interested-anymore way. At the end of the day Henry always wanted to see the shows, for which the tickets were already sold out, or he desperately craved for the beautifully presented cakes in the windowsill of a closed shop. When it turned out later that somebody returned their tickets so we could see the show or Henry could have his dream cake the following day – suddenly he wasn't interested anymore. I was afraid his love life was determined by similar principles. Finally, I decided to use only black mascara and eyeliner with no eye shadow but I went for a juicy red lipstick that I bought in Madrid during my shopping spree. I preferred to look like a student than melt myself into the crowd of Henry's work colleagues. Besides I had to admit at least to myself I was kind of desperate. *Woman on the verge of a breakdown*, I thought looking at myself in the bathroom mirror. Even if Henry wanted to get back together, our motives were unlikely to be the same.

By the time I finished applying the lipstick and found an appropriate outfit for the day – a stripy dress á la *I'm sailing* that was masking my bigger only-in-my-head belly – Meg opened the door to Henry. Meghan Johansson had only been living with me for a week but my estate agent had already found her before I flew to Grenada. Henry's attitude towards renting a room in our house had been far from positive but I'd managed to convince him by saying that half of a year living separately would give us a reasonable amount of time to decide on our relationship, and in the meantime a tenant would cover a part of his mortgage. I also suspected that he would like to spend the summer in London where he was busy working for Spy Education.

He didn't have to drive all the way back to Dream Fields to sign the papers to rent the room, but he did.

"You know that I'm old fashioned and I don't like doing things like that online. I preferred to see the estate agency you hired. Have a chat with them, you know…" he was clumsily explaining but I knew he just wanted to use the opportunity to see me. I'd hoped he would have texted me beforehand so I could have said I was busy. Tough luck he knocked on my door and I welcomed him into a hallway, where I had my packed bags ready to go to Grenada.

"Are you going on holiday or is the tenant already moving in before I've even sign—?" he asked stunned.

"Oh, just a short holiday," I said flippantly while feeling butterflies in my stomach. *Please don't ask for more. If you keep asking, I'm going to lie to you and it will be your fault!*

"Are you going alone?" he asked still standing in the doorway and staring at me with disbelief. I somehow managed to forget he had been my boyfriend for five years, and was now working for a company with "spy" in its name.

"I'm going alone. I need some time ALONE to think about my life… about us…" I said decisively, thinking *You've got what you asked for!* I wasn't entirely ready to burn all the bridges for a future with Henry, especially since I now knew the reason why he had acted so weird. I also saw Grenada as a test for Hugo and me before we would be set to go on our journey around the world.

Two weeks passed, and I came back from Grenada confident that I wanted to spend the rest of my life with Hugo. Four days after that, on the Thursday night after seeing doctor Cromwell, I was equally confident I should forget about Hugo and focus on trying to make a family with Henry. *It's not that I'm indecisive*, I was thinking. *I know exactly what I want but it's just not the same every day!*

I wasn't ready to tell Hugo the truth. I wasn't ready to cross him out of my grand life adventure but at the same I didn't know whether in my current state I could accept all the risk that he was bringing into my life. Henry was the less exciting option but at least he came with a clear insurance policy – I'd known him for five years! As I was walking off the plane at Madrid, I muttered to myself: *I'll never trust anybody again. I'll never love anybody.* I should seriously take the word "never" out of my dictionary because it only brings me bad luck.

On Sunday Henry materialised in my hallway like a genie. I only managed to think *Henry* and he was everywhere. He brought a bunch of yellow tulips and a bottle of my favourite rosé, which I couldn't drink, or tell him why I wasn't drinking. He stood for a long moment between a console table that we had chosen together and our framed picture from a university ball, which I had been tempted to smash against the wall only a couple of weeks ago. He also brought his hungry puppy eyes, which were as useful as the wine. What was I supposed to do with them? All I had for him was hope.

Henry was wearing a light blue jacket and a white shirt without a tie. *You're looking good but probably not as good as...* I thought with nostalgia and quickly chastised myself. In the last few weeks my relationship with Henry had changed more than it had during the previous few years. We both had our own carefully guarded secrets. We had built separate worlds that were coexisting with each other, but at the same time had become more independent than ever. If the worlds were once again to overlap, it wouldn't be without injury.

* * *

Don't die for a Selfie removed any hidden desires I had to self-promote through my own photos. But it wasn't the main reason I decided to suspend my Facebook profile that night. I wasn't going to *never* use it again, it was only until "further notice". In order not to instil any suspicions in the middle of the night I put on my page over fifty odd links, among them, "the nudists' right to go on the tube as god created them" and "the gold fish believers demanding to become officially recognised as a new religion." At the bottom of my page I posted a comprehensive explanation about my Facebook profile being hacked and with the deepest regret I was forced to suspend it. By eight o'clock in the morning I received more than five hundred sad faces and three hundred comments. Most Facebookers were determined to help me in catching the hackers but I also got tens of messages from people confessing to attacking my page alongside pathetic threats: "If you keep posting such everyday nonsense like 'I cooked a fish pie today', your account will be hacked again." After reading such negative and ridiculous comments I removed my profile without regret.

Atlanta didn't believe for a minute in me being a victim of any cyber offenders. She kept calling me the whole morning until I finally budged and answered.

"Fine, you're right," I snapped sitting on my bathroom floor just after I'd thrown up again. "I don't want Hugo to see me with Henry, and annoyingly his students keep posting our photos everywhere and tagging us both."

"I thought that Hugo doesn't use social media."

"I convinced him, but I shot myself in the foot by doing it. He's already posted our photos from Grenada but I quickly untagged myself. I don't want Henry to see me with Hugo either. There's no point complicating my life even further…"

"Does it mean you have two boyfriends?" she asked amused.

"Well, I don't think so… I mean practically… maybe I have but… it's not illegal, is it?"

"No, just kind of wrong."

15

SATURDAY, 20 JUNE
(A WEEK EARLIER) GRENADA

It was only a fifteen-minute stroll between our hotel and our favourite restaurant on the island. Our feet were moving smoothly on the soft sandy beach, a line of palm trees on one side and a calm warm sea on the other. If not for the full moon and a few stars it would be pitch black. As we were walking to the restaurant for the first time I'd regretted not stealing some cutlery from breakfast as a weapon but after two weeks on the island I felt safer at night on that deserted beach than in our village in Oxfordshire.

All Grenadians we'd met were friendly and welcoming. Tourists didn't appear to have annoyed them yet unlike in so many other popular destinations all over the world. Every Grenadian loved to have a chat – whether we were travelling with them for five minutes on a bus or strolling with somebody for half an hour on a beach, and they always asked about our names. If they happened to meet us again they always remembered our names and pronounced them correctly. They seemed to be genuinely interested in our lives and they were eager to share their stories about the island. Grenadians talked fondly about their beautiful home that wasn't always the paradise it seemed to be on a warm summer evening with the sun slowly going down.

Hurricanes didn't often affect the island but when they did they were truly devastating and impossible to erase from memory.

The best opportunity to meet true Grenadians was through a cricket match – something that I would have never even considered going to if it wasn't for Hugo, who was madly excited about such an event. I treated it as a long-term investment in our future together – Hugo really wanted to see the match, I wanted to keep seeing Hugo, so I sacrificed half of a day on the beach and to my surprise I didn't regret it at all. I'd never seen cricket in England but I knew that it was a family game so I expected a peaceful and relaxing atmosphere. I hadn't imagined, however, that it would look like one huge Sunday picnic. I didn't understand much when it came to the rules of the game and I found the slow pace of cricket ridiculous. From my amateurish perspective a group of men-in-white were walking around the pitch occasionally doing something with the ball, something which I hadn't quite comprehended – mainly because I couldn't be bothered. Far more interesting were the audience that appeared to be more alive and vibrant than the players themselves. Grenadians were chanting, singing, dancing, eating and drinking like they were at the best party in the universe. They were chatting and laughing, only sometimes looking at the direction of the pitch or commenting on the game. Some were having a nap, it appeared to be perfectly normal to snooze in their chair just like I would on a hammock at the back of my garden. A man sitting next to us, and dressed in the most yellow trousers I had even seen, fell asleep after gulping the entire contents of his thermos. We assumed that what he drunk probably hadn't been water or orange juice and expected him to wake up with a terrible headache, or worse, vomiting over a person in front of him. In fact, he woke up later in the afternoon in a great mood and full of energy, just as everybody but us was tucking into their home-made lunches. He looked at us, saw our lack of catering and said stone cold sober, "Would you like some food?"

Our jaws dropped to the cricket pitch. We both nodded, although Hugo mumbled politely, "No, thank you."

"Are you sure? I see you haven't brought anything today and I've got enough for the three of us..."

I kept wondering if it was the weather or the paradise scenery that made the Grenadians so good-natured. It is said that people are the best versions of themselves when they aren't worried and don't live under constant pressure; plus frequent exposure to nature calms our body and mind. Even if they don't have less to worry about than people in other parts of the world, maybe it's easier to cherish life when you can pick bananas straight from the trees, hear the sound of a waterfall, and the air smells like cinnamon.

When on the last night of our holiday we were walking through the beach to the restaurant, the only thing I was afraid of was stepping on one of the small yellow crabs that inhabited the local sands. I knew that it was ridiculous – the crabs were harmless and more scared of me than I was of them but I couldn't stop thinking, *What if they don't notice my foot descending?* During the day crabs were regularly organising meetings around our sunbeds but as soon as we put the tips of our toes on the sand they immediately evacuated. *God, they could teach Tiggy a lesson in evacuation,* I was thinking, *she was always the last to leave the office when we had a fire alarm.* She always insisted on packing her laptop and diary first.

We were only a couple of minutes away from our destination when all of a sudden we got caught in a downpour. We stormed into the restaurant soaking wet, leaving our footsteps on its wooden floor and small puddles next to our chairs. A waiter brought us a menu without a word of comment on us flooding his workplace. Hugo and I looked at each other and burst into laughter.

The restaurant was alongside a massive rock from which a man-made waterfall cascaded. Most tables, including ours, had a good view both for the illuminated waterfall and the beach framed by palm trees against the backdrop of a loud dark sea lit only by the moon. The interior was simple but cosy with almost everything made of wood. We ordered our favourite dish – codfish with local grilled vegetables and mashed potatoes.

"I'm going to miss the island," I said which brought a tear to my eye. "I don't have a habit of going back to the same places but…" I hesitated looking around.

"It's so unique," Hugo said enthusiastically bringing a massive smile to my face. "Let's come back here one day!"

"Deal," I exclaimed.

"I'm going to miss the view of all the exotic fruits growing on the trees and the tiny little shops spread along the windy roads in the jungle…"

"With their shop assistants all sitting outside seemingly mulling over life," I added. "God," I sighed. "Me too! But do you think that "turning right" is some kind of a joke only known to the locals?"

"Women are always so suspicious," Hugo laughed out loud while taking a bottle of rose from an ice bucket and pouring it evenly to our glasses, while our waiter was chatting and giggling with another table. "At the end of the day we found our way to the hotel."

"But it was in the middle of the night!"

"Well, on the bright side we were still back on the same day, it was just before midnight. I was afraid we would have to spend the night in the jungle and sleep in the car."

On our first trip to the jungle we went with a small group of American tourists, a local tour guide and a driver of a jeep that was so old it might have seen the first Grenadians settling on the island. The views were so mesmerizing that we quickly forgot what we were driving in – waterfalls cascading from green hills, local daredevils jumping from the top of them into plunge pools. We stopped for a dinner hosted in the home of a local Caribbean family, dipped our sunbathed bodies in a sulphur spring and visited a rum factory, where we both were brave enough to taste seventy-five percent rum – too flammable to take on the plane. A week later we hired a decent four by four to explore the island ourselves and go to St. George, the islands' capital. We only wanted to "pop to the jungle for an hour" or "have a quick drive around to see how the locals live." We only managed to find our way out after eight hours, and this place didn't have ice cream and pizza shops on every corner like when I got lost in Venice with Henry. If we couldn't get home, it wouldn't be too tough though because we could pick our food from the surrounding trees.

We had enough time to notice that in the middle of the island there was no divide between more or less affluent districts. Large gated villas with their closed shutters stood right next to little wooden houses with people relaxing outside. On the narrow windy roads there weren't many cars but we kept meeting people sitting on rocks swinging their legs and watching the world passing by. They all smiled to us and were eager to help with directions, when we couldn't count on the map that we got from the hotel. The scenario was always the same: we would lean out of the car window and ask for directions and everybody would just say with all apparent sincerity "straight and right" irrespective of where we were on the island. Inevitably we ended up in the same places – except those who had shown us the way had moved on. Somehow, we guessed our way out of the jungle.

"I was more afraid that we might have been kidnapped when our mini bus drove off the main road and stopped in a random place—"

"Oh yeah!" Hugo laughed out loud and hit the table so enthusiastically our wine glasses and cutlery played a short loud tune. "Me too! But I didn't want to say anything so as not to scare you. I was really uncomfortable seeing those guys with their massive spades getting on the bus! Dear god, I was relieved when the mini bus driver said they were his friends and he was just giving them a lift.

"In my imagination I saw them asking us to leave the bus and pass them all our belongings and—"

"Maybe you should be writing crime novels, instead of working for a travel magazine."

"Hmmm…" I rested my chin on my right hand. "I was actually thinking that I would prefer to become an underwater reporter."

"What?" he asked while trying not to spit out the rose.

"I could snorkel and dive every day to report on the Caribbean coral reef… and you…"

"I could be your muse?" he said with a cheeky smile.

"More practical than that," I said decisively. "You could be my cameraman."

"Deal. When we come back we should send our proposal to a few TV stations."

"I'm all in," I said and we clinked our glass. "I'm so glad that you convinced me to go snorkelling, I would have never thought that you could see such vibrant and colourful sea life so close from the shore!"

"I'm so glad you were so easy to convince. The last time I came here my ex-girlfriend preferred to lie on the beach for the whole time. She wasn't interested… Sorry, what a stupid idea to talk about exes!"

"You mean Paulina?" I was pushing.

"Yeah but lets' talk about…"

"Why did you leave her?" I had already drunk a couple of glasses of wine so the question that had been haunting me for the last few weeks came out naturally. "You said you were with her for how long? Six years?" I was acting like my gran Betty. I knew exactly how long.

"Something like that but look it's our last night here—"

"I was with Henry almost five years and just when I thought we would get engaged he dumped me at the airport like some unwanted luggage, his ballast…" I was saying this while looking at him and watching how his face was gradually changing from someone very reluctant to discuss our previous love lives to someone who was becoming increasingly curious. I didn't feel like talking about Henry but it seemed to be the only way to get something out of him about Paulina. There might have been another better way but it was difficult to be particularly clever so late at night with a full stomach and a head pulsating from heat and wine. Obviously, I was clever enough not to mention anything about Henry's new career and the fact he wanted to get back together. "Are you saying you left Paulina because she wanted to marry you? How rude of her! She should've managed her expectations," I said outraged, feeling sudden solidarity with the woman who I'd never seen and never wanted to see, but I was grateful for her not being good enough in Hugo's mind to tight the knot with.

"Of course not! She never really pushed me to get married but I knew it was what she wanted. We talked sometimes about children, we both wanted them some day. but…" he hesitated, "the thing is after six years I should have known… I mean I should have been sure that I wanted to get married and I wasn't."

"So why didn't you split up with her earlier? Was it too difficult to find a convenient time? Of course! How can you tell somebody that you don't want her anymore when you've just had sex, not the best in your life but still… or when she's just cooked you a three-course dinner or got two tickets for a cricket game or—?"

"Olivia stop it," he said calmly. "I'm not Henry, and it's not like I planned to waste her time. I wanted her to be the one but she just wasn't."

Are they all exactly the same? I was thinking while staring at him and anticipating him to say something that would prove otherwise.

"If I didn't leave her, you and I, we wouldn't be together now," he said with a faint smile.

Who knows! Maybe you broke up with her after you met me. Maybe when we had our romantic rendezvous all across Europe she was still waiting for you and texting frantically. I've heard that every man is like a monkey – he doesn't let one branch go before he can firmly hold another; he also tends to hold them both as long as he can to minimise the risk of falling.

"But you're not one of those men who are scared of commitment?"

"Most men aren't afraid of commitment," he snapped. "It's just a flimsy excuse. I've got many friends who claimed that they didn't want to commit but when they met the right woman they did, sometimes after only a few months."

"So…" I suddenly regretted saying anything.

"So, I would like to get married one day and…" he paused probably regretting saying too much, "and also have children," he gasped as if I had been torturing him.

"Good. Good for you."

Jeez! What am I saying? Good for you? For you and who? Me? I've drunk too much.

Understandably Hugo laughed at me.

"So how many?" I continued my investigation.

"Nothing crazy, two would be plenty but I'm still not quite ready for kids."

"I think you can't really be ready for kids. One of my best friends who's got a child says that the journey that they – the kids – take you on it's so personal and unexpected you'll never know you're ready."

"All I'm trying to say is that children mean great responsibility and I don't want to have that just yet. For now I would like to focus on running my businesses and travelling."

"I get it. I also want to boost my career and do more travelling first."

"Then we're on the same page," he said and reached for a toothpick only to chew it for a minute while looking into the distance.

Right, I was frantically thinking. *We need a good couple of years for dating and travelling, at least a year to move in together and see how we get on, a year for all the engagement faff and organising the wedding and then more time to try for a child... And what if he dumps me just before the wedding? I totally need to freeze my eggs.*

16

MONDAY, 6 JULY
LONDON

I was lying comfortably on a sofa that seemed to be made to measure for me, perfectly supporting my one hundred and sixty-six centimetres. There were only two things sticking out of the couch – my long ponytail, dangling in front of a large floor lamp, and my ten-centimetre-high heels pointed towards the entrance. After a long day at work I was struggling not to fall asleep. *I need some eyelid holders*, I thought staring at the smooth white ceiling on which played the shadow from the bulky round lamp. My nostrils were flooded with lavender from burning incense sticks, and my thoughts were slowing down in tune with the sound of ocean waves and seagulls that were emitting from a speaker behind my head.

Arleta made sure that her room wouldn't be distracting for her clients. All walls were painted pastel green and had no pictures on them. The peaceful green was only broken by long heavy curtains that were hanging in two Victorian windows. The curtains, sofa and an armchair on which Arleta was sitting were in the same shade of ecru. On a couple of oak chests of drawers and one chunky sideboard there were only incense sticks and white candles. No flowers, no photo frames, no useless knick-knacks. I wondered whether she had an interior designer who advised her to adopt the minimalistic décor or she did it all by herself.

"Close your eyes. Put your hands down your sides. Inhale and exhale while listening to your body," Arleta said calmly, nearly whispering.

When she said 'listen to your body' it was like switching on a button in my brain that unravelled all the voices rumbling in my head that I so desperately tried to put on mute, at least for the one evening – for the one hour I was paying for. I wanted to listen to *the inner me*, not everybody else! But suddenly all I could hear was Atlanta saying that I needed the break with Henry to reflect on our relationship and make it better. Unusually for her, Freya agreed with Atlanta nodding after everything that she told me. "I knew you would eventually be back together," Freya was saying. Then there was my mother, who even on the phone couldn't hold back her enthusiasm, "That's wonderful news darling. Do you know that your father and I also split up once?"

"Mum, it's not quite the same. You split up for a week when you both were still in high-school!"

My mother wouldn't be herself if she didn't share the wonderful news with all her neighbours who were eager to listen, so they were now sharing Arleta's sofa with me. Their preaching voices were making them the number one irritating *ghosts* of that evening. I had goosebumps on my arms as I was having flashbacks of a twice divorced mother of four children from number seven saying: "Young people wait too long now, far too long, to get married and have a family. That's why their relationships fall apart so often," or an owner of a chain of luxurious hair salons at number three, whose children were brought up by a herd of different nannies: "Nowadays women put their career first, and then what? They wake up old and lonely!"

There was also Hannah, whose conversation on the phone kept being interrupted by a sudden cry, giggle or simple "mummy I'm bored, will you play with me now?" The last time I talked to her she was bending towards the Henry-solution too: "Hugo might be fantastic for now but you still don't know him that well. He's certainly great dating material but is he good father material? You said he wouldn't be thrilled to have a child now. Imagine if you had to chase him all around the world to ensure he pays for the child." I couldn't imagine that my Hugo could abandon his own child but she was right, I didn't know him well enough to start a family. The problem was that the decision wasn't quite up to me anymore.

"Love is not enough" was rumbling in my head like an overly loud and irritating song being played everywhere I went. The more my body was sinking into the soft couch and my senses were bombarded with the lavender and the sound of the ocean (doesn't quite match! I had never seen lavender on the beach), the more I was finding myself somewhere on the edge of reality and dream with all the voices spinning in my head, hammering my brain and leaving a dull pain.

Then suddenly Henry's voice became the loudest: "Are you pregnant? Darling, that's great news. I'm so happy!" When Henry found out by chance I was pregnant he instantly assumed it was his. That voice was followed by an unaware Hugo simply saying: "I miss you."

The only voice that was absent was mine. I wasn't sure whether there was no more space for it or I didn't want to hear it. Either way I hoped that Arleta would solve the problem.

"Olivia, are you ready to face your problems?" Arleta interrupted my contemplations. "Are you ready to—"

"Yes, I'm ready." *Jeez! That's why I'm here.*

"Open your eyes now but stay in the lying position. What are you feeling right now?"

When I slowly opened my eyes all I felt was how heavy my eye make-up was. My mascara, eye shadow and eyeliner were as heavy as my thoughts. I crossed my hands on my stomach and I started. "Fear," I said the first thing that crossed my mind.

"How strong is the fear on a scale from one to ten when one means being a bit afraid and ten is blind panic?" Arleta was talking while fiddling with her pen ready to make some notes in her golden diary.

"That depends. Currently there are several scenarios going through my head, but I can breathe easily so… I would say that my fear is about a four. But that's here relaxing on your couch. For most of my day I feel something between six and seven—"

"So, six or seven?" Arleta rolled her eyes.

"Six," I said unconvinced. "And last night my fear hit ten and would have gone further up—"

"It's a scale from one to ten, it can't go further," she rolled her eyes again. "Tell me what happened yesterday?"

"I went to the theatre with my friends to see the show Dilemmas of Marianna De Fontaine, have you heard about it?"

"I have but I haven't seen it yet. Tell me about it," she lowered her voice and leaned towards me with her hands resting on her knees. "What were you so afraid of? Why ten?"

"Gina Smith, the actress performing Marianna was incredible, very convincing. I felt like somebody's real life was happening just in front of my eyes. I've never identified myself with any character so much..." I was talking while hardly taking any breaks for breathing. "Marianna had twenty-four hours to decide whether she would have an arranged marriage with a wealthy and respected aristocrat or she would have a misalliance with the man who she loved but who was poor and couldn't provide for her and..." I put my right hand on my stomach feeling sick, "for her and her illegitimate child who was to be born in a few months..."

"Hmmm... so you said that you strongly identified yourself with Marianna," she paused waiting for me to keep talking but at that moment I felt ready to listen. Her business was registered as Arleta Newman, fortune-teller and psychotherapist so she should have known better why I identified myself with the main character – she should have known better than me. I suddenly decided to talk predominantly about the state of my mind and stop providing Arleta with too many details about my most recent problems and life challenges. She had great reviews among women, especially those working long hours in London and feeling lost or heartbroken but you can never be too careful. According to her website she should have known why I was there!

"Yes, I did. When she had only a half an hour to decide whether to go on a boat and sail away with her poor lover, she couldn't stop weeping and I started crying with her. Soon after my heart was pounding like a jackhammer, and my breath was getting shorter. I suddenly panicked that I would suffocate there. I wanted to leave the stalls but we were sitting in the middle of a long aisle and it was the beginning of the play's climax. When Marianna was shouting like a lunatic, "What should I do? Oh heaven, tell me what should I do?" I felt like the darkness surrounding us was squeezing my throat, all the people in the audience were trying to take my breath, and Marianna's' yell was pressing on my chest. I was afraid that if I'd tried to leave, I would have made a scene and… well, I made one anyway. Freya, after she noticed how much I was sweating, sobbing and nervously breathing, emptied her paper shopping bag and passed it to me saying "inhale and exhale". The last thing I heard was "we need to take her out of here". I was glad I was able to use pregnancy as an excuse.

"You already know what decision you should make and you need to be prepared to take destiny into your own hands," Arleta was saying with her eyes closed and head resting on the back of her armchair. She looked as if she was communicating with ghosts.

"So, you're thinking that what I'm thinking right now is good?" I asked timidly.

"It's the best possible choice that you've got at the moment. The situation might change soon but for now follow your mind, not your heart, and see what happens."

"Sorry…" I said with a hint of irritation, "but I think you've just said I needed to take destiny into my own hands not—"

"That's correct. When you make a rational decision, which you consider less risky, you put your fate on a certain path but then you need to wait and see how the situation develops."

"I see," although certainly I didn't *see* as much as I hoped for. "Do you think that I should move somewhere abroad soon?" I needed blunter tips. It was all a bit too vague for £150 per hour.

Arleta closed her eyes again, leaned back on her chair and moved her hands along the armrests. I wondered for a minute how she managed to keep the ecru upholstering in such an immaculate state.

Has she just bought the furniture or does she throw them all out and replace every month? That would at least partly explain the high rates for her sessions.

"In the nearest future you go somewhere across the sea but you won't necessarily move there. The trip will bring a lot of good into your life and will give you some important answers that you've been looking for."

"How long will the flight be? Is it going to be short or long haul?"

"It doesn't matter how long the flight is. It's completely irrelevant now," I sensed irritation in her voice. She was rather moody for a psychotherapist. Maybe the fortune-teller element of her job was making her more emotional. "What does matter, however, is that you shouldn't be afraid to take the journey. It might completely change your love life."

"I will but—"

"Unfortunately, our session is coming to an end. I would love to keep you longer but in five minutes I've got another patient."

"I only wanted to ask very quickly whether the man I'm currently with is a good person?"

She sighed while slowly rising up from her seat, "he's a good man who sometimes make bad choices. We can analyse him during our next session."

Hold on, am I with Hugo or Henry at the moment? I thought but I didn't have a chance to clarify who she meant because she cut me off saying: "It would help if you could bring his photo next time or a short film – even if it's with your phone." Then she looked at her watch again and opened her diary, "Next week at the same time?"

"Please," I said not thinking straight. I had planned to only pay for one appointment, it was expensive enough. I had no intention of making it a regular thing but *what if she could tell me something important about Henry... or Hugo.*

"Done," Arleta said shutting her diary with a bang. "I just wanted to say quickly that if you need emergency advice before our next session you could purchase my text-advice services. For only a hundred and twenty pounds a week you can ask me a total of six questions that I'll answer on the same day by text. If you decide to go for a monthly package, it will only be a hundred pounds a week," she smiled as if she was offering me freebies.

"Thank you, I'll definitely think about it."

It was tempting because in the messages I could also ask about Tiggy and my job. The only obstacle was the cost. I had far more important expenses, *although she could potentially advise me also on my financial matters...*

I couldn't wait to get home before I texted Henry. I stopped just outside of Arleta's office, located in her white posh house in St John's Wood, to quickly type:

```
Ok, I'll be at yours tomorrow.
```

I wanted to tell him personally that I would go with him on his business trip to New York.

17

TUESDAY, 7 JULY

LONDON

I t was a stuffy summer evening. After an hour spent crossing crowded London's streets, sweat drops were trickling down my spine. My straightened at six o'clock hair was breaking into unruly waves, and all that my hairspray managed to achieve was to make the city dust even more likely to stick to my head. I slowly started regretting that I hadn't used the underground. Fifteen minutes spent fighting claustrophobia suddenly seemed to be a better alternative to presenting myself to Henry in I-have-just-run-a-marathon version. On the bright side, I was carrying only my own sweat drops which wasn't a given from the underground. But soon it was about to get worse and I was going to look as if I had run a marathon in the rain. I was so lost in my thoughts that I hadn't checked the weather forecast as I would normally do in the morning on my way to work. I hadn't even looked at the sky, which would actually be enough to realise I needed an umbrella. When I stood outside of the gate to a three-storey house with a small attic flat where Henry was now living alone, I was completely drenched but I kept smiling to myself. It could have been worse, at least I hadn't been hit by lightning that was illuminating the city like fireworks welcoming another new year. *I'm going to start a completely New Year, a new chapter in my life*, I thought pressing on the intercom. I was pressing it for the third time when I suddenly noticed next to me a trembling soaked wet woman in her early twenties. She tried to put her hand to her leopard pattern Birkin bag without opening it too wide and drenching the contents, "Where's the damn key?" she said loudly.

"Let's get inside," I said when Henry buzzed me in without saying anything through the intercom.

"Thanks, Ben is late and I can't find my key," she said and her teeth started chattering. Her white top was sticking to her slim shaking body. When we got inside of the house I noticed she created a small puddle on the staircase where she was standing and looking for the key.

I wanted to be alone with Henry but I couldn't just leave her alone in such a state, "Would you like to come to us to dry your clothes and have some tea?"

"Oh, no thank you. It's really nice of you but Ben should be here any minute," she smiled gratefully and reached for her phone to type something.

"Okay but if he's not here anytime soon, don't hesitate to knock on the door of the flat at the very top."

Henry was waiting for me in the door with one hand keeping the door open and one holding his mobile next to his ear, "One of my students, it won't be long," he whispered," and left me in the hallway.

I couldn't even remember when the last time was that he waited for me like that – for the last couple of years I was using my own keys. *Once it was my home too*, I thought with nostalgia. Then one Sunday afternoon tired from the constant commuting between our flats we finally decided to move in together. It was a short conversation with a quick practical conclusion – he didn't pack my key in a box with a ribbon or ask me during a romantic dinner whether I wanted to live with him. He just said out of the blue while doing the dishes, "let's stop wasting time on the commute and save some money for a deposit to buy our own place later."

I threw my handbag on the floor and rushed to switch on the coffee machine. I leaned back against the black kitchen worktop and looked around. As I was viewing the place in hindsight I wasn't surprised that we'd had so many arguments in this flat – most of which were pretty trivial and I couldn't remember. There wasn't enough space for two people who sometimes liked to be left alone with their thoughts. To be honest, even the most agreeable couple who enjoyed each other's company twenty-four seven would struggle. A small kitchen, with a round glass table, opened onto the living room, which included an L-shaped sofa, a mini coffee table, one wall covered entirely with white bookshelves, one with a small round window, and one dominated by a large TV – too large to watch from such a short distance. In the kitchen-lounge area we also had a black freestanding hanger and there were two doors – one leading to a tiny bedroom and one to a bathroom. In the bedroom, where Henry was now speaking on the phone, we had proudly squeezed a double bed, with no bedside cabinets, but with fitted wooden wardrobes on both sides and cupboards over the head end. The storage-maximizing bed frame made me feel like I was travelling on a boat, in an economy cabin. The bedroom had a small window but it was so close to another house that it gave us barely any light and we kept the blinds down most of the time.

I sat at the kitchen table on one of four white plastic chairs. I couldn't wait for the coffee machine to finally welcome me with a latte. It was taking ages to heat up, *Henry must have forgotten to de-scale the machine. Again!* The white plastic chair seemed to have some magical powers as within few seconds it took me on a trip back in time showing me with astounding clarity some unwanted scenes from my life with Henry. I saw how we were arguing about who would work at the table and who would compromise by sitting with a laptop on the couch. We had regular quarrels about which pair of friends we should have invited for dinner first as we had a table that could accommodate only four people. Before that we'd had a table for six but we'd argued every day whether the table should have been posi-tioned close to the kitchen annexe or the bedroom door. Both Henry and I moved it so often that we made a long scratch on our wooden floor. I looked down at the floorboards, the scratch wasn't that obvious anymore – Henry must have painted it with varnish. If he was really going to leave the flat he would be worried that the owner would charge him for that from the deposit.

Irritated from the accumulation of bad memories and the ridiculous wait for my coffee, I stood up abruptly and realised that my high heels made another scratch just next to the old one. *Damn it, Henry will be delighted, he hates DIY and he most certainly classifies using varnish as DIY!*

I bloody knew it, I thought on discovering that the coffee machine didn't work because its container was maxed out with used capsules. "How many times do I have to repeat it to you that coffee capsules don't miraculously disappear but you have to bin them regularly?" that was the question I used to ask Henry at least twice a week. I was throwing out the capsules when Henry, free of his phone, finally showed up smiling and saying, "I no longer have the excuse that you drink more coffee than me," but his smile quickly faded away when he saw my wet handbag making a small puddle on the floor.

"Sorry, I'll take the bag to the bathroom in a minute," I said irritated and I heard Henry's voice in my head saying: *In a minute? In a minute the floor will be permanently damaged!* But nothing like that was said this time.

"Would you like to change your wet blouse?" he asked holding in his hand his favourite blue polo shirt. Indeed, my silky light blue blouse was soaked and exposing my pink bra underneath.

"Good idea," I said and he got closer to me – so close that it could have been recognised as intrusion of my personal space. I felt chills down my spine and it had nothing to do with the actual cold.

I took Henry's perfectly ironed T-shirt and to his disappointment moved straight towards the bathroom. Henry trodded back to the bedroom to make another call. *Darling, you haven't deserved yet to see me half naked*, I thought and smirked, when I heard the doorbell. *Seriously, why now?* I walked reluctantly to the front door and looked through the peephole. I saw the girl from downstairs, Ben obviously was taking his time. I felt cold wind from both the staircase and the girl's face expression. *No wonder, she must be pissed off that Ben is so late and she's all wet and tired.* I invited her in and offered some coffee, without much thought I also suggested her taking the t-shirt, which Henry had just given to me. When Henry appeared and saw her, a weird squeak came out of his throat. His face made a grimace that I'd never seen before – it was a mixture of: his face during turbulence, the time when after six months of being together he found my pregnancy test, and something else that I couldn't quite identify.

* * *

"No thanks. You'll need the dry T-shirt more than me as I want you to leave darling. Right now," she said to me. *Flabbergasted* wasn't enough to describe my state of mind at the time. "Please don't make this even more difficult. I need to talk to Henry in private."

For a short minute I thought I was dreaming and none of this was happening.

"Blanca, what the hell? How have you managed to get inside? And what are you doing here in the first place?" Henry was now shouting with a slight panic in his voice.

"She let me in," Blanca pointed at me triumphantly and laughed forcefully.

"She told me she was waiting for Ben and she was drenched and… How could I not?" I was explaining myself to Henry as if I'd done something wrong.

"Ben went to Chicago a week ago and I bet Blanca knows that," Henry was trying to control his trembling voice.

"He did," she snapped. "I also know you'd never let me into your flat but just as you said she's incredibly naïve."

"Now I understand everything. It's all because of her, isn't it?" I shouted.

"You're a naïve but nice woman," Blanca said and I thought for a second that she was about to tap me on my shoulder. Did she feel mercy towards me? "Could you please leave us alone and don't turn into a hysterical woman. I really don't like it when women get hysterical. It's kind of pathetic and so unnecessary—"

"You're leaving right now," Henry yelled, his right hand pointing at the door. "Get out now!" he shouted again, I didn't recognise this yelling and decisive man standing next to me.

Henry's gesticulations caused his fingers to brush her wet top, he suddenly jumped away from her and bent back with his hands covering his horrified face.

"Don't you dare touch me!" she screamed as if Henry had tried to molest her right in front of me. "Don't you dare put your sticky little fingers on me!"

Henry and I stood still. Neither of us would dare move a finger against her demands, but our bodies were shaking against our will. Blanca was pointing a gun at us. First, she was aiming at Henry's chest but quickly she moved it towards my head.

"I told you, you better leave lady! I told you. Now I'll have to... I'll have to..." she was still pointing the gun at me, her body trembling, her cheeks flooded with tears. "Fuck it! In every war there's collateral damage. Every day there are good people losing their lives, while others try to fight for the right cause."

I lost my voice due to an invisible cord suffocating my throat. I was looking at a woman on the verge of a breakdown who had transferred all her anger into one small black pistol and she wanted to fire it. Fire it to feel some relief. I closed my eyes.

"Just tell me what you want," Henry said calmly taking deep breaths. "Let me fix everything. Give me one more chance and whatever it is, I'm going to fix you... I mean fix IT. Trust me," he didn't seem to be talking to somebody who wanted to blow his head off, but rather to a person who he was trying to persuade from jumping off a building.

"You destroyed my life you son of a bitch!" Blanca was now targeting Henry's forehead while not taking her eyes away from me.

Henry put his hands up in a give-up gesture, "You've got your whole life ahead of you. It's not worth it."

"I had. I had my whole wonderful life ahead of me and you took it away from me."

"I can help you Blanca, you know I can. If you kill me I won't be able to help you…" Henry was losing his confidence again.

"You son of a bitch, I'm not going to believe a word that you're saying. My mother was right, when a man promises you a lot, you can be sure he's not going to fulfil any of it.

"I didn't have a choice—"

Blanca fired the gun. There was an ear-splitting bang and after *a touch of silence* another bang. Then there were some aftershocks – the bang of the TV falling off the wall and smashing on the floor. I'd always wondered how it would sound. I'd always wondered how it would sound to pull the TV off the wall when Henry wasn't listening to me, totally immersed in one of his historical TV shows. Now I knew, courtesy of one of his students. The glass in the window shook but remained in its old wooden frame. I heard a rustle of a poster sliding down to the parquet floor, Einstein's face in black and white moving towards my feet. Again, came the silence but this time it remained. I didn't dare look at Blanca or the place where Henry was previously standing. My eyes were fixed on the poster saying: *"The definition of insanity is doing the same thing over and over and over again but expecting a different result".*

"For god's sake, she's pregnant with my child," Henry was saying and weeping like a small scared boy. Neither of the bullets had even scratched him. There was however a large hole in the wall, in the place where once hung our too-large-for-the-flat TV. Also, Albert Einstein had a hole in his head. "Have mercy for the child, she's completely innocent!" Henry even in a moment of terror didn't forget that he wanted to have a little girl.

"I don't believe you. She's not pregnant," Blanca was weeping no less than Henry, her breath became faster, her face redder and her hair, which had managed to dry a bit, was hanging messily on both sides of her childish round face. Her ruffled locks started getting into her eyes and sticking to her cheeks. She held the gun with her left hand while trying to get rid of the hair from her face with the right one. I could tell she wasn't a professional killer – she looked like she was holding the gun for the very first time in her life, her thin trembling hand could barely take the weight of the pistol. I felt confident, though, her being amateurish wasn't going to stop her from killing us. If anybody needed proof – there were the two holes in the wall.

Any word or wrong move could provoke her to pull the trigger. Blanca's face was full of rage but at the same time filled with some deep pain and fear. She was standing there between us like a wounded animal ready to attack at any second. My gut was telling me there was no way to approach her without causing casualties and I wasn't going to be one of them.

"Next to the hanger there's my handbag," I said pointing in that direction with a gentle movement of my head. "Inside in my purse there's a picture from my last scan. Have a look if you don't believe I'm pregnant."

"Fine, I believe you, and what?" she shouted in a gravelly voice.

"You're a good person Blanca," Henry nearly whispered. "You don't want to hurt anybody, especially an unborn baby."

"Bullshit! You don't know as much as you think you know and that's exactly the problem. You do something because you're convinced you know something, that you know everything and... and then..." she couldn't finish the sentence, maybe even she didn't know what she was trying to say.

"You're right but everybody deserves a second chance. I'll change, we both can..."

"Shut up professor! Blanca aimed the gun again at Henry's chest. "You're right I'm not going to kill her and her baby but why would I save you?"

Henry and Blanca were looking at each other like a bull and matador. I suddenly saw them dancing in a ring but it wasn't clear to me who was the one holding the red blanket and who was going to run into it. She held the gun to kill him but he seemed to have some strength that I hadn't been aware of before. Henry moved his eyes to look somewhere above the entrance door and then above the fridge.

"Seriously?" she laughed hysterically putting her right hand on her shaking belly. "Are you trying to say that you've got the cameras on now, even when you're at home? I didn't know you're so twisted," she was finding it more and more funny. "They must be dummies to scare somebody away."

"When you find they're real it's going to be too late. On the bright side, you're only twenty-one so when you go to jail now, you might have a few years out of prison at the end of your life."

"Oh Henry, I've just said that you always assume that you know everything but the truth is you don't know shit!" she was laughing louder and louder repeating *shit* like a child who had just learned a naughty word. "So, as part of your last enlightenment – as you're not going to experience your last rites – I'll tell you something interesting before I blow off your smug face. We both know the cameras are dummies because you're too mean to spend money on real ones. You think however that I would be mad to kill you and let your girlfriend live to identify me later."

"That's not what I'm thinking," Henry said sheepishly.

"But you do think I'm crazy."

"It's not—"

"It's fine, I'm crazy and what would a crazy person do?" she smirked, put the pistol close to her face and examined it from both sides. "I've got here enough ammunition for two people, even if I miss a few times – although in such a small space it's probably safe to assume that one shot will be enough to get rid of you forever," she smiled with her red lips tightly closed like a clown. "By the way how could you two live together in so few square meters? They really don't pay you well at uni."

"We wanted to save up for—"

Oh, shut up Henry, I thought.

"Oh, shut up Henry," Blanca snapped irritated.

"Blanca, I beg you…"

"So, what would a crazy person do now? What Henry?" he opened his mouth but she didn't let him make even a sound, "yeah, that's right, a crazy person would shoot herself later. That's why I don't give a crap what your ex tells the police later. And if the cameras are real – even better because I don't mind somebody posting this on YouTube, I've always wanted to go viral," Blanca talking in a slow and confident way seemed to be scarier than when she was laughing and sobbing interchangeably.

She was a ticking bomb and the only way to survive her was to blow her up at a safe distance before it was too late.

"Do you have a last wish Henry?"

"Yes, I would like to…"

"He would like to see the scan of his child. That's the reason I'm here."

"Wow, you can't even have the last word at the end of your life," Blanca laughed hysterically.

I looked at Henry begging him with my eyes to do what I said.

"Olivia just knows me well enough to know what I want," he said confidently.

He would have never said that if a crazy person wasn't aiming her gun at him.

"The scan is in my bag, in the small pocket on the inside," I was instructing Blanca, who was going through my handbag with her right hand, while holding the gun with her left hand and aiming it somewhere between me and Henry.

"I can't find it. Hopefully it's not some sort of stupid trick that you think might save your life. You better remember where it is before I change my mind and shoot you too. You think I'm not going to do that but…" she didn't finish the sentence before we heard another loud bang.

Blanca collapsed on the floor weighed down by the metal hanger, which a few seconds earlier had been standing above my wet hand-bag. The hanger also used to be a source of many arguments with Henry. I'd always been afraid that the heavy unstable hanger standing on the uneven boards and loaded with lots of coats could one day fall down on somebody. Henry thought I was exaggerating and never screwed it to the floor as I asked him to do on numerous occasions. I would have never thought that him being stubborn could have ever saved our lives or at least his life. My bag was caught around the leg and any light tug would cause the hanger to fall over. Blanca had tugged.

Everything happened in a split second. Blanca collapsed on the parquet, making the sound of an animal in agony, her pistol slid to the other side of the kitchen-lounge area and fired itself. It made a hole in the leather sofa – the only piece of furniture I bought myself for the flat. There was no need to subdue Blanca, she wasn't able to move on her own. As we found out later in hospital she broke a leg and her nose. She also had a concussion and multiple bruises. She left spots of blood on the floorboards that we weren't allowed to clean before the investigation was completed. The police arrived at the same time as an ambulance. As soon as they took her on the stretcher the flat got yellow-taped. Blanca refused to say anything without her lawyer but Henry and I were eagerly reporting everything to the police, trying not to miss any details while we still remembered. We were talking over each other like market sellers, vividly gesticulating and quickly catching our breaths. I needed somebody to share the weight of the experience with me, and I suppose Henry felt exactly the same.

There was nobody to confirm our version of events. Ben who worked with Henry at the university and lived on the first floor was giving lectures in Chicago. The basement apartment was vacant, and a family of three occupying the second floor had gone on holiday the night before. The cameras turned out to be dummies and there were no signs of forced entry. Thanks god neither of us had been tempted to touch the pistol.

* * *

"Now I'm thinking…" I broke the silence, "we should've rented a bigger flat away from the centre. We would've lost some time commuting but probably not more than on all those arguments that we had here.

I was lying on our shot sofa, staring at the two holes in the wall, which were getting progressively bigger as more and more plaster and orange paint fractured and fell away around them. My head was resting on Henry's knees. He was stroking my hair in silence.

"You're right," he whispered and we returned to silence.

I suddenly thought about Arleta saying, "You'll go somewhere across the water, but you won't move away just yet. The journey will bring a lot of good into your life and a new beginning to your love life."

"I came today to tell you that I would go with you to New York in September."

"I'm really glad," he said unemotionally and automatically.

It wasn't the reaction I'd been expecting. I turned on my back to be able to see Henry's face expression. He was staring numbly at the place where a few hours ago hung the large television. Then his face twitched, he moved my head off his lap, got up briskly and walked towards the only window there was in the room. He stood with his back to me, I could see his shoulders gently rising up and hear him sighing. Then he turned to me sideways occasionally gazing at the brightly shining moon behind the dusty looking window.

"Would you like a cup of tea?" I suggested not having a clue what to do with myself.

"No, thanks," he snapped. "Why don't you ask now what you really want to know?"

"It's two o'clock in the morning," I said defensively. "It's not the best time to—"

"Why not? You do it every time, can't you see that?"

"What are you talking about?"

He crossed his hands, spread his legs on the floor and started talking in a way that made me feel I'd been invited to a principal's office for something much worse than running too fast in the school's corridors. "You're always afraid to ask about something difficult just in case you don't like the answer. You'll go away as if nothing happened, not saying a word for weeks, then finally explode like a volcano. You normally wait so long that I can't even recall the detail."

"That's really lucky because this time neither of us should have a problem with recalling the night. Worse case we can always ask the police for a detailed report."

"I don't want to talk about it in in two or three months. I want to talk it through and forget about it."

193

"Good for you but I'm definitely not going to forget. And what exactly are you talking about? Do you mean your ex-lover who wanted to perform the last scene from Romeo and Julia in your flat?"

"I'm glad you're exploding now when I can at least expect it," he said flippantly.

"Jeez Henry!" I shouted feeling an irresistible urge to throw my shoe at him. *Don't they say that aggression causes aggression?* "I'm chuffed for you! You managed to provoke me – well bloody done you! So, who is the woman who wanted to kill us?"

"One of my students, definitely not my ex-anything."

"The two aren't mutually exclusive, in fact normally the total opposite in your world, they work together like a horse and carriage!"

"Only a student. She was struggling with her exams—"

"Do you want me to believe that she wanted to blow your head off because she failed at applied linguistics? The Shakespeare University is a fantastic setting for a crime series. First the Cheaters Gang, then Blanca. What's next?"

"Bingo!" Henry said joyfully making me even more confused. "Blanca was struggling with her exams until... until she suddenly was at the top of her class. Our company caught her essay dealer. It was over a week ago. She's already been expelled from the university, she paid a fine and she's on a black list of students who can't study at any university in the country. I happened to talk to one of her friends in a pub a couple of days ago. Blanca's long-term relationship fell apart and her parents blocked her trust fund. Instead, they suggested she works as a waitress in one of their chain restaurants in Rome."

"She only has herself to blame."

"True but I do feel bad that my work exposed you to such danger. Now you've seen what I'm dealing with and why I desperately wanted to keep you away from all that—"

"Stop! Crazy people are everywhere! But..." I hesitated.

"What?"

"You said that students don't know that you work for the company chasing cheaters... As far as I remember you said that you just inform the customers, you don't confront the cheaters."

"Normally, but in this specific case it was me who had to tell her the bad news. She was one of my students and she must be thinking now it's my fault entirely. She overestimates my power as a professor."

"And what are the chances she knows about your secret job?"

"It's not impossible of course and I'll have to investigate it first thing in the morning. She was furious when I told her she was expelled. She was yelling that I hadn't understood anything including how demanding her parents were and what kind of pressure they put on her whole life. Apparently, she always wanted to be a model or an actress and she never wanted to study."

"She should be grateful then that you made her free from the ballast of such unnecessary education. You opened a range of new possibilities for her!"

"The possibility of becoming a serial killer?" Henry laughed and we both quickly felt better, as if none of the terrible events of that night had ever happened.

Unfortunately, I woke up in the morning full of doubts and questions that had been bothering me before the night chat with Henry. How did she know where Henry lived? Was it a coincidence that Henry was the only tenant in the whole building that night? How did she know the cameras weren't real? When I was leaving the flat I noticed that at the front gate there were no names on the buzzer. Next to the number two was just Ben's initials. How did she know Ben lived there too? I wanted to believe Henry, I wanted to believe him so badly but I had not expected it would be so difficult.

18

THURSDAY, 27 APRIL

(TWO MONTHS EARLIER) LONDON

"Today we'll talk about what *interpersonal communication* is and what we can do to make it more effective..." Henry was giving his lecture in the biggest auditorium of Shakespeare University. "We'll start from defining the word *communication* and reviewing the most popular models of the communication process. Then we'll consider the question why we so often struggle offering our thoughts and intentions to others, as well as why we are such bad listeners. We'll also identify some factors that can disturb interpersonal communication..."

I was sitting in the second to last row trying to split my attention between what Henry was saying and what was happening around me. The lecture hall, which could accommodate three hundred people, was full. I couldn't spot a free chair. Psycholinguistics was obligatory for all students reading philology and applied linguistics. Those who studied other subjects, like journalism, chose the lecture voluntarily from a long list of optional modules. I was wondering how many of the students occupying the chairs felt forced to listen to the guy walking around the stage with a mike in front of ever-changing slides. Most people, I could see, were staring at bright screens of their laptops seemingly treating Henry like a busker – they wouldn't throw him any coins but he wasn't particularly bothering them either. For them he was just a noise. Except that they or their parents had already thrown loads of heavy coins to the university hat at the beginning of the semester. Henry was one of a few professors who let his students use laptops during his lectures. He quoted his students saying that nobody handwrites anymore so why should he prevent people from typing their notes on the computer. He also argued that if somebody didn't want to listen to him, taking the laptop away from them wouldn't solve the problem anyway. I'd agreed with him until I had a chance to participate in one of his lectures. It started dawning on me that the majority wouldn't know what to do with themselves without their screens, the continual clicking and scrolling. They would have probably started involuntarily looking and listening to the funny guy sweating on the stage and putting all his energy into trying to explain them something – something, bless him, probably only important to him.

"The word communication comes from the Latin word *commūnicāre*, which means *to share* something..." Henry kept talking but his voice was getting more and more dispersed in my thoughts, it was disappearing somewhere within lecture hall B13.

The Internet was offering a whole range of possibilities during this ninety-minute lecture. A few girls in the row in front of me were shopping. One of them was purchasing a week's worth of food and a year's worth of alcohol. Another one was educating herself on expensive moisturisers, and a third girl dressed in a silver shiny top was searching frantically for a pair of shoes – each time she zoomed in on some stilettoes I sighed with admiration. I took my diary out of my bag to note the name of an Italian luxurious shoe brand I hadn't known before. *How useful and educational!* The shoes were a bit pricy but women shouldn't save on their looks.

"In repair?" a golden-haired boy asked me all of a sudden.

"I'm sorry I don't—" I started thinking that I must've missed something he said previously.

"Mine broke a week ago. I had to have it repaired and I lost it for six hours. I felt naked!"

"Mine? Yours?" I asked stupidly. "Oh yeah," suddenly enlightened, "my notebook exploded last night, apparently it was due to overuse!"

"I'm sorry to hear that," he said in a tone appropriate to somebody who had lost their beloved dog.

He glanced at me full of compassion and mercy and then returned to editing his photos on Instagram. He wasn't a blond version of David Gandy but he definitely had a better face and body than the national average. When he finished with photoshop he also posted several of his pictures on his blog. There I could watch him in every possible fashion variation: the golden-haired boy in a tailored suit, the golden-haired boy in posh wellingtons, green quilted jacket and chequered beret... the golden-haired boy in... I leaned towards his computer to see him only in his tight white boxer shorts.

"Here you are," the golden-haired boy passed me his business card saying David Blueberry, trendsetter.

"Thanks," I whispered and felt like I was starting to blush.

I turned instantly to my right to see what a girl next to me was doing. The slim brunette in heavy dark blue glasses was constantly typing. On the pretext of taking something out of my handbag I bent down to my right. The brunette was busy translating some marketing slides from French to English. *Working from "home", eh?* I thought as she gave herself a break to have an energy bar and a stroll through her Facebook page. I was about to stop staring at her and get a snack myself when I noticed she was looking at a photo of Henry and me standing next to a lit palm tree. *Our holiday last year to Crete,* after a moment lost in nostalgia I didn't have a chance to further reflect on my sweet memories because the brunette elbowed another brunette on her right and said, "Have a look Tatiana how funny our Harry looks in a shirt buttoned all the way up to his chin? And the woman next to him might be pretty but why would she choose such flat granny sandals?" she pouted and finished with a loud and slurred "Ew".

"His name is Henry," I said.

"Oh, I thought that Harry and Henry is the same," she said brushing me off.

Why would he let his student befriend him and then post our private photos? Does he really have to schmooze with his students?

"I can provide many examples on how intercultural differences can cause some misunderstandings in my relationship..." I heard a female voice with a melodic accent.

"Fantastic," said Henry and passed his microphone to a short girl dressed in a tight white t-shirt stretched over large boobs.

"I'm Bianca. My boyfriend Eliot is English, and I come from Italy," she said so loudly as if she'd forgotten she had the mike and the whole room burst into laughter.

My brunettes from the right looked at each other and rolled their eyes simultaneously.

"I'm bored with the Italian geek," said Tatiana, or maybe Titiana.

"Me too but I'm grateful to her that she speaks for three hundred people," said the other brunette and giggled while almost choking on her chocolate bar.

"I thought for a while that Eliot's neighbours are just rude..." Bianca said squeezing tightly the mike in her left hand. "To be fair they don't seem to be kind either... although it might be just me being Italian and not fully understanding the local customs... Each time when we meet some of his neighbours they always finish with "you must come for dinner", but they have never actually invited us. They keep saying it, we keep replying "sure" and it never happens. After the first time I went to buy a new dress. Eliot looked at me mercifully and said the dinner would probably never happen. How could I know that "you must come for dinner" is just a kind of salutation similar to "how are you", when nobody is really interested in how you are.

"Why don't you invite them?" somebody shouted from the audience.

"Oh, I do... I do it on a regular basis to be polite, just like they do," she said seriously but the corners of her lips twitched. "I'm just more creative than them. I say "you must come for a drink. Eliot makes a fab sex on the beach", and "you must come to see our new exotic aquarium". Obviously, Eliot only drinks beer and we only have one gold fish, but who cares? They're never actually coming over."

Before Bianca passed the mike to Henry she managed to have a selfie with him – with the mike and with the whole audience in the background. Henry smiled politely and said nothing. A few minutes later I was looking at their selfie on the laptop belonging to the golden-haired boy.

19
WEDNESDAY, 8 JULY

LONDON

"Olivia, you can't be so sure it was her," Freya was shouting on the phone.

"I thought I heard Bianca, but now I'm pretty convinced it was Blanca. I can't remember her face from the lecture but the big boobs, the accent, the loud husky voice—"

"Oh, come on," she cut me off. "What's the chances at one of the most international universities in London you find an Italian girl with good size boobs? I'm also sure they're loads of girls with names starting from *B*. You experienced something traumatic, no wonder your head is now full of conspiracy theories. You need some time to be yourself again."

"Maybe you're right," I said concluding that all my explanations were pointless – Freya was completely, if not ridiculously, adamant that my idea, which formed the very morning after the terrible incident in Henry's flat was nonsense.

The fact that somebody put a gun to my head doesn't have to mean that my brain has been scrambled and I need some time to fix it, I thought while fiddling with my carrot cake. After the conversation with Freya I lost my appetite. I had to get ready for work so I shovelled the cake into a plastic bag with goodies prepared for the local ducks.

Several hours later I was sitting with Hannah in an outdoor café in Regent's Park. The afternoon breeze chased away the scorching heat that only an hour ago had been giving me a headache. Some birds were entertaining us with their singing while others were infuriating us by picking food from the tables and treating the place like their open-air lavatory. I couldn't remember the last time when I'd enjoyed a warm afternoon in London, and definitely not in the middle of the week.

When I showed up at work in a creased skirt and top that I'd been wearing the previous day, Tiggy asked me to immediately come to her office. *Oh heaven, I'm going to get a lecture on personal hygiene and ironing my clothes. Oh, and washing them too,* I thought glancing at my knees where there were some small drops of blood, a reminder of a nose bleed I got when Blanca was leaving the flat on a stretcher. I took a seat in Tiggy's office feeling nothing but ambivalence to what she was about to say. *What's the worst that can happen? Does she keep a gun in her drawer? And if she does, is she going to shoot me for looking like a slob?*

"I know what happened," she said coldly. "I'm going to give you three days off so you can pull yourself together."

"Has it already been on the news?" I asked amazed.

"Don't be ridiculous. Nobody shot you last night."

"Oh, I'm sorry that nobody shot me last night," I mumbled to myself but she managed to hear it.

"Go before I change my mind," she was saying while typing on her laptop.

"But how—?"

"Henry called me. Goodbye Olivia," she said pronouncing every word almost too clearly and too loudly. "You've got so much leave this year, and you're getting an additional three days. Some have it lucky," she whispered to herself.

I felt an almost irresistible urge to respond to her outrageous comment, but I just managed to hold myself back. She was not worth any of my time.

Thank you, Henry, I thought leaving the office, *thank you that you let me return to normality and get occupied by something not-you-related.*

I called Hannah as I was going down in the lift. I pressed her number almost automatically, I needed somebody to talk to. She always used to say that she was bored with the everyday life of *the Real Housewives of London,* so I thought she would appreciate a juicy piece of gossip. I wasn't sure how nice or not-nice being a housewife was in London but I had a feeling that being a rich housewife could have some indisputable advantages. One of them was having Time – not the time to finally clean the house or shave your legs but the Time to leave the house without much hassle and spend a day with your friend, go shopping or have tennis lessons. As I accurately predicted Hannah called her nanny and an hour later she was out hunting with me in Oxford Street for some bargains. She got very excited every time she pulled out a pretty designer top from the piles of hangers and clothes (definitely not clothes on hangers anymore) that were building around the shops. I suspected she did it only for me – nice social thing to do when you are minted and your friend is not. When we finished, Hannah suggested that we should change into some of our new clothes. "Good idea," I said knowing that it was her way of getting me out of my creased and dirty outfit. *Nicely done Hannah!*

It took me a while to tell Hannah why I really called her. Judging by my look and the urgency of my voice on the phone she knew something wasn't right but she'd expected some more love drama. When we sat down in a café I was still not ready to return to the events of the previous night. I needed to focus on somebody else's problems and just for a minute forget about mine.

"Have you told Alfie about the child?"

She nodded and set her sad eyes on a cup of cappuccino as if she'd planned to read something important in the way a barista sprinkled some chocolate on frothed milk.

"By the look on your face I guess he wasn't delighted but maybe that's for the best if you want Oscar to be the father," I said thinking about Hugo, who still didn't know about me being pregnant. I kept procrastinating because I was afraid that his reaction would be far from thrilled and enthusiastic.

"I told him last weekend. I was afraid to look into his eyes and see anything less than joy so I called him."

"Was he surprised that you spoke to him after such a long break, it's been a couple of months, hasn't it?"

"No, he wasn't," Hannah said grudgingly. She obviously wasn't keen to discuss her love life. She might've also hoped that I would distract her. "He wasn't at all," she took a long breath, "and when he found out about the pregnancy he asked joyfully 'which week'."

"Seriously?"

"Yeap! But his voice quickly switched from *merry* to *mercy* – mercy for himself of course – when he heard *eighteen weeks*. When I said 'Alfie it could be yours' he stopped talking and then he suddenly exploded with 'what the fuck? You said you were on the pill with me'."

"Maybe he was in shock and that's why..."

"Well, a thirty-something man shouldn't be that shocked that when he has sex there's always a chance of making a baby," Hannah's right hand started trembling involuntarily causing a small silver spoon she was holding to hit the side of her coffee cup. It was quite rhythmical actually like she was playing a tune.

"Good riddance to him then. One less problem! Besides you've mentioned recently that Oscar is now a better father and he spends more time with Zoe."

"And Zoe often tells me about an auntie Rose, who works with daddy. Apparently, they spend a lot of time together and she's very nice..."

"Don't tell me you're going to spy on him again."

"No, I'm not going to. I don't have time for that and it would be beneath me."

"I'm glad to hear it," I said surprised at the sudden maturity of my friend.

"I'm going to pay somebody to do it for me. I might get a discount, because I'll also have another job for my PI," she said with a massive grin.

I almost choked on my second slice of carrot cake that day, maybe it was a hint I should stop stuffing my face with cakes, "Are you going to check out auntie Rose?"

"Of course!" she exclaimed. "But that's not only what I mean. My PI potentially will have to fly to Australia, it's going to be pricy but I have no choice."

"Now I'm getting really curious," I said putting my cake fork down.

"I've got a feeling Alfie is running away from responsibility. He said on the phone he was going to quit his desk job and move to Australia to become a scuba diving instructor!"

"You never said he could scuba dive."

"He can't," she shouted fiddling with the wine menu. I suddenly felt like a glass of rose or better, a whole bottle of rose. "Apparently he'd been planning it for ages. I say, Alfie you can't even scuba dive. He says, but I'll learn quickly. I say Alfie, you leave the pool after fifteen minutes claiming you're tired and need a beer. He says, that's right I need to work on my body and do something with my life before I've got children. I say Alfie, you might be a father soon and all he says is *oh* and switches to talking about getting the best ticket price to Australia."

"Let's hope he'll get eaten by an idiot-hungry Australian shark!"

"And then my child might not have a father," she said gloomily.

"Oh."

When I thought Hannah had finished reflecting on her potentially unfaithful husband and dick ex-lover, and I felt ready to talk about Blanca, it turned out she was just getting started, "We think that our biggest problem is making the right choice between Mr A and Mr O, or in your case between Mr H1 or Mr H2, but the fact is that we might not have a choice at all. Can we assume that they'll always be there waiting for us?" she was saying this as if she'd suddenly discovered men also had something to say regarding relationships. "My best-case scenario is a choice between Oscar and being lonely."

I nodded but it made me irritated that she put my boyfriends in the same basket as Oscar and Alfie the kid. It was even more irritating when I thought she might be right. Hugo easily understood that I wasn't able to meet up with him anytime soon, he hadn't even mentioned leaving my job and going with him around the world. I didn't have to make up complicated excuses for him to understand that I couldn't go anywhere yet because of my family issues. He kept texting and calling me saying that he missed me and would wait patiently until I was ready. Men in love have many things in common but one of them is definitely not patience. And since when does missing somebody get fully expressed in a single text: *"te echo de menos."*?

"And then Oscar spends so much time with auntie Rose now," Hannah was saying as I realised I had missed part of her monologue.

"So, is she Oscar's close auntie? That would be a bit sick. How old is she?"

"Are you even listening to me? Zoe calls her auntie. Oscar has never asked Zoe to call his friends auntie or uncle before! It stinks! And once they both took Zoe out for lunch... So, I'm thinking now that I'm going to end up as an old spinster."

"You can't be an old spinster anymore, just a divorcee. I can be an old spinster and I'm starting to think that it's not the worst thing in the world. There's been research that concludes single women not only live longer but they also enjoy better physical and mental health," I said knowledgeably.

"Then it's definitely something to consider... but Henry is not going to leave you unless you told him it might not be his child," she paused for me to answer but I said nothing. "Olivia, have you told him the truth?" she screeched questioningly, successfully scaring a few pooping birds around us.

"Of course not. I don't entirely trust him right now."

"It's understandable after what he's done to you but to be honest I don't even trust myself entirely, maybe that's the healthiest way to be."

"Something happened last night..." I started feeling butterflies in my stomach. I tried to imagine that I was giving a report on something I wasn't involved in, it was the only way I could keep myself together. I aimed to be as coherent as possible talking without being overly emotional. I was staring at some cake crumbs on our table and I was talking and talking until I got to the point when I was trying to convince Hannah that Bianca and Blanca was the same person. Similarly to Freya, she found it difficult to believe and mentioned a few times "after shock" and" conspiracy theory" but unlike Freya she wasn't completely dismissive about my idea.

"Okay, so let's say the girl who you saw during the lecture and the one who tried to kill Henry and you is the same person, so what? What does it change?"

"The girls called her a geek, you still don't understand?"

"Because maybe they're two different women..." she said hesitantly, almost apologetically that she'd tried but couldn't quite believe me, "and Henry didn't lie to you."

"Or she was deliberately very active during the lectures not to instil any suspicions about such good exam results," I was thinking aloud.

"It would mean Henry was telling you the truth... provided they're the same person of course."

"I don't know, Henry was inferring she was pretty dumb."

"But she wasn't saying anything particularly wise or knowledgeable. She was talking about her boyfriend."

"She didn't make the impression of a woman who is emotionally unstable. I find it hard to believe that expelling her from uni would make her so furious."

"Again providing that Bianca is Blanca..." Hannah couldn't resist the temptation of stressing in her every sentence that I might be wrong, "looks can be deceiving. What's one of the best weapons of a murderer?"

"That they don't look like one?"

"Exactly," she clasped. "Has she always been nice and smiled to everybody? Does she say good morning even to strangers?"

"I saw her talking to some people after the lecture, she seemed to be very nice."

"Bingo! They're the people we need to be most afraid of..."

"Are you inferring I should be afraid of half of my village?" I asked but Hannah seemed not to listen.

"People who no one would ever suspect! They don't stand out in the crowd—"

"Except that being a geek sort of makes you stand out."

"They're always NICE, always NICE," she continued not paying attention to me interrupting her occasionally. "It's like with all the lovey-dovey couples who make you jealous about their magical connection, and before you know it, they've split up with a bang! So the always NICE people who help old ladies to cross the street and say 'hello' to everybody are those who really spend their time silently plotting their perfect murder. They never say they don't like something, they seemingly agree with everything, while they just accumulate their anger and keep lowering their self-esteem until bam, bam, bam – they explode!"

I had nothing to add to Hannah's monologue so I felt relief when my phone loudly beeped in my handbag. "It might be something important," I leaned over to my bag without looking at my friend to read aloud:

```
The company FYF with Arleta reserves the right
not to reply to messages that are considered to
be inappropriate in accordance with paragraph...
```

"What's FYF?" Hannah asked.

"Face Your Future with Arleta," I replied embarrassed. *Couldn't she make up a less embarrassing name for her company?*

Hannah looked me with wide eyes while I kept reading:

```
Olivia, if you don't trust my skills and you're
trying to test me, please don't waste your money
just to see how I deal with such awkward
questions.
```

. . .

Hannah put her hand over her opened mouth, also covering her nose, and asked in a weirdly altered voice, "have you paid for a text-service with a freaking fortune-teller?"

"How do you know?"

"Darling, if you were the only person who uses the company, she would have gone bust by now. I wish she would! What did you ask her?"

"Who put the gun to my head last night?" I said matter-of-factly.

"Shouldn't you put a bit more detail in the message?" she asked shyly.

"The questions can't be longer than ten words."

"So you can't really ask for more than one thing and waste more of her precious time," she nodded. "If you've got money to waste, I can give you the number for my PI, but be careful it's more addictive than chocolate," she giggled as if she'd drunk a glass of wine. Maybe she got drunk just from reading the wine list.

"I hoped to find out whether Blanca was Henry's lover."

"It's what I used to say 'I only want to find out the one thing', and before you know it, you've got a whole list of things you want to find out. I needed to check Oscar just the one time, now I'm going to investigate him again, and aunt Rose, and Alfie..." she said sounding like she had no other choice but to employ a PI.

"Do you still care about Alfie?"

"Not after our last phone call but I would like to know where he is and what he does if the child turns out be his and one day asks me about their father."

"Do you really think he would run so far away?"

"I have no idea. I probably spent too much time concentrating on his second brain while I should've really been paying more attention to the first one," I looked inquisitively. "His penis! I spent too much time on his penis!" she exclaimed and I felt several pairs of inquisitive eyes on me, I blushed.

"Of course... do you have eh..."

"My PI's business card?" she dived energetically into her huge designer bag without waiting for me to respond. "But I would try first to collect some evidence on your own before contacting any professional. Put a decent amount of time into googling Hugo. You've still got a key to Henry's flat and thanks to him also a few days off that you can use very productively," she smirked.

My phone buzzed again. "It's my mother. I'm afraid Henry might've called her. Why does he always have to be such a bloody Santa's helper when I don't want him to be?"

"You can't keep avoiding her," she said in a singing voice and kissed me goodbye on my cheek, which was red with anger.

* * *

"Hi mum," I said reluctantly hoping that Henry hadn't told her about Blanca's murderer-to-be-mystery. "How are you?" I forced myself to sound joyful but the effect I probably achieved was suspiciously enthusiastic.

"I've just been cleaning out the attic with your dad. Goodness me, I think we haven't done it for years and years..."

"Well done you," I kept my joyful voice. "Have you discovered something particularly useful or precious? Something that you could sell for loads of money?" I was honestly happy knowing that Henry hadn't told them anything.

"We're cleaning your old Lego in the bath."

"I thought that Philip said he didn't want them for Sebastian. Aren't they made of something toxic that's not allowed nowadays?"

"No, no... Not the toxic ones, we've already binned them. I mean the pink ones," mum said suspiciously joyful. "They'll be lovely for a little girl," she squeaked and I would swear I heard her clapping. First, I got petrified thinking that Henry told them about me being pregnant but then I realised that she must have meant Philip, "Oh my god my big brother will be a dad again!" *I guess we can save on a baby-sitter having kids the same age. There's always a silver lining.*

"What are you talking about darling? Dad and I—"

"Am I going to have a sibling? Oh my god mum, are YOU pregnant? Why wouldn't you use contraception? Although... you keep saying that the only reliable contraception is lack of sex. So, are you still having sex? Oh my!" I felt I needed to leave the café because I was generating too much unwanted attention.

"Don't be silly. I'm fifty-five—"

"Well you never know. You're not that—"

"I'm fifty-five and a whole life ahead of me to enjoy, think about all the cruises around the world, crazy parties, carefree sex without worrying about getting pregnant and—"

"So, what are you saying?"

"Why didn't you tell us darling?" Mum's voice softened.

"I forgot to? And how do you know?" I asked really knowing the answer. *Henry! Of course! How could you?*

"Well, we've known for a while but forgotten to tell you," mum said confidently. If I didn't know her so well, I probably wouldn't feel the little irony in her voice.

"I'm only eight weeks pregnant, I just wanted to wait..."

"I totally understand my darling, but Henry was so happy he simply couldn't hide his joy. We're all thinking it's going to be a girl!"

I clenched my fists thinking, *Do I really need a PI or just a hitman?*

"Are you still there my darling?" she asked innocently.

"When did he tell you?"

"He called us in the morning and said it by mistake," as usual she was trying to defend him, which infuriated me even more. "He thought we already knew."

"And why did he call you?" I asked, my voice trembling, jaw shaking and right hand squeezing the phone so hard that it might have looked like I wanted to suffocate somebody.

"Oh, don't be angry. He was right to call us. He's been worried that recently you've been very stressed with your job and generally..."

"Generally – was that the exact word he used?"

"Yes it was, why? He was right, you're so stressed right now you're acting a bit weird. It's not good for your child."

"Poor Henry was so worried that he forgot to mention that so far he's been the BIGGEST source of my stress!" I yelled.

"Darling you need to forgive him at some point. Have I told you that your dad and I also split up once?"

"Nooo, really?" I asked and cut her off as soon as I heard her voice. "You have said it too many times!"

"Anyway my darling, I also agree with Henry that you two living apart isn't a good idea when you're expecting your baby girl. It's so annoying that the woman... what's her name? Ahh... Meghan... it's so annoying she doesn't want to move out. Is there something I could do? Pay her or—?"

"I've never asked her to move out. We've signed a deal for six months."

"I've got some money and time. I tell you what, let me find her a nice place and I'll pay her first month's rent and the cost of a removal van," she said happily. Poor mum was really convinced she was somehow saving me from nasty Meghan, while it wasn't her I was afraid of the most.

"No thank you," I said coldly.

"I understand," she said sounding almost insulted. "But remember that the offer stands." She gasped, "Oh, Olivia... if you just weren't as stubborn as your father. Henry is so calm and patient, he would be so good with you now when you're—"

"Mum I know I'm pregnant. Stop mentioning it in every sentence! And I'm sorry but I can't be not-as-stubborn-as-my-father. You made me with him so it's your fault how you decided to mix your genes and contaminate them with his stubbornness—" I felt like I was back in time to the days when I was still living with my parents and going to high school.

"Fine, but wedding planning can also be stressful, especially when you're..." she paused. "I mean it would be just easier if you weren't travelling to each other so far, especially in the summer, in the awful heat when you're..."

"I'm not going to travel to him. Has he mentioned any wedding? What else did he tell you?"

"He didn't mention the wedding but it goes without saying..."

"I need to go, I'm getting on a tube," I lied. "I'm losing my reception. Byeeee"

In fact, I was so red-hot I got lost twice before I found my way to Baker Street station. I did not believe in any coincidences when it came to Henry talking to my mother. He told her about me being pregnant by mistake? Phi! There were no accidents in anything that Henry had ever said! The only accident was how he found out about my pregnancy – and the answer was Meghan! Having her as a tenant and housemate had plenty of benefits. She was a plumber and a brilliant handywoman who could fix nearly everything – she was saving our household money and time. Thanks to her I didn't have to search on the Internet for any random handymen and invite a potential house burglary. Polly from work called once for a professional to fix her water softener. The guy who turned up wasn't even a plumber. He found the job simply too complicated and decided to pass but he asked her all about the contents of her shed and more specifically how many bikes she stored there. Then there was the carpenter who didn't know how to cut a kitchen work surface but got very chatty about the alarm system in her house – apparently, he wanted to install a similar one in his cottage.

Meg was also a perfect housemate for a few other reasons. Her clothes were at least a couple of sizes larger than mine, which made my wardrobe safe from unwanted borrowing. I still got angry thinking about my flat mate from university who would secretly borrow (temporarily steal) my dresses and contaminate them with strong perfumes and cigarettes. Meg was a lesbian, which meant our house was not disturbed by any unnecessary male beings or problems caused by them – no shoes kicked around in the hallway or wee around the toilet.

The biggest benefit though was that I had an excuse not to live with Henry. I had time to think about us instead of making any rushed and potentially regretful decisions. I could also call Hugo without being afraid Henry would overhear. We still talked a couple of times a week.

Any disadvantages? Just one – thanks to Meg, Henry found out too early about me being pregnant. A few days ago Henry had decided to surprise me – it was a double surprise because he had never done anything like that before. He pitched up at our house in the evening with my favourite curry, my favourite bottle of wine and a large tray of Brownies. I bet his mother made the cake and she didn't mean for me to eat it – nobody was good enough for her son! Bad luck had it that on that evening I had to stay longer at work so Meg let him in – led him into our lounge and then left to make him a cup of tea. Bad luck had it the phone rang and doctor Cromwell's secretary left me a message reminding me about my next baby scan.

First Tiggy, then my parents! Henry, you find it far too easy to spread my secrets! And I've got a feeling you're hiding something more, I thought while sitting on the metro and going through my bag to find Hannah's PI card. I didn't have a choice anymore, I had to use it. On a small creased piece of cheap white paper was written in black simple font: Gatsby Reynolds, Private Investigator, and a mobile number.

20

TUESDAY, 21 JULY

LONDON

My brother Philip and his wife Veronica kept saying that having their son Sebastian was like having twins, if not triplets. To be honest, I had babysitted many of my friends' kids but I'd never met any four-and-a-half-year-old with as much energy as Sebastian. At first sight my nephew was a well-behaved young man always remembering to say *please, thank you* and *good morning.* Despite still not being able to reach a kettle he always offered guests a cup of tea never forgetting to ask how much sugar and milk they took. He cleaned up his toys, took his shoes off when he entered a house and ate practically everything that was served to him. He would certainly win a competition for Child of the Year – if not for the fact that his day had to include at least thirty different activities involving every person around him, start not later than six am and finish no earlier than nine pm. When any of the criteria weren't met and Sebastian got bored – the Eliot's house was turned into a living hell.

Most of the drama now took place in the Eliot's house because Sebastian had been expelled from a few nurseries in London. Nobody was told how many exactly. I couldn't understand how professionals from prestigious nurseries were not able to tame that child. He painted faces on his class mates when they were sleeping, so what? The paint was not specifically for face use, but they didn't suffer too much except for a bit of a rash. "He was bored out of his mind, he didn't want to sleep in the middle of the day as the rest of the kids," I said defending him to my brother. He ruined a few meals when he broke into the nursery kitchen, so what? "They should have kept their eyes on him, it was their job!" said our mum. Philip and Veronica decided eventually to employ a nanny. Sebastian was thrilled, "I'm glad I won't have to go there anymore. I'm bored with going to the same place over and over again."

He was currently on nanny number three. The first one was fired after my nephew managed to smuggle two fish out of the Eliot's large exotic aquarium into his bubble bath. Both fish died, quite abruptly – one hundred and fifty pounds each, plus VAT and the cost of their shipping from Hawaii. Another nanny quit when Sebastian presented her with a post-mortem examination of a mouse – caught and brutally killed by Maya, Eliot's cat. The third nanny seemed to be doing fine but recently had been taken sick so Philip asked me to babysit. I'd already booked my appointment with Gatsby and because his diary was full for the next few weeks I decided to kill two birds with one stone – I invited Gatsby to my brother's house. I was well aware by then that Sebastian wouldn't go to bed at seven pm when my PI was planning to appear, so I'd prepared a whole entertainment box for the challenging four-and-a-half-year-old. I got him five cartoons on Blu-ray, all for age seven; a pack of organic chocolate cookies and three editions of a child's magazine for future vets. Each magazine included a plastic set of operating instruments and a made-in-China rat, pig or dolphin. I was sure that the entertainment box, which my brother and his wife would have never allowed, would make wonders and give me all the time I needed to talk to my PI.

I was actually glad I could meet with Gatsby in somebody else's house. I didn't have a reason not to trust Meg but I was afraid she would judge me for hiring a PI to spy on my boyfriend. I'd told her how Henry broke up with me at the airport and how on the very same day I'd met Hugo in Madrid, but as with Freya and Atlanta she was firmly on team Henry.

The doorbell rang and soon after I heard a sound of small feet on the stairs.

"What would you like to drink?" Sebastian asked, standing in his pyjamas and face covered in chocolate as he opened the door and welcomed our guest.

"Darling, I've told you that your auntie has a very important meeting—"

"I know but I've already done all the post-mortem executions," he said matter-of-factly, and Gatsby stared at me, his eyes wide open.

"He means post-mortem examinations," I said, but Gatsby was still staring at me with anticipation. "Sebastian would like to become a vet. He's been playing with some toys from magazines for future vets," I explained confidently, I didn't want to instil any suspicions as the kit was aimed for children from the age of twelve. I turned to my nephew again, "You did the rat and dolphin but I've also got you a pig. If you don't disturb us I might have a couple of other surprises."

"It's not my business..." started Gatsby, obviously feeling like it was his business. Many people once they become parents feel like they have bought some rights to *parenting* everybody around. They just can't resist acting like they've been the only one enlightened by the God-of-perfect-parenting and now they're on some kind of mission to spread their wisdom. My blood boiled as I knew all he wanted to do was judge my parenting, or rather babysitting skills. "Shouldn't he go to bed soon?"

"He was up late today," I said quickly and involuntarily I almost put my hand on Sebastian's mouth knowing his response.

"I was up at six am!" he shouted proudly. "Half an hour before daddy!"

"Well done you," I said and dragged Sebastian upstairs.

When I returned Gatsby had already made himself comfortable in the lounge on Veronica's rocking chair, which she bought when she was pregnant. *I'll need to add that to my baby shopping list*, I thought and sat down in front of him on a designer rock-solid sofa, which in less than ten minutes gave me awful bum-ache.

"I'm sorry for Sebastian. He's been very hyperactive today. I think it's the weather, something to do with the pressure..." I suddenly realised I was using the standard excuse that my parents fed everybody who got a little bit overwhelmed by their grandchild's behaviour.

"He's nice and very considerate. I've got two small boys, six and ten and they've never asked me whether I'd like to drink anything. As far as they're concerned I'm there to serve them the whole time and I don't need to drink," he said and we laughed, but as soon as I reminded myself why he was here I stopped giggling like at a tea party and felt deeply uncomfortable. I was close to calling it all off and saying there had been some misunderstanding or that I'd actually managed to solve the issue myself.

"I tell it to all my clients and I'm also going to say it to you – you don't have to feel guilty. I'm not here to judge you, but to help you," he was saying this while chewing a piece of brownie made by Henry's mother.

I wouldn't have even thought about using Gatsby's PI services but Hannah insisted he was a decent man and one of the best PIs in town. She convinced me that him not liking Henry could only work to my advantage. "If it's personal, Gatsby might be even more determined to get some dirt on Henry and work harder. Besides, he's likely to become your friend by thinking you potentially have the same enemy." According to Hannah there was also no point in reflecting on how weirdly he acted at Madrid Atocha – after all I'd lied to him about Henry, for which he might have taken offense.

I contacted several PI agencies in London but when I crossed out those who were busy for the next three months and those who were obviously milking the wealthiest citizens in the country, I was left only with those who wanted to meet up in some dodgy part of the city after dark or Gatsby. He didn't have years of experience and worked only part-time but I trusted Hannah, she and her city girlfriends seemed to be very experienced at hiring PIs.

"I don't feel guilty but..." *I do feel awfully guilty while you're eating the cake made by Henry's mother.*

"If you don't want to do it, I won't charge you," he said kindly. "That's despite driving here today all the way from Cambridge. My wife will be whinging again that I work too much and I missed the kid's birthday..."

"Have you missed your child's birthday?" *Now I feel guilty!*

"No, not mine. There're so many kids on the new development where we've just moved to that there's no day without somebody's birthday... Anyway, you can still change your mind and I'll give you, completely free of charge, the information I've managed to obtain to date. I don't really know yet how to charge for such small jobs. They're so rare because people always end up wanting to know everything."

"I didn't expect you to find out anything so soon," I said surprised and greedy for any kind of information that could clarify who the hell Henry was!

"Soon? It's been a week since your last call," he said with a smug face and pushed another piece of brownie into his self-satisfied mouth. "Blanca comes from Naples and she's twenty-one. She studied within two faculties at Shakespeare University before she was expelled – Applied Linguistics and Business Management.

"Let me guess—"

"I'm here so you don't have to guess," he said sharply. "She used to buy essays for Business Management, which she'd never wanted to study but her parents insisted that Linguistics just wasn't enough."

"So, she's just a cheating student, not Henry's lover," I said holding my hands ready to clap.

"The two are not mutually exclusive," he said mysteriously.

"Oh." *Thank you for building up the suspense and misleading me, it's exactly what I need right now!*

Gatsby stared at me for a few long seconds. He waited for a dramatic reaction before continuing any further. *Tough luck, I'm not going to be a hormonal drama queen tonight, I've gone through so much recently that Henry having an affair with a student is not going to wipe me off my feet!* I started understanding why Henry didn't have particularly warm feeling towards him. I was just not sure whether Gatsby was malicious, as Henry said, or just a bit peculiar.

"For over a year Blanca was Ben's lover. Ben is Henry's landlord and he's also a lecturer—"

"I know Ben," I cut him off impatiently. "I was also renting the flat from him. So, it was Ben who helped her somehow to pass the exams?"

"I would rather suggest that she wanted to use his help but he was very resistant and she finally decided to choose a different route... but you told me on the phone that Henry had been acting weird, what did you mean?"

Again, I felt an urge to call it all off but Gatsby had driven all the way from Cambridge, had already started working on my case and missed somebody's birthday. Besides Hannah wouldn't have forgiven me if I gave up so easily. "Olivia you need to make a decision – you either choose to trust Henry and stop poisoning your life every day by mulling over him being a potentially unfaithful thug, who has god knows what else on his conscience; or you don't believe a word he's saying and you pay a PI to find out whatever there is to find out," she said at the end of our most recent phone conversation – at the very end actually because I didn't have much to add, she was right.

"I can't really explain it but I've just got a gut feeling that something is wrong..."

"You want me to investigate whether Henry has been cheating on you?" he stretched both his arms on the back of the rocking chair and crossed his legs. I imagined him lighting a cigarette but he simply took another bite of the cake saying, "this brownie reminds me of my childhood, I think somebody's mother used to make these, delicious," he licked his fingers loudly. "Again, you've got that guilty look in your eyes, which is completely unnecessary – most of my job ends up focusing on unfaithful men."

"I didn't say he's un—"

"Fine, but you think there's a possibility. Any clues, which could help me to continue the investigation?"

"Well..." I hesitated. "I've searched his flat." He looked at me with a mixture of surprise and admiration. "We don't live together anymore but I've still got keys to his apartment."

"Have you found anything suspicious?"

"Nothing, which to be honest is suspicious in itself. I mean I haven't had enough time to search everywhere but I did it when he wasn't around and—"

"Has it crossed your mind that he could be just a normal boring guy?" Gatsby laughed loudly from his little joke. "No offence, it's good to be boring in certain ways."

Henry thinks you're boring, and that has no positive connotation.

"I've also downloaded on his phone an app that lets me monitor his position provided he's got 3G."

"Any particular discoveries?" he asked while ostentatiously yawning with his mouth open. "Have you caught him red handed with a lie?"

"Not quite but I found it weird that many times when we talked on the phone he was in a shop, just going to one or coming back—"

"And?"

"The app always confirmed what he was saying."

"Do you think his lover works in Tesco or in a fancy boutique, or maybe both part time?" he asked it in a way that meant I couldn't tell with certainty whether he was joking or being serious. "Or do you suspect that they meet up for sex in a dressing room or somewhere between the aisles—?"

"Where they sell haemorrhoid wet wipes, thrush treatment and tablets for trapped wind?" I snapped. "Ew! I haven't thought about it that much."

"Olivia," he sighed. "Has something happened recently? Has he changed any of his old habits, found a new hobby? Is he doing something in a completely different manner?"

"He's got a few business trips to the US planned and a few weekends abroad. I know he could send somebody else to go instead but he insists he'll do it better."

"Hmmm... Most people like to go abroad when their company is paying. With all due respect—"

"The thing is, Henry had always avoided business trips when they involved flying, the idea of even spending a couple of hours on the plane always makes him nauseas." *Or vomit!*

"Many people finally decide to face their fears, especially when they stand in their way to progress in their career," he said calmly explaining to me the obvious like a father to a small child.

"Do you think I'm paranoid?"

"No, of course not," he denied rapidly, probably reminding himself that I was a business opportunity – his chance for a decent amount of money for relatively little effort. "It makes me think I need to get going to continue working on the case as soon as possible. Like many women you probably have good intuition and if you feel something is not quite right... But of course, if you're not interested, there's no pressure. It's not a big deal I missed the birthday and—" he was saying this while slowly getting up from his chair and moving towards the door.

"I'm interested, I am," I said. *I'm interested to keep losing money on my paranoia.*

"I'll start working on it first thing in the morning. We'll be in touch."

"Gatsby..." I said when he was already outside the front door impatient to get to his car, "how long do you think it's going to take you?"

"It's really difficult to say. Sometimes it's a few days, sometimes it might take weeks or months. If Henry has something to hide, it all depends on how far he's gone to hide it."

"It just... it would be great if you could have something for me by the twenty-ninth of August."

"What's going to happen on the twenty-ninth of August?" he asked intrigued, fiddling with his car key.

"I've got my birthday. I'll be thirty and I think it's a good time to sort out my life."

"Any time is good for that but I promise I'll try not to miss your birthday."

* * *

As soon as I shut the door behind Gatsby I heard the cute little voice that I'd almost forgotten about, "Auntie Olivia…"

"What darling?" I asked and before Sebastian managed to answer I kissed him on his cheek saying, "thank you sweetie for not interrupting us. You're probably wondering what else I've brought you today?"

"I need to show you something," he said so flatly and so seriously that I didn't dare to protest.

We entered his kingdom, a big yellow room with matching dinosaur bedding and curtains. It smelt of chocolate, strawberries and candies. I looked again at his bedding standing petrified – it was all covered with sweets and even without touching I could tell it would be all sticky. *Veronica is going to kill me! She paid her interior designer to find that bedding in Rome!*

"Don't worry, we'll change and wash the bedding before your parents are back."

"What? Why? That's not what I meant," he said with a grumpy voice so similar to his father and his grandfather it struck me. "Maya am Dudu," he said with tears in his eyes and one chocolaty finger drilling a nostril.

"What are you talking about darling," I asked softly and instantly felt guilty for giving him the cartoon for seven year olds. "Have you watched something scary?" I asked and he nodded.

"Maya am Dudu," he shouted but this time pointing at something in the room with that chocolatey finger now with a booger at the end. He was getting to the point of having a meltdown and I had no idea what he meant.

I looked at the place where he was indicating – in the left corner of his room there was a small child-height table and on top of it was a rounded metal cage with a tiny door swinging open. Next to it, on a red plastic chair sat the family's fat ginger cat called Maya. She was looking even fatter than usual murmuring with contentment and licking her mouth. *No, no, no...* I was thinking in panic while staring at a tiny little feather sticking out of her mouth.

"Where is Dudu?" I asked suddenly realising that Sebastian had already explained it to me numerous times. In Polish baby language *am* meant *eat! Due to my total and unjustified negligence something had died!*

"I've said, Maya am Dudu!"

"Sebastian, what is the cage even doing in your room?" I was talking loudly but calmly, pushing my anger away each time it wanted to materialise and yell at my disobedient (but also neglected) nephew.

"Is that really so important right now?" he stopped crying and put his hands on his hips. His confidence nearly threw me off balance. "Dudu is dead! Dudu is dead!"

"Calm down darling. Please calm down," I was trying to hold him but he wouldn't let me. "Maybe there's something we can still do," I said without much thought.

"I know!" he said and looked around the room as if he'd just experienced some kind of miraculous enlightenment.

"What are you thinking?" I asked intrigued by the four-and-a-half-year-old.

Dudu, rest in peace, was a baby canary belonging to Veronica's best friend Amanda, who often brought the bird to Eliot's house when she was away. Dudu was always kept in his cage and normally put on one of the kitchen shelves, where he was safe from Sebastian's little hands and he could entertain the whole family with his beautiful singing voice. I had no idea how Sebastian managed to smuggle him to his room. Have we all missed how his arms could now reach much further, or has he finally worked out how to climb on a chair and stand on the kitchen surface?

I let down the poor little bird who has died tragically while looking at the fat cat's palate. I let down Sebastian who now will be traumatised after witnessing the brutal murder. It's all my fault, I was thinking with tears rolling down my cheeks. *Oh god, it's true, I had become more emotional.*

"Auntie Olivia, we don't have any time to lose. Bring me a pair of scissors, dad's shaver and a sharp knife – but the real ones, not the plastic Chinese tat for kids.

"I'm going!" I turned back towards the door and ran down the stairs.

I got to the bottom before I started thinking properly and returned to being a nearly-thirty-year-old grown up woman. I ran back upstairs twice as fast.

"Why do we need any of these things?"

"Auntie Olivia, I said we don't have much time, Dudu won't last that long!"

"Are you suggesting that we should—"

"Get him out of Maya's stomach before she starts the process of digestion! If we're quick enough we should be able to sew Dudu back together. He'll be safe and sound and I'll become a hero," he raised his right hand as if he'd been holding a sword, his mouth shining with a full set of milky teeth and ears getting red from excitement.

"Sebastian Eliot, have you deliberately let Maya eat Dudu so you could undertake the surgery?"

"The magazines you gave me were nice but it wasn't real. It's all for kids. I wanted to tell you that but you asked me not to interrupt you."

Before Philip and Veronica were back from their romantic anniversary dinner I managed to grip the chaos I'd caused. First, I called my mother, who was an expert at employing various replacement pets to mystifying success after their predecessors died, more or less tragically and more or less accidentally (Claus my Fish, rest in peace). She found a friend of hers who had a canary and brought him to us within an hour. She let us borrow him provided we would return the bird in a few days, warning us subtly her Daisy was chipped.

"Mum I have to ask, Jack the hamster didn't really live twelve years, did he? How many Jacks did I have?"

"A few darling. We couldn't tell you, it would break you. You were so upset when you dropped him from the balcony or when you tried to bath him and—"

"This family's children shouldn't have any pets, it's just wrong!"

There was only one problem left – Sebastian believed his grandmother when she said she put the cat upside down, shook him and the canary fell down onto the bed.

"So maybe we should shake Maya again in case there are some other little animals still living in her stomach?" asked Sebastian with sparkles in his eyes. "I'll try tomorrow," he said before turning on his left side and falling asleep content.

One crisis "Maya and Dudu" had ended but in its place came another one – *how am I going to take care of my child? I can't even look after my nephew for one evening. What sort of mother am I going to be?*

"What good have I done?" I said to Hannah on the phone that night. "I brought Sebastian cartoons and toys that were from the age of seven – his parents would never allow that. I fed him with a bag of sweets – again, his parents would never allow that. He was probably acting hyper all the time because he was so high on sugar! That's why he had such crazy ideas! Then I blackmailed him saying that if he left me alone, I would reward him later. Well, it worked out, I should be proud of myself! Completely undisturbed by any child I found out that my boyfriend told me the truth and I was just paranoid. But feeling guilty for wasting Gatsby's time I decided to go further with my paranoia and throw more money on the Henry-project. Meanwhile the poor animal was being murdered on my watch…"

"Olivia, don't be so dramatic. I understand what you're going through but—"

"I'm dramatic? Tomorrow Maya is going to poop Dudu and it's all my fault!"

"No," she said unmoved by my misery. "Your nephew shouldn't be anywhere near animals."

"But I let him," I cried.

"They shouldn't leave any animals in the house. From what you're saying Sebastian is dangerous."

"Hannah, he's four-and-a-half years old, he's not a freaking Dexter!"

"Okay, calm down and tell me what's the matter because it's not about Dudu and Sebastian."

"I can't even spend a few hours with a four-and-a-half-year-old and—"

"Nope, I'm not buying it. It's something more. People with a degree in pedagogy can't control the child. You'll be a wonderful mother."

"I can't even choose a father for my children."

"Well, you did but you just don't know who he is... Anyway, it's just one child, you don't have to have more of them with Hugo, Henry or whoever it is."

"Whoever it is? Thanks really! Oh, I've forgotten to tell you. I'm expecting twins."

"Damn it!" she exclaimed and paused. "I mean damn it, it's so damn amazing! Congratulations, double joy!"

"I also saw Gatsby today," I said gloomily.

"Henry's got a lover? Olivia, I'm so sorry..."

"No, he probably doesn't and he was telling me the truth about Blanca."

"So, if that's good news why doesn't it sound good?"

"I need to break up with Hugo. I've been delusional by thinking that a holiday fling could have ever turned into a serious till-death-do-us-part relationship. He'll never drop all his plans to be with me and two children, who most likely aren't his.

"What if the twins are his?"

"Statistically I've still got a better chance for a happy future – or just a future – with the devil I know."

Meeting Hugo was like an unforgettable journey into a wild and unexplored land. Being with him was like staying in a wonderland, which I'd not even known existed. Although, I was still not sure whether it actually existed or my imagination was messing with me and the magic would soon be gone. I wondered if I stayed there longer, whether the place would keep impressing and enchanting me, or eventually I would become disappointed, discovering it wasn't so different or special after all. I needed time to find out but nobody and nothing was prepared to give me that time so I had to make a decision and I did – I chose Henry – something nice enough, well known and safe. I knew sometimes it would rain and get cold, or I would just get bored, but it was something I could be prepared for. It wouldn't be cloudless skies and over thirty degrees but equally I wouldn't have to worry about a sudden hurricane that would destroy everything and turn my whole life upside down.

21

SATURDAY, 29 AUGUST

THE BIRTHDAY PARTY

"I don't like surprises" I kept saying this to my parents and Henry for so long that they finally gave up and let me take full control over my birthday planning. I rented a small house for a week on one of the Canary Islands. I loved the Canary's eternal spring, you could always plan for good weather without being disappointed. I dreamed about an outdoor party that would last all weekend long. I kept imagining how during the day we would be lying on sunbeds under large parasols and enjoying colourful drinks with umbrellas, some stolen by the wind. At night we would be sitting around a bonfire watching stars and sipping Sangria. I chose Lanzarote because I found there a perfect villa that was nearly in my budget. It had only two bedrooms but most guests were coming on Friday evening and going home by Sunday. The rest of the week was booked for Henry and me to recover after the party and *recharge our batteries* – Henry hated the phrase as much as lying in the sun but he relented for my big birthday. I thought that the plan minimised any risk of nostalgia from both getting older and saying goodbye to my youth.

The villa was situated on a hill with nothing within a couple of miles but mountains painted by nature in different shades of greys, browns and reds. There were also some juicy green cacti vividly contrasting against the sunburnt rocks they were growing from. The landscape reminded me of Mars from NASA pictures. The villa had a good size garden with plenty of exotic plants, a view of a crystal clear sea with tiny yachts pushed by the wind, and Lobos Island in the distance.

* * *

The sudden realisation that my birthday wasn't only a great opportunity to party but it meant another year of my life had passed hit me when I was twenty-five; a short while before I met Henry. It was the moment I decided to remove my date of birth from Facebook – to huge disappointment of those who couldn't tell anymore whether I looked good or bad for my age or whether I'd achieved so much or so little in terms of life and career. Back then I decided to set some goals I wanted to fulfil before I reached thirty. At that time I felt young, full of energy and invincible, and I was still enjoying making plans – blissfully unaware that it would bring on me far more misery than joy. During a girl night with Freya and Atlanta – when we were having some deep conversations about the meaning of life with our noses dipped deep into glasses of red wine – Freya suggested us defining and framing our goals in the shape of a so-called *dream map*. She read in a woman's magazine that such visualisation would help us to achieve the seemingly impossible.

"Let's try," I shouted while diving into all my furniture to get some crayons and watercolours from primary school, highlighters that I'd last used at university, and a pile of magazines that had accumulated in my bedside cabinet – never entirely read but never entirely ready to be finally binned. Our work reminded us how much we never stopped liking to draw, paint and create collages. We also promised ourselves to attend one of the events called drawing with – here put any alcohol you like – vodka, sangria, wine, cocktails etc. But we'd never found the time or enough drive to do it – maybe we had to drink first to generate motivation to build our art. It was hard work indeed, I cut the magazines with such passion that I got blisters on my fingers. Final result? Five years ago – there were our smug faces, one hundred percent certain that our dreams would come true and three pieces of art that definitely would sell for a ton of money if we just happened to have the right names! Reality five years later? From my perspective there was a defeated face, I was a hundred percent sure that the visualisation didn't work and it might as well be a worthless pile of ash. A few days before my upcoming birthday I called Freya and Atlanta for the ceremonial burning of my dream map in a bonfire while sipping ginger tea with lemon and eating dry crackers – butter made me vomit, which at least was good for my waist.

"I have to admit that your map definitely looks the best," said Freya staring at the large piece of paper covered in a my-first-day-at-nursery collage, which I had put on the grass and was illuminating with Meg's torch.

"It looks the best because, contrary to you two, I started working on it before my second bottle of wine."

"Maybe but I see something in it," Freya continued with a very serious face expression. "I see something deep there. I wouldn't burn it just yet... And I don't agree that the visualisation failed."

"Let it go Freya. It's time for the art to be consumed by fire," I said equally seriously not quite realising how stupid it sounded. "It's probably more art-like when it's burning."

"Hold on a minute. You wrote here that you would like to have two children, including one before your thirtieth. Well, you'll have two only half a year after your birthday," Freya giggled. "And here two cute babies, one girl and one boy," she was waving her finger above my dream map. I would swear she had added something to her ginger tea or drunk something a little stronger.

"I wish I knew who their father was," I said matter-of-factly without feeling sad or angry.

"Oh, never mind," yelled Atlanta who definitely had at least one glass of wine before our lovely evening commenced. "It says here," she pointed at the map with her nose preferring to keep her hands crossed, "First exotic holiday with my prince charming," she said trying not to burst into laughter, making me wonder whether we were five or twenty-five when we created the damn maps. "So at least that dream came true!"

"I think that it was my first and last holiday with a prince."

"Never mind," said Atlanta again. "You wanted to have your own house by thirty and a career at a travel magazine. Done! Two big fat ticks."

"True but I've got a mortgage with a man I don't trust and I'm not quite sure I want to spend the rest of my life with. The only reason I can keep my job is because I got unexpectedly pregnant. Besides, I don't travel anywhere anymore unless I pay for it myself."

"Never mind," said Freya.

"Never mind," repeated Atlanta. "Everything came true. You just weren't specific enough about your dreams. Maybe you should make another map saying – I would like to have little plump children and know who their father is. I would like to have my own house without any tenants in it. I would like to—"

"Exactly! You need to make another more precise map! I would also add, just in case – to own my own house, which is not occupied by squatters and has no travellers camping in my back yard… and it didn't previously belong to a drug dealer who had put dead bodies under the floorboards or—"

"Maybe, but first let me burn this one, a collage we could re-name *never mind*."

I threw the map onto the fire, watching silently how my dreams disappeared in the flames. I felt burnt out, I'd lost every sparkle of hope for a life that my twenty-five-year-old self had imagined. I had to try hard to push my tears back. I wasn't even that disappointed and frustrated that I hadn't achieved everything I wanted by my thirties. I didn't feel like crying because my life wasn't going according to the script that I'd written five years earlier. I was crying through fear that I might not have enough time or another chance to write a new script and follow a different path, instead I would likely just be carried through life reacting to hasty choices.

"Even if I somehow manage to take a degree of control over the total chaos I brought on myself, I'll be dealing with the consequences of my most recent choices for the rest of my life."

"Olivia, I know you're pregnant and not exactly in the right place at the moment but you're being overdramatic," Freya said but I didn't respond. I only imagined how dramatic she would become if she were in my place – she was the girl who panicked each time she was late two days despite being happily married, having one happy child and living in a house without a mortgage.

"Even my dream birthday party couldn't happen," I changed the topic for something less deep and dramatic. I was upset about it but not as much as everybody thought.

A month before my doctor had advised me against the four-hour flight – it wasn't only because I was expecting twins but I also had raised blood pressure. The pressure returned to normal but I preferred not to take any unnecessary risks and so with a heavy heart I cancelled the villa.

I felt like crying, and it wasn't just because I couldn't go to Lanzarote. More than missing the Canary Islands I missed *myself* – the ME I used to be five years ago when I still thought that everything was possible with a good action plan, some effort and faith. Five years ago I was absolutely sure that all my dreams and goals would eventually come true – woe betide anyone who would have dared try to stop me! The feeling that the world was my oyster gave me a kick of energy every time I needed it. I had an appetite for life – that was what I missed the most about myself. I missed the wind in my sails that seemed to come from nowhere and push me effortlessly towards a better future. Now I felt that no matter which way I positioned myself I wasn't able to move my boat on my own, I was chaotically drifting at sea, my destinations subject to a whim. I missed the blissful peace of mind from believing that I still had time for everything – the time that enables me to fix anything that needs fixing or start all over again. I would love to return to that moment when silence was collecting thoughts and dreaming about the wonderful tomorrow – not dwelling on the potential difficulties of the future.

* * *

On the day of my birthday I woke up with some unidentified ache – alongside symptoms including feeling a little depressed, overwhelmed and too heavy to get out of bed – Google said it was most likely something many romantic poets used to suffer from – the Pain of Existence! *Gotcha!* I thought feeling sorry for myself.

"Olivia, get up darling," Henry was shouting from downstairs. I'd agreed he could move in for my birthday weekend but I'd already started to regret it.

I was lying in my king-size bed looking at the ceiling when Henry, obviously very impatient, walked briskly into the room to drag me out of my kingdom. "I'll put the blinds up," he said rushing towards one of the two large windows in the bedroom. It reminded me why we loved the house so much – its high ceilings and long windows provided a lot of light even when outside was miserable. "Although there's no rush to put the blinds up," he forced himself to smile. "You can't pretend you don't know anything about the party..." he stood in front of the bed, his arms crossed, legs spread wide on my mustard rug, "you didn't want a surprise so you can't pretend now—"

"Why have you suddenly decided to leave the blinds down?" I asked although I knew exactly what the reason was. "Is it raining again?" I said with a pillow on my head. I just wanted everybody to leave me alone.

"It's not raining, there're only small drops dripping from the clouds," he was saying with fear in his voice.

"I'm not three but thirty," I snapped irritated.

"I've checked the weather," he said now confidently. Of course, he did, he always started his day from checking the weather. "The clouds will be gone by early afternoon. Besides it's eighteen degrees. At least nobody will get sweaty. Nobody will complain that they'll get sun stroke, sunburn or sun-anything. We won't have to put anything into the fridge except beer and ice cream. I see only positives!"

"Good for you!" *And what an interesting twist in your character!*

"I know you're still angry the Lanzarote party didn't work out.

We'll go there next year, I promise you. And I know you're going through a... a sort of age crisis. I really get it. I had exactly the same—"

"I'm sure you had," I said bitterly. *I'm sure, as you were pregnant with twins not knowing who their father was. You also broke up with the man who seemed to have all the qualities of the Mr Right of your dreams except he didn't pester you after you said you wanted to finish the relationship. Not at all – nada! On the contrary he took it very well, no pain of existence or any emotional regret at all.* "I just haven't slept well, that's all. I talked until late with Freya and Atlanta."

When I called off the villa and lost my deposit I also lost any desire I ever had to organise anything. I would be the happiest by celebrating the day like every other day of the year but I knew it wasn't going to happen – if I didn't come up with an idea, the others would do and the chances were high I wouldn't like it, so I invited friends and family for a barbeque! I'd never understood the phenomenon of BBQ – personally I preferred to fry my burger on a Panini press grill and take it to the garden – less fat and less faff. There was no mess, and my hair and clothes didn't smell like burned cow. However, the barbeque created a great opportunity to kill two birds with one stone, or rather fry two birds on one grill. People kept asking me about a housewarming party and I finally had the answer – my birthday and housewarming party in one – two in one like shampoo and conditioner – less effective but very practical. The undeniable advantage was that I didn't have to try to squeeze my arse into a too tight dress and dance with a glass of water around people who were completely wasted. The friends and family got very emotional about my idea, far more than I'd expected. "But you don't like barbeques!" shouted my surprised mother. "Since when are you a fan of outdoor grilling?" asked Freya with disbelief. "You practically despise barbeque!" said Atlanta. I didn't change my mind but I let them prepare my barbeque birthday and housewarming party. One small problem – I didn't have a barbeque! But it wasn't a problem as Henry offered to buy me one for my birthday – of course he did, he loved barbeque and he could also kill two birds with one stone – how practical!

* * *

When I walked into my garden just after having a small brunch prepared by Henry – which had never happened before – I felt like Olivia in Wonderland. My parents had asked me to move in with them for a week, which I guessed was an excuse to do some work on my house but the results went far beyond my highest expectations. I kept looking around, nervously anticipating somebody would suddenly jump out of a hedge with a microphone and introduce himself as the presenter of the show *Garden Makeover* – I could almost see the short chubby guy with sheep-curly hair and his smug face shouting in my ear "surprise!" I immediately regretted not wearing a better dress, ideally less tight, and significantly more make-up. Luckily nothing like this happened.

When I moved in, the garden only had a narrow stone patio, a large piece of well-mown grass and a small wooden shed that had waited too long for somebody to finally move in and paint it at least with some varnish. Now on a significantly widened patio there was a large rattan garden set in dark cream, it included a large L-shaped sofa for eight people, two armchairs and an oval table. The patio was now so big that it could also easily take a new massive parasol covering the whole outdoor lounge area, a freestanding patio heater and two lavender plants in marble pots. On both sides of the garden were red maple trees and at the end a couple of blue spruces that would be perfect for Christmas. The shed was still standing in the far-left corner but somebody had painted it thyme green – I knew the exact colour because I'd chosen it myself and included it in my dream garden plan months before I bought the house. I'd spent many evenings going through garden design magazines and websites making notes and cutting out or printing the best pictures. I'd been trying to relax and remind myself that buying a house wasn't just a nightmare of dealing with developers and mortgage companies – there was a lot to look forward to.

I couldn't believe my eyes – it was perfect and exactly the way I'd imagined. At the back of the garden and in the middle of the lawn there was a yellow stone fountain with four lion's heads pouring water into a round pool. Just next to it stood a smart metal bench with a gold plate, and on it was written in black letters: „*Twenty years from now you will be more disappointed by the things you didn't do than by the ones you did. So throw off the bowlines. Sail away from the safe harbour. Catch the trade winds in your sails. Explore. Dream. Discover.*"

"My favourite quote! Mark Twain!" I said with tears in my eyes that had nothing to do with the pain of existence. *Does it make me a materialistic girl?*

"Actually, I've recently discovered that it was said by the mother of another writer – H. Jackson Brown Junior," said Atlanta, who like another thirty-something people was now standing in the garden looking for my reaction.

"You know I don't like surprises," I said seriously and looked around in silence.

"If you don't like it," said Sebastian. "I can take the bench and the lion fountain! But dad said he wouldn't bloody move it ever, ever, ever again if you don't like it so you'll have to pay for some removal guys. I've got some pocket money..." he didn't finish because Veronica put her hand on his mouth, which I thought wasn't particularly didactic or kind, but I wouldn't dare to ever say anything – after all he killed something during my last supervision session.

"I don't like surprises except the great ones. You've made me an amazing surprise and I just want to hug each and every one of you right now."

"Don't hug me, I don't want to have twins!" Sebastian screamed and before Veronica pressed her hand against his mouth again he was already jumping in front of me.

"What are you talking about?" I asked more intrigued than offended.

"Mum said last night that two of her friends and you were pregnant with twins so maybe it's bloody contagious and... And she hoped she would stay non-pregnant for at least a decade!" everybody laughed except poor Veronica.

"If you don't like something, don't hesitate to change it even though we all spent a fortune on it and worked so hard," Philip said, probably to make everybody forget about his son's comment. It did work, everybody was laughing now with Philip.

"It's wonderful, how did you know?" I was so moved that I couldn't say anything more.

"We know how much you like spending time outside," Freya said.

"We wanted to get a smaller table but Henry insisted that it needed to take at least eight people so you can invite a few couples at the same time," mum said smiling to Henry.

"It's perfect," I said to Henry and he blushed – I hadn't seen him like that for a while.

I was already in seventh heaven but the best was yet to come. In the evening the patio was lit up by large glass lampions, and the rest of the garden by small gold lights hanging along the fence and on the blue spruces. It was magical. The food surpassed the requirements of even the most pampered and picky guests. Burgers decorated with herbs, salads alongside specially cut and shaped vegetables, more art than food. Shashliks, chicken drumsticks and grilled vegetables were presented like meals in a fine dining restaurant – served on white and silver china and hidden carefully in colourful salads. In silver ice buckets there was both alcohol and alcohol-free wine and champagne, all clearly labelled. For the whole evening we had two waiters walking around with silver trays, wearing black waistcoats over white shirts with red bowties. They were Henry's students who wanted to make some extra money – very handsome and in their early twenties they made me feel a bit old, but thanks to an avalanche of surprises I didn't have time to reflect on my age and I quickly got over it.

My birthday cake was served when only the stars were illuminating the cloudless summer sky – apparently everybody had agreed that it would create the most effective cake-entrance. If somebody had described my birthday cake to me, I would have thought 'cheesy' but actually the four-layered cake with the first two bottom tiers representing suitcases, the third one being a globe and the top in the shape of an aircraft was a confectioner's masterpiece. I loved the chocolate pins that were marking all the places I'd been on the globe –

the fattest one was stuck to Grenada – which made me feel like I was choking on the chocolate, or like somebody was pushing the whole cake down my throat screaming 'eat what you made'. I'd never told Henry I went to Grenada with Hugo or any man actually. He still thought I went there alone to have time to think about our relationship and reflect on my life.

"Wow," I screamed putting both hands to my cheeks but I quickly stopped in fear that I would rub off my make-up.

"It's so much bigger than mine," Sebastian said and glanced disappointed at his parents.

"Because your auntie is bigger than you," Philip rushed with a silly explanation.

"Well, it's not the right time to lose weight, now your auntie can only become bigger and bigger," I said with a forced smile, one of many recently.

"Not what I meant," Philip said quickly. "When we said in the cake shop how many candles we wanted to put on, they advised us to choose at least four layers so you don't feel overwhelmed by your age."

"Oh, shut up Philip," Veronica said and elbowed him so hard he jumped.

"Time to think of your wish," Freya squeaked and clapped her excited hands.

And then just like that I looked around and felt happy, loved and appreciative of everything that I had. I suddenly felt no need to wish for more. I realised I was surrounded by friends and family, who I could always count on. The family was soon about to expand by two more people to love. On that day I had next to me my grandparents from Poland, it had taken them less time to fly from Krakow and then drive from Heathrow than my other grandparents who drove to my birthday all the way from the Lake District. My group of friends had also recently expanded to include Hannah and Meghan. Freya and Atlanta knew exactly which friends from work I would have wanted to invite. Henry didn't insist on Tiggy, who he seemed to like for whatever reason and who he often tried to defend by justifying her most ridiculous behaviour. The only invited guest who couldn't make it was Hannah's husband – his excuse was work but she said he'd never been anywhere for her. I was afraid to make any unspecific-enough wishes. *Look what happened with the two children and the house – what a mess!* I thought and smiled gently still not knowing what to wish for. I was terrified that I could make a wish that would actually turn out to be bad for me, or bring more chaos. Don't they say be careful what you wish for?

I leaned above the cake still thinking.

"Come on sis! I bet – as every woman – you've got thousands of wishes and you just don't know which one you want to pick."

Why have I ever wondered why Sebastian is so difficult? Contrary to what my mother wants to believe – it's definitely not because of Veronica, her daughter-in-law! Like father like son!

I thought a wish – a simple, materialistic and safe one. It came true only a half an hour later.

"Is it mine?" I exclaimed.

All guests held their breath, and grandpa Edward asked for a glass of water with some ice.

"Of course, it's yours," said Henry and then whispered in my ear, "brand new, fully paid off and all toys included."

"You bought me a car, this car?" I still couldn't believe it. He'd never bought me anything for my birthday that cost more than twenty pounds and now he'd bought me a car?

"I know you sold yours to go to Grenada. You wanted to get away to have some space, think about us and it was all my fault."

"Oh Henry."

"And I'm glad you went there. It was what you needed the most."

"Oh yes," tipsy Atlanta giggled in my ear. "Oh yes," she repeated as if she'd been caught in some love ecstasy. "You needed to make passionate love to the hot Spanish guy on that Caribbean island. Nobody can take it from you."

"For god's sake, stop!" I snapped.

"Oh, come on, nobody has heard me." Nobody except my grandmother Betty, who in typical fashion, frowned her eyebrows when she was eavesdropping and glanced at me with curiosity.

"Now you'll need the car even more and have a look what you've got inside," Henry enthusiastically opened the back door to show me two funky baby car seats that reminded me of race seats, "I chose red and green because we still don't know whether we're going to have boys or girls or one of each."

"Oh, it's so sweet," I heard a female voice.

Happiness and guilt were mixing in my stomach giving me some butterflies alongside slightly painful cramps.

"What a car!" shouted grandpa Edward putting his head inside my new red Jaguar F-Pace, and other men followed suit.

"I just love the colour," said grandma Betty.

"Is there something that the car doesn't have?" asked my father rhetorically.

"They gave me a good discount for taking the full package," Henry said and winked at me.

I looked at my Jaguar and I imagined myself driving it on a sunny day with two cute babies in the back. In the very vivid daydream I was tanned, after a business trip to Hawaii, I had an amazing new haircut and I was even slimmer than before I got pregnant. I was driving my babies to a nursery set up in a company that I launched all by myself. Then I saw myself walking out of a gold lift, stomping on a marble floor with my red soled designer stilettoes and heading straight to my office with a plaque on the door 'CEO Olivia Eliot'. Tiggy, who I employed out of pure mercy after the bankruptcy of I-Heart-Travelling, was bringing me some coffee and I was telling her off for not pouring enough milk, before she cleaned my floor-to-ceiling windows with a view of the Thames.

* * *

"Pretty good birthday for somebody who doesn't like surprises," I said to Freya while we were sitting on the new rattan chairs admiring a sky full of bright stars and the twinkling lights on the fence. Grandpa Edward was playing on a guitar and singing *What a Wonderful World* at the back of the garden, next to the fountain, I felt so blissfully happy and relaxed.

"Olivia, will you be my wife?" Of all guests only grandpa Edward didn't hear the question and kept singing louder and louder – so loud that I was expecting some letters of complaint from my neighbours the next day. Henry went down on his knees holding in front of me a small blue velvet box engraved with Tiffany&Co. I had seen the box before. It didn't happen in the middle of the spring but at the end of the summer. Not in Madrid, but at the back of my garden. I wasn't sitting in a boat swinging on Retiro's lake, but on an English rattan chair. We weren't alone but surrounded by my friends and family. We weren't drinking wine but water. The proposal was nothing like I'd imagined and everything I could have wished for. It was a hundred-fold better because it completely took me by surprise. "Olivia will you be my wife?" he repeated.

"I can't hear anything," shouted grandma Sofie in a strong Polish accent and she tossed a cushion at grandpa Edward, who had been singing the same song over and over again like a broken record-player. He then suddenly stopped to have a glass of wine and Philip put on *Just Say Yes* by Snow Patrol on his phone.

"Yes," I said baffled, and everybody started clapping and hugging one another like after a match well won.

Henry opened the blue box and put the ring on my finger. Not a simple platinum one but a gold one with tiny flowers engraved around a single stone. Not a big shiny diamond but a massive red stone. Not a classy one that I'd seen in his library but a cheesy one that I would have never chosen. It was nothing like I'd imagined and nothing I would have ever wished for.

"I hope you like it. It belonged to my mother," said my future mother-in-law.

22

SUNDAY, 30 AUGUST
DREAM FIELDS

"I would like you to see us the way I do. I still believe I can become a part of your *Reality*," I read the note attached to a painting that I unpacked the next morning. *Why now Hugo? You couldn't choose a better time,* I was thinking while staring at a beautifully framed reproduction of *People's Flowers* by Richard Estes. Full of anger and sorrow I ripped off the red paper on another present from Hugo. It was a tin of hot chocolate from Churreria los Artesanos with a note saying, 'delicious but it doesn't taste so good without you'. He also sent me an album full of our photos from all the trips we made together. On its first page there was a picture of me standing on a wooden bridge in Retiro, and one with me and Hugo with the Temple of Debod in the background – the one where I was concerned that the older man taking our photo would steal Hugo's camera. I closed the album with a bang without looking at another photo and threw all the presents into the big grey box they were delivered in. I left the bathroom, where in a dirty laundry basket Meg had hidden the parcel. "It's from Madrid," she said lowering her voice last night, a couple of hours before my surprise engagement. "I thought you'd like to open it in private." I smiled gratefully not knowing what to say, she was so thoughtful.

I just wanted to run away and hide from everybody for a while but the option was not even on the menu – especially as there were now three of us and we were getting bigger and bigger – so I did what I did every morning and headed downstairs to make myself a coffee. The only difference today was my husband-to-be waiting for me. *Damn you all!* I pushed open the kitchen door overly aggressively into Henry holding two flowery mugs full of freshly made coffee, and he staggered back spilling some of the contents. The set of twelve kitschy mugs was a housewarming present from a woman who worked at the same university department as Henry – she loved everything flowery, always had a smug face and a daisy in her long blond hair.

"It's hot," he yelled. "Are you okay honey?"

"Yeah, absolutely fine," I said quickly pulling off my smart white dressing gown and throwing it on a chair. "I'll just have to use some bleach."

"Sit down honey. I'll put your robe in the washing machine and make you another coffee."

"You can chill Henry. My birthday is over."

"I've forgotten, you're not an early bird," he said trying to hug me but I pushed him gently away and moved towards the cupboard where I stored coffee capsules. To my despair he wasn't giving up, "I've read recently that American scientists had discovered that getting up early can cause a kind of shock – it's the transition between night and day, returning to reality..."

I still believe I can become a part of your Reality – the words were rumbling in my head like drums, getting louder and louder just like grandpa Edward singing the night before.

"Waking up in the morning can cause some people a shock similar to the one that a baby experiences when they're born..." he continued standing so close to me and the coffee machine that I felt he was glued to my right arm, I couldn't get rid of him.

"Really, American scientists can always explain everything," I said drinking my first sip of coffee and sitting down on a high chair.

"Oh, you only made coffee for yourself," he suddenly noticed.

"Sorry," I said not sorry at all. "I thought I only spilt one of them."

"Why are you so..." he paused waiting for me to choose the most appropriate adjective to describe my mood but I only opened my eyes wider in anticipation, "so moody like when you're on your period."

"Better! I'm pregnant Henry and I can't have a period," I snapped. "Why did you propose to me yesterday?"

"What are you talking about? I thought it was exactly what you wanted me to do."

"I did but before our... my trip to Madrid. Before you decided to abandon me at check-in."

"I've already told you why. I'm still really sorry but what's done is done. I can't turn the time back so what's the point reflecting on it? And you said yes!"

"And what could I say when you literally pressed me to the wall by proposing in front of all my friends and family, on my birthday that you so carefully planned and arranged."

"You could've said that you'd think about it? Nobody put a pistol to your head and made you say yes," he shouted it out and then he must have quickly realised what he said because he looked at me petrified.

"That wasn't the best metaphor," I said calmly and took another sip of my coffee, which didn't taste good that morning.

"I'm sorry, I didn't mean to..." he sat down on the second bar chair next to me, lowered his voice and looked deeply into my eyes, "I know you find the whole situation hard and you still don't trust me, but I promise everything will be all right from now on," he wanted to hold my hand but I gently moved it back.

"You know you can't promise me that. I don't understand why people promise something that they can't control. It's ridiculous!"

"I promise," he repeated and again tried to reach for my hand but without success, "I promise that I'll do—"

"You're lying and I can't pretend anymore Henry. I wasn't going to tell you now because I still haven't processed it but..." I covered my face with my hands, "I just can't..."

Henry looked questioningly at me but he wasn't surprised. He slowly got up from his chair and walked around the kitchen like he used to walk sometimes on stage during his lectures with his hands together and resting on his slightly bent lower back. He rolled and pressed his lips together.

"I opened a parcel today..."

"I'm sorry," he suddenly livened up. "I was about to give it to you but I'd just forgotten. I didn't hide it or anything..."

"God, so you did hide it!"

"What are you talking about? I've just said I didn't!"

"Last night Sebastian brought me your leather bag. He was embarrassed because he hid it after he got angry with you. How could you tell him that he couldn't be a vet because he killed animals and that he was more cut out to be a poacher or..." I stopped because I was running out of breath being so angry, "or do animal testing. He's just a little boy!"

"He massively exaggerated, you know him," Henry said, his lips still pursed together, face reddening. "You know how manipulative and naughty he can be. I've been looking everywhere for that bag."

"Well, you could've asked me if I happened to see it but you obviously didn't because of what you were hiding there. When were you going to tell me the truth?" I was standing in front of him with my hands on my hips.

"I don't understand," he said sitting back on the same chair but this time no position was comfortable enough and he was jiggling and wriggling like a small child during a boring lesson.

"When were you going to tell me about your businesses? It was how you got the money for my car, wasn't it?" He sat still and set his eyes on the floor. He most certainly didn't expect I would have found out. He didn't have any excuse, which was so not like him – the man who always had an answer for everything. "In my wildest dreams I wouldn't have suspected you of being so two-faced... I don't know who you are anymore. Why would you sell exams questions and essays and at the same time chase and punish those who buy them?"

"Olivia, I've recently sold a few exams, that's it. I'll explain it to—"

"Explain me something by coming up with more lies?"

* * *

I got up in a great mood, it was after ten and Meg had already got on the road to Wales to see her parents. I was lying in bed listening to Henry making noises in the kitchen and imagining how our mornings would be when Meg moved out. I got up tempted by the subtle smell of coffee coming from downstairs. I felt a bit of breeze from an open window so I immediately reached for a dressing gown lying on our fluffy bedroom carpet. Only when I was tying up the robe did I glance at the floor and remind myself that the night before I'd covered it with the contents of Henry's bag. It was his work handbag in which he always carried some students' work to correct. According to the students' questionnaires he was the most organised lecturer at the university, never late checking essays and exams. He reached for the bag to do some work whenever he had a spare moment.

"Auntie Olivia, can you give this to Henry tomorrow? He's been looking for it," Sebastian said with a guilty face. Of course I didn't believe that he found it as he initially suggested. "I hid it because I was angry with Henry. He made me upset..." I understood them both – Sebastian because Henry hurt his feelings; and my fiancé because my little nephew required a great deal more patience than an average child. I was sure that Henry wouldn't say anything nasty too him without reason.

I had recently got into a bad habit of searching through Henry's belongings and I wouldn't stop myself on this special opportunity. *Gatsby promised to provide me some relevant information before my birthday. I see I can rely on him like most of the men in my life,* I was thinking this while undoing the buckles on Henry's leather bag. In the main compartment there was his mobile, a diary, a well-used notebook, a dull grey paper file full of essays and a pile of pens. I was reaching for the diary when suddenly my eyes moved towards a smaller compartment with some loose papers and letters squeezed tightly with probably quite a lot of effort. To get there I had to first have a proper fight with the zip that didn't want to cooperate with me. *Oh, let me look inside, you stupid and malicious zip!* It eventually did but I cut my forefinger and a few drops of blood landed on a big white envelope, small win for Mr Zip. *How will I explain it to Henry now? I was looking for the nail file in your bag. Sebastian! I'll have to say that it was Sebastian's blood! He put one of his operated animals in there! Eureka! Oh, I'm such a bad example for kids, such a terrible aunt! What sort of mother am I going to be?* My thinking was suddenly interrupted by what was written on one envelope – the realisation that I wouldn't have to explain myself to Henry, but rather he would have to explain himself to me was not, however, a pleasant relief.

It's my letter from Gatsby! I opened it leaving more of my blood on the envelope, then I put my finger to my mouth and started sucking it. I was left with an unpleasant taste in my mouth and I wasn't sure whether it was a consequence of the blood or what I was reading. Gatsby had discovered that Henry belonged to one of the Cheater Gangs. He was able to prove my fiancé had been working as an exam and essay dealer for the last five weeks but he was convinced he had started a long while before, and he was determined to further back it up with strong evidence. Henry didn't lie about Spy Education catching Blanca on cheating, and he was the person who managed her case. The problem was that he had sold her several sets of exam questions and at least seven essays. I sat on the carpet and read the last two paragraphs in Gatsby's report, which for some reason he didn't want to send to me by email:

1. Good news is – Henry is not a cheater. I mean he is but not in the meaning of the word you had suspected him to be!

He's got a really peculiar sense of humour! I thought before moving to the next point:

2. Whatever you're going to do, don't go to the police with this information! At least not yet! I appreciate that you might feel like taking revenge on him (I would if I was you!) but leave it for now! The Cheater Gangs are serious criminal organizations with plenty of money and influence.

I was sitting on the carpet moving backward and forward like in a trance when my phone beeped and I read a message from Meg reminding me of my parcel she had hidden in the laundry basket.

* * *

"How *recently* are you talking about? Few months? A year? It actually doesn't matter at all. You're a liar and a criminal."

"I'm not!" Henry shouted looking offended, I wasn't sure whether it was more grotesque or pathetic. "I agree that I've been very lost recently. I didn't get a penny from the aunt who lived in New Zealand. Apparently, they found a new and more recent last will. She gave everything to charity. I had nothing for our house deposit and I found out about it after we'd already committed to buying the house." I didn't want to believe a word he was saying but he looked genuinely upset.

"That's not an excuse. You've got a decent job. You don't have to lie, steal or smuggle anything to feed your children or get them out of a cardboard box under a bridge – not that it would be an excuse but—"

"I love my job at uni but—"

"The one in which you teach, sell exams or catch the cheaters or maybe all of them together as they so wonderfully complement one another. You're like a spy who goes abroad to do the job for his country and as soon as he gets there, he starts working for the foreign nation. Do you know what Russians do with such spies? They shoot them," I yelled and I saw on his face the same look like when Blanca was aiming her gun at him. Did I exaggerate? Probably. Maybe. Definitely.

He cleared his throat, took a sip of coffee and started sheepishly, "I've always loved giving lectures, engaging with students, listening to them and even giving them advice. I love teaching, the opportunity to constantly absorb new knowledge and challenge myself. I love my job but I've been feeling frustrated for a while now. I've been working so hard to get my PhD and become fluent in a couple of foreign languages while also working full-time. And what have I got? I can barely afford to rent a tiny apartment in the city and go to the cinema a couple of times a month.

"Go on holiday every year and—"

"By Bryan Airways! Do you know how much it cost me—"

"I've told you so many times that when you book early enough or don't forget to print your boarding pass at home it's not so—"

"I mean how much it cost me to fly with them knowing they might not have enough fuel or—"

"Oh, come on! It's Europe, they have to comply to certain rules and regulations."

"Yeah, the bare minimum. You have no idea how many times I had the same nightmare before flying with them, when there's an emergency on board I need to pay for my speedy evacuation and my credit card gets refused because it's been maxed out that month."

"And let me guess, it's maxed out because you printed your boarding pass at the airport or you had to bail yourself out from prison after you got caught helping your students to cheat?"

"You don't really get my frustrations but you've always been angry I couldn't understand yours," he said hurt, and I had to admit that for once he was right – obviously only to myself as it wasn't the time or place to admit to him he might have been right in anything he was saying. "Many of my friends got their jobs only through the right connections or pure nepotism. They've been farting in their designer chairs and they've managed to fart out properties worth a couple of million pounds. And every day after they complete their rituals of farting in their designer chairs, they move their arses to some posh London bars to make further connections by drinking their arses off so they can fart out more money and build useful links."

I had never heard Henry use the word *fart* before, he would always say *break wind* – *fart* in his mouth sounded like a terrible swear word. I was staring at him not knowing whether I was more concerned or amused. "You can't base your whole knowledge about London's corporate life on one example of a friend of yours who you clearly dislike and you've been jealous of since high-school."

"I'm not talking just about Gatsby," he snapped. I thought he would beg for mercy and apologise but he was desperately trying to justify what he had done. It started dawning on me that I'd spent all these years with him but I really didn't know him. "And it's not all about me. My students are also terribly frustrated. I'm not the bad guy here, and they're not the bad spoiled kids but there's something significantly wrong with the whole system we're currently trapped in. Before I sold my first exam questions, I had a thousand conversations with students. They kept asking me how to survive in a world where employers expect from twenty-something candidates thirty years of experience, solid education, being available twenty-four-seven and working for peanuts. I knew most of my students would end up working on a till in the evening just to be able to afford six months of unpaid internship in London with no guarantee of a job at the end."

"Why don't you try to change the system that you're a part of instead of breaking the law and risking your whole career? I used to be really proud of you Henry," I said feeling as if I had been slapped on my face by the same person again. *I should have never let him come near me after what he did at the airport.*

"I did it for you. I wanted to save our house, buy you the car. The moment you told me about having our child and then..." his voice started cracking, tears appeared in his eyes, "And then two children... I was thrilled but my immediate worry was money. I wanted to give you a better future than Henry-the-lecturer could offer you. We live in such times—"

"Seriously? How long are you going to continue your teaching on moral relativism?" I asked flippantly, and headed towards my newly fitted larder to grab a biscuit. I had always liked sweets, but in the first few months of pregnancy, carbs and sugar were constantly on my mind.

"No," he said matter-of-factly, his tone switching from begging to irritated. "Maybe now you tell me something about your moral relativism," he said while taking away from me a box of wholegrain biscuits, violently unpacking one of them to shovel it quickly in his angry mouth.

"Excuse me?" I shouted taking the box back from him.

"When were you going to tell me that you don't know who the father of your children is?"

The question seemed to stop the blood in my veins from circulating. I felt like my brain suspended.

"Are you all right?" he asked with concern.

"I got a little bit dizzy but I'm fine," I sat down and took a sip of water that Henry passed me.

"I'm sorry, I should have been more considerate. You're pregnant."

"How do you know?" I yelled, and Henry looked at me with even more concern, like my brain really had stopped functioning properly.

"You told me."

"Not that I'm pregnant!"

"Gatsby is as much a professional PI as me," he laughed and for a very short moment I saw something evil in his smile.

"Did you see him following you?" I had to admit Gatsby's face wasn't one that could easily melt into the crowd – strong cheekbones, chunky nose and big round eyes. He is one of those people who are neither pretty or ugly but tend to attract attention. I was beating myself up for listening to Hannah.

"Don't worry, I made the same mistake," he said and sighed without a trace of a smile.

Don't worry about what – being equally stupid as you were – or don't worry, Gatsby didn't tell you everything about my currently messed up life?

"I don't understand," I said getting more curious than angry.

"Gatsby used to temporarily work for us in Spy Education. I asked him for help because we needed an IT specialist pronto."

I was about to say again that I didn't understand what he was talking about when I suddenly got enlightened. "You sent him to Madrid after me?" Henry nodded. "Why did you want him to follow me? It was you who left me."

"He went to Madrid to deal with a completely different case."

Case, I'm his case now!

"Meaning?"

He sighed. I had to drag every word out of his mouth. He was now probably regretting he told me the truth. He had no choice – he had to tell me everything now or come out with more lies. "I was going to Madrid with him. I had an important meeting planned with a dean at one of Madrid's biggest universities. She wanted to discuss utilising the services of Spy Education. But then we had a bigger problem as I had already told—"

"Were you also on the hunt for some new dealers or planning to sell some exams to students so terribly affected by the system in Spain?" I laughed but then I quickly realised something else and my smile faded away. "I thought you wanted to go to Madrid because of me! You made me believe that I was the whole reason why we were flying to that damn city, while the truth was that you were going there anyway, with or without me."

"First, there's nothing wrong trying to connect business with pleasure. Second, I've only sold a few exams. I've told you that it's big money."

"If you can get a Jaguar by trading a few exams, it's probably a better business than selling cocaine – so if I were you I would be afraid of some serious competition."

"I was only planning on selling a few but then I got tempted and sold more. It's addictive like cocaine but I'm going to stop!"

"Why did you ask Gatsby to follow me?" I changed the topic because I realised I would never find out from Henry how far his illegal business had evolved or if he was ever going to stop before being caught by the police.

"It was an impulse," he said and it was the first time that morning when he sounded genuine. "I saw your picture on Facebook with this guy and I got scared you would do something stupid. I knew you would be vulnerable after I left you. You weren't yourself. I called Gatsby and he was already in town."

"Thank you for being so considerate and protective of me! But you know what? I think the vain part of you was simply angry I could've forgotten about you so quickly. Well, I had a great time and I did manage to forget about you so maybe that says something on its own," I took another sip of water but it tasted metallic so I poured it into the sink. I should have installed a water softener but Henry the Scrooge had convinced me it was an unnecessary expense.

"I'll never forgive myself for how I treated you that day at the airport."

"Good, you shouldn't," I snapped to his surprise. "You asked Gatsby to follow me not because you were afraid Hugo was a serial killer but because he was cute enough I might sleep with him," I said with satisfaction as his jaw looked like it was about to suddenly collapse on the floor. He clenched his fists and looked out of the window. "Guess what? It was already too late." I started laughing but I didn't know whether I was genuinely amused by the whole situation or it was just a way to release the tension from my body. "By the time Gatsby saw me at Madrid Atocha I had already had the best, the most passionate sex in my life. It was like—"

"Fine, I get it," he shouted and put his hands on his ears. "I don't know about passion but it was definitely one of the most fruitful ones if the children turn out to be his."

I'd never thought I would have a conversation like this with Henry. Other people yes, but not us – we might've had our problems but we'd never talked to each other like this – not trying to solve issues but throwing anger and envy at one another simply to cut the other side deeper than we were cut; a battle to leave the other side speechless and hurt.

"Even if you worried about me being kidnapped or killed by Hugo, it turned out there was a bigger threat waiting for me in your flat, after you helped Blanca to cheat, then kicked her out for doing it."

"It wasn't the plan," he lowered his voice and explained calmly. "My colleagues tracked her down and it was too late for me to even warn her."

I didn't trust him and again I knew I wouldn't find out the whole Blanca-story from him, so I moved to a less painful issue, "Why did you stop working with Gatsby?"

"We found another IT specialist – cheaper and more effective. Gatsby also wasn't particularly good as a detective, it was more a hobby for him. I found out that most of the jobs he had been getting involved in were unfaithful husbands, and guess what? He drank with most of them in the City. He didn't have to be a detective, he was just a disloyal friend who betrayed his mates for money from their wives. In fact most of the wives weren't working so technically the men were paying him to tell their wives they were unfaithful. Hilarious!" he laughed out loud.

"Are you trying to say he also knew about your illegal business?"

"Yeap," he said and we stood for a while staring at each other not knowing what to say. I felt I had completely run out of steam to argue and I thought he had also had enough. "Olivia, we were so happy yesterday…"

"We were because everything was going according to YOUR plan. You told my parents I was pregnant before they had a chance to find it out from their own daughter, but at the same time you somehow didn't mention the incident with Blanca. Then you proposed to me in front of everybody. I feel I'm suffocating around you."

"You can leave whenever you want but I did it all because I love you and I've been terrified I could lose you."

"More terrified than flying with Bryan Airways?"

He smiled. "Of course," but I knew him well enough to know he was lying over that as well. "Olivia you're not any more honest than me. You've been waiting to find out the children are mine so then you don't have to tell me anything but it doesn't make it right. I've been avoiding telling you the truth for the same reason as you have – I've hoped that ultimately I would somehow get away with it. Just like you I did something stupid, I do regret it and I don't want you to start perceiving me through the one mistake I've done."

At this moment the last thing I regretted was meeting Hugo and getting pregnant but I passed over that part of our conversation in silence. "Well, at least I'm not a criminal."

"Well, at least I'm not a slut," he snapped and stood still. We both went quiet and the silence felt worse than when we were arguing – we couldn't mask our painful disappointment with words. "I didn't mean to say it. Can't you just see how much you want me to be the bad one while neither of us has a clear conscience. Were you even going to tell me the truth if the Spaniard turned out to be the father?"

"Hugo, his name is Hugo." It annoyed me how easily Henry assumed that Hugo was only a fling, a mistake that I wanted to rub out of my life.

"You know," he said rubbing his chin, "I've thought about it and I wouldn't leave you if the Span—, I mean if Hue was the father."

"How generous of you," I raised my voice and my hands up. "And his name is Hugo."

"But only if you told me the truth," he put his forefinger in front of me which I found comical.

"Well, we won't find out now, will we? You already know there's a chance the children are not yours."

"True but I still have faith in us and I hope you'll give us another chance," he said in an unnaturally deep voice. "I know it's my fault because I left you at the damn airport. But did you really have to jump in bed with the Hue?" he muttered through tight lips.

"There's been so many secrets between us, I just—"

"I'll tell you everything you want to know but give us another chance," he switched again to his please-forgive-me mode.

Why did you give me your grandmother's ring, what happened to the diamond one I found in your flat? I wished I could've asked about it but I wasn't in the mood to explain why I'd searched through his stuff before he dumped me. There was, however, another thing that had been bothering me for a while, something I hadn't asked Gatsby about. All because deep down I was afraid he would take it as proof of me being a paranoid, over-jealous woman and he wouldn't have treated the case with the right level of seriousness.

"Who's Tiggy Brown to you?"

He didn't instantly shout *'nobody'* as I'd expected him to do as some form of pathetic defence. He didn't ask *'why would it even matter now'* as I'd imagined.

"I see Gatsby managed to track something down on his own," he said with a smirk. I was confused by how quickly he was switching between the guilty Henry and the full of irony and angry one.

"You said you would tell me everything I wanted to know," I said matter-of-factly with my hands crossed.

"Fine, just don't jump too quickly to any conclusions. We studied at the same uni, as you probably already know from my dear friend Gatsby," he said while walking around our small kitchen. "We weren't very close friends but we bumped into each other from time to time. Sometimes we'd socialise with the same people. The world is so small," he sighed. "She was a friend of a friend of—"

"Stop procrastinating! I know what you're doing, you're just giving yourself more time to make up some lame excuses!"

"I helped her once to pull herself together after *a bad* romance," he over- accentuated *bad*. "She wasn't able to study for a couple of weeks so I wrote an essay for her for one module."

"And?"

"Why do you want me to say something you already know?"

"Because I want to hear it from you!"

"Fine, I asked her to employ you and what? I helped her, she helped me."

"Why didn't you tell me about it?" Now I was pretending to be angry while in reality I'd expected something much worse and his answer actually came as a relief.

"So you would feel better about getting the job all by yourself! But get real Olivia! Nobody gets to I-Heart-Travelling from nowhere. Even their internships aren't just unpaid – the interns have to pay the magazine to take them," he laughed clearly amused with himself.

"I wish you told me. Did you want me to keep the job so badly because you thought I wasn't good enough to get anything better?"

"The competition is high, and what counts now are good connections. I just didn't want you to be disappointed."

"Well, I am now because you lied to me."

He seemed not to hear what I'd just said. "By the way, Tiggy called me and they won't fire you after all. She apologised to me that she was a bit too harsh on you. She's also pregnant and… you know how it is," he smiled.

"She apologised to YOU? I think I also need to apologise to you – I'm sorry. I'm not going to have breakfast with you. I need to get some air."

23

TUESDAY, 1 SEPTEMBER

MADRID

"Welcome again to Madrid," Cristiano was beaming from behind his counter in the newly opened Madrid Fairy Boutique Hotel.

"Wow, this place really is some sort of fairyland," I said with my jaw wide open and my eyes wandering around a hallway with golden walls and lifts, crystal chandeliers, heavy velvet curtains and a granite fountain in the middle of the lobby. It was a bit too opulent for my taste but I was looking forward to spending a few days surrounded by such lavish interiors. Unlike Henry, I didn't want to feel at home in a hotel, I liked to be taken to a different world. "No surprise it has *fairy* in its name."

"Indeed, it's *fairy*, it's *mágico* and I love being here but the name comes from the hotel's owner Señora Fairy Gonzales. She's an *increíble* woman!" Cristiano said blushing.

"How long have you been working here?"

"Only a month but I'm sure I'm going to be happier here than in Madrid Kings. Here at the reception there're always at least two of us for just thirty rooms, in Kings there were often only two of us for three hundred rooms," he said passing me a magnetic card to my room.

I entered my apartment straight from the largest golden lift in the building. My suite was at the top on the tenth floor and it was the only one in the hotel that had a private lift and roof terrace. I walked on a soft oriental carpet through a light living room, with a modern mahogany dining table and eight chairs upholstered in green velvet. At the end of the living area there was a wooden double door to, as I accurately predicted, my bedroom. I pushed them gently and while standing in the doorway I enjoyed the moment – the feeling of being a princess, or just a rich woman. Before I threw myself on the king-sized bed with a white canopy and silk bedding I *visited* the bathroom – yes, marble on the walls, gold taps, a hot tub in the middle and double-everything including sinks, showers and toilets, it looked like it was fit for a palace – although after a few minutes of careful consideration I realised the second toilet was actually a bidet. If not for Cristiano, I wouldn't have been able to afford the suite even for one night.

On Sunday soon after our argument, Henry drove to Heathrow to catch his flight to the USA. The moment he shut the main door I was climbing the stairs to search every possible drawer in every room of the house to find Cristiano's business card. "Here you are my little darling," I exclaimed taking out the crumpled card from the bottom of my bedside drawer. I decided not to lose a minute typing texts or emails and immediately grabbed my phone to call him. It turned out he hadn't only changed his job but he had also been promoted to head of the marketing department in the hotel. He was only working part time at the reception desk. "Let's make a deal..." he started cheerfully. He offered me three nights free in the hotel's best apartment and in exchange I would write about the Madrid Fairy for I-Heart-Travelling. My job had some perks after all, I just couldn't get most of them directly from my employer. I called Tiggy the very same evening and booked my tickets on high-speed trains from London to Barcelona and Barcelona to Madrid. Tiggy was initially reluctant to let me go anywhere, then she insisted on going there herself, but for a change she didn't scream at me but expressed concern about me travelling so far while pregnant with twins.

Pot calling the kettle black, I bet you've already checked the hotel on the

Internet, I thought irritated but said calmly, "American scientists said that twins travel better because they've got company."

She didn't even laugh once but instead said seriously, "Makes sense," and then added quickly, "My husband also keeps saying that pregnancy is not an illness and he doesn't mind me going anywhere. However, Henry might take issue with it."

"Well…" I started patiently, "we're free women Tiggy," while on the inside I was screaming, *Why would it matter what men think?*

"But they're also his children."

Possibly. "I met Cristiano during a travel networking meeting in Madrid and he wants me specifically to write about the hotel."

"Fine then but when Henry asks—"

"Tell him I insisted," I snapped this time not without obvious irritation in my voice.

Tiggy was right – I felt exhausted after the journey. Having two small passengers travelling in my body was more tiring then dragging twenty-kilos of luggage. I had significantly less energy than in my pre-pregnancy life and I needed more sleep. No wonder the most attractive part of the apartment appeared to be its soft bed. I threw my handbag on the floor and lay on the bed fully dressed with my trainers on. I only managed to think how wonderful it would be to have such a big bed and canopy at home before I was gone into my own fairyland.

The first part of the journey on the route London-Barcelona wasn't the relaxing train experience I'd hoped for. I regretted trying to get to Barcelona within one day, which meant a twelve-hour journey with one change and a four-hour stopover in Lyon. I could've changed trains in Paris but the idea of taking a taxi between the stations Paris du Nord and Paris Gare de Lyon didn't particularly appeal to me – I would be stressing out about traffic jams and other adventures that would delay me. Unfortunately, the Lyon stopover that sounded like a nice opportunity to stretch my legs, have lunch and maybe even do some shopping ended up being a four-hour survival exercise. Lyon's international train station didn't have a chain of smart coffee shops and boutiques like St Pancras or a botanical garden with turtles like Madrid Atocha. I found a few places selling delicious French pastries and baguettes but there was no place to sit and enjoy them. I gave up looking for a table and spent over an hour walking around the station and outside in the immediate neighbourhood trying to find somewhere just to sit. Tired of fighting my way through the crowds of travellers rushing in all directions and in permanent fear of pickpockets, I eventually found a busy coffee shop with many people eating their lunch on their knees. I bought a cup of coffee, a cheese and ham baguette and stood in a corner waiting for somebody to leave their seat. After a quarter of an hour I was sitting on a piece of leather sofa between two small tables and two couples having loud conversations in French. I put a napkin on my knees and was ready to take my first long-awaited bite of French bread when a tall fat guy threw his soft gym bag next to my feet and ran away. Nobody noticed anything. I immediately got up ready to shout but I stopped myself, seeing the same guy shovelling into his arms as many sandwiches from a fridge next to the counter as he could carry at once. I was so shocked that I didn't make a sound as he put them all into his bag and left. I sat down flabbergasted, I had my lunch and spent another couple of hours on that seat tightly squeezing my small luggage and handbag, checking every ten minutes whether I still had my passport and purse.

When I finally arrived at a cheap hotel in Barcelona I went straight to bed but I didn't get much sleep as my balcony looked over a busy street dominated by nightclubs. I was peeved I hadn't bothered to read any reviews before booking it. On the following day I had only three hours on a train to get to Madrid but it felt like thirteen. At least I had bought a first-class ticket – it was one of my best purchases of the year. I made myself comfortable next to a window with an empty seat on my left. The train began to move with the compartment half empty and I closed my eyes hoping for a sweet little nap. The next thing I heard was a loud noise of somebody taking or putting their bags above my head and then shouting between several people in a language that at first I didn't recognise. *The doze made me even more tired,* I was thinking while leaning out of my seat to see with blurred vision what was going on.

"Are we in Zaragoza?" I asked a conductor with a thick moustache, who was passing smoothly through the wide first-class aisle. Zaragoza was the biggest city which the train stopped at on its way to Madrid.

The conductor stopped and gave me a curious look, then he leant towards me so nobody else could hear and he said clearly and slowly in English, "We're still in Barcelona Señora." He must have noticed my astonishment and embarrassed face because he didn't move but asked, *"Todo bien?* Everything all right? As soon as we move we'll be bringing coffee."

Naturally I felt like an idiot, a very tired one. The train wasn't moving and I was already starting to feel sick. I took out a paper bag stacked at the back of the seat ahead of me and I made a few deep breaths. I stopped when I heard a warm voice saying, "Ladies and gentleman welcome on board. Our journey to Madrid will last two hours and fifty minutes…" I closed my eyes, my feet squeezing my small suitcase, both hands on my handbag resting on my lap. I was desperate for some sleep but a few rows in front of me a group of foreigners were having a vivid conversation which only stopped on rare occasions to make some space for booming laughter. I last heard a similar language at one of my favourite Chinese restaurants in London. I went there with Henry in May, not long before our planned holiday to Madrid. I was watching him eating lemon chicken with chopsticks and wondering how we would look together in ten or twenty years. I was staring at him more and more intensely but struggled to imagine anything, I blamed it on him procrastinating about our engagement and promptly forgot about it.

I wished Chinese was more popular when I was at school because I hadn't had enough time or motivation to learn another language since I graduated from university. I was dying to know what the people were so enthusiastic about. Were they laughing at us, the Europeans, of how silly and weird we acted or were they just joking about some random stuff? A few weeks before I listened to a presentation at I-Heart-Travelling concerning the most recent trends in travelling and the characteristics of how other nations travel. A large part of the meeting revolved around the Chinese, which in 2014 were at the top of the list of nationalities that spend the most money on international travel.

"Chinese people prefer travelling in big groups," said Bob an expert invited by Cecilia. "If you want to target the market in China you need to focus less on couples and families but think about group travel…"

My newly gained experience was telling me that we should aim to change the trends rather than just support them, they were so loud. Although I knew it was not fair for me to judge an entire people from a group of roughly twenty, my travel buddies reminded me of a high-school bus trip except nobody was supervising them.

How the hell did you manage to plan the journey across Europe in such a large group without constantly arguing what and when you should see? Do you get up every day at the same time? Is one of you in charge of your timetable or do you vote when you can't agree on something? Have you been friends before or have you just met during the trip? All these thoughts were passing through my mind as I was resting with my eyes closed.

"Europeans are more likely to travel solo than in a large group." Bob was saying during his presentation. "When I think of Europeans, I think of individualists, who would rather choose to go away alone to search for themselves and their inner happiness than try to get closer with other people."

Would the Chinese be interested in Hugo TorTillas? Would they even need it? I was wondering, then I reflected that the person who probably needed it the most on the train was me. I took the phone out of my handbag and typed 'Amigo, habla conmigo, Madrid'. I preferred to fill out a detailed questionnaire than provide some kind of confession to the professionals at the restaurant. I was struggling to make up a name that sounded real – I tried five and all of them were already taken. *How many English people have already registered for Hugo TorTillas?* I typed Tiggy Brown. *Done! It worked!* I whispered to myself and wrote a sentence on what I wanted to be the main topic of my conversation: 'I don't know who the father of my child is (two possible candidates) and I don't know which one of them I should choose (for the sake of the children [expecting twins] and for the sake of my future happiness).' I opted out from all questions that weren't marked with red stars and I moved to my preferences – mostly I ticked 'don't mind'. I really didn't care whether I would be chatting to a man or a woman, to a Spanish, English or Polish person; somebody from a city or a village; with basic or higher education. I didn't want to close any options – god knows who could turn out to be my best advisor. I ticked two age groups: '25 to 30' and '30 to 35'.

I was putting my phone back in my bag when the trained stopped in Zaragoza. Outside of the window I saw a Chinese man with a plastic suitcase on wheels. He was wearing a brown leather vest and a beret. He was standing there completely still like a statue and staring at the train. Suddenly a woman belonging to the loud group stood up and ran out of the train to drag the surprised man with his beret inside. The train moved just as the man walked into our carriage. The Chinese group welcomed him with clapping and laughing.

"I bet trains in China open their doors at every station and don't require you to press for entry," said a woman behind me with a strong American accent.

"I bet he's got a butler at home…" responded the woman's husband, "or knowing the Chinese they have it so advanced the door opens when somebody approaches. Anyway, I can't believe how smooth and fast this train is moving. In the US my arse would be bruised by now from the train jumping down the track."

Everybody was amused by the Man in Beret except one very stern business woman who also got on the train in Zaragoza and took the single seat on my left. She was surrounded by people but acted as if she was alone in her office. She began her journey from arranging her table like it had been her desk. On her small table, where most people kept their newspapers and plastic cups with hot drinks, she carefully arranged a laptop, smartphone, thick diary, a collection of pens in various colours and a pair of glasses. She spent her whole time on the train shouting down her phone and gradually crossing out some notes in her diary.

I got out at Madrid Atocha with a slight headache, carrying with me a melody of Chinese language and Spanish swear words. I headed straight to a taxi and felt relieved as I passed my taxi driver the address of my hotel. I couldn't wait to get there and finally put my head on my pillow. I was so sleepy I reached for my mobile to keep myself awake for the rest of the car journey. I tried to connect to the Internet but it didn't work and then I reminded myself that I only paid for 4G roaming on my second mobile, which I used to contact Hugo. Previously I had a very good wi-fi on the train. I threw my UK mobile into the bag, ignoring messages and missed calls from Henry, and started searching for my Hugo-phone. I hadn't used it for over twenty-four hours and I had already managed to forgot where I had hidden it. In vain I dug through my red Kelly Hermés bag – another present from Henry that he gave me on my birthday after all the guests were gone. *Again, I've hidden something so effectively that I can't find it!* I called myself, put my ear to *Kelly*, then to my suitcase sitting next to me on the back seat. *Nothing! Nada!*

"You've got to be kidding me! They've stolen my phone!" I shouted but the taxi driver didn't even twitch. He either didn't understand English or didn't care, "Last time I was using it was in Lyon." I said this time quieter, at this point the taxi guy rolled his window down, put his elbow outside and started smoking. *Seriously?*

I woke up in the hotel room after a good seven-hour nap. It was ten o'clock in the evening. In England at this time my only chance for a dinner would probably be MacDonald's or a street Kebab but not in a city that never sleeps like Madrid. I didn't rush to leave the room. First, I had a shower, put some make up on and had a chocolate bar from the fridge. I also found two small bottles of juice practically hidden among a wide selection of free mini bottles of various alcohols that I couldn't try. An hour later I was getting in a taxi again, but this time it smelt of a lavender instead of cigarettes – Cristiano knew which company to call.

"Hugo Tor*Tillas* please," I said excited with my heart skittering.

"It's my fifth ride to the place tonight. People have gone mad about it," he said looking at me by glancing in his rear view mirror. "So which Hugo are we going to?"

"Hugo Tor*Tillas*," I said loudly. "There's only one Hugo Tor*Tillas*."

"Last month they opened a new one and—"

"The old one please then," I cut him off impatiently.

When I entered the large hallway in Hugo Tor*Tillas*, the cuckoo clock was just striking midnight. I stood there in the middle of the lobby having some second thoughts. *Maybe it's the wrong idea. I should've gone to the second Hugo TorTillas where I had no memories.* All I could think of was the night I spent here with Hugo. I was about to leave when I heard a firm voice in my head – *Are you really going to chicken out? Just like that? Somebody is waiting here for you, and maybe she or he needs the meeting even more than you.* I took a deep breath, pulled out a compact mirror to check my teeth and lipstick, then straightened my dress feeling as if I was going for a job interview. I approached a handsome dark-haired man at the reception. He was wearing a black sleek suit and when I saw him I thought that my heart would jump out of my chest and start running around the lobby.

"Welcome to Hugo Tor*Tillas*. How can I help you?"

"My name is Oli—, Tiggy Brown. I've booked a table for quarter past midnight," I said, my voice slightly shaking, my hands sweating.

The man in the suit typed something on his shiny laptop, "When did you fill out the questionnaire?"

"Today in the morning. Is something wrong?" I asked with relief that I would be able to run away and have some tapas in the city instead.

"Would you mind speaking in Spanish with your *Amigo* tonight?

"No, not at all."

He sighed with relief. "Then everything is perfect," he smiled. "I thought that it might've been a mistake because people generally want to speak in their native language... Your Amigo will be Nicolas, and he'll be waiting for you in room C. Have you been here before?"

I nodded, "Room C is upstairs?"

"That's right."

Unlike in May, when I wasn't dressed up for my visit, this time I was wearing glossy tights, red stilettoes and a little black dress that was cut just below my knees. I had pulled my hair into a straight ponytail and done simple make-up. My Kelly bag was matching my shoes – according to some it was currently a fashion faux pas but I didn't care – I looked classy. I preferred to turn up smarter than my *Amigo,* than be ashamed of a too casual look. I had deliberately chosen such a late time because I assumed that Hugo would be sleeping or at least would have left his restaurant by then – from what he was saying a few weeks ago he needed to get up early to run the increasing number of business meetings.

I hadn't expected crowds after midnight during the working week but all tables were occupied. Most of the seats were either taken by men in shirts without ties, their jackets hanging on the back of their chairs or women in tight sleeveless dresses – I could've easily melted into the crowd. I had a moment of panic when I saw a waiter walking briskly in my direction with a massive grin on his face – I was afraid it might have been Rogelio and I was wondering whether he would recognise me as Hugo's date. I started breathing again when the waiter stood in front of me. *Oh, thank you heaven, I've never seen this guy in my life!*

"Good afternoon Señora, are you taking part in our programme *Amigo, habla conmigo* or is it just dinner tonight?"

"Amigo habla conmigo, por favor," I said thinking that I had spent two days on the train to get to the place and now I just wanted to leg it.

I followed the tall thin waiter to the table, where Nicolas was already waiting. He was a slim, middle-height brunet with bushy hair and a dense beard which for some reason didn't work on his face – it looked almost like it was fake. I couldn't say how old he was but instinctively I put him into the 25-30 category. Unlike other people that night he didn't look like he had just left his office. He was wearing a red tartan flannel shirt, dark jeans and red well-worn trainers. He was obviously influenced in his dress and all-hair-style by the recent fashion to look lumbersexual. We both clearly liked red which was a good start I thought. I felt like we were meeting up in a pub to have a beer rather than about to have a serious chat in a smart restaurant.

He offered a friendly smile when he saw me, stood up and shook my hand energetically. "I'm Nicolas, simply Nicolas," he said in English.

When we sat down and ordered some drinks he spoke loudly with a warm beaming smile, "You're probably wondering who the hell reads the questionnaires and whether it wasn't some sort of a mistake." He glanced at my lightly rounded stomach.

"Well, I trust they're professional but we won't be able to share our mutual experience regarding morning sickness or swollen ankles."

"You're jumping quickly to conclusions," he kept smiling.

"Are you…" I cleared my throat. "Does it mean that you're a…"

"A woman going through a sex change?" he asked seriously and I shyly nodded. "I had all my children before my sex change."

"Oh, fascinating," I said surprised and intrigued.

"Tiggy, I'm fucking with you," he said suddenly in English and broke into laughter. That was the moment I lost any hope for a serious conversation that could help me to solve any of my problems but at least I relaxed expecting a pleasant evening. "But, you still don't know who is hiding under this beard…"

"Do you live in Madrid?"

"Is your real name Tiggy?"

"You still haven't answered my question," I said as a new waiter suddenly appeared.

"Good evening, my name is Eugenio and I'll be accompanying you tonight."

"But I hope not for the whole time," said Nicolas with exaggerated fear in his voice. "I ticked in my preferred age category 25-30, and with all due respect you look a bit older."

Eugenio didn't look even a little bit offended – he couldn't be more than twenty-five. Most likely he was a local student, trying to make some extra money for the expensive life of Madrid. Neither of us even looked at the menu. Nicolas ordered some sea food, and I asked for salmon with a medium spicy chilli sauce. He ordered another glass of Chardonnay, and I chose non-alcoholic ginger beer and still water.

"Yes, Tiggy is my real name," I lied without blinking. Apparently the more we lie, the better we can mask it.

"Original," he nodded and I got the impression he didn't believe me. "I'm not sure whether it suits you," he kept watching me like a painting, "but I gather you didn't come here with that problem."

"Cheeky," I leaned back in my chair and gave him a long stare. "I think something else brings us here, not our funny sounding names."

"Nicolas is not funny, it's my nickname, I'm sorry to disappoint you," he said strongly accentuating "r" in sorry like in *Zorro*. Not-Nicolas was about to say something more but Eugenio brought our drinks. Not-Nicolas started again after taking a sip of his wine, "I live in Madrid and speaking about things that matter I'm gay..."

"You don't look like one," I said before I managed to bite my tongue.

"So how should I look according to you? Should I be sitting here with my pink handbag and wearing a too tight pink T-shirt?" he said amused by himself.

"That's not what I meant, just... I always wanted to have a best gay friend?"

"Of course, every woman wants to have her best gay friend. But I won't be your *bestie*, your gay-shop-friend."

"I like going shopping alone. You can't ever get an honest opinion from another woman and I hate when other people are waiting for me looking all bored," I said in one breath, thinking, *But I think I would enjoy shopping with my best gay friend if I had one.*

"I'm glad to hear that, I don't want to put your hopes up," he laughed warmly. The fact I fancy men doesn't mean I actually like any of the activities, which are stereotypically assigned to women like shopping, manicures or watching romantic comedies. I'm an engineer, I design bridges and road tunnels. I don't like cats and I love football."

"Watching or playing?"

"I don't watch much sport, I prefer to play."

It took us a while before either of us revealed why we had decided to come to Hugo TorTillas – it was sometime between the main course and dessert when Nicolas began all of a sudden, "My father has never accepted me being gay. Initially he wanted me to go to a doctor to cure myself from this shameful disease," he laughed bitterly. "He kept arranging dates for me with his friends' daughters. I felt like I let him down. For years he wouldn't take any of my explanations that nothing would ever change me. He used to say I was just confused. Finally, he asked me to pretend in front of our friends and family and I did exactly as he asked me to. I was pretending I was just picky – I would meet up with women for a date so people would see me out, but later after I drove them home I would secretly go to a gay club. Most of my relationships fell apart quickly because my partners didn't want to pretend and I didn't blame them for it."

"I'm really sorry," I said genuinely moved by his story. "How old were you when you told your father you were gay?"

"Fifteen, and I told both of my parents at the same time. Mum wasn't even particularly surprised. She was okay with it from the very beginning, while my father was furious. That's why I've always had mixed feeling towards him – I simultaneously loved and hated him. This year he had a serious operation and... And I lost my father," he said matter-of-factly without much sorrow in his voice or eyes.

"I'm really sorry," I said, feeling like my mind was blank and I couldn't come out with anything better. *He didn't meet up with you to keep hearing you're really sorry! Try to think of something more constructive, supportive, anything...* "I can't imagine how hard it must've been for you to lose him before you actually managed to solve your problems. I mean his problems – because he had a problem with you. I mean you weren't actually his problem, he had a problem with himself…" I paused feeling exhausted and thinking, *Holy moly, I should have stuck to 'I'm really sorry… Let me just collect my thoughts on that, ideally by typing them on my phone…*

"Sorry, that's not what I've been trying to say," he said and gurgled half of a glass of wine in two seconds. I looked at him confused. "My father is not dead."

"Oh, so is it good or…"

"His surgery was postponed because they needed more of his type of blood before they started, and the blood transport was late. They asked me whether I would do it. I've always had an issue with needles but I felt guilty not helping my father – I didn't want anybody to think my reluctance was some kind of revenge. Plus the nurse had such amazing hazel eyes and toned legs and—"

"So, you're bisexual?"

"No," he said slowly. "Why did you assume that the nurse had to be a woman? There're plenty of male nurses."

"I'm sorry," I said sheepishly. "Did you donate your blood?"

"I did but they couldn't use it. It turned out he wasn't my biological father."

"No way," I said with my mouth full of chocolate cake.

"In my entire twenty-seven years of life my mother never found a convenient moment to tell me such a small, irrelevant detail."

"Did she have any particular reason for not telling you the truth? Was your biological father in prison or a womanizer, a drug addict or—"

"Are you trying to defend her?" he asked flatly.

"Of course not!" I exclaimed. *Of course I'm not defending anybody… I just… yes maybe a little bit!*

"She really hurt me. The closest people in my life keep hurting me. First my non-biological father, then my mother…" he rubbed both his eyes with open hands, gasped and squeezed his hairy cheeks before he was ready to continue, "It turned out that my biological father didn't even know about my existence. I mean he knew I existed. He was my mother's first husband but he thought I was a child of my mother's lover, who later became her second husband. Are you following? I know it's a bit of a *telenovela*, but it's actually really simple."

A red light went on in my head. I suddenly knew why an expert in Hugo Tor*T*illas thought I was a good match for Nicolas!

"Have you met your biological father?"

"I have and he accepts me as I am – he doesn't care whether I'm hetero or homosexual," he said cheerfully but soon his smile faded away." I don't understand why she would let me believe for all those years that the man, who later became clearly ashamed and disgusted with me, was my father. How could she? She destroyed the whole family. My stepfather has now left her, I practically don't speak to her."

"Did she have at least a good reason why she did it? Have you ever asked her?"

"Of course, I asked her Tiggy. How could I not? I wanted to believe that maybe my father was somebody she wanted to protect me from! I didn't want to lose them both at the same time."

"So what—?"

"She was afraid to lose my stepfather and she didn't want my actual father to be involved in her new family. She's simply been selfish all the way through."

"And now she's lost everybody, it's so sad," I wasn't actually sure whether I felt more sorry for Nicolas or his mother. I just wanted to find her and cuddle her. A few months earlier it would be a no brainer – I wouldn't even try to defend or understand the woman, but my life had changed. I had changed and I still didn't know whether it was for better or worse – I was worried it was probably going to be the latter.

"Do you know what's saddest in all of this? Each time I was upset about my father not accepting me, she asked me to give him more time because he was apparently just old-fashioned and struggled with change – and she kept saying that for twelve years never mentioning—"

"She must've been really scared."

"Ironically she wasn't worried about her son's self-esteem while being brought up by a homophobe." Nicolas kept his voice down but I saw tears in his eyes, and his jaw was trembling.

"What was your stepfather like before you told him about you being gay?"

"He was…" Nicolas stopped to take a few breaths. "I actually have to admit he was great," he said as if he surprised himself. "He always listened and had plenty of time for me. He was supportive and encouraging. I was his only child, and I loved our relationship."

"Bingo! Maybe your mother thought that he would be the better father and she wanted the best for you and that's why she—"

"It wasn't for her to decide," he snapped. "I can only think that she thought my biological father wouldn't have had so much time or money for me. Unlike my wealthy stepfather, who makes a living renting numerous properties around the world, my biological father had to work hard. He's done well but he's never even been close to the wealth of my stepfather, who inherited most of his money. I've never thought about my mother being materialist but then I don't really know her, do I?"

"What does your mum say about your biological father?"

"We haven't talked about it yet. She had over twenty-seven years to tell me. Now I need a decent amount of time to digest the revelation."

"I don't want to defend her but…"

"So don't," he snapped and I wondered why he told me all of that if he didn't want to listen and he'd already made up his mind on every possible topic.

"There must be something important she hasn't told you yet. Maybe it would upset you even more. Besides she's not the same woman as she was twenty-seven years ago."

"Which doesn't justify her lies by any means. She had no right to prevent me from knowing my biological father. If my father was some kind of monster she should've left him before she had a second child with him. I'm not the only child as I'd believed until recently. I've got an older brother, who lived with my father as a child," he said with a smile on his face.

"I do agree with you but I think you should listen to her. I don't say she deserves listening to but do it for your own good to know the whole truth."

"Tiggy, are you also pregnant with your lover's child?" he looked at me as if his eyes saw through me, saw exactly what secrets I'd brought with me to share in Hugo TorTillas.

"Not exactly, I'm not married..." *I don't even know whether I'm still engaged – technically yes because I didn't break up with Henry but it's only a matter of time...*

"Just unfaithful?" he snorted with disdain.

I thought that guests in Hugo TorTillas weren't meant to be judgemental. I started thinking that maybe trying to identify and connect two people with similar problems was a mistake. *Should I write an anonymous letter to Hugo?*

"Not quite," I was afraid to say anything – it was like deliberately throwing myself into a cage with hungry tigers.

I guess there's no point in asking you now whether I should choose the best possible candidate for my husband and father of my children and stick to that plan irrespective of the DNA results. Lies aren't always bad! Whatever other people say, sometimes the end does justify the means, doesn't it?

He sighed looking impatient, "You've accidentally got pregnant with Mr A, but you don't know whether you want to be with him or not because there's also Mr B, who's probably your long-term boyfriend, am I right?"

I nodded.

"Tell me, it didn't even cross your mind to pretend that your *chosen one* is the biological father?" he said in a more judgy tone than Henry. I suddenly felt that Nicolas was one of my unborn children who had decided to pop out for a minute from my body and give me a lecture. *If it really happened the children would definitely be Henry's!*

I took a spoonful of my chocolate cake with raspberries, and then seeing Eugenio two tables away from ours I raised my hand to beckon him over.

"Let's just pay and go home," I murmured. "That will be best for everybody."

"Fine," he snapped but before Eugenio materialised at our table he quickly said. "We haven't come here to judge each other."

"No kidding," I snapped in a more bitter and angry tone than him.

"Would you like something else?" Eugenio asked with a wide genuine smile that quickly turned into a forced one – he could feel the tension between me and Not-Nicolas.

"Just the—"

"Another glass of Chardonnay for me," Nicolas cut me off abruptly. "No sorry, two ginger beers and two slices of the chocolate cake with raspberries. Thank you," he said quickly to stop Eugenio from looking at me.

"Maybe I don't want another ginger beer or more cake?" I asked more surprised than irritated. I could easily have another cake.

"If you don't want it, I'll have both," he said matter-of-factly. "Now, why are you here Tiggy?" his voice got softer and ready to listen.

I took a deep breath, "As you correctly predicted I'm pregnant and I don't know who the father is."

"More than two potential candidates?" he asked as if he was doing a phone questionnaire, devoid of emotion.

"Three… maybe four but I think the first three are the most likely to be the father," I said seriously.

"You don't look like," he leaned back to eye me up and down.

"So how should I look according to you? Should I be sitting here with my boobs falling out of my too small dress?" I tried to look insulted.

"Yyy… no, it's not what I mean…"

"I'm kidding, Not-Nicolas," I laughed and I saw genuine relief on his face. "There're two potential candidates," I started again seriously, "but it's still one too many…"

"Ginger beer and chocolate cakes," Eugenio seemed to appear out of nowhere.

"Don't hesitate to tell me if you don't want your cake because you need to care about your waist," Nicolas said with a cheeky smile.

"Are you kidding? Now when I've got the best excuse ever I'm not going to go off cake? Besides the fatter I get the more likable I become for other women!"

"True! Enjoy then!" he said enthusiastically putting a small silver fork into the chocolate cake. "And now, I'm all ears."

I told him how I was unexpectedly dumped at the airport, went alone on holiday and met somebody I quickly fell in love with. Then I briefly expressed my concerns about Henry's illegal business without going into too much detail, although Nicolas was very curious. I said I was worried that Henry might have been involved in some sort of work scam.

"Does something else worry you about the Spanish boyfriend other than the fact you don't know him well enough?"

"He's not my boy—"

"Let's just stick to the idea you've got two boyfriends – it's easier this way, otherwise you make it all too complicated," he said waving his hands.

"I don't know him well enough, that's for sure."

"From what you've been saying you've known him for a shorter amount of time but actually you might know him better than—"

"It's something I could keep debating for months as it's not only choosing the right man for me but also the right father for my children."

"I think you don't have that luxury anymore. Your children have a father, you just don't know yet who he is – and you know what?" he leaned towards me, resting his elbows on the white cloth, which was covered with bits of squashed raspberries and chocolate. Somebody watching us from a distance could think he wanted to kiss me.

"What?"

"You'll be able to tell them who their father is."

"But then there's a fifty percent chance I'll be a single mother of twins because *the chosen one* won't want to bring up children that are not his, and the biological father might not want to be my second choice," I said realising how selfish it all sounded – the truth was, however, I was just scared of bringing up the boys on my own.

"Even if I were bisexual I wouldn't get into a relationship with a woman."

"What do you mean. The fact men can't get pregnant?"

"Men don't make everything so complicated. Give a woman a piece of string and she ties it in so many different ways that it won't even resemble string."

"What is your advice then, Mr Uncomplicated?"

"You know best what you need to do. You just prefer to pretend not to know because that way it's a hell of a lot easier."

"I've seen a therapist and fortune teller in one. I hired a PI to follow my fiancé... I mean I don't know whether he's my fiancé anymore—"

"I know, he broke up with you at the airport," he was rushing me and at that moment I was grateful that Not-Nicolas like most people wasn't a patient listener.

"I made friends with a woman who is in a similar position to me. I spent two days on the train to get here and speak to you, and I still don't know."

"Because you don't need anybody other than yourself to tell you what to do," he was practically whispering but it felt like he was shouting out every word to me.

"I wish I could employ somebody to do some form of risk assessment."

"Do what?" he laughed, his eyes amused and wide open. "Do you want to predict the weather for the rest of the year only by looking at the few clouds above your head? There was no way for my mother to know that I would be gay or that my stepfather wouldn't accept it. You can't predict every possibility, you just have to do what's right."

"I feel the burden of the responsibility – potentially my decisions could make so many people unhappy: my children, myself, a good man who cares about me... Do you think that your mum has ever done DNA tests?"

"I don't think so but I can't tell for sure and choosing not to know something doesn't make you free of the responsibility."

. . .

I drove away from Hugo TorTillas through the wide streets of Madrid's centre – the *madrileños* were slowly waking up on Monday morning with the street lights ending their shift and sunlight gradually replacing them. The taxi driver made me listen to an energetic Spanish song that made me feel like I wanted to open the rooftop, stand up and dance. We were passing runners dressed in tight bright outfits and people in suits rushing towards metro stations. Many tourists were waiting for their cabs outside their hotels with bags on wheels and their eyes set on their phones and watches. Men in wide yellow vests were sweeping the pavements to prepare them for another day in the city. Each one of the people was carrying their worries and decisions. I knew what I needed to do. *It would be easier not to know but I do,* I thought while resting my head on the backseat and waiting to get to my next destination.

24

WEDNESDAY, 2 SEPTEMBER
MADRID

I threw my beige summer coat on the stairs to use it as a cushion – for the very first time I didn't worry how creased or dirty it would be later. I had more important issues on my mind than dry cleaning a designer coat. I took a sip of hot chocolate from a paper cup and looked at my compact mirror. *I doubt somebody will stumble across me here in the early afternoon,* I thought. *But if they do, after sleeping for barely three hours, I look like a homeless person.* Nobody would believe me if I told them I lived in the best suite at the Madrid Fairy Boutique Hotel, or in fact in any respectable hotel in the city. I took a big bite from my still warm Churros.

The only thing disturbing my perfect lunch and affecting my appetite were the millions of thoughts flooding my head. I couldn't stop dwelling on the night I told Hugo it was definitely over. It happened the day after I saw Gatsby at my brother's house. More and more convinced about Henry being an honest man, and me descending into worse and worse paranoia, I typed a message to Hugo informing him that I wasn't able to go with him for the trip around the world. The reasons I gave him were my difficult family situation and an unexpected promotion at work. The first was a half-truth, so practically speaking it was a lie close to the truth – I only missed the part that soon he could be part of my immediate family. The latter was a full-blown lie – a rapid demotion was far more likely than any kind of promotion at present. Hugo called immediately after I sent him the message and he kept calling continually for at least five minutes. I was afraid that if I'd heard his voice I would've changed my mind so I decided not to answer. Then my phone beeped and I knew he left me a voicemail. I lay on a soft rug in the lounge staring at the ceiling – I was trying to switch off my thinking and just for a very short moment feel nothing, but my phone kept vibrating with new messages every few seconds. I wasn't strong enough even to put it on mute.

```
Why are you not answering? Does it mean it's all
over between us? If so, can you at least tell me
that instead of texting me? I don't believe
you're such a coward.
```

I called him, which hadn't been part of my plan, and before he managed to say *hola* I started quickly with "I'm sorry but it's over." I kept my eyes closed and by doing so I could almost pretend none of this was real – I wasn't breaking up with Hugo, it was only a bad dream. It took me a while before he believed that it had nothing to do with Henry. "Really? Are you getting back together with the guy who treated you so badly?" he asked in disbelief.

I replied shouting, "Of course not!" I was too embarrassed to admit that it was exactly what I was doing. Finally, out of pure desperation I said, "Look Hugo, I've been promoted after writing the article about Madrid, Barcelona and Avignon."

"I'm glad I could help. Good luck then," he said dryly and it was the last thing I heard from him. He didn't let me say goodbye and he had a damn good reason for not doing so.

I thought that it would be easier for him to forget about the bad-Olivia than about the good one albeit who had some significant problems and was very confused. It worked. He hadn't called me since then. *Nada!*

I suddenly jumped on my beige coat spilling a bit of hot chocolate on it. The lift, which I was sitting next to, had made a similar sound an hour ago. However, it was a false alarm that again only caused my heart to race. Somebody got out on the floor below. I was camping on the top floor, where there was only Hugo's tiny studio and a three-hundred square meter penthouse with a roof terrace. I studied its impressive layout on the fire map hanging just next to the lift.

I didn't call Hugo to say I was planning to visit him because:

(a) I lost the only phone which had his phone number in Lyon,

(b) I was afraid he wouldn't answer or say he was busy.

I called, however, one of the Hugo TorTillas saying I'd had an appointment with Hugo Torilla and I couldn't get through to him. It worked! A head manager said that Hugo had been working from home for a few days and asked me to give them a call on Monday. He also promised to pass on to Hugo my message. I introduced myself as Tiggy Brown, a journalist. He gave me Hugo's work phone number but I had nothing to write it on and I thought that was pointless anyway. I just had to go and see him!

* * *

The hours passed and nobody appeared on the top floor. I imagined Hugo silently approaching his door, peering through the peep-hole and deciding not to leave his studio. My arse had just started aching from sitting on the hard surface for the last two hours when suddenly the door to the penthouse flew open and a tall blonde smiled to me gently saying something so quickly in Spanish I didn't understand half of it. It also didn't help I was very nervous.

"I'm sorry, I just...yyy..."

"Everything all right? If you're waiting for Luciano he's gone on holiday," she switched to English without any effort.

Has he moved out of the studio? I thought anxiously. *Of course! He must have done – his business is doing better and better so he probably got himself a nicer flat! Does she know his new address?*

"Actually, I'm looking for Hugo Torilla."

The blonde sized me up with eyebrows set in a frown. I imagined she was a dog running around to smell my arse to understand who I really was.

"Please come in then," she said gesturing me to get inside with a smile. "Hugo will be at home in the evening. I think he should be back by eight o'clock."

At home? What the hell? Which home? Does he live here? He lives HERE? What?! And who are you? His new girlfriend?

"Please don't take your shoes off," she said when I bent to my trainers wishing I had packed a pair of stilettoes into my bag. "It's not that clean anyway."

I glanced at the black and white chequered tiles in the hallway – I couldn't see a spot of dust, a crumb or a single hair. *I bet you've got a cleaner otherwise you wouldn't want to waste your work!* The hall was the size of a decent bedroom or a standard lounge in England – in the middle there was a white shining piano and wide wooden stairs – everything was so shiny as if somebody had just polished it. The woman asked me to follow her inside. She was wearing tight grey jeans and a simple white T-shirt and she looked like a top model. I wonder whether her lightly tanned and perfectly smooth face didn't have a gram of make-up on or whether she had some expensive and difficult to detect foundation. I wasn't into women but she was a head-turner. We walked through the hallway and a huge living room – full of carboard boxes, all with the name of the same removal company – to finally get to the kitchen. The mysterious girl pointed to four bar chairs alongside an island with a granite worktop. The kitchen with long white glass cabinets was a mixture of modern and traditional and was bigger than the whole studio where I had expected to see Hugo. *Exactly, where is Hugo? What's going on?*

"Sorry, I haven't even introduced myself. My name is Olivia Eliot."

"Paulina de la Fuente," she said and rapidly approached me to squeeze my hand. I felt a flow of heat going down my spine. I got a bit dizzy and I had to sit down.

"Everything okay? You don't feel well?" she asked with concern. "I'm sorry, our air-conditioning isn't working in every room. They should fix it tomorrow."

"I'm absolutely fine. I just felt a little bit dizzy," I said while automatically putting my right hand on my lightly rounded belly and the left on my lower back.

"You're pregnant!" she exclaimed happily as if I'd been her bestie and she just heard the big news.

"I'm… yyy…"

"I'm so sorry, it was rude of me. I shouldn't have—"

"It's fine. It's the third month so I can talk about it now," I forced myself to smile. "I've got used to hiding it so much that I still find it difficult to talk about," I lied.

"I totally understand," she said adjusting her long straight ponytail. "My friend Gabriella had to recently go through something similar. Now she's five months pregnant. She kept drinking water with ice and pretending it was vodka! She even faked on a couple of occasions being tipsy. I was impressed," she said and we laughed like two old friends.

"I haven't faked being drunk. I've never really been drunk my entire life so people would probably find it very suspicious. I've claimed, however, on a few occasions that my cranberry juice was a Cosmopolitan."

Paulina gave me a warm smile, "Oh, I can't wait to become an auntie. Gabriela will have a girl, I would love to have a little girl," she said looking across her large stylish kitchen, suddenly turning to me again, "Do you know what you're having?"

"I don't know yet," I lied to cut the topic that was starting to annoy me.

"I mean it actually doesn't matter whether it's a boy or a girl. I'm glad I'll be able to get some experience with children before I've got my own kids," she said beaming.

I bet you've got veneers. Please, stop showing them off, I thought putting my lips into a smile. *I've had enough of the chit-chat, I'm going!* I looked at my watch, it was seven twenty. *Perfect! If I go now, the chances of bumping into Hugo are small. In fact, I'll go by the stairs...*

"I think I'd better—"

"Are you meeting Hugo for business?" she asked, looking very convinced that could be the case.

"Oh sorry, I should've told you why I'm here but I was sure Hugo would've done anyway," I said nicely switching off Paulina's annoying smile.

That was the first time she looked at me suspiciously. "He's probably mentioned something but I've recently been so busy with the move that I must have forgotten," the effortless smile was back on her face as if it was glued to it.

"I work for a travel magazine in London and I'm going to write an article about Hugo TorTillas."

"That's wonderful!" she clapped her hands.

Suddenly something clicked in me and I decided to stay a few minutes longer to interview her before Hugo got back.

"My photographer would also like to take a couple of photos of Hugo but you're also very welcome to take part in the photo session. In fact, a family photo would be ideal, are you married?" I felt somebody was suffocating me when I was saying the word *married.*

"I'm not his wife," she said happily.

Thank you heaven!

"Oh, sorry I thought—"

"We're engaged and currently looking for a venue for our wedding," she squeaked and almost jumped. "Sorry, it's just so exciting."

My whole body screamed on the inside leaving me almost breathless.

"That's wonderful!" I exclaimed too loudly, hoping that her engagement was as true and relevant as mine to Henry! "How did he propose? I love such romantic stories." I probably sounded fake but it didn't matter. She thought I was just a journalist who wanted to get some juicy details from Hugo's private life.

"It happened two weeks ago. Hugo got us a surprise trip to Lanzarote..." I must've looked a bit funny as she added quickly, "one of the Canary Islands. He rented a yacht in the local marina and proposed to me there after our dinner, which he cooked all by himself," her cheeks looked red hot and I took some pleasure in imagining her as a poor village woman working hard milking her cows. "We only spent the weekend there but we plan to sail around the Canary Islands during our honeymoon."

How dare you steal my dreams?

"How lovely. So romantic!" I exclaimed joyfully.

"I wake up every single day feeling so lucky and I wish every woman in the world to feel the same..."

I know how you can do it! Give him back to me! I thought feeling lonely and pathetic.

"That's wonderful, truly wonderful."

"Hugo is so romantic and creative," she said proudly. "*Amigo, habla conmigo* is a great example. Initially, I was afraid it was a risky business but it's been less than a year and Hugo has already paid off the loan."

"I thought that his step father financed the venture."

Paulina hesitated for a moment as if she had been caught on a lie or lack of knowledge. "It's true but only for one of the Hugo TorTillas, not all four of them... I'm sorry I haven't offered you anything to drink, it's so rude of me. I've got some non-alcoholic wine—"

"Water would be great. Thank you."

"Sparkling or still? Lemon, lime or maybe both? Would you like some ice?"

Too many questions... but do I want to know all the answers or should I leave?

"Still with ice and lemon please."

A few ice cubes fell down from a fridge ice dispenser into a beautiful cut glass tumbler. "The glasses are our engagement gift from our close friends," she said without looking at me, saving me a forced smile for later. Then she reached for a glass bottle of water from the fridge – the bottle was rectangular and light blue. *Even water needs to be extraordinary here!*

She passed me the glass and despite being thirsty I only took one slow sip.

"I'm sorry. I must sound so boring but I'm just so happy right now and I struggle not to share it with the whole world... Oh, I've forgotten the lemon!" Before I managed to say that it was okay she started slicing a perfectly oval and yellow lemon.

I was watching her carefully for a few seconds. No wonder Hugo was back to her. I'd always been slim but Paulina had the body of a fitness instructor. Hugo had mentioned once that she was very successful in her job. Besides she had an amazing smile and she was just so bloody nice! The only question was – was she real?

"I'm sorry for the mess," she said when we were sitting comfortably on her large white L-shaped sofa on the balcony of her penthouse. "I'm trying to unpack, work full-time and organise the wedding. My life is complete chaos," she laughed. "Hugo is right we need to look for a wedding organiser and find a housekeeper."

"If you knew what chaos my life is," I said laughing and for the first time it was a genuine laugh – a laugh of despair – I felt like weeping and laughing interchangeably.

"Would you like to talk about it?" she asked seriously and for a moment I forgot that we weren't meant to be friends – now or ever.

"I'm also trying to organise my wedding before I get so fat that somebody will have to roll me to the altar!" I said seriously and we burst out laughing but quickly became silent to admire another stunning sunset over Madrid. I was trying to stop thinking about all of the sunrises and sunsets that I'd spent with Hugo, while Paulina seemed to be entirely immersing herself with dreams about her future life with him.

"I get it," she said all of a sudden. We also want to get married as soon as possible. Hugo proposed to me after being together six years and I can't really wait any longer," she laughed. "I want to have at least two children..." she was talking but I'd stopped listening. I couldn't focus on her words when so many other thoughts were flooding my more and more confused head. *Has Hugo been lying to both of us about his feelings? Did he even break up with her while he was with me? But who am I to judge? I'm not any better than him!*

"Madrid is amazing, especially the area where you live. I'm jealous about this view you've got," I said. *The view and at least a couple of other things!* "Where did you live before?"

"I moved here a few years ago but…" she hesitated and I could see genuine pain in her eyes, "I decided to leave for a few months."

"You packed quite a few things for a few months," I said and immediately regretted it – it wasn't her fault I wanted her fiancé, but nobody could blame me either for wanting him so badly, he was a one in a million type of guy – although completely aware of it and using it to his advantage.

Paulina seemed to be encouraged by my remarks, "We argued just after our friends' wedding. Gabriela and Fernando had an amazing party on Fuerteventura. I got a bit tipsy and while we were dancing I asked him whether we would ever get married.

"He wasn't ready?" I asked thinking, Just like Henry!

"Something like that so I concluded that I wasn't the one! Come on! Is six years not enough to know?" she looked at me and I nodded with understanding. "So I asked him for a break."

"And you packed all your things! You didn't want him to think you were just bluffing."

"Exactly! I went for three months to India. For the first six weeks I didn't use any phone and spent most of my time doing yoga and meditation."

I sighed, "I wish I'd done that myself when I still could. It's just what I needed when I broke up with my fiancé."

"But you're happy now? Enough to want to marry him?" she asked with concern. Was she trying to dissuade me from spending the rest of my life with Henry? "I know you're pregnant but—"

"Oh no, it's not because of that. We got back together before I found out I was pregnant."

"Oh, that's really good," she said but I knew she didn't believe me for a minute. "You should try meditation anyway. I'm sure you'll find some good classes in London, and when the baby is a bit older you could take a few days for yourself and go for a little trip. I don't mean India but—"

"Sure. It's a great idea," I said joyfully but I could see she wasn't buying it, she knew something was wrong with my relationship. "So how did Hugo manage to convince you to go back to him?"

"Well…" she started blushing, "he got on a plane to India in July." I found it hard to swallow, something was suffocating me. He didn't bother to fly to London to try to convince me to take that trip around the world with him because he was on his way to India. "He explained that it wasn't me but him. He said he found it hard to believe in marriage after his parents got divorced. He was afraid that marriage could destroy something between us but when I left and he realised he could have lost me he decided to go and see a therapist…"

I bet I was his bloody therapy! He would've chosen her anyway! I must've been delusional thinking he only wanted to respect my decision and would be waiting for me. Sometimes I wanted him so badly to stand in my door, while all that time he was pulling himself together to be ready to stand in her door. She's the type you don't give up on so easily!

"Would you like something to eat?" she suggested just when I heard the sound of a key turning in the lock. I held my breath.

"It must be Hugo. I'll let him know we've got a guest," she said and before I managed to make a sound she was gone.

* * *

I jumped up from the sofa to look out from the glass balustrade at the street below. It was way too high to jump. I felt so desperate that if there had been another balcony below I would've probably tried to get there. *There's no way out*, I was thinking, looking down at the wide tree-lined street. I saw a man in a dark suit. He was walking fast and talking into a mike on his headphones – he looked like he was talking to himself. Then he suddenly elbowed a young guy in jeans and a grey hoodie who was innocently strolling along with his arm embracing his ginger girlfriend. The guy got irritated and screamed that he should've at least said sorry but the man in the suit ignored him. Suddenly I had an idea. I called my friend.

"Hannah, I'll explain later but can you please call me as soon as I put the phone down and keep calling me until I answer?" She agreed but sounded totally baffled.

Hannah did what I asked and within a couple of seconds I heard some heavy footsteps moving on the tiled entrance hall and then across the wooden floored lounge; my phone was vibrating and playing some loud rock music while my heart was bumping like mad. I grabbed the phone while standing with my back to the terrace door. "Really? You've got to be kidding me. Are you sure?" I was almost shouting while Hannah was calmly asking me to call her again later and explain everything. She was also saying Henry was torturing her with phone calls and messages and if I didn't come back soon, she would have no choice but to accuse him of stalking her. "Does it have to be now? Right, I'll be there soon," I kept talking loudly as though I was trying to sell something at a market – *two melons for two pounds!* I began pacing through the lounge trying not to look up when I walked straight into a wide male chest. My phone hit the wooden floor and made an unexpectedly loud noise. Then followed an uncomfortable silence before I slowly raised my eyes up in terror.

"Olivia, it's Luciano. He's back earlier from his holidays and came to fix our air-conditioning.

Luciano said *hola* and threw himself on the floor to collect his tools that I'd pushed out of his hands by bumping into him. My phone was fine, just its cheap plastic cover was cracked in two places. As I picked it up, it immediately began to play the same annoying ring tone. I could always count on Hannah.

"So Luciano lives in the studio opposite your penthouse?" I asked Paulina when her personal handyman was gone to fix things around her royal apartment.

"He does. Hugo offered him his old office space when Luciano was struggling to find anything cheap to rent in the area, and we needed somebody close to look after the house as we're away quite a lot. Why did you think Hugo lived there?"

I glanced at my watch pretending I didn't hear her. "I'm really sorry but my boss has just called and I need to get back to my hotel to send her something that I've only got on my laptop. I'll call Hugo soon!"

"I'm really sorry he's late today. It must've been something important because he hasn't even texted me yet."

"No problem. It was very nice to meet you."

Paulina was standing in her double entrance door – probably wider than my garage door – waiting for me to disappear into the lift. I planned to get out on the first floor and use the stairs in case Hugo wasn't coming back home that late after all.

It *turned out to be A Little Crisis in Hugo's relationship, his therapy, a break*, I was thinking while walking out onto the street to get wherever my feet took me. I walked for a while before it even crossed my mind I didn't know what time it was, but I decided against checking my watch – it wouldn't have made any difference. *Who cares? It's definitely not an hour I want to remember!* I didn't even feel like crying. I felt nothing and I somehow enjoyed the kind of stupor and ambivalence – it was totally new for me not to be too emotional.

"Señora, don't wipe the pavements with your beautiful coat," an old lady in a housecoat was looking at me impatiently. Her white terrier was also staring at me with a certain anticipation, putting his head to the left, to the right and to the left again.

I suddenly looked at my dirty designer coat that reminded me of a well-used cloth. The lady wasn't going to leave me alone until I stopped dragging my coat on the pavement and moved it up my arm. I did it but it felt like a lot of effort.

"Thank you. I mean Gracias," I said.

"Do you need something?" she continued in Spanish. "Have you got lost?"

"Everything's fine," I said in an anaemic voice.

"Don't think about him. Don't be preoccupied with a man, who's obviously not worth you."

I thought there were a lot of don'ts coming from a woman who had just seen me for the very first time in her life, "Who do you mean?"

"The man you're thinking about," she answered with such certainty that I thought for a moment I'd stumbled across a fortune-teller, a psychic, a ghost or worse – was she just my imagination?

"I'm not thinking about any men," I lied.

"You won't deceive me darling. I'm too old not to recognise a broken heart," she said making me smile. "Let yourself cry for a little while."

"Sorry, my Spanish is not very good – are you saying that I should cry?"

"Of course. You need to get it all out to make space for all the new good feelings, for a new man in your life. You need to cry and mourn because nobody will do it for you. Nobody will ever feel sorry for a young beautiful woman."

"You do," I said flippantly.

"I don't," she snapped, "you're too young and beautiful to feel sorry for," she exclaimed raising her leash-free hand and we both laughed. Her little white terrier in his red coat barked and waved his tail for goodbye.

Late in the evening I ordered some take-away Spanish tapas from the place that Cristiano had recommended and I locked myself in the room to have a little feast for my belly and allow Beautiful-and-young Me to feel sorry for myself – as the old lady with the dog had ordered.

Hope is like GPS – most of the time it proves to be very useful but sometimes it takes us off a cliff or straight into a river. I had an irresistible feeling that my Hope was screaming for me to end up somewhere I didn't really want to be. There was no perfect news out there for me anymore. Even if Hugo was the father, he obviously didn't want to have a family with me, he'd already made his choice. That didn't stop me from fantasising about him calling me as soon as Paulina told him I came to visit. I wasn't able to fully immerse myself in my sadness and cry everything out because I couldn't convince myself it was all over. *Maybe he doesn't want to call me when Paulina is around. He'll probably call me when she's deep asleep or... Or he does it first thing in the morning when he leaves the house. He could get out on the stair-case I suppose or give me a ring from the lift – I bet their lift has reception... but he might consider it too risky. What if he can't get through because he only tries the pay-as-you-go phone I lost in Lyon? He still should have the phone number I gave him during our first night in Madrid, it's not like I asked him to burn it – it's probably still somewhere among his contacts – maybe he's saved me as OliviER Eliot so as not to instil Paulina's suspicions. But just in case I need to unblock my Facebook account... Paulina must've told him I was pregnant. Maybe he needs some time to think... or maybe... maybe he just doesn't give a fuck about you Olivia!*

There was still Henry and we were still technically engaged but it was becoming more and more apparent that Mr Safe Harbour was a cover for Mr Shady Business. I also didn't believe that Henry would like to raise a couple of children who weren't biologically his. He would stick with me trying to convince me about his love as long as there was hope the children might be his.

25

THURSDAY, 8 OCTOBER
LONDON

"Olivia, have you found it? We'll miss our train," Meg was shouting from the hallway while I was nervously searching the house for my company's tablet.

"I'm starting to think I lost it on the train last night," I screamed from the staircase getting shivers, imagining how angry Tiggy would be if it turned out to be the truth. She would have yet more proof that I should have been fired a long while ago. Sometimes I was convinced she had a little black book with my name at the front where she diligently collected all my sins – writing each one out in detail with a massive grin on her face.

"I've got it! Come to the kitchen and look!"

I would run but in my current state I was afraid of slipping on the stairs so I moved cautiously downstairs.

"Who put it in the fridge?" I asked surprised.

"You!" Meg laughed. "You did the same last week with the remote control."

"Did I?" I asked rhetorically because I'd just reminded myself about doing that. I didn't know whether my absent-mindedness was caused by the pregnancy, but if so I was doing pretty well anyway avoiding other more unpleasant symptoms like feeling nauseas, dizzy or extremely emotional. I was just walking with my head in the clouds and that was it for the fifth month of my pregnancy. "Hopefully it's fine," I murmured and quickly typed in my password.

"It looks like it's all good, the cover kept him warm," Meg said cheerfully and we moved to the hallway to get our autumn coats and shoes. All of my jackets had started being too tight except one designer buggy orange coat that I'd hunted down during a sale and at the time was two sizes too big. I love the colour and it was a great bargain. "Hmm... It still fits me. All women should have one emergency coat that is a bit too big for them just in case—"

"Just in case they get unexpectedly pregnant with twins?" Meg laughed.

"Something like that... or just very bloated" I said while opening the door and feeling on my face a sudden blast of cold air. "Brrr... All I feel like doing right now is jumping into my new cosy pyjamas and getting under a warm blanket to sip hot chocolate and read a chick lit."

"And that's not what you do for most of your days now?" she asked with a hint of accusation in her voice.

Meg was right, since Tiggy had let me work three days a week from home I'd been spending a lot of time under a warm blanket with a large mug of orange hot chocolate in one hand and a chick lit or remote control in the other. Often, I started my work in the afternoon as I found it hard to motivate myself to do anything requiring much effort before midday. I still had many deadlines to meet but I didn't have to be constantly available on my phone or email. Besides, I liked the idea of spending long autumn evenings doing some work. It prevented me from obsessing about my future or spying on Henry. The very same Henry, who seemed to be worried about me, and who had encouraged me to persuade Tiggy to let me work from home. In my wildest dreams I wouldn't have come up with such an idea on my own.

"Why don't you just ask her? She's pregnant herself, she should understand," said Henry when once again I was trying to justify my gloomy mood through tiredness from a relentless London commute. He had no idea about my little visit to Madrid and I wanted it to stay that way.

"She'll just laugh at me," I snapped irritated. "But maybe you've got some other friends that owe you a debt of gratitude and who would be eager to employ me?"

"I thought we've moved on from that," he said not even moving his eyes away from the book he was reading on the couch. "No harm in just asking her."

I did what Henry suggested and to my surprise Tiggy instantly agreed. I couldn't work out whether she loved the idea of not seeing me so often or that Henry had participated in the decision by reminding her how much she owed him.

"Olivia..." Meg had said to me the previous night, a stern expression painted all over her face, her eyes set intensely on me. "I'm not so sure whether Henry did you a favour. You don't leave the house except for the two days a week to go to work," she said putting her hands on her hips. "Would you like to go with me to the Home Building and Refurbishing Exhibition tomorrow? I've got two tickets because a friend of mine has to stay at home with her sick child."

"I would love to," I lied, "but I'm working tomorrow. Work from home is still work."

"You don't start till at least midday. You forget how often I've had my lunch at home. Phi! You don't even seem to notice me sometimes!"

What I did notice, however, was that Meg had more and more work in Dream Fields and Haven-on-Thames, since she became fully qualified as an electrician and started training in carpentry. She couldn't have lunch out in her work outfit because the minute she sat down anywhere women kept constantly offering her work. Most of them lived alone or stayed at home with the children. Meg was so busy she got herself a secretary and was thinking about expanding her business by employing other handywomen. I wished her well but in my selfishness I was afraid she would soon move out to live in her own house, probably three times bigger than mine. She wasn't only my excuse for Henry not to move in but she had become a good friend of mine. I was thrilled when she wanted to sign a deal till February. Henry agreed as he seemed to finally understand I needed more time to decide on our future together. We postponed the wedding to an unspecified date after the twins would be born. Henry lived predominantly in the London flat but he spent most weekends in our house. He also travelled a lot to the US so I had all the space I needed. I believed him when he said he had nothing to do with the Cheaters Gang anymore. I believed him because it was easier to live that way and not get overly stressed while expecting my babies.

"Come on Olivia!" Meg looked like she wasn't going to give up anytime soon. "It's going to be fun. You might find out something interesting that proves useful when you want to put an extension on your house. We could also have dinner in the city. You'll miss it after you give birth!"

She convinced me – I knew I wouldn't be able to make such sponta-neous decisions when I had small children – so there I was marching in a perfectly fitting orange coat to catch a train to London for a reason other than seeing Tiggy Brown. Initially I wasn't particularly excited about the exhibition but I thought that spending the day with Meg could be fun. She was full of positive energy that I needed like never before. She was bringing something new and fresh to my group of girlfriends. She taught me how to change a tap washer, kept updating me on building and tech news, and also showed me how much fun computer games could be. We didn't play much but enough to occasionally escape from the worries of everyday life, and give my brain a little break.

I didn't feel like I was a building or property expert but I wasn't a total amateur either. During the last few weeks while I was at home, I had watched enough free TV to educate myself on the major building trends and the current property market. Whenever I switched on TV and flicked through channels, I couldn't avoid programs about building or renovating a house – creating a dream space to live in or maximise selling potential. I watched countless people wanting to buy a property in the UK or overseas – making their cheeky offers and life changing decisions. I watched people who couldn't decide on a villa in the sun that was supposed to be their second home, and those living in a campervan while scraping and saving to finish a house on time before a child was born.

Conveniently the exhibition was aimed to attract both professionals and people interested in DIY projects, so even without any of my TV-knowledge I would have been able to enjoy it and talk freely to the traders without a need to pretend I was a professional. It wasn't long after we got to the London ExCel that I grabbed some free stationery and began making notes about anything I could introduce into my house or a future extension.

We were just admiring the newest hydro massage baths when I heard a familiar voice. I slowly turned back to see a handsome dark-haired man talking in Spanish about a hot tub he wanted to install in his house.

"I thought you're currently not interested in men, or at least you're trying not to be," said Meg in a chastising tone of voice.

"Just looking," I snapped. "I would swear I've seen him before."

"Yeah, I suppose he's a bit similar to Hugo," she nodded now staring at him in a way that her lesbian partner would have found threatening.

"To be fair any dark-haired man speaking Spanish reminds me now of Hugo. I can't help it. Last week I was staring so much at one Spanish guy in a London store that he told me with a beaming smile he was already taken. Can you imagine? So embarrassing," I said and turned on my feet to start walking.

"So arrogant of him," Meg said, disgust painted all over her face.

"Tiggy? Tiggy Brown?" the familiar Spanish voice now made me jump.

Meg looked at me, then at the guy and at me again completely baffled, "Is that not the name of your boss? Maybe she's spying on you to prove that you actually don't WORK from home. From what you've been saying I wouldn't be so surprised and—"

"Not quite," I interrupted Meg with an open palm, thinking, *Please, just shut up because you're making this so much more difficult for me.*

"Nicolas?" I said feeling like my throat was narrowing and that the whole ExCel building was closing in on me. "Meg can you please get me some water? Actually no, I'm fine."

"I tried to call you so we could meet up in London but the number you gave me didn't work."

"I really need to see something in the plumbing section. Give me a call when you finish here," Meg said in such a way I knew what she was thinking – Nicolas was a third candidate for the father of my children. *Oh heaven!*

"I… yyy…"

"Don't worry I get it. You didn't want to see me ever again and that's absolutely fine," he laughed.

Nicolas would have never gotten through to me because I'd given him, totally by mistake, the number to my Hugo phone, which I'd lost. I would have given a lot to be able to talk to him during the last few weeks. I'd regretted so much not taking his number.

"I've got a new number, which I'll give you right now," I reached for the phone in my handbag.

"Seriously Tiggy, it's fine. I also understand if you're in a rush now and—".

"Can I get you some coffee? Please," I looked at him with a begging face because I was convinced he didn't believe me.

"It's nice of you that you don't try to ditch me in person."

"Seriously I—"

"I'll give you the benefit of the doubt. Where do they make the best coffee here?"

"You've changed," I said to Nicolas when we were sitting at a small round table, me drinking a large ginger latte and him slowly sipping a double expresso. "Your face looks so different without the beard."

"I got bored with my lumbersexual image and somebody impor-

298

tant to me, who came with me to London prefers me shaved," he said slightly blushing.

"Who's the lucky one? I can't wait to hear all about it," I took a sip of coffee and rested my chin on my hands.

"I'm sure it's not as interesting as anything that is happening in your life. So, have you told him about the baby? How did he react?" Nicolas straightened in his chair as if he had suddenly remembered about his doctor telling him not to hunch his back.

"I haven't because..." I hesitated and then somebody shouting *Stefano* didn't let me finish. Nicolas turned in his chair and waved with a smile to the Stefano-screaming guy. "Oh, I'd forgotten, Nicolas is not your real name. Well, it's time to tell you that—"

"Tiggy, this is Hugo Torilla," he smiled proudly. Yes, the Hugo Torilla who has—"

"I know what he's got" I snapped. "I just didn't know he's gay!"

Hugo was staring at me still as a statue. I would swear his eyes weren't even blinking.

"Oh no," said Stefano-Nicolas. "He's my brother."

"That's even bloody better," I whispered but both brothers heard me very clearly.

"Hugo..." said Stefano-Nicolas cheerfully, "this is my friend Tiggy Brown, who I've told you about. I mean..." he said looking at me, "not in any detail of course." Neither Hugo nor me made a move. "I'm sorry Tiggy, I should have told you that my brother owned Hugo Tor*Tillas*. And *por supuesto* I didn't tell him all our secrets."

"He told me everything," Hugo said seemingly without any face expression. It was like he was pretending to be a robot or a street mime.

"I didn't," said Stefano high-pitched.

"Tiggy, hmm... very original name," Hugo smirked and sat down on a chair between me and his brother.

Suddenly I was flooded with flashbacks from the last few months – the dinner in Grenada when I was talking to Hugo about Tiggy, my boss-from-hell; the night when Hugo insisted on sitting down next to me in the tapas bar in Madrid or us drinking hot chocolate in the morning on the balcony of the King's Hotel. I could easily imagine myself dropping everything and running away with him to the other side of the world in a heartbeat – wherever it was and whatever it took. *Stop!* I told myself. He played you! *He had never had any intention of being with you. You were only his Break, his Therapy! Don't you forget!* I preferred not to remember because it hurt like a bitch but unfortunately I had to.

"Stefano, as we're friends now I should probably tell you my real name is Olivia Eliot."

"You're friends, how wonderful," Hugo said and smiled in a forced manner that I had never seen before on his face. It wasn't any of the five distinctive Hugo-smiles. "What a relief that my brother prefers *los hombres* so I don't have to worry about what sort of friendship you mean."

"*Oh dios mío!* Hugo, what's the matter with you? I also didn't tell her my real name. She accidentally gave me the wrong phone number, that's why I couldn't get in touch with her. It's not like she tried to avoid me."

"That's not what I mean."

"So you did tell him everything. Stefano, you bloody gossip girl! Why would you talk to him about me? I thought that the whole point of *Amigo, habla conmigo* is to keep secrets!"

"But he didn't know your real name. Actually, the whole time I called you the English Girl. I used Tiggy maybe once. It's not like you're a celebrity or you knew each other before. I just talked to him about a complete stranger... a completely random girl!"

I slightly pushed myself back from the table to bend down and pick up a plastic lid from my coffee that I'd dropped on the floor when I was nervously fiddling with it. I put the lid back on the table feeling two pairs of eyes on me. Hugo was staring at the place where my rounded belly was pushing against the small white table. "Stefano this is Olivia Eliot, the friend of mine I've told you about recently – and as it has just turned out the one who shares some characteristics with our mother," he said emotionlessly and leant back on his chair with his eyes set on the ceiling and hands on his forehead.

"Fuck! Oh fuck, fuck!"

"Stefano, we're in England – the word *fuck* here is much stronger than in Spain," I said feeling stupid but I really had no idea what to say.

"Tell me Olivia, did you dump me because you thought I wouldn't be good enough as a father? You didn't want a guy living in a studio apartment and starting a risky business to bring up your child?" he said calmly but with a certain disdain that I hadn't seen before on his face. I would have much preferred him to be angry. Instead, he treated me like an employee he wanted to fire but didn't have enough evidence on, or a neighbour whom he tried to avoid but annoyingly kept bumping into at every corner.

Except for his face expression Hugo looked exactly the same as when I last saw him. He hadn't grown a beard or moustache, he hadn't shaved his head or let his bushy dark hair grow unrestricted until it met his shoulders. His stomach was as flat as it used to be. He hadn't started wearing tight T-shirts or too loose hoodies. Even his light tan seemed to be the same as when we got back from Grenada – but of course he and Paulina had had a chance to catch some sun in the Canaries and god knows where else he had also been with her. In contrast to him, I hadn't forgotten about his existence – but I'd been slowly adjusting to the idea of not having him in my life. I was getting gradually better at it or at least I thought I was but when I saw him *Operation Forgetting Hugo* was gone with the wind.

"I was afraid to tell you the truth."

"So much you preferred somebody else to bring up my child?"

Your childREN actually but no need to mention that part just yet!

"Of course I would tell you if the DNA tests showed you were the father but I need to wait with the test till I give birth."

"And it didn't even cross your mind that while having no idea about your pregnancy I haven't put my life on hold to wait for some ground-breaking news from you?" Now Hugo sounded angry. "News that would completely turn my whole life upside down."

"It did but it was probably too late," I said thinking about the day I met Paulina. "I didn't tell you because I was afraid that you wouldn't be able to look at me the same way. I wouldn't be the girl you'd want to be with but the girl you'd feel obligated to "

The truth is I didn't tell you because I was terrified you would give me hope of a family with you and then drop me like a stone when you found out that the children weren't yours and I wouldn't even be able to blame you for that.

"I wouldn't have rushed into marrying you because you're the mother of my child if that's what you mean," he interrupted me.

"Thank you for being so considerate," I snapped.

"Yeah, your proposal would really hurt her feelings. Totally unacceptable reaction to the whole situation," said Stefano-Nicolas and for a brief moment I felt he might have been on my side.

"That's fine because I wouldn't dream about marrying her now."

PART TWO

2016

'It is never too late to be what you might have been'

George Eliot

26

THURSDAY, 11 FEBRUARY

OXFORD

I'd always been convinced that the day I gave birth would have been similar to what I'd seen in American movies. I'd been imagining how I would have been chatting to my husband, a work colleague or a shop assistant when suddenly I would have looked at a puddle under my legs and scream "my waters broke!" From that moment everything speeds up. I immediately forget what I've been talking or arguing about. Somebody helps me to get into a taxi that moves with a squeak of its tyres. We drive fast overtaking many other cars, jumping curbs and not stopping at any lights. We might even be chased by the police, who eventually give us a fine but not until my fast and furious taxi driver stops in front of the hospital. As we drive like maniacs I'm screaming at the top of my lungs from pain, the driver is also screaming but for me not to give birth in his car and mess up his new upholstery. In hospital somebody is taking me in a wheelchair to reception where – here the script slightly changes because I'm in the UK, not in the USA, so the receptionist doesn't ask me for my insurance details, but instead asks me to take a seat and wait without saying for how long, she also kindly offers me paracetamol. I decline the paracetamol as I know punching somebody on the face would dull the pain more. It's the UK so when I finally get examined they say I'm not sufficiently dilated and they kindly suggest I should go home, get comfy under my duvet, run myself a bath and watch TV. I decline as it's hard to watch anything with three minutes between contractions that make you see the world through a kind of mist – I based this on Freya's experience. Then before going into the delivery room a doctor asks my husband, who was with me for the whole time or has just landed in his helicopter on the roof of the hospital, whether he would like to stay with me throughout. If it's Henry we simultaneously say *no* because we both know that it would end up with Henry passing out or even passing away from a heart attack and as always making the whole event about himself! If it's Hugo, he immediately says *yes* and I immediately say *no* because I don't want him to see me as I curse the entire world. But he stays with me anyway and I do curse the entire world but only for five minutes – because that is how long I need to push. After five minutes it's only my beautiful babies who scream, not understanding why they got evicted from their little cosy home.

And then life happens and nothing is like I have ever imagined. My water didn't break and nobody was speeding so I wouldn't give birth in the back seat of their car. My Caesarean was planned on the twelfth of February and I checked into hospital the day before. The whole adventure began with a male receptionist, with sleek dark hair and a bulky Rolex, asking me for my credit card as I was in one of the best private hospitals in the country. Hugo had driven me slowly to Oxford and stayed in a hotel nearby, my parents and Philip with Veronica were planning on being there as well for my *Delivery Day*. I had a private room with a second bed for somebody to stay with me the night before and after the birth. I asked Hannah to be with me the first night.

It was almost four o'clock in the afternoon when Hannah and I were drinking camomile tea, me sitting under a heavenly soft duvet and silky bedding and Hannah on a green chair with her legs up on a matching green foot stool. I put the blinds up to have an amazing view of Oxford covered in snow. The hospital was on a hill and the whole city was spread in front of us.

"Thank you for staying with me tonight," I said.

"Are you kidding? It's a pleasure! I feel like I'm in a five-star hotel and I wouldn't miss the chance for a girls' night!" she laughed.

"Except we've got two boys with us and I bet they're listening to everything that we're saying… When you open the funky red fridge in the corner you won't see a range of small bottles of booze but three types of mineral water. Oh, and the cupboard next to the fridge is full of different nappies and several types of organic formula."

"Then I feel like home," said Hannah who had only given birth to her son Nicolas on the sixth of December. She also had to have a C-section but it was in a private clinic in London and she had her husband with her the whole time. "Did you even have to think about buying anything or does the hospital provide you with everything?"

"They provide everything that a baby needs in the first few days of their life. Wet wipes, sleeping bag, sleepsuits in three different sizes. I had to pack only a few of my things but they even offered to shop for me."

"Oscar would never pay for such a luxurious package," Hannah pretended to be angry – we both thought the luxurious package was overpriced and really unnecessary but still a nice touch.

"Well, at least he was with you the whole time," I said looking out of the window.

"I'm sorry Henry couldn't get back in time, but on the bright side you've got me and I know I'm dream company!" she giggled. "And you've got a very hot guy in the hotel, less than five minutes away from here."

Hannah was totally enchanted by Hugo, if not smitten, as were all the nurses who had a chance to see him. One of them tried to dig deeper into what form our relationship was. I didn't wear the engagement ring of Henry's grandmother. Sadly, it had to be cut off my finger when pregnancy expanded my fingers into two sets of sausages. I went to the first jewellers I found on the high street in Haven-on-Thames. They did warn me the main jeweller wasn't in, it would have to be an apprentice but I didn't care – the ring was painfully digging into my finger making me hate it even more. As a result of the cutting, the ring lost its stone and re-fitting it would be so expensive I bet Henry wouldn't be keen to spend so much money in the foreseeable future, a small win.

"How's your Internet?" I asked. "My phone is so slow today."

"Let me see," Hannah reached for her handbag. "Tell me you're not going to search for anything C-section related."

"I would like to check the weather in New York. I've heard on the radio today that it isn't snowing there anymore and all airports have already re-opened."

"Darling…" she looked at me with mercy, "even if all the airports are now open it doesn't mean Henry will be able to get a flight tomorrow. Many other people will be desperate to get out of the city at the same time," while she was explaining all that she was actually just verbalising my own thoughts.

Hannah was right but Henry could have tried harder or maybe drive to a different city to fly from there. He had found out about my C-section two weeks ago and he still decided not to change his flight, which meant he would be back at the very last minute, on the tenth of February. He insisted that New York wasn't as far away as Australia and even if for some reason he missed his plane on the tenth, he would definitely be able to get back by the twelfth. I also didn't try too hard to change his mind because Hugo had no intention of missing my *Labour Day*, and the three of us could well create our own Bermuda Triangle, where somebody goes missing without a trace.

Henry was becoming more and more irritated with me for keeping in touch with Hugo. It also didn't help that Hugo was engaged, that he was only interested if they were his children and he'd never forgiven me for the way he found out about my pregnancy. The truth was I had no idea whether Hugo had forgiven me or not. We hadn't talked about it since the building exhibition in London. I didn't often talk about Henry and I appreciated he tried not to mention Paulina too much. We didn't even talk about Hugo potentially becoming a father. Although most people couldn't believe it, he behaved like an old good friend. We talked once or twice a week on the phone to chat about our jobs, global issues and complain about the weather and traffic jams.

We didn't have a problem with conversation, which at times got pretty abstract like how big my goldfish would grow in the wild. The week before I went into hospital we had a vivid hour of conversation about the global warming impact of cow farts and the benefits of becoming vegan.

"Cows aren't particularly pretty or cuddly so do you think you'll only see them in a zoo some day?" I asked.

"Possibly," Hugo said and paused, "although I know people who would die for a good steak so it might not happen anytime soon."

On other occasions when I couldn't sleep because of my new shape and size or some thoughts disturbed my rest, I would call Hugo and he would read me a book in Spanish or try to summarize the one he was reading.

* * *

"Are you sleeping?" I whispered to Hannah at midnight without much hope she would reply. It was her first night without her baby waking her up every couple of hours.

"Annoyingly, I also can't fall asleep," she whispered and got out of her bed to sit in her big pink dressing gown next to me on the green armchair.

"Please distract me with a story, the weirder the better. I don't want to think about tomorrow's surgery or the results of the DNA tests. I can't wait to see my boys, but I'm also freaking out."

"The good news is you'll know who the father is within the next few days. The nightmare of not knowing will be over."

"Have you ever regretted that you didn't do a DNA test while you were pregnant?"

"Nope. It's considered to be relatively safe but it's still not worth it."

"True," I sighed. "After I met Paulina I knew that there was no ideal solution anymore."

"Oh, I've got one," she said all of a sudden.

"You've got what?"

"I've got an interesting story for you. Although it might make you think about Hugo and Henry."

"Well, it's still better than thinking about a C-section!"

"I've told you Nicolas' father is Oscar, right?"

"Oh my god! You faked the results! How did you manage to do it? Hannah, why?" I didn't know whether I was more impressed or disappointed with my friend. *Maybe you could do it for me if necessary, hmm?*

"Do you really think I could do something like that? Oscar is his father and he's a good father. He plans to take three months of paternity leave. I know, I would never think—"

"I'm so happy for you Hannah, and also for Zoe who will finally have her father around."

"Zoe… hmmm… she's the subject of my story actually…"

"You're kidding me… I mean… I don't want to accuse you of something again…"

"It's not what you think."

"So you're not such a floozie after all," I said and immediately regretted my silly joke when I saw Hannah's face expression.

"Speak for yourself Miss Mother Theresa! Actually, my story is a bit similar to yours…"

I bet it's not at all. "Okay, I'm listening."

Hannah took a deep breath, "The story begins with the day I accidentally discovered that Oscar's mother faked my signature, which she needed to validate our prenup. It happened a few weeks before our first wedding anniversary."

"Damn her! She's a real mother-in-law from hell… but hold on a minute, did she also fake Oscar's signature or he—"

"She didn't have to do it," Hannah set her sad eyes on the wooden floor of the hospital bedroom. I could see it still hurt her.

"What a cunning pig or… or rather what a nasty pig and her nasty little piglet!"

"I couldn't phrase it any better," Hannah laughed bitterly. "I thought exactly the same or worse but let's not swear around children. When I found out I immediately packed my bags and drove to my parents."

I nodded with understanding, "But how did you find out about the prenup? And more importantly, why are you two still together?"

"Oscar's mother is a famous judge, and his father is a prosecutor. They're really wealthy people, who not completely without reason have been obsessed that somebody would try to marry into their family to boost their material status. Apparently, it almost happened once but it was a while ago and not important now. How did I find out? We were at Oscar's father's birthday party. Brits struggle with an abundance of free booze, don't they? Some guy ended up in a pool in a white outfit exposing his red thong. Even Johanna got drunk and she never drinks. She's always on her antibiotics, or driving or breast-feeding or not in the right mood—"

"Who's Johanna?" I interrupted her conscious that we didn't have the whole night for the story, sooner or later I needed some sleep.

"Weird, I thought I've already mentioned her. Anyway, she's the wife of Oscar's brother, the older one. So, where was I?"

"At the birthday party with all the drunk people," I said impatiently.

"Most of the guests were socializing in the massive living room of their enormous summer house in Cornwall. I went outside with Johanna to get some air and have a stroll in the garden from which we had an incredible view of the black sea with the only light being a perfectly round moon and a small lighthouse. I had a glass of red wine and I felt wonderful. I was breathing in the fresh sea air – the mixture of salt, fish and wet sand… I almost regretted I hadn't left the house alone because drunk Johanna kept complaining about her husband and destroying the moment. She repeated the same sentences over and over again without realising she had already said it. I got bored and was just about to suggest going inside when she said, 'I can't even get the divorce because I agreed to sign the fucking prenup'. I asked why she would ever have signed one, realising quickly it was completely unnecessary as she had already done it and my comment would only make her more upset and feel even more stupid. But she wasn't upset, she was angry and said something I wasn't expecting at all, 'Why did you sign your prenup?'"

"You signed a prenup?" I asked shocked not remembering Hannah ever telling me that.

She rolled her eyes and gasped, "Of course not but Johanna was adamant she saw one on my mother-in-law's desk when she was snooping around at the party. She said it was signed by both Oscar and me."

"He preferred to fake your signature to avoid a confrontation," I said. "You would have never found out unless you wanted a divorce and then his mother would have been right!"

"I couldn't believe he would do something like that to me. He said something once about a prenup but seeing my astonished faced he quickly recovered the situation by saying it was only his mother's stupid idea and he would never ask me to sign one. When Johanna inevitably disappeared somewhere in the garden's bushes to throw up, I stormed inside the house to confront Oscar."

"In front of everybody?" I gasped.

"No, I asked him calmly to go with me outside. He didn't even try to deny it but the fact I had found out took him completely by surprise. I left him astonished under a tree. He didn't even try to chase me. Later he would tell me that he didn't want to make a scene at his father's birthday. I packed my bags and took a taxi to my parents who live in Bath. Over four hours of driving on a night tariff – I could have flown to Singapore for the money I paid but then I just didn't care. I used Oscar's credit card. I thought it was my last present from him before we would get divorced and in accordance with the false prenup I would be left with nothing."

"But then you discovered you were pregnant and went back to him?" I asked although Hannah ignored my question.

"I hadn't talked to Oscar for almost two months and I filed for separation. When my neighbour called me saying that Oscar went for a business trip I went back and packed most of my things to take them to Bath, where I lived with my parents and spent most of my time with Tony."

"Who's Tony?" I exclaimed so loud that a nurse knocked on our door to check whether everything was all right. She advised us to go to sleep, I felt like I was on a school trip.

"My best friend from childhood who lived on the same street as my family. We used to walk to school together and make cakes with his mum. To the surprise of many, one day he just grew from a primary school sweet little doughnut into a high school cutie, who later became an even more attractive man. We started going out in high school and my parents were okay with that until..." she paused for a moment looking angry, "until I told them that Tony wasn't going to university because he wanted to become a chef. The more they tried to convince me he wasn't an appropriate match, the more I felt I wanted to marry him. Unfortunately, the aversion of my parents to Tony quickly changed into Tony's parents' aversion to my parents and even towards me.

"Sometimes love is not enough," I nodded. "Your parents destroyed your relationship?"

"Not immediately. We both moved to London but we couldn't live together. My parents would never pay for my flat if I lived there with Tony, and we couldn't afford to rent in the city without their help. I studied law and had barely time for anything else than law school, sleeping and eating. Tony was also working hard to earn a place at a prestigious culinary school in France. We thought our love would survive everything but our families dislike of each other plus the distance and our busy schedules eventually put an end to our relationship. By the end we started arguing a lot about the smallest and the most irrelevant things, on reflection it was like we were desperately searching for an excuse to break up. I then met Oscar, Tony also started seeing somebody in Paris and well... *C'est la vie!*" she sighed.

"But you met him again when you left Oscar."

She nodded, "And it was the first time since we broke up, during one rainy weekend in London when Tony came back to England for Christmas... In Bath I spent a week with my parents but then I quickly realised I also needed a break from them. My mother was angry with my father that he had become obsessed about me marrying a guy with a prestigious job. I kept blaming them both for destroying my love with Tony – deep in my heart I knew it wasn't really them but I needed to blame somebody but me. I remember screaming out to them, while I was packing my bags, 'You've got what you wanted. I married a lawyer and guess what he turned out to be an arsehole who lies even outside of the court room!'"

"I guess the pregnant hormones didn't help."

"Jeez, I wasn't pregnant then," she snapped. "I moved to my sister on the other side of Bath and for the next two months we made up for not partying enough when we were students. Zoe – my daughter is named after my sister – she is an artist who designs fabrics and furniture, so our night life didn't interfere with her career. She works from her studio at home and usually gets up late."

"Your parents were okay with her being an artist given the way they treated Tony?"

"Obviously they've never approved of it but Zoe just didn't care and had enough strength and courage to do whatever she decided herself. She was doing art school part-time and working. Now she's significantly wealthier than many good lawyers. But coming back to Tony, where was I?"

"Every night you went to paint the town red with your sister!" I laughed.

"Yeah, except that we only went to classy places," she smiled with a sparkle in her eye so I knew Tony was about to reappear in her story. "On occasion Zoe booked us at her favourite restaurant in Bath. And guess who was the chef?" she asked enthused.

"Justin Bieber?"

"Bingo! How did you know?"

"What? Who?"

"Sorry? Yes, Tony himself! I spent every day in Bath with him after that. I used to go to the restaurant when it wasn't too busy or it was still closed and he would teach me cooking and… and we talked about our last five years while we hadn't really heard from each other," she said blushing.

"Did you have sex in the restaurant's kitchen?"

"No!" she yelled at me laughing and I knew she was lying.

"Gross, and the people buy the food from the—"

"Stop it Olivia. Nothing happened in the kitchen except I baked a few tarts and stirred some soups in massive pots. The worst thing was the temperature in the kitchen – it melted my waterproof make-up."

"Did you tell him everything about Oscar? The marriage, the prenup?"

"It would be difficult not to include Oscar when talking about the last five years of my life, no matter how much I tried—"

"So, he knew you were still married but separated."

"I filed for separation but it wasn't official, these things take time and…" she hesitated.

"Hannah, you don't have to lie to me. You can trust me and I'm not going to judge you."

"I told him that I left my husband after I found out he faked my signature on our prenup."

"So, Tony thought you were divorced," I said decisively.

"Yes, it was what he obviously concluded and then we both gladly found more interesting topics than our exes. This was the same time I graduated from law school looking to get my first job. I knew it would be much more difficult without Oscar's and his family's connections although I was still naively optimistic."

"You were walking on the clouds because you were in love again."

"I was although at the time I didn't want to admit it. One night when we were sitting in a thermal pool of the Bath Spa, drinking champagne and looking at the stars, Tony said he had never stopped loving me…"

"So romantic," I sighed.

"They were only words but they made me feel incredible, like I had turned back time and he had never left me… When my sister went away for a weekend I invited Tony in…"

"Nice! Fifty shades of Tony to discover!"

Hannah didn't look half as excited as I was, "After Saturday night fever, I was taking a shower on Sunday morning when Tony opened the front door after hearing the doorbell."

"Oh God, don't tell me it was… Why would he open the door if it wasn't his flat?"

"Oscar was shouting 'I know you're there! Your parents told me!'" Hannah was saying with a deep voice that made me laugh. "I'm still your husband. You can't keep avoiding me forever!'"

"Tell me Tony punched him in the face."

"Tony walked out of the apartment wearing his dressing gown and holding his clothes under one arm. I'll never forget his look. All he said was, 'I'm not quite sure whether I really don't know you or you've changed so much I don't recognise you anymore – in either case you're definitely not the woman I used to love.'"

"I'm so sorry Hannah. But why would you go back to Oscar?" I asked already knowing the answer and thinking that our stories had more similarity than I'd originally assumed. It just felt different when I looked at it from somebody else's perspective. "Did he tell you his mother drugged him and asked him to sign it?"

"She tried to force him to sign the prenup, which she obviously wrote herself, threatening she would disinherit him, and I know she's the sort of person who would do it. Oscar claimed that he felt awful asking me for it and when he saw my disappointed face he knew exactly what to do. He went back home and threw the papers on his mother's desk saying he loved me and she could disinherit him if that was what she wanted because he wasn't going to lose me."

"Right," I said unconvinced, "he said exactly what you wanted to hear but—"

"Oscar said that when he found out his mother wrote the prenup and faked our signatures, he went to confront her but she insisted that she did it only because she loved him and it wasn't a big deal as I would never know unless—"

"Unless you left him. By keeping quiet the coward managed to maintain a good relationship with both you and his mother."

"I noticed at some point he became colder towards his mother but I just assumed it was because he was married!"

"Hannah, he lied to you! It was a disgusting fat lie and you can't know for sure he wasn't involved in faking your signature."

"And the witnesses' signatures," she added.

"She also forged their signatures?" I asked in disbelief.

"I mean not quite. They agreed to sign that they were witnessing me signing it but of course—"

"Anyway, Oscar said that his mother finally destroyed the prenup or at least that was what she told him."

"And you believed him because it was the most convenient solution after you found out you were pregnant and—"

"And Tony wanted to have nothing to do with me. He quickly found consolation in a new girlfriend. In the meantime, Oscar kept begging me to give him another chance, and I relented the day I did eight pregnancy tests."

"Is Zoe… is she Oscar's daughter? Did you do a DNA test?"

Hannah bit her lower lip and shook her head looking like a little girl who had just done something naughty. "I didn't have to. I can count and she looks just like Tony when he was little.

"Oscar has never suspected anything?"

"He can also count but we didn't touch the topic until Nicolas was born. It's been a taboo subject. It's not funny at all but it does amuse me when my mother-in-law keeps saying Zoe looks just like her father and is as bright as Oscar. Proof that people see what they want to see," she said without a trace of a smile and took a deep breath. "My family is so fucked up beyond the norm!"

"I don't get it. Why? How did you manage not to talk about it for so long?"

"The silence from his side was like telling me he took the blame for me leaving him and—"

"And having unprotected sex with your ex and getting pregnant with him! Has he ever said it?"

"He didn't say anything until Nicolas was born. Very quickly I noticed he treated him differently to Zoe for whom he never seemed to have much time. Oscar would buy her everything she wanted but wouldn't give her more than thirty minutes a day. He's recently told me he threw himself into work to avoid thinking about the fact that Zoe was looking more and more like my ex. He knew what he was signing up for but he didn't think it would be so hard. He loved me so he thought he would love my daughter too but—"

"Zoe deserves a father who truly loves her," I said thinking about the poor little girl.

Hannah again seemed to ignore my comment, "He also couldn't stand the fact that Tony didn't know the truth. That's why he spent so much time away, and I thought he was having an affair."

"Why didn't he say anything earlier?"

"He was afraid to lose me and Zoe. We were getting deeper and deeper into our lies and it was just harder and harder to find a way out. What were we supposed to say to our friends and family, and most importantly to Zoe?" Hannah pulled her knees towards her chest, she was shaking a little bit probably with stress and tiredness. "Now Oscar has three months of paternity leave. We're going to see a child psychologist and discuss what's best for Zoe. Then we tell her and Tony the truth.

"Do you know what's going on with him now? Does he have a family?"

"I've done a bit of Internet research. He doesn't have a wife or any children, at least as far as social media is concerned. I think he spends most of his time working. Maybe I've got a gift to make men workaholics! He has opened two restaurants, one of them has two Michelin stars. He's also been running a business called *Get Boney with Tony.*"

"What is it? A fitness club?"

"A catering firm that brings you four healthy meals a day after a personal consultation with a dietitian," she said with such an enthusiasm it was as if she was advertising it.

"Wow, I bet your parents didn't see it coming!"

"I should have never cared what they were seeing."

"I thought you didn't."

"On reflection I think that I've always had their words at the back of my head that Tony wasn't good enough for me and look what's happened – it's completely the other way around, I'm not worth him."

"Don't be so hard on yourself," I said still thinking about what she had done to little Zoe. I had a feeling that her story wouldn't have a happy ending so I tried to redirect our thoughts before she completely fell apart the night before my C-section – it wouldn't have been the kind of distraction I had hoped for. "Oh, I've forgotten to tell you something."

"What's that?" Hannah opened her mouth in a gigantic yawn.

"When I was packing for the hospital I discovered something interesting," she looked at me almost bored like none of my life stories could ever be more interesting than what she had just told me. "I've found the cosmetic bag I had with me in Madrid, when I met Hugo, and the contraceptive pills that I had..." I stopped to look at Hannah's reaction but she was fiddling with her gel nails feeling sorry for herself, "so they were actually folic acid pills. The packs looked almost the same, especially when you're drunk."

"No kidding!" she suddenly livened up. "Are you saying the chances for Hugo being the father have increased to fifty-fifty?" she said the odds like we were talking about horse-racing and the fate of real people weren't actually involved. "But..." she bit again her lower lip.

"What?"

"It shouldn't really matter," she said shyly.

"I know, Hugo is engaged and we need to go to sleep."

"Olivia, we've spent far too much time wondering who could be a better father for our children but we seem to forget about what kind of mother we want to be."

27

TUESDAY, 16 FEBRUARY

OXFORD

"Patrick and Dominic, I love their names. Oh, and the tiny identical faces, double cuteness!" Freya was staring at the boys swaddled in blue blankets embroidered with white clouds. They were lying next to each other, arm to arm, in their transparent plastic cot that was put just next to my bed. They were still sleeping very well, recovering from their big Delivery Day.

"Patrick and Dominic sound almost the same in English and Polish," I explained.

"And in Spanish," my brother added with a smirk on his face. I had the impression he was rather amused by the whole situation. His always-saint sister had got herself into such trouble. Besides, contrary to my parents and Veronica, he'd never had particularly warm feelings towards Henry, while he'd liked Hugo almost instantly.

My parents celebrated Philip's comment with a few long minutes of silence. Naturally they'd been shocked when I'd revealed to them a couple of weeks earlier that I would have to do DNA tests to find out who the father of their grandkids was – but they couldn't be angry with a pregnant woman.

"Well, it doesn't change the fact I'm their grandfather so who cares," said dad finally, while my mother needed slightly more time to digest the information and stop lamenting. "We've failed as parents. That's not the way we brought you up," she kept saying like a mantra – luckily I knew her well enough to know that she didn't feel guilty about how she had raised me but she was trying to make me feel guilty. When my mother saw her grandchildren, it was the first time in two weeks that her hard-hearted face expression faded away to make space for an honest smile.

Only Sebastian looked a bit disappointed when he saw the twins. "They're all right," he replied when my mum asked him how he liked his cousins. "But they're looking a bit lazy. They've just got out of your belly and they're not even excited about it. They sleep and sleep and sleep..." he didn't believe he had been the same only five years ago.

Henry wasn't with me when the boys were born. He didn't come to visit us the day after or even five days later when we were about to find out the DNA test results. I had no intention of waiting for him to get back from America to do the test. As soon as I gave birth I gave Atlanta the keys to Henry's flat. In two plastic freezer bags she brought his comb with a few blond hairs and nail clippers with a piece of his toe nail. "Yummy," I said taking the hair and immediately throwing away the nail clippers, only to realise later that they were designer silver nail clippers from Harrods that he got for Christmas from his parents. By day five Henry had seen the twins only once on Skype. He glanced at them and said blankly they were sweet before quickly returning to making excuses about why he was still in New York.

"Oh please! Just say it! Say that you don't want to see us!"

"It's not quite like that," he said biting his lips. "The truth is I don't want to get used to the thought they're my children and then lose them just after I start loving them." I nodded with understanding. At least I knew that if the twins turned out to be Hugo's, Henry would leave me and save me the pleasure of perpetually racking my brain on whether we would ever have made a good family.

"Why are you here Hugo knowing that they might not be your children?" I asked him the same day I spoke to Henry.

"Because I wouldn't forgive myself if they're my *niños* and I wasn't here to see them in the first moments of their life."

"I hope you don't hate me when... when..."

"I think you put a spell on me. I tried to dislike you after the exhibition in London but it didn't work," he said with a genuine but sad smile. "It doesn't mean however that I've forgiven you."

"I've started thinking that you've put a spell on my mother. She surprised herself by liking you when she definitely didn't want to," I laughed reminding myself of how she told the nurses Hugo was the father. Initially I thought she was embarrassed that there was no definite-father around or she was just angry with Henry for not turning up, but later I realised it might've been more than that.

Each time Hugo was holding one of the boys the corners of his lips were rising up, while his eyes were narrowing and bringing the tiny wrinkles around them to life. I'd missed his contagious smile that made me feel that everything was possible and life was better than it had seemed to be only seconds earlier. When I was alone with Hugo and my little boys I wanted the moment to last forever. Hope was back – it never really dies, it just pretends to be dead to survive and then comes back even stronger. I regretted that I'd chickened out and run away from Hugo's apartment not telling him that I was potentially expecting his children – it wasn't something any good mother would do for her children. It wasn't for me to decide whether he should be with the boys the moment they were born.

I felt incredibly anxious about the paternity test and I would lie saying it didn't matter after I gave birth, but seeing my babies was making me feel happier than I'd ever been. I was, however, exhausted and the painkillers were making me lethargic. I decided to stay in the hospital for a few days longer and nobody protested, on the contrary they were very welcoming about me spending there as much time as I wanted. I wasn't surprised by their eagerness to keep me for longer – every night cost several hundred pounds from Henry's account.

I planned to leave the hospital on the fifth day after giving birth and it wasn't a coincidence, I also expected to get the results from the paternity test on that day. The results were confidential, but I was afraid that when Hugo stopped coming to visit us the staff would know he wasn't the father. Freya and Atlanta were accusing me of being paranoid but I was convinced one of the nurses overheard me talking about the tests and she leaked my scandalous story to the rest of the staff.

"Letter for Miss Eliot," said a nurse with long blond hair put into a ponytail. She clearly accentuated the word *miss* but I said nothing thinking that it would only be confirmation for my friends that indeed I was over-paranoid.

"Okay, you might've been right," said Atlanta. "She looked at you like you'd slept with her husband."

"I bet she fancies Hugo," said Freya looking like she'd just discovered a juicy secret.

"Let's get down to the business," said Atlanta matter-of-factly. "Do you want me to open the letter for you?"

"Don't you think Hugo should be here with me now to find out first, before everybody else—"

"No," they shouted simultaneously.

"You think it's Henry," I said and they both rolled their eyes sighing. "Freya, I heard you once whispering to Atlanta that Dominic looked like Henry."

"Say a word and we'll leave but it was you who called us to come here today and—"

"I don't want to be alone now," I said slowly opening the brown envelope.

When I touched the white paper inside it felt like it would burn my fingers and I could only hear the loud beating of my heart. Bum, bum, bum – the sound was filling my head and making me deaf to the surrounding world. I could see Atlanta moving her lips but I couldn't hear a word she was saying. My sweaty wet fingers were staining the piece of white paper still mostly hidden in the envelope. I took a deep breath but it didn't help – I still felt dizzy and the whole room was covered in white fog. I was sitting on my bed petrified and not able to make a move.

"I can't stand the tension," Atlanta shouted and took the letter from me. I didn't make a sound of protest.

"Promise me that you won't faint when we tell you," said Freya staring at the red button next to my bed that I needed to press to get help.

"I do."

"It's Hugo," shouted Atlanta. "It's Hugo," she repeated louder and going closer to the door so somebody from the staff would definitely hear.

"Give me the paper," I suddenly got my voice back.

"Hugo," I said and burst into tears. Freya and Atlanta came to hug me and I could see tears silently rolling down their cheeks.

28

TUESDAY, 16 FEBRUARY

DREAM FIELDS

There is a Chinese proverb saying that when God wants to punish us, he answers our prayers. *Is that what's happening just now?* I was thinking as Hugo was driving me and our boys to the house in Dream Fields. *My children will always think they were the result of a brief affair. I guess it's still better to have a father who from the start isn't married to your mother than see your parents going through a terrible divorce. At least, there won't be any bad blood between me and Hugo. We'll stay friends.*

Hugo was going to stay with us for at least a few days before going back to Madrid. We planned to talk about the details of our shared custody but first we wanted to just enjoy the arrival of our children. I didn't ask Henry about his opinion on Hugo staying in our house. I couldn't get in touch with my ex-fiancé-to-be and I wasn't going to inform him about anything in a text message. I had no doubt that Henry would leave me now.

"Paulina doesn't mind if you stay with us for a little bit longer?" I asked when we put the boys into their double cot and sat down on the floor in their room. Later we would carry the cot to my bedroom but first I wanted to clear any traces of Henry so as not to make the whole situation even more uncomfortable and awkward than it needed to be. He shook his head. *Gosh, the woman is really flawless, no wonder he wants to marry her.*

Sitting in the nursery for the first time I was happy Henry had had nothing to do with it. I didn't have to feel guilty looking at the walls painted in warm peach complementing the classy grey furniture. It was a team's work. My brother painted the room, Meg assembled all the furniture, Veronica made curtains with bears on, and Hannah painted and framed three pictures of animals – I didn't know she was so talented.

"I should have painted the room. Isn't it what dads do?"

"More important is that you're here now. Besides you sent plenty of things that are in the nursery."

"I can only see a few cuddly toys, did Henry bin the rest?" he asked seriously.

"All clothes, shoes and toys have been carefully arranged in the wardrobe and the chest of drawers," I pointed at the furniture that I'd chosen with my parents. "I wouldn't let him throw anything away," I said although the truth was Henry thought I'd bought everything myself and I didn't deny it.

"The clothes are from a new baby brand only sold in Spain."

"He would never notice anything like that. Why do you keep asking about him? Henry is not going to be a problem if that's what you're worried about." *As I'm sure he's going to disappear from my life soon. He might've done so already. He's too much of a coward to tell me it's all over.*

"I guess I just feel sorry for him now, that's all."

"But you still haven't answered any of my questions about Paulina."

"Because there's no Paulina," he said flippantly in a way one would respond to a stranger asking whether you had a lighter or could change some money for a bus.

"But when we were driving to the hospital and somebody called, you didn't answer saying it was your girlfriend and you would call her back later."

"It was my girlfriend, Claudia. She broke up with me when she found out the boys were mine. She said it was too much for her and

I'm not really that surprised, we've just started going out and she's six years younger than me."

"Claudia, seriously? That's her name?"

"Yes, I like her name actually. Never mind, she's out of the picture, and I'll have to speak to Henry when he gets back from New York."

"He's out of the picture. But Paulina told me everything. Why would you lie about her?"

"Do I have to remind you who the liar is here?" he snapped irritated. I felt the only reason he didn't raise his voice was for the sleeping boys.

"Fine," I said while standing up. "It's the second of September last year. The door to your penthouse is opened by a charming blonde," I said strongly accentuating the word penthouse. Hugo's face suddenly changed, his eyes opened like an alien had just landed, his jaw shaking. He opened his mouth to say something but I didn't let him. "By the way I love the fact you made me believe you lived in the little studio, which is actually where your butler lives. Yes, I met Luciano too," I was whispering loudly. "The beautiful woman invites me in, suggests I have something to drink and then among her hundreds of cardboard boxes we're having a conversation about your engagement on Lanzarote. Didn't she mention anything about a journalist who came to interview you about Hugo TorTillas? Nothing about a pregnant English woman, who was writing about you for a travel magazine?"

"No way!" Hugo also stood up and started walking around the room rubbing his forehead. Then he stopped, held my arms and looked straight into my angry eyes. "Paulina is a habitual liar, that's why I had to end our relationship."

I brushed his hands away, "Really? You've never mentioned that to me."

"And why would I talk to you about my ex? Isn't it one of those topics that men aren't supposed to touch, especially at the beginning of a new relationship? Why would I lie to you in the first place?" he said loudly and we both glanced at the boys but they were still sleeping after their big feed, looking blissfully happy in their milky-coma. Hugo suddenly sat down in my comfy armchair bought for baby feeding, while I sat on the soft carpet with my legs stretched out and head resting on the wall.

"Oh, I'm sorry. Sit hear."

"I'm comfy here," I snapped. "You told me about your break-up when we were on Grenada, why would you omit such an important detail like her being a habitual liar?"

"I said as much as I needed to say to stop you asking me about Paulina. If not for Gabriela who we met in Mercado de San Miguel we wouldn't have talked about her at all."

"Why? Because you've never really left her but you had a break—"

"Oh, give me a break Olivia from all your accusations. You dumped me on the phone, don't you remember anymore? Then you kept ignoring my messages and calls. Now you're engaged to Henry. You can't have us both."

"I ignored your calls for maybe four or five days and then you just gave up on me. Would you really give up so easily if you cared about me?"

"I knew it was about Henry. What were you expecting me to do – have a fight with him?"

"You couldn't have known for sure, it's just an excuse."

"You asked me to try social media and I did. Very good news channel, much more reliable than Paulina."

"You're bluffing. First, I blocked all my social media accounts and then when I started using them again I didn't post anything."

"And who said, I was looking at your accounts? Henry is definitely more *social* than you and he updates the news from his life on a daily basis."

"He would have never befriended you," I laughed.

"I sent him an invite pretending I was one of his students. Easy! He's got over five hundred friends so I thought that he wasn't particularly picky or discriminative and I was right," Hugo said with a smug face. "My favourite photo was the one where he embraces you at the party... What was it? *Don't die for a selfie* or something like that."

"I'm happy for you and your little investigation. You saw me with

Henry in one photo and a few days later you were re-heating your feelings for Paulina, obviously the flame wasn't quite dead."

"One photo? And what about your birthday party where he proposed to you? Nothing special, right? Just a silly engagement that can be broken?" I was stunned he'd been spying on me online for all this time. I was staring at him not knowing what to say next. "Yes, I was watching you on Henry's social media accounts like your psychofan. You and a guy who I'd never met before."

"Why didn't you just talk to me? I mean I didn't answer your calls for some time but you could've come and seen me like…" I wanted to say *like you went to see Paulina in India* – but I thought it was obvious I was just not that important.

"I know from my own experience how difficult it is to leave some-body when you've spent years together planning your future, even after the person notoriously lets you down. You're afraid to lose them so you give them the benefit of the doubt, another chance, but the best you get back is just another ray of hope that – you gradually come to realise –never brings anything."

"You're right, you can't simply accept that you've wasted half of a decade on somebody who doesn't deserve it. Five bloody years torn from the peak of your youth… so you try hard to fix every breakdown that appears but for some reason nothing works properly. Then one day you realise that's because it's unrepairable and you just need to get a new model."

"You can't get back the time you've already lost but you can stop wasting the time you've still got," he said looking into the distance and then suddenly turned to me, "Do you remember the first time we met?"

"How could I forget?"

"Didn't you think it was odd I had no phone and watch with me?"

"I don't know anybody who leaves a house nowadays without a mobile."

"The day I met you I had a massive argument with Paulina and I told her we were over. I'd done it before but we always used to get back together. That night I was convinced it was finally over."

"As far as I remember you didn't look particularly depressed, on the contrary—"

"Because I felt relieved. When Gabriela and Fernando got married, Paulina became obsessed with us being engaged."

I felt some solidarity with Paulina. "Well, if you didn't want to spend the rest of your life with the woman, why would you keep leading her on all those years? The whole idea of a fling is that it shouldn't last a decade!"

"I know it's not the best explanation but I just followed my heart without putting much thought into the character of our relationship. I did love her and I wanted to believe that one day my love would change her into the honest person who I desperately wanted her to be. I managed to convince myself that I didn't believe in the institution of marriage because my parents got divorced when I was little. The truth was I couldn't imagine marrying the woman who kept feeding me with lies every day. The poker face that she mastered for years made her a great businesswoman. God..." he sighed, "she would be such a good actress."

"She's definitely got the look," I murmured. "But I still don't understand... so you split up but then got back together to get engaged on Lanzarote to break up again—"

"When I asked her to start packing and move out from my apartment, she suggested us having a break. I said categorically no and I left the house. Later that night I met you."

"I've never understood the break idea. You either want to be with somebody or not."

"That's exactly why I wanted her to move out as soon as possible."

"Did she?"

"She did pack some of her things but only enough to go to an ashram in India. She left me a letter in which she asked me to once again think everything through."

"So, you thought it through and bought her a diamond ring."

Hugo rolled his eyes but ignored my comment to continue his version of the story. "The meditation didn't change anything. She remained the old Paulina who couldn't miss an opportunity to tell you her twisted version of every event. She stayed in the ashram three months and during that time called me regularly every couple of weeks to check whether I missed her and couldn't live without her."

"Was that what she told you?" I thought thinking he was getting arrogant.

"No but Fernando did when even Gabriela, Paulina's best friend, finally stopped believing her lies. Paulina told her we had some troubles in our relationship but she never mentioned us breaking up. That's why Gabriela was so unpleasant and suspicious when she met you at the Mercado, which was only a couple of days after Paulina called her saying she was going to India to have a break from our constant arguments."

"What was she doing in your apartment then? And why would you lie to me that you lived in the studio opposite your penthouse?" I raised my voice but the twins didn't even twitch.

"She was finally packing up her stuff to move out, and anticipating your follow-on question, yes she knew exactly who you were. Gabriela told her she met me with a pretty brunette at the Mercado – her description must have been sufficient for Paulina to recognize you from the photos I'd framed in the flat and some that I put into an album. I hid them in a box in my walk-in wardrobe but when I came back from my short trip abroad – I found the box wide open and lying in the middle of the bedroom. She didn't even bother to put it back and hide the fact she went through my things."

"You framed our photos? You put them into an album?"

"What's so strange about it? Would it be better if I posted them on social media?" he snapped.

"It's just… I didn't expect it," I said moved. *You don't frame pictures of people who don't mean anything to you.*

"Why would she lie? Just for fun? Was it some kind of revenge on you or me?"

"Her lies are pretty calculating. She knew you became important to me and all she wanted to do was ruin it for us."

"There was nothing to ruin at the time, we weren't speaking to each other."

"Fernando knew about my trip to England, he told his wife and Gabriela must've passed the news to Paulina—"

"Wait a second, when did you go to the UK?"

"In September after I saw on social media your engagement to Henry," he said gloomily like he still couldn't believe it. "I needed to make sure you knew what you were doing. It was one thing to leave me, but to marry the guy who abandoned you without a word of explanation at the airport? I thought that if I let you go back to him sooner or later you would realise he wasn't the right man for you, but I hadn't expected you to marry him."

"In September, hmm… so you're saying that… oh my god you weren't coming back home that evening. She fooled me." *I knew she was too perfect to be real!* I thought angrily. "And I thought you didn't want to have anything to do with me anymore. That you were happy with Paulina."

"Didn't you get my birthday present? I bet Henry checked your post first," he said looking annoyed.

"You're wrong. I got it and that's why I went to see you."

"And then you met Paulina and you quickly concluded that I couldn't make a choice just like you couldn't about me and Henry? Did you think you were my back up plan?"

"You draw your conclusions way too quickly for the man who created *Amigo habla conmigo*."

"I've never said I'm good at true and meaningful conversations," he said without hesitation. "So how did you explain to yourself the fact that I sent you romantic presents while at the same time I apparently proposed to Paulina?"

"You sound as if I was completely unreasonable. Well, I'm so sorry for being so stupid to believe your fiancé in your flat."

"She's never been my fiancé," he said through gritted teeth.

"I assumed you sent the present maybe a month before I received it."

"I sent the parcel by courier the week you had your birthday. I've got the receipt on my email," Hugo reached into his pocket for his phone.

Why would Meg lie to me that she took the parcel a couple of weeks before my birthday? It doesn't make sense.

"Have a look here!" Hugo was pointing at an email on the screen of his smartphone. "It was sent on Monday, the twenty-fourth of August and you received it on Friday, the twenty-eighth of August at seven am. I don't know why I'm translating it for you from Spanish. You speak very good Spanish, something that you somehow forgot to mention to me when we were together. If not for your meeting with Stefano, I would've had no idea."

"Initially, I wanted to hear what you were saying about me to other people when you were off guard thinking I couldn't have understood a word."

"I love the fact you treat me like a liar while it's you who—"

"I've never lied to you, I was just waiting for the right moment to tell you—"

"Oh, please save such explanations for... I don't know who actually," he interrupted me irritated. "You were going to tell me but only if you found out I was the father. I would've missed the birth of my own children," he said looking insulted.

"For god's sake," I snapped. "I didn't want to destroy your relationship because I thought you MIGHT have been the father of my children and in my mind the chances were definitely less than fifty percent. I was giving you thirty percent," I said confidently.

"I don't know how you managed to estimate the exact percentage of the probability and quite frankly I don't want to know, but casual sex doesn't decrease the chance of conception," he said sounding like a scientist on TV.

"Casual sex? I was your casual sex?"

"That's what you're inferring. Clearly Henry had a seventy percent chance to be the father because in May you were still in a stable and meaningful relationship."

I wanted to scream and let myself be furious but it wasn't worth waking up the boys – nothing was worth that. "You don't seem to understand anything," I said throwing a cork coaster on the carpet which hardly made any noise but released some of my anger.

"Paulina was pretending to be my fiancé because she wrongly assumed I would have gone back to her if you had left me. Answering your other question, in May I lived in the studio because my apartment was being refurbished at the time and I didn't think to mention it – we had plenty of other more important things to talk about."

"Just admit it – you were afraid I might've been a gold digger."

"I'm sorry," he snapped irritated. "So only you can be suspicious? Only you have a right not to mention some details like being fluent in Spanish, not really leaving your long-term boyfriend or—"

"I'm working on it. I'm going to leave Henry soon. I mean… to be honest I think he's already dumped me and if it's not the case… although I think it is," I was speaking quickly, "I'm going to leave him anyway, and it's not because I'm delusional about you and me becoming one happy family but because I don't want to share my life with somebody like him. Hugo, I want us to—" I didn't have a chance to finish as somebody knocked on the door.

I expected it was my neighbour who I met outside of the house when I was coming back from the hospital. Mrs Blueberry had said she would come to drop off a little something later. *Mrs Blueberry it's so nice of you but why now?* I was thinking going downstairs. At the same time, I heard Hugo leaving the nursery and picking up his phone, it was like the whole world was acting against us so we couldn't finish the conversation.

"Henry?" I asked standing in the door and not making space for him to come inside.

"You look like you've just seen a ghost."

"Well, you've been acting like one recently."

"Let me come inside so I can explain," he said while stepping into the doorway but I didn't move an inch.

"Look Henry…" I started and quickly cleared my voice to begin louder and with more confidence, "now is not the right time. I'll call you in the evening or tomorrow and we'll come up with some dates when we can meet up and talk."

"Olivia…" said Hugo, who suddenly materialised in the hallway. I was angry with him for leaving the boys alone in their room. Besides I did not want Hugo to meet Henry like this. I had no energy for dealing with both of them now. I was not prepared for it!

"Henry, this is Hugo as you probably already know…" I said lazily and sighed. "Hugo this—"

"They've just called me from the hospital, there's been a mistake," Hugo's voice was cracking.

For a brief moment the three of us were still and silent, fossilised. Henry's wet coat was slowly making a large puddle on my outdoor doormat, which did not seem to absorb any water. I felt like I had not enough strength to pull my hair back that was getting into my eyes, and Hugo just kept staring at his phone.

"My congratulations," all of a sudden Hugo broke the silence and I felt like I was struck by lightning.

"That can't be—" I started through a squeezed dry throat.

"They've repeated the tests. They got it wrong because Henry and I – we've got the same initials. Henry is the father."

Henry Thyme, Hugo Torilla, I'd never even thought about it.

Henry is the father, father, father… The words were echoing in my head.

Hugo didn't even lace his shoes. He grabbed his jacket, left the house pushing past Henry and slamming the door. My whole world was shaken again. A minute later, I heard a quiet knocking on the door and Henry complaining he was cold and wet. I wasn't ready to let him in.

29

WEDNESDAY, 17 FEBRUARY

HAVEN-ON-THAMES

I had no regrets that I met Hugo. I appreciated and cherished every moment I spent with him. He reminded me how it felt to fall in love. In the short time I spent with him he also showed me how important it was to support one another to become together better people and bring out the best and the most valuable in each other.

Henry claimed he forgave me for 'the brief affair', as he called it, but he made it clear he wanted me to face all the consequences of my choices (and his!) completely on my own – even when it was no affair; and even if it meant abandoning me the whole time I was in the hospital to give birth. He did it without knowing Hugo would be there and despite the fact the twins could have been his children. He paid for the private hospital but it was the most he was able to do for us.

Henry secretly got me my first decent job but he never let the job be just the start of my career. He'd stubbornly advised me against looking for something else, although he knew exactly how much I hated the atmosphere in the company and how I would never get along with Tiggy. He'd never believed in me and he hadn't even tried particularly hard to hide it. Sometimes I felt my dreams were amusing him and he treated me like a small girl bubbling about her future as a princess. I couldn't blame him, however, for the lack of progress in my career – it was my fault I'd relied so much on his opinion and I hadn't trusted myself enough to initiate any meaningful changes in my life without his approval. Henry was himself frustrated with his job – and when his frustration sky rocketed one day, he went as far as committing a crime, which could have caused us both our lives. I let him convince me that in the difficult times we happened to live in, we were somehow justified to take a no-holds-barred approach. Hugo, on the other hand, tried to change the world instead of making it even more flawed. *People can't talk anymore? Let's provide them with the right environment to do so.*

Did I fantasize about Hugo and me getting back together despite all odds? I did, but now my priorities had changed and number one was making sure my children were safe and happy. I wanted to become a better person for them. I wanted them to be proud of me one day. I had to give up on the idea of a full happy family – I couldn't be with a criminal and a perpetual liar. I needed to stay strong and put an end to the relationship that had been draining me of all positive energy, self-esteem and... And could expose me to being associated with Henry's crimes.

"Listen Henry, the fact that Dominic and Patrick are your children doesn't make us a family. I'm not coming back to you," I said in one breath imagining myself old and lonely one day after my boys had got married and moved out from home, one to Australia and the other to Malaysia. I was struggling to remove from my head the vision of me sharing a tiny retirement flat with two fat grey cats.

We were strolling in Haven-on-Thames moving slowly towards the park I had planned to visit for over a year. I – the one who recently had a C-section – was pushing the twins in their blue double pram, while Henry – who regularly went to the gym – was walking next to me, straight and unmoved like a soldier on a parade. It didn't even cross his mind to ask me how I was doing after the operation. He and his mother, my mother-in-law-NOT-to-be, kept saying that giving birth was the most natural thing in the world and women were designed to recover practically immediately to be able to look after their offspring. Henry was saying something but I was too distracted to listen to him. I tried to focus but at the time anything seemed to be more important than his analysis of the future of our relationship. When two French bulldogs passed us, one wearing a fluffy bear outfit and the other dressed like a ginger fox, I was mulling over whether they would be good dogs for small children.

"They look ridiculous," Henry snapped suddenly.

"It's chilly. French bulldogs need to be wrapped up warm because they can't regulate their temperature."

"I would never buy something like that. I want a proper dog who barks and weighs more than a bird."

"It's lucky then that we're not going to be together because I consider French Bulldogs to be proper dogs and I don't feel like dealing with big dogs and their big poo."

In one of the shops on the high-street there was a sale on baby clothes so I started thinking about weekend shopping with mum. Then I was thinking whether I made the right choice about my pram and pushchair – I had insisted on one which enabled both boys to see the world from the same perspective without a brother's bum in front of their eyes, but the pavements in Haven-on-Thames were so narrow that I struggled walking around the town.

"You are not listening to me at all," Henry said looking surprised.

"I am, I'm just multitasking. I'm listening to you and thinking about something else at the same time," I said with a smirk reminding myself all those months ago when he wasn't there for me and I practically had to fight for his attention.

Henry opened his mouth without saying a word. He was truly flabbergasted I was not listening to him anymore like some sort of guru.

"So, what's your point Henry?"

"I keep telling you that you've never actually broken up with me. You've also lost some weight and it should be enough for you..." he eyed me from my toes to my head and back, "to start wearing your engagement ring again. Mum is worried that you might have lost it. I keep telling her it's not true but—"

"No please don't"

"Don't what?"

"Don't lie. I've lost it," I said nonchalantly.

"You've got to be kidding me?"

"Besides I'm going to put on weight again – it's going to be my fat-protest so you leave me alone."

"Okay," he tried to be calm but I could see in the corner of my right eye he was fuming so much from the inside I could practically see smoke billowing out of his ears and nose. "I chickened out. Yes, I did," he was trying to slow down his breathing. "I admit I should've been with you at the hospital and I'm sorry," he had never been good at apologising and even now he said *sorry* much quieter than everything else. "But you said on skype that you had understood me," he went back to his accusing tone.

"Maybe most other men would do exactly the same."

"Exactly, that's exactly my point," he made a small jump while walking.

"But they're exactly the sort of men I don't want to be with."

"Here we go again," he rolled his eyes. "And I just thought we were making some progress."

"You must be mad then if you're thinking like that."

"We shouldn't waste any more time arguing. For the sake of our children we need to bury the hatchet and work on being a loving family," he said looking proud of his words.

"Don't use my children in your evil plans."

"Don't forget that they're also my children… and what evils plans are you talking about? Is it evil that I want to marry you?" he said so loudly that a couple of teenagers sitting on a bench in the park looked at us, whispered something to each other and giggled.

"It would be evil because if you marry me you'll most likely ruin my life."

"Be patient Henry, be calm," he was repeating like a mantra, warming up the cold air with his breath. "Inhale and exhale. She's just given birth. Her hormones are still raging and making her completely unreasonable."

"Quite frankly I don't care how you want to explain it to yourself," I said sitting down on a bench as far away as it was possible from the staring teenagers.

It was a sunny but chilly winter morning. The grass was still covered by a thick layer of white frost. The twins were sleeping quietly in their pram totally unaware of the surrounding chaos. Dominic really looked like Henry in the pictures from his childhood, which his mother once showed me. He was almost bald, had a perfectly round face and round nose. Patrick, however, I thought looked like me – he had dark dense hair with a couple of curls around his little forehead. I wondered whether it meant I looked like a small boy or my son's pretty face had some girly features.

"When we finally get through this difficult period, I would like us to change the day of birth on the boys' certificates," Henry broke the short but blissful silence.

"What the hell? What's wrong with you?"

"I found out they're mine on the sixteenth of February and then we started our life together so—"

"The fact you weren't somewhere doesn't mean it didn't happen. Anyway, it would be impossible to do. Were you just speaking metaphorically?" I said suddenly feeling silly.

"No, I'm deadly serious. I've got a friend who—"

"No! I'm not going to forge the date of birth of my children for your own pleasure. The sooner you get this idea and of us getting back together out of your head, the better for your own good. I'm going to pack all of your things today if you don't do it yourself and I'll leave them outside the house."

"I don't understand you Olivia. When I break up with you at the airport and hide a criminal act from you – you forgive me. When I tell you the truth of why I decided to stay longer in New York, you want to leave me. Do you prefer me to lie to you?"

"I might've forgiven you of some things but it doesn't mean I can forget all about it in some magical way."

"Look, we both have our past, we've made some mistakes that we regret. You also put me through hell, or have you already forgotten?

Last night was the first time in a very long while I slept without waking up every couple of hours covered in sweat, thinking about a random guy taking you and my children away from me," he looked moved, my heart was telling me he was being honest, but reason and instinct didn't let me believe him.

"Right, you slept very well not giving a damn about me getting up every couple of hours to feed the twins! You aren't the man I thought you were, and I'm not the woman you want me to be. Simple. Should our future be a constant battle to forget the past and change what we don't like so much about each other?"

"You're being very melodramatic now but I get it, you've just given birth. I love you Olivia, and now when Hue is gone we can start everything from the very beginning."

"His name is Hugo," I said through gritted teeth. "Do you remember—"

"How we met each other?" he gave me a wide annoying smile.

"Do you remember the moment when Blanca fired the gun? Do you still have the poster of Einstein with the hole from the bullet?" he nodded surprised. "There's a quotation on the poster saying that it's madness to do the same over and over again expecting different results. It beautifully sums up our relationship."

"It's such a shame because now we finally have a chance to get back to normal."

"I don't want normal – *your normal* – anymore. I don't want anything to be back the way it was before."

"God, you've changed Olivia. Is family not the most important thing for you anymore?"

I wasn't even looking at Henry because I started watching a young couple with their small child dressed in a yellow snowsuit and duck hoodie. The father crouched down, his knee nearly touching the frosted grass – he was holding the baby who was rapidly wriggling his or her legs. When the woman standing a few meters away from them shouted, "Sophie are you ready? Three, two, one. Go!" the man put the child on the ground and she started walking on her wobbly legs towards her mum. The proud parents were cheering and clapping.

When the baby girl finally reached her destination – the arms of her mother-in-seventh-heaven – the woman stood up holding her little daughter and kissed her on both cheeks. Soon after the man joined them and they all headed towards the gate in the park. Maybe they had a difficult past. Maybe they argued a lot when nobody saw them. Maybe they weren't married. Maybe one of them was a step-parent. Maybe they didn't love each other anymore but at that particular moment they looked very happy together. I was certain that I wasn't going to marry Henry but I knew I would have to make a huge effort to have a good relationship with him for the sake of our children.

"Do you still think Hue will want to bring up children who are not his?"

"I'm sure he won't," I snapped. "I'll be fine on my own and don't worry I'll let you be involved in their life. They're your children and I want you to have a good relationship with them. I'll never stand in your way."

I thought about Hugo who had called me in the middle of the night. I'd never heard him so depressed. He apologised he left so abruptly but he was shocked and hurt. He told me I could always count on him and call him even with the most trivial problems. Henry was snoring in the guest room when I put the phone down and started weeping silently into my pillow. I felt confident I could stay in touch with Hugo and call him about anything – I trusted him and I knew he really meant it – but I had to stay realistic, I could only keep that kind of relationship for as long as he didn't have a new girlfriend. Sooner or later he would find somebody, marry her, go on honeymoon to the Caribbean, have his own children, get a French bulldog and forget about me.

"You've got a problem with my criminal past, as you keep referring to it, but you've never had an issue taking advantage of the money that came from my... yyy... my unconventional job. Do you—"

"Hugo has got an unconventional business, you broke the law."

"Jeez, the Hue again," he sighed loudly. "Do you think I could pay for you to give birth in a private hospital or buy a brand-new SUV just from being a lecturer?"

"Well, you can't buy a house with your dirty money, and I don't want to know how you bought the car without attracting attention from the tax authorities."

"There's a bit of truth in what you're saying but I've also got some savings that I would like to keep for our boys. I've never been a big spender."

"I've noticed," I exclaimed. "You've been a proper Scrooge at times."

"Some people would say that I just don't like blowing money. Anyway we—"

"We don't want your dirty money. You'll have enough to pay us child support from your job at the university."

"I'm afraid it's not going to happen," he said calmly. "If you don't marry me, you might not even get that."

"Excuse me? Are you really blackmailing me?" I stood up, took the brake off the pram and started walking away rapidly.

"Wait!" he ran after me. "I didn't want it to sound like that. I'm in serious trouble, actually we all are," the way he said it made me feel we needed to move our discussion home.

After I'd fed the twins putting them again into their milky-coma, Henry and I sat in exactly the same place I talked to Hugo the day before, but this time I took the armchair and Henry sat cross-legged on the carpet.

"Where should we start then? Maybe tell me first whether there's a risk of another Blanca-event?"

"The police have tracked us down."

"Us?"

"Me, Ben and a few other lecturers who worked for the Cheaters Gang."

"Can you go to jail?" I asked still not quite comprehending how serious the situation was. *It's not happening to me. The father of my children can't go to jail! What am I going to tell them?*

"Yes," he whispered with his eyes set on his shaking hands.

"How long would you be apart from the boys? Because I'm not taking them to visit you in prison at their age."

"I have no idea," he said angrily. "Is that now your biggest worry?

How big they'll be when I get out of jail?" I didn't reply. I felt I had less and less to say to him and the best was to just let him talk. "My PIs are currently collecting data on how much the police know about us. We initially thought we would be able to get out of this without a scratch because one of our rich students was going to help us – we'd provided him with all the necessary resources to pass his MSc. Unfortunately, his father who had a different approach to education found out and threatened to disinherit him."

"Are you saying his father is wrong?" I smirked.

"Now is not the best time for your sarcasm. We found out a couple of days ago the guy won't help us because of his angry daddy and we have to act alone. It's likely we'll go to a trial."

"I hope that for the sake of our children you tell them I knew nothing about it and I won't be dragged into court. That's what a decent father would do."

"I'm afraid it's more complicated than that. The police have found out that you hired the PI to follow me. They'll want to know what you learned from Gatsby."

"It's easy," I shook my shoulders. I learned that you didn't have a lover as I had suspected. Full stop. End of story."

"If they find out you're lying, you can be accused of perjury, collaborating with me and god knows what more out there."

"Wonderful," I murmured. "Do you have any idea how to get out of this? Do you want me to live with you on the run, change our identities, have our hair dyed? I was speaking quickly feeling sick to my stomach. "Do you have a mate who can give us new passports, forge our date of births so we can fly to Africa or China and try to melt into the crowd?"

"You're not going to melt into any crowd there darling," he smiled. "It crossed my mind we could run away and start again somewhere like New Zealand but—"

"Stop with the fucking starting again!"

"But I thought it through and I think I can get us out of this."

"You think? How lovely."

"Basically…" he cleared his throat, "Olivia, marry me. I love you and I want to spend the rest of my life with you," he practically recited it in one breath without a trace of emotion.

"What the hell?" I said but I did let him put a new diamond ring on my finger. It wasn't as beautiful as the one I found hidden between his books but so much better than his family ring.

"I knew you would make the right decision," he said cheerfully and I felt like I wanted to smack him on his stupid head.

"When we get married I won't have to testify against you."

"I knew you would understand, you're an intelligent woman and a wonderful mother," the smile wasn't fading away from his face. "But of course, I want to be your husband for a million other reasons."

"Let me guess, does it also involve your tax issues or any similar agenda? I'm not going to marry you for a million and one reasons but I'll keep the ring because it looks expensive and I need the money to pay for a lawyer."

"Olivia, you need to understand me. I… we don't have another option."

"For the last year I've been constantly hearing that I need to understand you. If you put as much effort into trying to understand me as I've put into understanding you, we wouldn't have to deal with any of the problems we're facing now so—"

"So, marry me and then we'll think it all through once again," he begged. "I promise I'll change."

"Excuse my language Henry but your promises are so useful that you can't even wipe your arse with them."

"What will you say when your sons ask you one day about their father?"

"Do you think they won't let you out before the boys start talking?" I asked seriously trying to stop the corner of my lips from rising.

Henry's face was slowly reddening. "Is it so funny for you?"

"Not at all. There's nothing to laugh about… although you're quite amusing if you're thinking I would ever marry you."

"I can go to jail for five years."

"Oops," I said covering my mouth with my hand. "Who knows maybe they release you earlier for good conduct."

"You'll have to give the car back."

"It's too big to park in Haven-on-Thames anyway. At least they can't take away my time in the private clinic."

"You'll also be amused to hear that you're going to lose the house."

"It's my house. I put down the entire deposit and I pay off the mortgage every month."

"That's correct..." he said with satisfaction, "but my name is on the deeds and on the mortgage. If I need to get any money back, the court will put the house up for auction and take my half."

"You won't have any half," I said trying to catch my breath, while taking off my blue cardigan as I suddenly felt a flow of heat.

"We bought the house as joint tenants so no matter how much you're paying, I legally own fifty percent of the property."

"You can give me your part of the house before the trial. We can make an appointment with a solicitor this week."

"My attorney advised me against it because it would like I'm guilty."

"Because you're guilty and it's all your fault."

"Marry me and I'll give you a divorce as soon as we get through this..." he hesitated and rubbed his chin, "this difficult phase in our life."

"God, you told me you were done with selling the exams and you were back to your normal job. I've been so stupid believing you."

"I wouldn't say stupid but you were definitely too absorbed having fun with the Hue... or Hugo the Spaniard. I did finish that job – as I said it was only temporary – but I finished with it just a tiny bit too late," he rubbed his thumb against a finger like he was adding salt to his meal. "Anyway, if you hadn't employed Gatsby, you could've pretended that you knew nothing."

"I certainly had no idea how bad it was! I still had faith in you. I couldn't believe you were a criminal."

"Criminal? Is that how you're going to describe me to our children, a cri-mi-nal? Do you know what influence it's going to have on them growing up? Have you already thought about it? I didn't think so. There's been research on children having one parent in prison. Many of the poor kids later had some mental health issues and ended up breaking the law themselves."

"I'll take care of their upbringing. They'll be safe in my hands."

"Is that what you want now – to bring them up on your own without a father? Going back to the research – children of parents in jail had significantly lower self-esteem than their peers, had major problems with concentration when it came to learning and on average were more aggressive than other school kids," Henry sounded like he was giving one of his lectures. "Beyond that they were often stigmatised at school and in the playground by other children and their parents, who often asked their own children to avoid the damaged kids. Having a parent in jail is a traumatic experience for every child and normally has serious consequences for their future. Is that what you want for your boys? Never-ending meetings with psychologists? Coming back from school in tears or being constantly angry?"

"Stop it Henry!" I shouted and woke up the twins who started crying their lungs out. I knew they were fine but I still felt sad about them crying. I couldn't stand the idea that they could have a difficult childhood and that I didn't do everything I could to prevent them from such misery.

30

FRIDAY, 26 FEBRUARY
LONDON

When I got so big that going out became an effort, and I felt the most comfortable lying on my bed with a u-shaped pregnancy pillow between my legs, I started fantasizing about the time when I would be back to my size and have a night out with my girlfriends. For weeks as soon as my head hit the pillow I was lost in dreams about getting into a tight black dress and thirteen-centimetre heels, which I bought especially for my first night out. The pregnancy limited my clothes choices and consequently reduced my urge to buy new dresses but I made up for that by getting a new pair of high-heels every month. I imagined going out with Freya, Atlanta, Meg and Hannah to a funky bar in London, sip colourful drinks and chat about how wonderful our lives were, and that looking after children was not as hard as everybody said. We talked about our exciting journeys abroad, the places we'd travelled to and the destinations we still planned to visit. We discussed books that we'd recently read and those we were going to buy. We scored men from one to ten when they approached us to buy us drinks – we always refused because we were all in happy relationships.

Two weeks after giving birth, Freya and Atlanta went on a mission to make my little dream come true and help me to leave the house on one Friday evening. I was more than reluctant – I still felt the most comfortable when lying on my bed but now with the u-shaped pillow behind my back. I didn't go through a miraculous recovery after my C-section – although my doctor said I was doing significantly better than most – and I wasn't in the mood to leave for anywhere.

"I'm so tired that I couldn't be bothered with a free trip to Hawaii," I said when Freya and Atlanta were standing in my kitchen, and my parents were already taking care of the boys in the lounge. Mum and dad turned out to be very keen to collaborate with the girls.

"They sleep well at night. You don't breastfeed them. Come on!" said Atlanta while sipping her second glass of formula milk. She had a crazy party the night before with her husband and his work colleagues and insisted on drinking something nutritious that would help her to recover.

"Let's go before she drinks all your formula and we'll need to make a trip to the supermarket on a Friday evening. Do you know how busy shops can be on Friday evening?" said Freya looking genuinely worried and then she turned to Atlanta, "The milk will make you fat."

"Oh, shut up Freya. It reminds me of my childhood," she said with nostalgia.

"You said you were breastfed till you were three," I said surprised.

"I don't remember I was only three after all," she snapped. "Come on, chop, chop! It's not Madrid. Most places close at midnight."

I felt like literally hitting myself to avoid going out with them and the feeling intensified when I was standing in front of a large mirror in my bedroom and hectically trying on all my dresses. "Nothing fits me!" I screamed from the top and within seconds I heard Freya running upstairs to storm into my room and dive into my wardrobe.

"This one," she pulled out a black knitted dress. "It's cold outside."

I laughed loudly, "It's my pregnancy dress."

"I know because I've seen you in it a few months ago but no one else will be able to tell."

I hesitated, "Oh god, really?"

"It takes time to—"

"You're not thinking about wearing your pregnancy dress," said Atlanta walking into my bedroom and Freya hissed at her.

"No one fits in their old clothes just a couple of weeks after giving birth," she said angrily and Atlanta raised her hands up as if Freya had been pointing a gun at her. That was the moment I noticed Atlanta was sitting on my bed with a tight silver sparkling dress while Freya, who normally liked to show off her great body, was wearing a pair of jeans and a loose silky salmon top.

I took the dress from Freya and searched in my drawer for a pair of slimming tights. I regretted not listening to Hannah who had advised me to buy some spandex for the afterbirth period, she even offered to find me some. Unfortunately, she couldn't make it for the evening, she already had some plans for the weekend. Oscar and her were going away to talk about their future, or rather decide whether they still had any future together. Meg was also busy – she had her first date with somebody I knew nothing about yet. She promised to show up when the date proved to be an utter disaster. Meg had no patience for dating, if she didn't like somebody immediately, she made up some lame excuses or just disappeared half way through a dinner or after one drink.

When we finally made it to a bar in Covent Garden I replaced my grey boring pumps with a new pair of purple high-heels, which I had managed to squeeze into my handbag just before we left the house. My feet were not swollen anymore but they were still struggling to accept anything more than flat wide granny shoes. Making a trip to the bathroom and back with the high-heels was an achievement. I changed the shoes several times that evening because we kept bouncing between various clubs, pubs and bars in the same area – first the music was too loud, then it was too quiet, too cold or too stuffy, there were either too many people or not enough people to experience the buzz of the evening out... Finally, we ended up in a mysterious but charming place, which we found by complete coincidence when I stopped to squeeze a tissue in the back of my right pump where it had been rubbing my foot.

"My feet still feel like they've been treated with a meat tenderizer!" I shouted with despair. Freya nodded with understanding.

Atlanta rolled her eyes in disbelief probably thinking I was massively exaggerating. "What about this place then?"

We went through a narrow unassuming door placed almost randomly between an entrance to a loud club and a large café that was already closed. To get into the place we needed to walk down winding concrete stairs with a wooden rickety rail, which we didn't trust in the slightest so we kept holding the whole time to old dusty brick walls, covered with cobwebs. The stairs were so long that I wanted to turn back but we suddenly saw another entrance and decided to at least push the door and see what was inside. The bar was divided into three separate rooms, all maintaining a similar atmosphere. In one of them there was a large group of people, consisting mainly of thirty-something male individuals dressed in jeans and T-shirts, gathered heavily in front of a glass bar lit with warm yellow and orange lights. The second room had a non-working chimney, colourful poufs and metal gold tables – there was nobody there except for two girls arguing, so we moved to the third room, which was filled with comfortable quirky armchairs. That room was the largest and full of couples sipping wine and listening to smooth jazz. Freya quickly glanced around and decided we were staying, "There're four chairs in the corner. I'm taking them before somebody else does."

"I hate artificial flowers and candles," Atlanta said with disgust looking at the candles spread evenly on dark wooden shelves, hanging from bare brick walls.

"They look real enough to me and I'm glad they're artificial because can you imagine getting out of here in a fire?" Freya was saying while making herself comfortable on a green armchair by fiddling with two embroidered cushions.

I was soaking the unique atmosphere of the place, which reminded me so much of some bars in the basements of Krakow's old town. It had been a while since I'd been there. The last time was to see my grandparents and go out with a group of old friends from childhood – the group that for years had been getting smaller and smaller was now finally reduced to just three girlfriends who stayed locally and always had time to meet up with me. Suddenly the bar in Covent Garden evoked in me a longing to visit Krakow in the winter. I wanted to walk across the Market Square to pass stalls with fresh flowers while people gathered around the Adam Mickiewicz Monument, a famous meeting point for the locals. I wanted to see the roofs of bright and colourful townhouses being slowly covered with snow. I could almost hear the sound of horse carriages taking tourists around the town centre and whisking a bride and groom from Saint Mary's Church. I thought that if I'd been there in January I could have seen all of that and more in the glow of a massive Christmas tree that the Polish decorate as late as the twenty-fourth of December but often enjoy till the beginning of February. I fantasised about getting lost in one of the dark streets around the Jewish Quarter – with smoky street lanterns trying to light through the winter fog both gentrified expensive townhouses and old scruffy apartment blocks. I closed my eyes, I saw some footsteps in the snow, and heard the church bells breaking the silence on a frosty winter evening. Then, I thought, I would have found my way to a cosy café badly lit with real candles (causing even more of a real fire hazard) and I would order hot chocolate and mulled wine or a shot of *Wiśniówka*.

"What are you thinking about? Freya's soft voice managed to get through my daydreaming. "Do you feel like some food? They sell snacks here."

"I do actually," I said enthusiastically. I'm thinking *Zapiekanka* and salty pretzels."

"Are you all right?" asked Atlanta. "What are you talking about darling?"

"Zapiekanka and salty pretzels in Kraków are like bagels in New York."

"Tell me, you're not just going through some kind of postnatal breakdown. Why are we even talking about Kraków?" Atlanta screamed in my ear over the music and took a long sip of her Cosmo. I noticed they also got me one so I took a sip so small that it was probably equal to dipping my tongue in the glass.

"I know why," Freya jumped in her chair. "You want to get married with Henry in Kraków!" she said with a smug face.

"Nice and original," said Atlanta.

"I really don't think so."

"Why don't you look happy talking about your own wedding?" Freya eyed me as if she'd been a snake estimating my size to eat me. "Brides-to-be are normally ecstatic about their wedding planning."

"It would take a lot of time to plan the wedding abroad and we don't have the time. We want to do it sooner rather than later," I said taking a big sip of my Cosmo.

"What's the rush? You already have the house together and two kids," said Atlanta, and I knew they weren't going to let me get away without answering the question.

"You sound like you're going to take out your tonsils rather than get hitched," Freya frowned her eyebrows. "How soon?"

"Week, maybe two. Depends when you've got a free weekend and you can come," I said trying to stop my voice from trembling.

Both my best friends burst out laughing. For them the amount of quickly consumed alcohol made everything at least double as funny as normal.

Freya suddenly coughed and looked at me with her eyes wide open, "What the... you're not joking?"

Atlanta wiped tears from her warm red cheeks, "Olivia, what the hell is going on?"

"Nothing," I said as flippantly as I could, adding to it some waving gestures and a snort to enhance the effect of my fake nonchalance. "My grandmother insists on us getting married and she wants us to have a quiet wedding. We've already got two children—"

"Bullshit," snapped Atlanta. "Which grandmother? The English one who got married a year after your father was born or the Polish one who was unfaithful to her first husband with your grandfather."

"Yeah, what a hypocrite," said Freya.

Atlanta gave her a merciful look, "She's lying to us and she never lies to us so it must be something serious!"

"Henry has some problems, yyy... some problems of a legal

nature..." I took a deep breath, "and when we're married I don't have to testify against him. We can always have a bigger wedding later."

"Yeah, why not?" Freya started enthusiastically. "In Kraków or Las Vegas or Hawaii, or Bali or—"

"Or shut up Freya. How much have you drunk? One Cosmo and you're already so pissed? Haven't you heard? Olivia wants to marry Henry to prevent him from going to prison?"

"A gangster's wife. How cool is that?" Freya winked at me and then her head practically hit the back of the armchair and she fell asleep with her mouth open snoring loudly.

"What do you mean by *legal nature*? Has he recently bought a campervan and is spending a lot of time cooking in it? Has he befriended a weird-looking student of his?" Atlanta was loudly whispering.

"You've watched too much American TV."

"Think about it. Students would be perfect customers. It has long been known how they help themselves pass their exams," she raised both her eyebrows and nodded.

"Taking drugs to get through university is lame. People want to be fit and healthy nowadays, you've got to have the looks to have a high-flyer career. Those who've got money would rather buy their education than try to enhance their learning skills by drugging themselves."

"Do what?"

"Never mind, it's something I've heard. The thing is Henry might need to clear some debt... and lawyers are so expensive. The thing is, we're afraid that we would have to sell the house and it's the last thing I need right now."

Atlanta put her face into her palms and gasped heavily, "I told you not to sign the joint tenant deal. I told you to fuck being trustful and appropriate, didn't I?" she shouted, which made Freya open her eyes but she quickly went back to sleep. "Women have to be more careful than men. No matter how equal or unequal the world is – babies are catapulted through our vaginas or stomachs. We're more vulnerable, we—"

"Stop, I get it but it's too late to be sorry. I thought he was the one I would spend the rest of my life with. I was in love. Signing any different deal would be like writing a prenup. I didn't want to do it and I turned out to be wrong."

"Don't make another mistake. I beg you. You can't trust him, he might have some other debts you're not even aware of."

"Henry says that if I don't testify he's got a much better chance of getting away with whatever he did."

"And since when has anything that Henry said prove true?" she snapped. "Hold on a minute. You said *I was*. You said that you were. Aha!"

"I have no idea what you're talking about right now."

"Oh, you know exactly my darling. You said you *were* in love with Henry, so you're not anymore! Don't marry him and get yourself a good lawyer is my only advice!" she said in a begging tone. "I know a good lawyer, I'll call him tomorrow."

"But—"

"That's right, you need to take care of your *butt* and also the other two cute butts you've now got at home."

"I don't want their father to go to jail. Do you know what effect it could have on them?" I said and Atlanta only rolled her eyes as if it was completely irrelevant. "Talking about cute butts, I've taken some new photos of the boys in the bear outfits you gave us." I reached for my bag that was between Freya's right hip and the armrest. My hand only skimmed her leg but it was enough to wake her up.

Freya jumped. "Right, what have we been talking about?"

"Olivia is going to show us some photos of the twins."

"Brilliant."

I pulled out my tablet and typed in my four number PIN – I did it three times and each time it was wrong! I tried to unlock it with my fingerprint but it was not working. I was about to give up when I suddenly reminded myself that I had changed the password so Henry couldn't use it without me knowing about it. I tried for a fourth time with success, it was Meg's date of birth. *Henry would never guess*, I thought and smirked. The girls moved their armchairs closer to me and looked with anticipation at the screen resting on my knees. I touched the icon saying photos, set a slide show and asked Atlanta to pass me my glass of Cosmo that I'd been sipping for the last hour. In contrast to Freya I was perfectly aware I couldn't have drunk more than one drink without serious consequences. I moved the tablet to Freya's lap because I didn't want any water dripping slowly from the bottom of my glass to end up on the screen.

Freya giggled. "It must be Meghan's tablet," she said yawning.

"I'm so absent-minded now. It's because we bought the same orange cases."

"Wow, have a look at this," said Atlanta.

"Stop the slides for her. She'll miss it all," said Freya.

My eyes moved to the screen to see an average looking face with loads of make-up and a well-exercised toned body adorned only in skimpy red lingerie. The girl was lying on her side with her head resting on one hand, while with the second hand she was putting into her mouth a strawberry dipped in chocolate. The white sheets and her boobs – unusually big for such a slim body – were covered in drops of chocolate. In another photo the same long-haired blonde was kneeling on the bed with a half-full glass of champagne in one hand, and a bottle in the other from which champagne was spilling out onto the once snow-white bedding.

"She's making so much mess," said Freya outraged.

"It's getting juicier and juicier," said Atlanta looking at the blonde posing completely naked with the red thong in her mouth.

"We should switch it off. Meg would be furious," I said angry that my absent-mindedness exposed my flat mate to such embarrassment.

"Wait a sec, where's Meg?" asked Atlanta with curiosity.

"Why? Are you a lesbian too? No way. I don't want to see her naked! I couldn't *unsee* it later."

I looked away and reached for my tablet but Atlanta was not going to give up on it so easily and continued scrolling. The last thing I felt like was making a scene by fighting or chasing her around the bar. We were all a bit tipsy and not everyone in the bar had to know about it. I leaned back on my chair, Freya yawned and did the same. Suddenly

Atlanta closed the orange case from the tablet with a bang and jumped up covering her mouth with her right hand.

"I told you not to do it," I said with self-satisfaction. "Was it really worth it?"

"Does Meg not shave her armpits or—" Freya was nothing but amused.

"Stop, stop…" I put my hands over my ears.

"No idea if she does but *he* doesn't. Do you recognise this person?" she asked putting the tablet so close to my nose that initially I couldn't see anything.

"Take it away, you're suffocating me… Is it? Oh my god! It can't be…"

"What a little piece of shit!" shouted Freya.

"The shitiest shit!" added Atlanta giving me a pitiful look.

31

FRIDAY, 26 FEBRUARY

WITNEY

"Mum, are you sure it's her? Have a good look again. It's important." My mother reluctantly scrutinized the photo, which showed Henry resting his head on a pair of big boobs covered with nothing but chocolate and champagne.

"Don't you have any other photos or just this one with the plastic tits out?" asked my father in disgust. "If you want to know my opinion I think she's a prostitute," he added matter-of-factly.

"How do you know what a prostitute looks like?" mum snapped, and dad gasped.

"That's one of the best photos I've got." My parents looked at me both astonished and terrified. "I mean one of the most decent ones."

"Yeah, it's her," mum said decisively. "She's the estate agent I told you about. I've got her business card somewhere here," mum opened a cupboard hanging above her smart white desk in the kitchen to take out a silver box with a glass lid.

"He's not only been unfaithful but also stupid," dad murmured. "If I was cheating on your mother I wouldn't have any photos of my lover on our computer... or tablet or whatever you call it."

"I'm glad to hear that you would be clever enough to hide your affair."

"You know what I mean my darling," dad said affectionately. "I wouldn't have any photos but I would also never, never ever, have any lover in the first place," he said excessively loudly like he wanted somebody next door to hear him, and then he bent towards me and whispered, "You can't hide anything from your mother."

"I heard that Adam. I'm just not sure whether that's the best reason not to have a lover," mum was fiddling with a pile of business cards that she threw on the table from her box.

"Although I don't know whether you can't hide anything from her anymore, she's not as organised as she used to be," he said with a big grin on his face.

"Do you want me to help you or not?" asked my mother, the only totally sober person in the house. Dad's first reaction to seeing the photos was pouring us both whisky.

"When Henry takes a photo with his tablet, it automatically appears on my tablet, which for a while used to be ours because Henry didn't want to waste money to have his own" I was explaining as if it made any difference to our already ruined relationship. "He must've somehow switched on the Cloud back-up without even realising it…"

"I've got it," mum shouted proud of herself as if she'd been holding the key to the New York Federal gold vault.

I glanced at a black business card with gold letters, "Mum, have you never asked yourself why Henry employed an estate agent from Manhattan to see our house in Dream Fields? Kitty Allen? Hmmm… Is Kitty even a name or is it from Katherine?

"I don't understand it either," said dad and threw a couple of cubes of ice into his second glass of whisky. "Maybe if your mother wasn't so obsessed with you breaking up with Henry, which actually would have been the best decision saving us all this drama… although I love my grandchildren so—"

"I asked her for a business card and you have to admit it was a good move," she said proudly. "If it wasn't for me, we wouldn't know now who Kitty is! Not only that, I've got you the address and phone number of the company she works for."

"Now we also know how Henry combated his fear of flying. The temptation to see those massive boobs overcame his fear."

"He probably justified it in his twisted little head that he would survive anything by landing on that chest," said dad with a dead serious face.

"If the romance had been going since at least May, I don't understand why he would propose to you in the summer?" mum looked totally confused and she was normally very good at working out conspiracies – mainly due to her deep knowledge of South American telenovelas, which seemed to touch every possible domestic and love drama. "I know!" she exclaimed with her forefinger raised high in the air. "Henry has a twin brother! It makes perfect sense! You've also got twins with him, it must be hereditary!"

"Your mother is incredible. I've already told you that you can't hide anything from her," my father said full of admiration. "But..." he hesitated while flicking through more photos "maybe he did it because the woman is also engaged to somebody else."

"What are you talking about?" I asked.

"Oh, leave it," said mum trying to take the tablet from dad but he stopped her with his open palm.

"Look," he pointed to a photo I hadn't seen before. Kitty was wearing a big shiny diamond ring, which she was proudly showing to the camera.

"My ring!" I screamed.

"He's not worth you," mum tried to comfort me without any success.

"No kidding," snapped dad. "I'm glad we found out before you married the bastard."

"She'll play around with Henry and marry the other guy. Henry will end up sad and lonely with no one," said mum, who once used to be Henry's biggest fan and a cheerleader of our relationship.

"You don't understand anything," I was making small circles around my kitchen island. "Kitty is engaged to Henry. He gave her the ring. I saw the ring before our... before my trip to Madrid. It was hidden between Henry's books."

"But you said he wanted to get married as soon as possible so he must have changed his mind after the boys were born and turned out to be his. He must know bigamy is illegal. I don't mean to defend him but—"

"So don't!" dad interrupted her.

"He wanted to get married so I wouldn't have to testify against him," as I was explaining it my mother's neck was slowly getting covered in a red rash. "Henry was selling some exam questions and essays to students."

"He said he was chasing those who were doing that," dad was saying. "I don't understand."

"He did both actually. Henry is a man of many interests."

"Why haven't you told us earlier?" mum was lamenting. "Why do I always have to be the last one to find out?"

"I didn't know what to say! Hi mum. Hi dad. You're going to be grandparents but I don't know who the father is. Would you prefer A – a Spanish guy who I really don't know that well, or B – a criminal?"

Dad sighed and turned to mum, "When we found out that Olivia had to do the paternity tests I tried to explain to you it wasn't the end of the world, and always could've been worse. It turns out I also can be right some times," he smiled.

"My congratulations Adam," she snapped irritated.

"Now isn't the right time to argue. We need to think about how to put the bastard behind bars so our daughter and grandchildren are free from his toxic company."

"Adam, do you really want the father of your grandchildren to go to prison? Oh, I still can't believe it. He was making such a good impression of being a well-behaved man with a respectable job—"

"At least one of his jobs was respectable," he cut her off.

"How could I know about his other jobs?"

"Stop. It doesn't matter now," I shouted and we all went silent.

* * *

It was just after one when mum, dad and I decided that the best thing was to sleep on the problem and come back to the discussion in the morning. The issue was, none of us could fall asleep. I didn't hear my father snoring next door, but I could hear mum walking downstairs, listening to the radio and watching some old films from her collection of DVDs – she had her I-cannot-sleep routine. I was turning from one side to the other and counting Henry's imaginary and not-so-imaginary lovers: one – blonde with gigantic boobs and my ring, two – ginger with freckles and a Scottish accent, three – tall and slim model, four – fat clever professor from his university… When I finally fell asleep I woke up less than an hour later covered with sweat after a dream, in which I was thrown into a cell with Henry and a few other convicts – all bald with huge arms, tattoos all over their body and big eyes just staring at us. I got up, made one circle around the room, bumped into a chair, got a couple of bruises and texted Gatsby:

```
Why didn't you tell me Henry had a lover? Did he
pay you not to do so?
```

He replied quicker than I'd expected at that time of the night. Could he also not sleep? Was he bothered by remorse or conscience?

```
I had no idea about any lover! The affair must be
a very recent thing!
```

```
Can't be!!! She was in my house in Dream Fields,
while I was crying after him in Madrid!!!
```

. . .

From what I remember you weren't crying so much
and you weren't there alone for more than a few
hours ;)

I'm sorry. I've forgotten that during that time
you were still working for Henry and spying on
me!!!

He sacked me as soon as I was back from Spain. I
tried to convince him to tell you everything
about his new business but he only got furious
with me.

Why would you tell him about Hugo but hide from
me that Henry had a lover??? I know about
Kitty!!!

Haven't heard about any Kitty! Didn't tell him
anything about Hugo except that I met you with
him at the station.

And you also didn't know he was flying to the US
to see Kitty???

Gatsby didn't reply and I had a feeling that he had enough of my accusations. I didn't really blame him for that. It was four o'clock in the
morning and I was probably the last person he wanted to talk to. I was
making myself comfortable on my favourite right side – the one I was
advised not to sleep on while pregnant – when my phone suddenly

rang. I picked it up almost immediately, swearing in my head for not switching off the vibrate. Luckily the twins were deep asleep.

"Gatsby?" I asked as if I couldn't believe it was him and I moved to the en-suite bathroom not to tempt my luck and wake up the boys.

"Olivia, I didn't go to the States."

"I paid for your flight in premium economy."

"I gave you a fifty percent discount at the end. I would have even given you the information for free if I had it. The thing is Henry didn't pay me for my last job, and I still had to pay my bills. I switched to working part-time in my old IT firm because Henry had convinced me he would need me a lot more, and I would earn twice as much by working for him than in my old company."

"Well, you're not the only victim of Henry's lies."

"Is Kitty from America?"

"She is but... tell me how Henry found out that the twins might not have been his children? I mean how did YOU find out?"

"You don't know with whom you've got your children?" he screamed sounding genuinely surprised.

I felt a pinch of embarrassment. "I know now and Henry is the father... What I don't know is whether I can still trust you."

"Well, I've called you to see whether I can help you and I didn't have to. It's four o'clock in the morning, right? I've always liked you more than Henry."

"In Madrid you were quite brittle, if not even harsh to me."

"Women love going back to the past," he sighed and I knew at that moment he deeply regretted calling me. "I worked then for Henry. I was just angry with you that you'd given up on him so easily. I wasn't aware of the whole story, and Henry made sure he put himself in the best possible light. Anyway, as I said I did try to convince him to tell you the truth about his job. I told him the chances were that he would lose you otherwise..."

"Why would you care whether he loses me or not?"

I heard Gatsby taking a deep breath. "My wife is right. I shouldn't get involved so much in other people's lives."

"But you did and I'm glad you told me about his peculiar business,"

I used the word *peculiar* because I was trying at all costs to avoid mentioning on the phone that Henry was involved in anything illegal. Who knows who was listening. You can't be too careful when the stakes are so high. "Although maybe it would be easier not to know… It wouldn't have been so hard to marry him in a pre-Kitty world—"

"To marry so you can't testify against him?"

I was terrified to say anything and I regretted picking up the phone and waking up Gatsby with my texts in the first place.

"No, we've got children together, don't you remember?"

"Is Henry going to be accused of—"

"He most definitely needs a good lawyer right now."

"Okay, I need to finish. I've got a job interview in the morning," Gatsby was talking very quickly. "Then I'll need to call my lawyer and he's currently in Jamaica – I saw it last night on his Instagram. Damn it! Never mind, we'll be in touch," he didn't wait for me to say goodbye.

Once again I was left alone with my thoughts. I didn't trust Gatsby but something was telling me that he was more on mine than Henry's side and he really didn't know about the paternity tests or Kitty Allen.

32

MONDAY, 29 FEBRUARY

DREAM FIELDS

"How did he manage to convince you? Just tell me! How could you pretend to be my friend for so long?" I was shouting, while she was staring at me blankly. She didn't even try to move her lips to pretend that she wanted to say something in her defence. "Why would you do this to me? Did you desperately need money or was he giving you some exam questions?"

"Exam questions?" she asked confused.

"Never mind," I said as she most likely had no idea about Henry's *peculiar* business.

For a few long minutes neither of us dared to make a move. We were sitting on two armchairs in my living room and facing each other across a distance of not more than two feet, which was close enough to feel her quick breath, smell of sweet perfumes and a recently drunk coffee. I heard my loudly pounding heart and I was imagining hers was even louder. *I'm not going to give up even if I have to force it out of you with some kind of torture. I could tie you to a chair and put you next to a dripping tap, apparently after a while it gets painful. What a good torture for a plumber!*

"Henry blackmailed me to do it," Meg shouted all of a sudden as if she could read my mind and was scared of the dripping tap.

"Really? He barely knows you! Has it ever crossed your deceitful mind that I could have married the cheater and liar?"

"With all due respect you're not a saint either. How can you be so furious about Henry having an affair with Kitty while you thought you were pregnant by Hugo?"

"I've never been with both of them at the same time," I snapped angry that she didn't understand the difference between the two completely different relationships.

"I thought Henry was a good guy, who really cared about you—"

"And I was the bad one? I told you how he broke up with me."

"You also said that he had some serious reason to behave like that so I trusted you."

"Anyway, it wasn't your place to tell him Hugo might've been the father. You also shouldn't have lied to me about the time I received that parcel from Hugo. It was for me to decide with whom I wanted to be!"

"I must admit I let myself go too far," Meg, always so confident, now was talking like something was squeezing her throat. Her voice kept cracking, and at times I felt like she was about to cry. She put both hands into the wide pockets of her grey hoodie only to take them out from there within a minute and start fiddling with the drawstring. "Look, I was convinced I was rescuing you from making one of the biggest mistakes of your life. Henry was so wonderful to you on your birthday, and I knew then that the silly parcel from Hugo could ruin everything for you and Henry. I was right, as soon as you opened it, you went half way across Europe, pregnant and alone just to see a man who you barely knew."

"It's not your life. You're only my flat mate," I said through gritted teeth.

"I wish somebody had stopped me from making the biggest mistake in my life. I left my long-term boyfriend for an Italian who I met during a holiday with my sister—"

"Boyfriend? You left him for an Italian… what sort of Italian?"

"Do you mean whether it was an Italian woman?" she laughed. "Olivia, I'm not a lesbian."

"Of course you are not but if you were it's fine with me… It's wonderful. I wish I was a lesbian, my life would be so much easier."

"It wouldn't be," she snapped. "You've got a gift to complicate your life, and whether it's with a man or a woman in your case it truly wouldn't matter… And you totally thought I was a lesbian. I heard you saying it once on the phone to Hannah… and Atlanta, and Freya, and that male friend of yours who wanted to ask me out…"

"You're clearly a good spy."

Meg looked at me with pity, "When one day I build my own house I'll make sure all the internal walls are brick. It'll save so much drama."

"It does, especially when you live with somebody who's got an agenda and likes pressing their nosey ears against the walls."

"If it wasn't for me you wouldn't have a clue Henry had been having an affair." My eyes were wide open and once again I was confused on whose team Meg was – mine or Henry's. "When I found out about his affair I was shocked and I decided to link his phone and tablet with yours in the way that each time he takes a photo it appears on—"

"Oh my god, I thought he was so stupid he…" I was looking at her shaking her head with a smug face. "I've always been on your side. I really like you Olivia."

"I've really liked you too," I said feeling that I would miss Meg – or rather my old perception of her. "That's why I'm sorry you will have to move out today. I'll give you back the rent you've already paid for March."

"I need a bit more time. Could you give me a few more days to leave?"

"No and please don't try to use the deal that we've signed to give yourself another month. You've been spying on me, which is defi-nitely a violation."

"I wouldn't even dare… it's just that I've got loads of stuff and nowhere to go."

"I'm sorry to hear that," I said flatly examining my nails that needed a manicure. "You can store your tools here for… let's say a week, but I don't want to see you ever again in my house. I can't feel safe around you… Get yourself a hotel room, call some friends. I don't care."

* * *

24 HOURS EARLIER

I couldn't stop wondering whether Gatsby had been honest with me. Did he really have no idea about the paternity tests? If he was telling me the truth, there must have been someone else around me who had betrayed me. First my suspicion had fallen on Hannah, and then on Meghan – they were my newest friends and I really didn't know them that well. I was envisaging Hannah making me the laughing stock of her night out with some posh girlfriends in London. I got myself practically convinced she made up Oscar as the constantly busy guy so it would be easier for her to justify his notorious absence. *Does he even exist? And is Tony real?* Her story seemed to be a little far-fetched, especially when considering its similarity to my current life situation. She chatted me up when we were waiting to see the doctor, who happened to be late for the first time in fifteen years. Was it deliberate? Did she and Henry pay doctor Cromwell to be late or did they send a patient to keep him sufficiently busy so Hannah and I had an opportunity to bond and get each others numbers? Had Hannah been pretending the whole time she was putting sun cream on my back, while in reality she was plotting where to stab me silently without anybody noticing?

On Sunday afternoon, when many people in the country were having their roast dinner, I was standing in front of Hannah's door knocking on it impatiently. As soon as she opened it I was planning to shout out I knew everything and let myself rant at her on her posh staircase of one of the newest glass skyscrapers in Canary Wharf.

"Hi, I'm glad you're finally here because I'm starving. Have you been stuck in traffic or what? If my pizza is cold I expect a discount," said a tall unshaved man dressed in a red velvet robe and a pair of red matching slippers with a hole over his right big toe. The part of his face that wasn't covered with a few days stubble was pale and green-ish. I couldn't tell, however, whether the hoarseness in his voice was a result of over-drinking or a cold.

"I'm here to see Hannah," I said, which sounded more like a question than a statement. *Do I have the right address? It can't be.*

"So you're going to be disappointed," he said taking out a cigarette from his robe and lighting it so close to my face I thought for a second he intended to set fire to me. "Hannah moved out yesterday. She took the children and I don't know when or if she's ever going to come back."

"Are you Oscar?"

"I'm Oscar, and who are you?"

"Olivia Eliot, nice to meet you," I said stretching my right hand towards him. I held it at the height of his belly for a couple of seconds, then not getting any response I returned it to holding my handbag. "Oh…" I didn't know what to say, but even if I did I wouldn't have had the pleasure to speak as he slammed the door on my face. I was standing there for a minute in shock, while listening to him shouting behind the door, "bloody women, you're all worth each other."

When I got out of the building I was even angrier with Hannah for her not being there so I could've shouted at her. I called her without much hope she would answer but to my surprise she did after just one ring – then I quickly reminded myself she still didn't have a clue I was about to accuse her of snitching on me to Henry. She didn't hesitate when I said I wanted to see her and she invited me over to the apartment that she was renting in one of London's five-star hotels.

We sat down in her living room, while her kids were in the bedroom next door. The apartment was the size of a flat that most people weren't able to afford to rent in the city.

"Who's paying for this?" I started straight away from attacking her in spite of having absolutely no proof she was the snitch. "Is it Oscar or Henry?"

"Have you lost your mind? Do you think I'm having an affair with Henry?"

"I think… Actually, I know it for sure that Henry is having an affair

369

with Kitty Allen, but you've been telling him my secrets. I know you told him I didn't know who the father of my children was."

"Wasn't it Gatsby who told Henry?"

"That's what you want me to believe."

"Darling, I'm sure you haven't thought this through," she gave me a merciful look and took a cupcake from a silver tray – she had ordered via room service before my arrival. "Why would I spy on you? Henry has nothing to offer that would interest me. You need some sleep, you're tired and overwhelmed which makes you more vulnerable to be paranoid."

She might be right, I was thinking although I didn't like the bit where she suggested I was paranoid. Hannah had a law degree that she obtained long before Henry was involved in selling education. She had said recently her marriage prenup was invalid as she was able to prove her signature was forged. *But she could have been lying... Should I employ a PI to discover who has been spying on me? Or would it only confirm my paranoia?*

"I've got to the point in my life where nothing is a surprise anymore," I said and took a large bite of chocolate cupcake thinking I wasn't ready to lose any weight yet.

"How much do you trust your flatmate?" she asked all of a sudden as we were both stuffing our faces in the hotel cakes for two reasons – one, they were amazing, and two, they were a great excuse not to talk.

"Meghan?" I asked and she nodded energetically. "I can't make everybody a suspect."

"You've tried to make me into one," she snapped.

"Fair enough," I said thinking that I had to at least listen to Hannah's ideas.

"You said that Meg didn't even try to bargain over the price."

"Total opposite. She suggested paying ten percent more than other people who wanted to rent the room."

"And she probably lied to you about the time when you received the parcel from Hugo. She didn't get the days wrong, it was a few weeks. Have you asked her about that?"

"Hmmm..." I started wondering whether Hannah the spy could

pay Meg to pretend to be the spy, but then I came to the conclusion that I was definitely getting paranoid.

* * *

"I'm really sorry Olivia. I never meant to hurt you and—"

"What else have you got from Henry except free rent?"

"He hasn't paid my rent," Meg raised her hands up defensively. "I haven't got anything from him. He just blackmailed me, I've told you... Please could I stay here for one more day?"

"No way."

"There's something in your garden that I need to take," she said slowly and quietly, and I felt like my stomach moved upside down.

"Something like the bench you gave me for my birthday? Fine, but the plaque with the quote wasn't from you so I'm going to take it off even if it leaves a couple of holes in the bench."

"It's better for you not to know and trust me, you want me to get rid of this before the police come to search your house."

I swallowed hard and suddenly felt dizzy, "Is there a dead body in my garden? Oh my god! Oh my god..." I kept saying louder and louder. "I've got a corpse in my garden. Take it. Oh, my god, have you killed the person yourself?"

"Who do you think I am?" she asked calmly. "There's some money dug deep in your garden and when Henry finds out I don't want to cooperate with him anymore, he might tell the police."

"What have you done? No. Wait. I don't want to know... No, I should know what's been going on in my house."

"If you insist," she said nonchalantly like nothing mattered anymore and it really couldn't get worse so what the heck! "I left my fiancé for an Italian man I met during a holiday. I'd never been so crazily in love. I totally lost my mind... I must've done because we got married less than six months later on Sicily. Giuseppe was... he was... God, I would have never thought a man like him would pay any attention to me..."

"Oh, please Meg. True, you've let yourself go but one visit to a spa and a hairdresser would sort you out. Plus, it would help if you throw away the baggy trousers and stretched jumpers and got yourself a few nice dresses. I can go shopping with you… No, I can't…" I reminded myself. "I can't because we're not friends anymore."

"When I met him, I was also nearly a stone and a half lighter. When he was gone, I started eating through my pain."

"He wasn't worth it."

"He wasn't but my money was," she said matter-of-factly. "He left me with debt," she sighed like she didn't really want to reflect on the past. "He talked me into building our own house, which wasn't difficult because at the time I would have done anything for him. My grandparents left me some land in Wales, I knew I could do loads myself, I had great connections with builders and all the knowledge – why not, I thought! So, we took a loan."

"Ouch, I think I know where it's going."

"It might be worse actually. I took the loan myself because he didn't have a permanent job as a model."

"But as your husband—"

"No, I got the loan just before we got married. He said that we could use a small part of the money for our quiet wedding on Sicily. Long story short. We got married, at least that was what I thought because actually Giuseppe faked the whole ceremony with a friend of his so it wasn't legally binding, and then he took all the money and ran away."

"How much?"

"Two hundred thousand," she said with a squeezed throat and I couldn't stop myself from a squeal.

"I feel really sorry for you but it doesn't mean I can let myself trust you again."

"I'm well aware of that," she said with her eyes down. "The only thing I'm asking you to do is to let me take my ten thousand pounds, which I dug under your paving slabs when you were in Grenada."

"Another slap to my naïve face! And I thought you just wanted to help me with the paving."

"And you were right because I only got the idea after I started digging..."

"Why are you hiding the money?"

"As I said Giuseppe ran away with his beautiful lover," Meg looked ashamed and despite the fact she betrayed me to Henry I felt sorry for her. "I wasn't the first one who was fooled by that pair of con artists. It turned out that they had lived like that for seven years going around the world and hunting for their prey to fund their perpetual holiday. They eventually got caught and went to jail but banks aren't charities, and my ex with his girlfriend didn't have much money when they were finally caught by the police."

"I bet they hid the money."

"I wouldn't be surprised but the point is that I'm bankrupt, every month the bank takes most of my money and gives me just a small allowance to live on. The hidden ten thousand is my only chance to get myself something extra. My land was auctioned but I've still got almost a hundred grand to pay off."

"I would actually feel better if Henry paid you some money." *One fraud boyfriend paying for the sins of another*, I thought.

"Tough luck," she cast her eyes down again. "I wish he was paying me for the information but of course I would never do it just for money! Instead he caught me red handed when I was putting the money into the ground at night and ta-da – he suddenly had an idea!"

"What a dick! A lucky dick actually! But hopefully not for much longer."

"Initially, I thought he was just desperate and his primary goal was to save your relationship. I know from my own experience that people can be stupid and dumb when they fall in love. I quickly explained to myself that by protecting my money and my arse from going to jail, I was also helping Henry who was in love and overall had good intentions. I thought that you – just like me – lost your mind for a hot-looking guy who wasn't worth your love."

"How could you ever compare Hugo to Giuseppe?"

Meg ignored my question and continued, "But when you were in Madrid I met Kitty Allen."

"You did what?" I stood up feeling I wasn't able to stay still in my chair.

"She arrived here in the morning on the same day you came back from Madrid. You missed each other by just a few hours. She thought I was you and I was too shocked and confused to immediately correct her. She was also speaking very quickly not giving me any chance to say much. She introduced herself as Henry's fiancée."

"I don't get it. It was soon after Henry proposed to me, and why would she come here instead of the flat he was still renting in London?"

"Let's say Kitty was inspired by Henry's insta-story from your big birthday proposal. She said she needed to know what the hell was going on. Apparently, Henry proposed to me just after she rejected his proposal because – so she said – it was too soon to get married after less than a year of dating long-distance," Meg was speaking quickly and excitedly as if it concerned her own life.

"He cheated on both of us," I said suddenly having some warmer feeling toward the big boobs blonde. "No wait! What? He also proposed to you?"

"Kitty thought I was you," she gasped and I felt as stupid as a cow calmly chewing grass in a field. "But how could she mistake you for me if she saw me on Instagram?" I got suspicious again, reminding myself that anything Meg was saying might be a lie.

"The photos were taken at night and showed more Henry than you..." she was explaining quite sensibly. Henry had always been so narcistic it made sense. "Besides, Kitty was so furious it could've clouded her judgment. Remember that she flew trans-Atlantic just after she saw her fiancé proposing to another woman."

"To tell me Henry was hers?" I laughed out loud. "I can help her to pack his things and become their wedding organiser if it ensures he's gone for good."

"She's still married to somebody so it would be difficult..."

"Wonderful," I snapped. "That explains why she didn't want to rush into getting hitched with Henry. Paulina, Hugo..." I was counting loudly on my fingers, "Henry, Kitty, Kitty's husband, me. It's time somebody stops the adventures of this romantic circle."

"I was afraid how Henry would react if I told you the truth so I came up with the whole idea of connecting his phone to your tablet."

"Well, I'm grateful you did and I wish we could still be friends."

"Could I ask you for something?" she said sheepishly.

"Dig your money out tonight, but you need to leave in the morning."

"Thank you. Could you also tell Henry you kicked me out for another reason?"

"I'll tell him Hannah will be moving in with her children."

"The Hannah? Has she finally left Oscar?"

I wasn't going to share anything personal with her that concerned my life or the lives of my friends. We stared at each other for a minute before she realised our relationship had really changed irreparably.

"Right," she sighed. "I get it… I should probably tell you one more thing."

"More good news?" I rubbed my temples and took a couple of loud breaths like I was anticipating physical pain.

"When you were in Madrid, Hugo was here," she said and paused waiting for my reaction. All I did was widely open my mouth. "I told him you were away on holiday with Henry, and probably…" she hesitated again.

"I can't believe you. And probably what?" I shouted but she only shrugged her shoulders whispering silently *nothing else*. "Do you want me to tell Henry why I kicked you out?" I said through gritted teeth wondering how it could've got to this, me scaring other people with my evil ex-fiancé.

"I told him you probably eloped to have a quiet wedding on a beach with just witnesses."

"Never mind, it does look like the whole world has been acting against us being together. We're obviously not meant for each other."

"That's nonsense," Meg said decisively hitting the side of the armchair with her clenched fists. "He was amazing the whole time you were in hospital and after the twins were born."

375

"Just a real shame that you've waited so long to tell me that he was in my house in September," I said wanting to instil some guilt in her.

"Henry wanted me to convince you to marry him. It was my last task, then he promised to leave me alone. He texted me today. Olivia, he thinks you want to propose to him after you've already rejected him twice."

"That's more than ridiculous!"

"Initially I thought exactly the same but it's the twenty-ninth today, a leap year and—"

"And Henry's birthday," I nodded. "Then I can't wait to see his disappointed and wide-open gob... Meg, I want you to leave me alone tonight and don't come back before I text you. I'm sorry but you might need to dig your money out in the middle of the night." She looked at me questioningly. "I would like to prepare a special dinner for our birthday boy!"

* * *

Henry was a leap-year baby, who decided to celebrate his birthday only every four years. Once I got him a present and I gave it to him during a romantic self-made dinner on the twenty-eighth of February – it was a rare signed hardback and a designer shirt (bought at full-price!), which he kindly accepted but then equally kindly asked me not to do it again except on his real birthday. At the time I thought it was quirky, now I think it was stupid, rude and lacked any appreciation or empathy.

But when his 'real birthday' occurred, he wouldn't miss the chance to celebrate and invited all his friends and work colleagues to go clubbing with him in London. Like every well-organised person would do, he sent his invites just after New Year and suggested everybody take a day off the following day. While his old friends were amused, the new ones were stunned thinking it must have been a joke, and Henry always had to personally make a few phone calls explaining that he was serious and he wasn't going through any kind of crisis. People were stunned because everybody knew Henry wasn't a clubbing type of person. He was a pub crawl kind of person or sitting-on-the-couch-with-a-glass-of-wine type of person. Since I met him I had only participated in such an event once – it was four years before at his thirty-first birthday – we had known each other for just under a year and Henry already seemed to be my dream candidate for a husband and a father of my future children. At the time he was finishing his doctorate, worked full-time at a prestigious university in London and regularly took part in marathons in the UK and abroad. In his busy life he always found the time for me. We used to regularly go out for dinner or a drink in a nearby bar, see the latest movies in the cinema and the best shows in London. During our romantic dinners with candles, Henry kept saying he wanted to buy a house in the suburbs of London and travel around the world with his lectures. Our plan was that I would often go with him writing articles while on our crazy romantic and adventurous journeys. It was a real shame that one day Henry's enthusiasm started fading away to finally become just a sweet distant memory within our relationship.

It was sad to look at Henry paying from his own pocket for additional courses and qualifications, studying hard on the weekends and at night only to get a tiny pay increase and a word of approval from the dean of his university. Henry's frustration was getting deeper and deeper, which also had a bad effect on us – he became unbearably grumpy at times and incredibly moody, so when he received an offer to give some guest lectures in the US and he also spent more time with his students I actually felt relieved. I got to see him less often but once again I enjoyed the time we spent together. Unfortunately, just when everything seemed to be going in the right direction – he finally had the appreciation that he deserved and a decent pay rise – I felt we were millions of miles away from each other. He didn't listen to me, and I never heard again about going around the world – no feeding koalas in Australia, no selfies with penguins on the Falklands, no surfing in California and no trips to the jungle in Brazil. *Nada!*

* * *

When Meg left, I changed the boys' clothes for the third time that day, packed all their necessary stuff into two large bags, and drove them to my parents. On my way back, I quickly did some shopping and ended up with a bulky bag full of groceries, a new smart dress with some extra space for my still far-from-perfection belly, and a present for Henry. Before I unpacked everything at home, I sat by a big table in the lounge holding a mug of hot chocolate and thinking about Henry's last birthday party. My enduring memory was him dancing on a table at around two o'clock in the morning, shouting one of the Backstreet Boys' songs into a microphone and winking to all the pretty girls in front of the stage. I didn't recognise him then, but I quickly forgot about the whole incident blaming everything on him getting totally smashed. Four years later preparing his birthday dinner I was wondering how much I recognised myself from that girl I was before I met Henry Thyme and before he left me at the airport.

Then my thoughts returned to that last birthday when we left the last club that night and caught a taxi home at five o'clock in the morning.

"Have you been partying so much after you proposed to your boyfriend?" asked the taxi driver, while adjusting his baseball cap. "I've never heard before about the whole girls' leap year proposals thing but tonight I've already picked up three newly engaged couples and each time it was—"

"No," I interrupted him and burst out laughing. "I would never do it." I said and glanced at Henry making drunk-googly eyes.

"I think it would be rather cool if we could say one day to our children and grandchildren that—"

"No," I said this time even more categorically.

* * *

"Wow! Olivia, it all looks fabulous," Henry was pretending to be surprised while we both knew the romantic dinner was the bare minimum he expected that night.

"I just thought it would be nice to finally have a slow dinner, just

378

the two of us in the house we bought together. We haven't really had a chance to celebrate moving in – with so much happening in the last few months. And now we've also got your birthday – and we'll have to wait another four years for your next one... Hold on a minute, it means that we'll celebrate your thirty-ninth birthday but we'll skip your fortieth..." I was saying this with a forced sweet smile, while simultaneously wondering why I couldn't stop all the words coming out of my mouth. I felt like somebody had got into my body to talk to Henry, and I was shouting for them to shut up but nobody could hear me.

Henry seemed to be more focused on food than conversation. He was smelling the meals I'd previously unpacked from several silver trays, reheated in the oven and served as home-made. I binned all the packaging into a black bag, tied it tightly at the end and moved to the large bin that we stored in the garage.

"Wow," he kept saying. "This fish pie is even better than the one my mum makes." I gave my first and probably last honest laugh – such a compliment would have never gone through his throat if he wasn't expecting something big to happen tonight.

I lit candles while holding a remote under the table, he didn't notice they were not real. I poured him a glass of white wine and switched on a music play list he loved, and I just about tolerated. "I hope you don't regret cancelling your clubbing for tonight," I said innocently.

"I told everybody that we might join them later but it's entirely up to you," he said and I knew immediately he expected me to go out with him later and it definitely was not up to me.

Henry reached with one hand for a crystal glass that we got from his parents as our engagement present, while his other hand energeti-cally pushed a fork into the claimed-to-be organic but massively over-priced fish pie – I thought that even I could make a better one and I wasn't a particularly good cook. I could tell he was enjoying the meal and wine but he looked like he was mulling over something – it crossed my mind he might have even felt guilty about the affair with Kitty. While he was happily stuffing his face with the pie and quickly drinking his wine, I suddenly felt that all I wanted was to put an end to the whole sham – to stab the fork into his hand, push the bottle of wine down his throat and kick his arse out of the house, but last minute I managed to resist the temptation.

"Olivia you're amazing," he said through a full mouth, probably meaning that the food was amazing, not me.

"I'm glad you like it. I've spent a lot of time in the kitchen today."

"I love you, you're my one and only," he was saying this while staring mostly at his plate, and occasionally glancing at me.

I couldn't listen to his lies so before he finished the main course, I went to the kitchen to take a chocolate cake from the oven, which I was obviously only heating up as it got cold on its trip from the shop. The smell of the cake brought sudden memories of my childhood and I started wondering whether I would ever be able to create a normal family for my children, and whether my boys could still have the happy childhood I had.

When I was back to clean the table and make some space for the birthday cake, Henry was pouring himself a whole glass of wine, while leaving my glass completely empty. He kindly took his hands away so I could collect the dirty plates and cutlery. On the way to the kitchen I switched off the light in the living room and asked him to close his eyes – although I still had thirty-five candles to put into his favourite cake before presenting it to him.

"Can't I open them yet?" he was shouting from the lounge.

"Now," I said at least ten minutes later when I was standing behind his back with one shaky hand on his arm. Henry's eyes went wide open – as wide open as his mouth.

He looked so aghast I was confident he hadn't anticipated such a surprise. For a moment he totally lost his voice, which didn't happen very often – he always had something to say. *Tell me the truth Henry, I* was begging him in my head. *Tell me that you can't do it. Show me the last trace of decency in you.* I was staring at the cake with thirty-five candles squeezed clumsily around pink icing stating – *will you marry me?* It was cheesy and the letters weren't quite straight but it was the only ready-made-icing-marriage-proposal I managed to find at the last minute. The young male shop assistant could hardly stop giggling when selling it to me in the cake shop.

"Olivia, honey…" he finally spoke up. "Is it really what you want?" his voice was cracking, and I was becoming more and more confused as to whether he was pretending – because he was secretly recording the whole event to prove later in court that our marriage was genuine – or whether he was honestly surprised and touched.

I nodded and he quickly shaped his lips into a beak and closed his eyes. *You've got to be kidding me,* I thought. When no kiss landed on his lips, he opened his eyes and frowned his eyebrows.

"You still haven't answered the question," I said matter-of-factly.

"Oh," he gave me a beaming smile – too beaming for somebody who gets married only to protect his arse in court. "Of course, I will."

"Wonderful," I clapped my hands and rushed towards the window, where behind the long curtains I had hidden his present. It was large, flat and wrapped in blue paper with various modes of transport on it, predominantly planes – which I had once bought for Sebastian.

"You didn't have to. You're my biggest present," he said quickly taking the gift from my hands and impatiently ripping the paper off.

"It's just a little something. I framed some of our photos. I hope you like it… Do you?" I asked innocently when Henry had managed to unpack his birthday collage. "Surprise," I sang and laughed but instead of a smile on his face I saw how his lips rolled and eyes narrowed. "What's wrong? Oh no!" I said in a singing voice. "Sebastian was helping me," I lied. "He must have stuck some photos in of the wrong fiancée."

"Great surprise, I would never have thought you could be so—"

"Creative? Well, I only glued the pictures, I didn't take them," I said glancing at the half-naked Kitty rolling in white bedding with the diamond ring that was supposed to be mine.

He took a deep breath, "Look, she doesn't mean much… I mean she doesn't mean anything to me."

"Of course not. Nobody means anything to you but yourself, you lying-son-of-a-bitch-arse!" I exploded like a volcano realising all the emotions that had been accumulating in me for the last few hours.

"It's not what you're thinking. I'm currently going through therapy. It can be cured."

"There is a cure for being an arse? Wonderful but in your case it's too late. What you really needed was a vaccination against becoming an arse."

"It's not my fault I'm carrying the gene of infidelity," he nodded, "That's right. I know! I was also surprised," he said straight-faced.

I chortled, "Is your doctor Kitty Allen? Are you also carrying the crime gene? It could be useful in court and maybe we wouldn't even have to get married?"

"I've got a note from my doctor saying that—"

"Please, save it for your lovers."

"I'm going to take injections with oxytocin which will make me completely immune to other women's charms."

"Good luck Henry. I, however, don't need any oxyto-anything to be completely immune to your charms anymore. I've genetically modified and improved myself to be able to get rid of arses like you from my life with great success, *Capiche?*"

"You can't just get rid of me from your life. I'm the father of your children," he said standing up and putting his hands on his hips. "You'll regret it when you have to tell the boys—"

"The truth? Look where we've got with all the lies."

"Sometimes it's better to—"

"Leave now," I said decisively. "Leave before I smash the cake in your face."

"I know you Olivia," he said mercifully. "After I leave, you'll need the cake to ease the pain of being completely alone. The whole chocolate cake will be gone within a quarter of an hour," he said with a smug face – the face that had never irritated me so much before.

I didn't like wasting food. I always felt bad about throwing away even the last piece of stale bread – I would normally try to take it to some hungry ducks. I gave one more look at the cake wondering how much effort somebody had put in to make it, then immediately absolving myself I grabbed it from the table with one swift move and pushed it straight into Henry's face.

He snorted out some bits of chocolate cream and jam into his hand and clicked his tongue a couple of times in disgust. "Yuck, cherry jam!" he shouted and still shocked started wiping the chocolate and cherry from his face, hair and from behind the grey collar of his shirt.

"I never planned on you eating it," I snapped feeling relieved.

When Henry left with bits of the cake still on his face I literally jumped to the fridge to get a fresh piece of cheesecake and expensive wine that had been chilling in my new carafe. I giggled to myself thinking about the cheap apple wine that I'd poured into the empty bottle of the vintage Chardonnay that I kept all for myself. Equipped with the cake and wine I sat down on my couch smiling to myself. I'd rested my head back and closed my eyes when my phone beeped.

```
What have you done with the additional day of the
year? I never work on the 29th Feb. If I can get
away without working the extra day most years, I
can have the day off once every four years.
```

I typed back immediately:

```
Oh Hugo, it's easy when you're self-employed and
don't have any children.
```

Understandably he didn't send anything back pronto. Considering all we had been through during the last months saying how lucky he was having no children was a bit of a faux pas that I instantly regretted. The answer came when I was mulling over nervously what to text him next.

```
Lucky me, I guess? How was your 29th? Busy?
```

. . .

```
Very busy. I've been doing some stocktaking, got
rid of a couple of useless things that were only
taking space in my life. I feel a wonderful
lightness of being!
```

My phone buzzed. We talked for half of the night. He was drinking his wine, I was drinking mine – physically miles away one from another – but we talked like two old friends who had met again after a very long journey.

33

FRIDAY, 11 MARCH, LONDON
LONDON

I -Heart-Travelling actively practiced a family unfriendly policy, which meant that no matter how long you'd worked for the company prior to having a child you only got statutory maternity pay – unless you were Tiggy or Cecilia, of course. Given that situation and Henry potentially going to jail, or in best case going bankrupt, I was planning to go back to work six weeks after giving birth. I was angry with myself for not trying hard enough to change my job a couple of years earlier when I was only responsible for myself, but it was too late to be sorry. All I could do was forgive myself for being a coward and move on. There was also Tiggy, who had already informed me that if I wanted to keep my job with the same pay, I would have to get back to work quickly or they find somebody to replace me. She told me about it flippantly, when I was washing my hands in the bathroom with my large belly pushing against the sink and my tired eyes looking through the mirror – at my pale and slightly plump face eight months pregnant. She was speaking to me loudly through a green toilet door not caring in the slightest whether there was somebody else around who could hear her subtle threats. I did some proper gymnastics to bend my back down and see whether there were other legs dangling in any of the five toilet cubicles, but I

385

could only see Tiggy's flowery wedges. Before I managed to say a word, the toilet's door swung wide open and shook all the loo cubicles. Tiggy rushed to the mirror to freshen up some make-up on her self-satisfied malicious face. At the time I took it quite well. I'd already known Tiggy was a malicious cow, and at the time I didn't feel that alone – both potential fathers were well-off and ready to help. Luckily, I could also count on mum, who ran her own translation company from home which was growing quickly, employing more and more people.

"I'll stay with the boys until you… yyy… until you find a better job or win the lottery," mum had suggested.

I wasn't particularly surprised when Tiggy's name appeared on my phone four weeks after I gave birth, but I thought she really outdid herself when she asked me to see her in her office first thing the next morning. Tiggy had a year of full-paid maternity leave but for some reason wanted to work at least one day every week of it and she started just a couple of weeks after giving birth.

Tiggy made a gesture for me to sit down on the chair in front of her desk. I thought that each time my bum had touched that leather armchair I'd been in some sort of trouble. She was standing sideways looking out of the window at London's skyscrapers with the upper floors covered with grey dense clouds. Just when I had the impression that she'd forgotten about my presence she suddenly spoke up, "Do you know why I asked you to be here today?"

"Yes, you said on the phone you wanted to talk about me coming back to work in a couple of weeks and my new responsibilities. I'm well aware I won't be able to work from home anymore." *Especially when Henry, your bestie, and I are not together. I bet he told you,* I added in my mind.

"The situation has actually changed," she said crossing her arms and turning back to me.

I was staring at her arse pushed into tight black jeggings. Gosh, your *bottom has rounded after the pregnancy, getting the a la Kim Kardashian style both in its shape and size,* I thought, and for a moment I got scared I might have said it aloud because she turned to me abruptly with a furious face. "Do you really not know why I asked you here?" she repeated the question with her face reddening and jaw shaking. She rested her hands on her desk stretching them out and she leaned forward so I could also see her perfectly rounded boobs. *Must be breastfeeding*, I thought. *Or she has already had a boob job since the birth.*

"Shall I guess?" I asked meekly as if I was afraid of my own voice.

Tiggy took her hands off the desk leaving on its wooden surface two wet marks and disappeared for a few seconds under her desk. As she was getting up from her knees she hit her head on the side of the desk, swore loudly and before I managed to acknowledge what was going on she threw a magazine at me. I dodged the magazine, which flew across the whole length of her office, hit the door and fell down on the floor.

Have they published my article about Grenada yet? I thought making myself deliriously happy for one short sweet little moment. I hadn't expected it would happen that quickly and irrespective I hadn't suspected that Tiggy would find out anyway – she didn't seem to read anything else than I-Heart-Travelling or gossip magazines. I knew she would be angry – she always was – but this time she truly outdid herself. I got up slowly the whole time keeping my eyes on Tiggy, in case she planned to throw something else at me, and I tiptoed towards the door.

"That's all? You don't have anything to say to me, not even a word of apology?" she said with her hands on her hips, blowing at her fringe and lightly shaking her head. I imagined her exploding with fury and covering the whole office with bits of her too tight black jeggings and too tight blouse with mustard and black strips, which made her look like a seriously pissed off wasp – you wouldn't want to piss her off any more. The only way forward was a quick evacuation.

"As usual you react completely inadequately to the situation. I'm on my way to make an official complaint," I said with a confidence that surprised even myself. "You can't abuse me anymore or use physical violence against me."

"Excuse me? Inadequately? I'm the laughing stock at work, and my husband is getting legal advice on potentially divorcing me. And that's all your fault."

"I'm thinking that…" I cleared my throat, "what's happening here Tiggy is that – and please excuse my language – you're losing your shit. How can any of that be my fault, eh?"

"Was it revenge for me not publishing any of your holiday *memoirs?*" she said in an exaggerated French accent.

"No, I've just sent my articles to *Travel Happy* and they've already replied. That's it. Somebody has finally appreciated my work and offered to pay for the two pieces my monthly wage, so why would I refuse it?" I said calmly but chastising myself for explaining any of that to her. *I don't need to justify anything to you!*

"And what? You're thinking now you're some sort of Marco Polo and you can do anything you want including destroying other people's lives? I shouldn't have given you the job but Henry insisted and I owed him. You've never appreciated the opportunity you've been given—"

"Enough," I said and reached for the magazine lying on the floor. "I'll have something to read on the train," I murmured and then my eyes landed on the cover of something that turned out to be a weekly news magazine. I read its front page three times and my head span.

HUGO TORTILLAS AND THEIR PROGRAM *AMIGO, HABLA CONMIGO* BECOMES THE NEW VICTIM OF CYBER-TERRORISM. SINCE ITS CUSTOMERS' DATA LEAKED ONTO THE INTERNET LAST WEEK, MILLIONS OF PEOPLE HAVE BEEN FORCED TO FACE ITS DEVASTATING CONSEQUENCES.

* * *

"Now you catch my drift, Miss I'm All Innocent?"

I shook my head, "I still don't—"

"How dare you pretend to be me?" Tiggy punched the desk with her fist. "Ouch," she screamed and blew on her red hand. "You did it to get back at me for—"

"Stop," I shouted sitting down on the floor with my back resting against one of the walls, legs stretched in front of me and feet touching the rug in the middle of the office. I'd always had the feeling that Tiggy bought the rug only so people could trip over it and she had something to laugh at. I read the whole *Your Weekly News* article with Tiggy constantly staring at me, breathing heavily.

"Firstly…" I started after I rolled the magazine and was holding it like a baseball bat. "Why do you think I was pretending to be you? And there's nothing about you here except…" I opened the magazine again to read aloud, "Luckily most people who did their question-naires for Hugo TorTillas used nicknames like Yogi Bear, Elvis P., Tiggy Brown or Donald Trump."

"You were in Madrid and I know from a reliable source that you had to do paternity tests. My advice for your future – start writing a sex diary if you're planning on being a total slut!"

"But there's nothing—"

"Have you read the part saying that you can find the fully completed questionnaires online, and each time they block one website, another one pops up? And guess what? My husband has already checked the questionnaire of the person with – oh such a funny nickname – Tiggy Brown. Now he's going to do a paternity test!"

"Why are you so furious? You have nothing to worry about if it's his child!"

"Of course, the child is his but he claims – and he's right – that it doesn't prove my fidelity."

"They said that Tiggy Brown is a nickname. Do you think that Donald Trump is going to call me too because I happen to know Hugo?"

"I wouldn't be surprised if it was you who released all the data," she shook angrily as she was saying it, staring at me with piercing eyes.

"You're just being paranoid," I said thinking that it was probably a wrong move – you cannot tell a woman she exaggerates or becomes paranoid if you don't want to see her even more angry and paranoid.

"How dare you?" she shouted fully exposing her lower and upper gums. "On the website you can check when you filled the question-naire and visited Hugo TorTillas. Everybody thinks it was me because I was on a business trip at the time! And I was pregnant!"

"Just a coincidence," I said innocently. Even if I'd tried hard I couldn't have come up with a better revenge. *Karma?* I felt a bit sorry for her but not enough to suddenly expose myself and tell everybody I used her name at the restaurant. "I still don't understand one thing – why would your husband so easily believe you were cheating on him? Plenty of people don't like you and could've taken revenge on you," I said fiddling with my hair and trying not to raise the corner of my lips.

To my surprise Tiggy didn't respond. She walked across her whole twenty square meter office and bent down to open a cupboard with a small fridge inside. She rested one of her arms on the side of a double sofa, while the other disappeared inside the personal fridge. I thought life wasn't fair – Tiggy had the spacious and luxurious office that was used predominantly to abuse her whole team, while most people in the company were so squeezed at their desks that they were happy when a person sitting next to them wasn't at work – at least it meant being able to stretched your arms a little more than on the tube during rush hour. I was patiently watching how Tiggy was taking out the whole contents of the fridge and distributing it on the floor: soft cheese, fruit salad, two bars of organic chocolate, a sand-wich and two small bottles of whiskey. *Has she nicked them from a hotel?*

"Will you have a glass of whisky with me?" she said while unpacking two crystal tumblers from a carton box that was at the bottom of her wardrobe.

"No thanks. I don't drink whisky."

She consumed the entire contents of her glass in two large gulps, smacked her tongue and said, "You don't know what you're missing."

"Can you remind me why I'm still here?" I was afraid that if I made another attempt to leave she would throw another bombshell at me. I was praying for somebody to enter her office and rescue me from her claws.

"I just thought that we could have a drink together and gossip while pretending for a minute we're good friends."

"It's only three o'clock and considering everything you've told me—"

"It is what it is. Don't teach me when I should drink, Eliot."

"Are you not afraid that somebody comes into your office now?"

"Nobody comes in without knocking first. Well, nobody except you... I thought we're both currently going through a lot... having some personal problems and work issues..."

"I don't feel like sharing anything with you. Most of my problems have been solved anyway."

"Oh darling, it's only the beginning. You haven't been listening to me carefully. Do you really think I'll just let you get away with everything you've done to me?" she laughed loudly, reminding me of an evil witch from a cartoon. "Because of you I'll probably have to change my job, my name and my husband.... Maybe even the country."

"That would really suit me," I murmured so quietly she didn't hear.

"I'm not going to kick you out just yet – although I should do it... but I've got a big heart..." Tiggy's left hand touched the left side of her chest, "and you're a single mother of two small children, which is your own fault but anyway..."

"You can't fire me on my maternity leave or even when I get back to work. You really need to change the country if you want to become such a Boss-zilla."

"I'm not stupid, Eliot but..." she smirked, "where there's a will, there's a way. In two weeks' time you're going to give your notice. You'll receive a couple of thousand pounds of severance payment."

"Do you think I'm so stupid? If I give my notice, I'm not getting anything. You need to fire me so I receive the money."

"Normally yes but I'm going to convince the board to give you the money. I'll say that you're going through a really hard time at the moment and you're struggling with having twins, being heartbroken and a single mom," when I opened my mouth to say something she only got louder. "If you don't take the offer, I'll make sure that your job disappears, and everything you do will be handed over to a few interns. You wouldn't believe how many well-educated losers are ready to work for free. Then when you are back, you'll do the typical intern job for a wage that starts gradually decreasing: scanning, photocopying, bringing me coffee, typing data into spreadsheets, rubbing my feet."

"Do interns rub your feet?" I questioned. *Gross!*

"No but you will be," Tiggy said sternly with a clown smile glued to her face and walked briskly to her fridge to get another small bottle of something that this time looked like a mini gin or vodka, and a pack of chocolate buttons.

"I'll sue you," I said staring at the mini bottle – I recognised the label of an expensive vodka.

She laughed still holding the door to the fridge, "Where will you find money for a good lawyer? Do I need to remind you again that now you're a single mother of two with a mortgage?"

"Don't you worry, I'll be fine," I snapped. "You don't know me that well."

"I know more about you than you think. You see..." she sat down on her chair with her legs on the desk and vodka in her tumbler, which she hadn't even rinsed after the whisky. I was waiting for her to light a cigarette but surprisingly it didn't happen. "We've actually got more in common than you would think. We both lost to an American slut wearing fifty shades of pink, if she wears anything at all."

"Are you trying to say..." I took a deep breath and inhaled slowly.

"Oh yeah," she nodded and gulped down the glass of vodka.

Tiggy wasn't pretty but she had always looked after herself and she had known how to expose her good figure – until today when her big bum in the skinny jeggings would be considered a massive fashion faux-pas. Her arse that seemed to be at least three sizes bigger than only a few months ago was still a novelty to me. *Has she been drowning her sorrows in booze and chocolate? Was she the one going through a hard time?*

"I knew he slept with you," I bluffed. "He said it was only sex and not the best."

"Has he told you he slept with me on several occasions when he was going out with you. Last time maybe a year ago?"

"Of course, he did, he couldn't have hidden that from me" I replied without hesitation, while feeling a rushing flow of heat. "Is he also the father of your child?" I asked flippantly when all I wanted to do was throw up.

"Relax he's definitely not. Neither he or nobody…"

"What are you saying? Immaculate conception?"

"What the heck, everybody will know soon anyway," she said and I held my breath waiting for the revelation. "I paid for a sperm donor that I chose myself. Don't get me wrong, I love my husband and he's incredibly intelligent but we all know that this is the era of beautiful people. All they have to do to succeed in this world is take photos, put them online and rake in the money. I went for a tall, fit brunet with bushy hair, straight nose and big eyes." I was so flabbergasted my brain couldn't come up with anything good to say. "Oh Eliot, don't judge me, at least I know who the father is… You know we could have been friends now and bitch together about Henry choosing Kitty, such a shame you took revenge on me."

"How many times do I need to repeat it? I've had nothing to—"

Tiggy put fingers into her ears singing loudly like a three-year-old, "la, la, la, la…".

"Fine," I snapped and moved towards the door.

"See ya! Arrivederci! Hasta la vista and auf wiedersehen," she shouted waving at me with the hand that wasn't holding the glass while crossing her feet on the desk. "Oh, I almost forgot to tell you…" she managed to stop me again from pressing the doorknob, "your idea for a nursery in the office was fantastic. Sadly, we don't have any space at I-Heart-Travelling but I passed the idea to the company two floors below us. They're opening their nursery in a couple of months. They've just offered us eight places for half the normal price. They can't fill all the places because their employees get, in my opinion, insanely good maternity packages."

"Thanks, I'll put my boys on the list."

"You're giving your notice in two weeks," she smirked.

I shut the door with both relief and a trembling heart. I didn't need any more problems in my life but if I did I could always count on Tiggy, she would never miss any opportunity to make my life a misery. Tiggy – another woman who slept with my ex-fiancé.

"Tiggy is drunk, you've got to see it. And don't forget to take some photos," I threw it out to the people frantically typing away on the keyboards of their computers, and then to a group of girls smoking outside the building.

34

SATURDAY, 12 MARCH

DREAM FIELDS

"You won't believe who called me today?"

"I won't…" Hugo pushed his fringe up and gave me a beaming smile, "so tell me," his eyes opened wider and head bent slightly to the right.

"But first can you take the phone away from your face?" I asked.

"I thought you liked my face," he said pretending to be offended.

"I'd just like to see where you are now and your face is taking the whole screen on my phone."

I loved our video chats even if it meant I had to put more effort into how I looked - being a mother of new-born twins and looking good seemed incredibly difficult at times. When I was exhausted and had no time to put any make-up on I just dimmed all lights around me and whispered to Hugo pretending that the boys were sleeping, while in reality my parents or Atlanta were looking after them in a different room.

Hugo spun the phone around to show me the place where he had been running on Saturday morning before I called him – I recognised it immediately and sighed longingly. "I've told you, you should move here." For him everything seemed to be so simple.

Watching Retiro in the morning sun induced all the suppressed thoughts that I'd been trying to hide in the deepest corners of my brain. Suddenly I couldn't stop imagining Hugo strolling with me in the park and pushing the twins in their double pram. "Love it... I mean I love the idea but it's definitely impossible at the moment. Definitely."

"I agree it would be difficult but not impossible. The biggest barriers I think are in your head."

"I don't think we're talking about the same thing," I gave him a faded smile. "Anyway, how can you have so much energy after we spent half of the night on the phone?"

"And vice versa, you're a mother—"

"I know," I cut him off wondering why people have to tell me about it every single day as if I needed them to remind me. "I've just got a lot of help."

* * *

The day before when I left Tiggy's office I was wandering around London for an hour. I was self-pitying and it was absorbing me so much that at the time it didn't even cross my mind that Atlanta and Freya would have appreciated if I got back home and stood them down as nannies. Freya said that she'd already forgotten how tough it was at the beginning, while Atlanta was swearing she wasn't ready for children for at least ten years and irrespective she would have to have a full-time nanny. When the front door shut and I was finally alone I was mentally ready for another sleepless night but it didn't happen – well, at least not in the way I'd been expecting. Patrick and Dominic only woke up a couple of times – they seemed to be as exhausted with their babysitters, as the babysitters were with them. But instead of letting myself have a good night's sleep I called Hugo. I needed to learn first-hand how bad the situation was with *Amigo habla conmigo*.

He picked up without saying hello or any unnecessary niceties. "You've read the news," he gasped.

"I'm so sorry Hugo."

"It's actually not as bad as it seems to be. You'll probably read tomorrow that the situation has already improved. But I'm glad you've called. I could use somebody to talk to instead of running my arse off."

"Well, I'm sure it's good for your arse," I giggled.

"Undoubtedly but I'm now going home to soak my sore muscles."

"I'm not going to talk with you when you're naked in the bath."

"What's the difference? You can't see me anyway."

"Now when you've told me about it, trust me, I can! But what's going on with your TorTillas?"

"My tortillas? It's what you call…" he stopped joking to quickly get serious. "Oh, if not for the hackers I would never know that Hugo TorTillas has so many fans. This afternoon thousands of our supporters went through the streets of Madrid with banners saying *Pirata informático hable conmigo* and *Pirata informático necesita hablar con alguien*. They were shouting that nobody would stop them from coming to our *Amigos*. Luckily the questionnaires that we store on our system don't contain any personal data that could identify our users – unless of course they used their real names, which happened in some cases but even then, there is normally more than one person with the same name."

"Yeah, do you think that people often use the names of those who they don't like? Nothing malicious I mean… Just for fun?"

"I hadn't really thought about it. Have you… *Oh dios mío!* That's exactly what you did. Well, Tiggy won't probably ever know, our database is so huge—"

"You're right," I cut him off not wanting to talk about Tiggy at that very moment. I did actually feel guilty about embarrassing her. "So, what are you going to do now? Any clue who could have done it?"

"Not yet. I've got a press conference on Monday during which I'm going to apologise again and say that we've employed new IT specialists and have everything under control. Apparently Spanish people took the attack very personally – many claim that it was also an attack on their right to help each other. I wasn't looking for advertising but I think I might have found it."

"Are you saying that I shouldn't be sorry but actually happy for you," I said cheerfully and thought that maybe despite all the odds the world wasn't acting against me.

"I wouldn't go that far. It's still embarrassing for our company... But tell me how has your day been?"

"Tiggy wants to sack me from work but apart from that everything is perfectly fine."

* * *

"You still haven't told me who called you?" Hugo asked enthusiastically but I was not listening. I'd noticed he was strolling next to the pond and I was dreaming about being there with him. "Olivia?"

"Sorry, I've just had another phone call but I'll call them back later."

"Is somebody stalking you? Don't tell me it's Henry," he said irritated.

"Cecilia Anastasia Rice still wants me to work for them," I said in one breath.

Hugo stopped walking and exclaimed so loudly that a couple of people turned to look at him, "See? I told you last night they wouldn't let you go so easily. I've read your articles, they're really good."

"Don't you think that Cecilia is just afraid of me filing a law suit against the company? I haven't even got back from maternity leave yet and Tiggy has already threatened to make me unemployed without evidence." The night before I did eventually tell Hugo that Tiggy had found out about me using her name. I couldn't think of another reason for her acting so mad and I didn't want to lie to him. "And there's something else," I paused to build a bit of a suspense and let Hugo guess.

"Tell me they fired Tiggy."

"It would be a dream come true but for now she's only suspended till further notice for drinking at work and shouting something offensive at Polly – I haven't actually complained yet so that should add further colour and might be enough."

"Another great piece of news."

"Cecilia offered me Tiggy's position," I said blushing.

Hugo stopped walking again. I was surprised at how genuinely happy he was for me. "That's fantastic. Congratulations... Although..." his smile quickly gave way to a gloomy expression painted all over his face, "I still think you should apply for a job in Madrid! Your Spanish is excellent, and you love the weather and the city. Get some experience in Tiggy's role and then move here... Wait a second, will you get Tiggy's maternity leave? Then you could come here. When the boys are a few months old we'll have spring – it will be perfect weather for strolling around the city."

"It would be too perfect," I laughed. "I can get Tiggy's job but only because she's suspended and they need somebody pronto. But I could use a nursery in the same building when the boys are a bit older and I would get a large pay rise."

"Well, that's still great news."

"But I've thought this through and I'm not going back there," I said matter-of-factly.

"Don't tell me you've chickened out. If you're worried about the responsibility alongside children, just be prepared to delegate where you can. Employ more interns."

"That's definitely what Tiggy would do."

"She wouldn't pay them but you could, convince Cecilia that they're worth decent wages."

"I'm not afraid of anything. On the contrary, I haven't told anybody yet but a few weeks ago I received an offer from a magazine *Travel the World*. They're going to publish my article about Grenada soon, they've just paid me a good amount of money for it and they've asked for more... so I sent them another article about Madrid, Barcelona and Avignon by train and..."

"Why didn't you say anything?" he said and the screen went black. "Hold on a minute, I need to open the door."

"You can't be at home so quick," I said suspiciously. Recently I'd had some problems trusting anybody, even in relation to the most ridiculous things.

"The door to my car. I'm driving back so I have time for breakfast," he laughed. "Wait... okay... I've got you on the hands free... so why you—"

"I haven't told anybody because I wanted to make sure it was my decision. Then last week I decided to reject the offer because it's freelance and overseas."

"I get it, you're a mo—"

"Mother of two children now," I snapped. "And that's the most beautiful thing that has ever happen to me and there's nothing more important than my boys. That's why I said I couldn't do it. The job was everything I wanted before I was pregnant but in the current circumstances to leave a job with a regular wage sounds crazy, right?"

"Yeah... maybe... so you're not taking the promotion in I-Heart-Travelling but you also didn't take the freelance job for Travel the World... so what are you taking?"

"A chance," I said quickly.

"What?" Hugo shouted and at the same time I heard a car horn.

"Everything all right?"

"Fine, just a guy in front of me is driving like an idiot... Will you tell me what you're going to do?"

"I'll take a chance on me... something I should've done a long while ago... I'm going to accept the freelance job," I was shouting although Hugo probably could have heard me clearly enough in the car. "Tell me I've lost my mind but all the issues with Tiggy and motherhood only gave me more energy, which I hadn't even known I had in me. I'm going to do it!" I exclaimed feeling extremely chuffed with myself.

"Wow," he said and we went silent for a minute.

"Are you still there?" I asked.

"Sorry, I've just been thinking... and concentrating on the road," he sighed. "You're brave and I'm proud of you," he said flatly.

"You think I'm crazy and it's not the right time," I said and paused but he didn't reply. "It was you who told me that when an opportunity comes we need to take it because it might not happen again... even when we think it's not the right time because actually how do we really know what time is best..."

"Right… you're right," he said again without any emotion, and I thought I actually didn't need his approval. I didn't need anybody's approval. No man anymore was going to tell me what was best or worst for me, I knew better!

"Anyway, this is what I'm going to do," I said decisively. "I'll be able to work from home except for a few meetings in London each month. I'll go away from time to time but not longer than three or four days… I mean initially I'll also need to go away for a couple of months but it will probably be a one-off adventure… maybe several months actually but—"

"How long? Where?" he sounded surprised and judgy.

"Somewhere in Europe to work on a book guide but they'll help me find a good nanny and my family will be able to visit me a lot. They're thinking it might be Krakow."

"That's great," he exclaimed and this time he sounded genuinely happy for me. "Can I come and visit you? I'm glad that…"

"Glad that what?"

"I'm glad that… just generally glad for you." He was definitely hiding something from me but I didn't have any more time to dig into the topic because Hannah suddenly arrived from a walk with Zoe and Nicolas. Zoe ran inside asking who I was talking to and without waiting for an invitation grabbed my phone and said *hola* to Hugo. I could hear him laughing and asking her how she was and whether she enjoyed living with auntie Olivia.

Hannah undid her coat and stroked Nicolas' cheek while he was sleeping in his pram. I thought it was a risky game if she didn't want him to wake up but before I managed to say anything she passed me a letter. "I met your postman outside the door. He thought I was you," she giggled. "And you say that people who live in small towns and villages are more attentive to each other and blah, blah, blah… but my postman in London at least used to recognised me."

I opened a long white envelope and quickly read the one-page letter. Then I read it again and again. All my plans were going to hell.

35

MONDAY, 14 MARCH, LONDON
LONDON

"Olivia, can you hurry up? We've been here for over an hour," Hannah was sitting on a chair with her hands under her bum and nervously jiggling her legs.

"I know and I still haven't found anything," I shouted with my head in a wardrobe.

"Do you think it might be because Henry is just not stupid enough to keep any evidence of the crimes he committed in the flat to which you've still got a key?"

"Firstly, I bet he doesn't even remember I've got a key. I haven't been here since Blanca tried to shoot me. Secondly, he would never suspect I would do something like this," I smirked getting out of the wardrobe.

"Fine but we should go now. What will we do if somebody finds us here?" Hannah suddenly got up as if uttering her own thoughts scared her, and she moved towards the door to have a look through the peephole.

"Nobody is going to be here, chill. I've called Shakespeare University and they confirmed Henry is in New York, and Ben went to Tokyo. He doesn't even have a plant to water, and his parents live in Cambridge. Besides I haven't broken into his flat. I've got a key."

"Um… That's actually true," she looked calmer but still ready to go. "Why don't you anonymously call the police to search his flat?"

"It's not that easy. They need a good reason. Besides the police prefer to waste their time on innocent people like me," I snapped feeling a sudden flow of anger filling me up from the tips of my toes to the top of my head. "Look, you don't have to be here with me, I'll be okay."

"No," she said categorically. "I'm not going to leave you alone." Hannah crossed her hands, spread her legs on the wooden floor and shook her head energetically acting like a soldier on a mission.

I took my white gloves off, which I had bought on eBay and were designed for handling silver, I wiped sweat from my forehead and let my eyes wander around the tiny flat that seemed to be suddenly so big. Time was running out fast – after an hour I still had more than half of the flat to search, but I was going to check every corner of this little London home that once was also mine. If necessary I would look under every moving floorboard, behind every painting and inside every single box of cereal – and Henry had at least ten of them. I'd watched too many American TV shows to miss places like the fridge or a pizza box in the oven. I couldn't give up when my freedom was at stake! I had been expecting that I would have to testify in court but when I got the letter informing me I wouldn't be able to leave the country until further notice I was flabbergasted. Since then it had only got worse. The very next day after opening the letter, the police knocked on my door. They had a search warrant. Hannah was at her parents, and I called my brother to quickly take the kids to his house.

"What have you got yourself into?" he asked disapprovingly and I felt like bursting into tears. I managed to stopped myself from a breakdown, but only because I was afraid it would have made me look guilty in front of the police.

I was trying to stay calm while sipping my camomile tea in the kitchen as three police officers were going through all my and not-my belongings. I was embarrassed at the mere thought of me explaining to Hannah why her professionally packed and delivered moving boxes had been brutally torn apart, and their contents thrown around her new bedroom. Three cups of various tea infusions and one bar of chocolate later I heard a voice from the living room. I stood up so quickly that I knocked down one of the two bar chairs, which fell on the floor with a bang and hit my big toe. I imagined stars going round my head and my eyes rolling as fast as a carousel.

"Duck!" I shouted as I'd already got used to baby-swearing.

One of the three officers, the one with the largest belly and a light blond fringe touching his bushy eyebrows, walked into the kitchen with his hands on his belt, "Mrs Thyme, have you really been thinking you would get away with it?"

Despite a throbbing pain in my toe I managed to stand still and say decisively, "My name isn't Thyme. I'm Olivia Eliot, E-l-i-o-t, and I have nothing to do with Henry Thyme."

"What about your children?" he asked with a smug face, which quickly disappeared to be replaced by the face of a man who is trying to squeeze his fart in – frowny eyebrows, tense expression and held breath. "You know…" he rapidly started breathing again, "the one who you've been trying to frame with your illegal business?"

"Excuse me? Is this some kind of game you're playing to get more information out of me?"

"Detective Murray," said another policeman suddenly upon entering my kitchen. He had a round baby face with flushed cheeks but still managed to somehow make a profoundly serious and severe expression. He passed detective Murray a thick blue file packed into a dirty transparent plastic bag. Murray took out a pair of black gloves from his pocket and put them on his hands like a surgeon preparing for an operation. Before he opened the file he warned me not to touch anything, then he spread the papers on the table in front of me. He didn't feel it was necessary to explain anything else to me, he just showed me a few sets of exams questions with dates in the future and two MBA dissertations.

"Where have you found them?" I heard coming out from my throat.

"Exactly where you buried them, under the patio slabs in your back garden. You didn't think we would check there, eh?" Murray asked with satisfaction.

"Great, have you been digging anywhere else?"

"Bob?" asked Murray.

"We've checked the front garden as well but there was nothing there."

"I don't have a front garden, anything in front of the building belongs to the estate, have you got their permission or a warrant to do that digging work?" I asked without much thought. Obviously this made them angry but it was already too late.

Meg you cunning bitch! I kept shouting in my head as Murray was explaining to me I would have to go with him to the police station. I drove my own car, although it wasn't the best idea – my whole body was trembling as if I was hypothermic and tears that I tried to stop without much success were blurring my vision. I couldn't believe Henry would do something like this to me. I was the mother of his children! *Why Henry, why?* I tried to call him while driving but each time I only got to listen to his answer machine. Meg was also not answering.

"Mrs Th—, I mean Miss Eliot, the best thing for you is to tell me the truth right now," said Murray calmly sitting at the other side of a gunmetal grey table.

"But I didn't do anything," I whispered.

He sighed and opened his tired grey notebook with one of its corners bent, "How were you able to afford a brand-new SUV? Your wage in I-Heart-Travelling is just above the national average and you don't have another income... another official income. To be honest I doubled checked because I would think that a journalist in a respected travel magazine would make more money."

"I know how much I earn so please be so kind and stop reminding me about it," I snapped putting my hands on the cold table. "Henry bought me the car for my thirtieth birthday."

"It was bought in your name—."

"Because it was for me."

"We've got footage from CCTV in the shop and it was bought by a woman with dark hair."

"I've got a whole group of witnesses."

"Your friends and family?" he smiled mercifully. "We already know that you asked your ex-fiancé to pretend he bought you the car. He said he had been staggered but did it for you because he had believed you must've had a good reason."

I leant back on my chair and threw my hands in the air. "How can you trust the son of a bitch? I can't believe he told you that."

"Please calm down Miss Eliot."

"You need to get in touch with Megan Johnson. She lived with me for nearly a year. It was her who buried the files in my garden."

"You've just accused Henry Thyme of framing you and now you're saying that it's a Megan?" he said, with his arms crossed while yawning without covering his mouth.

"She was acting on his behalf!"

"Are you sure you want to keep making things up and defending yourself, instead of saving us all a lot of time by admitting what you've done?"

"First Meg hid some money in my garden. She was hiding it from her bank," I was talking quickly while listening to my heart running like mad. "You see, her husband took all the money that she'd borrowed and she had to pay off their debt for a house, which—"

"I'll check again," he scribbled something in his notebook, "but I don't think she's got any debt. "Let's talk about you."

"I'm not going to say anything more without a lawyer," I said suddenly feeling like my mind was getting clearer.

Later that afternoon Hannah arrived at the police station with the only lawyer she had managed to find within a couple of hours. It helped that despite not working she still kept in touch with her friends from law school. Her friend Alistair Dragon stormed into the interrogation room like a king into a royal chamber looking down at Murray like at his butler. A quarter of an hour later, after filling in some papers, the three of us were walking briskly out of the police station – Me still shaking in washed-out jeans and a stretched hoodie,

Hannah in a tight black dress with pearls around her slim neck and Alistair in his perfectly fitted dark blue suit and his shoulder-length carefully styled black hair.

Alistair advised me against doing anything myself and insisted on taking care of it all for me. "I've got enough information for now. I'll contact you if I've got any questions. Remember that every move you take, can act to your disadvantage. Take a bath, have a glass of wine or swim in a pool a hundred times. In other words, do whatever you feel like to relax but do not to try to call Henry or Megan anymore. Trust me and wait until I get in touch with you again."

The following morning, I was lying in bed in a stupor and staring at the ceiling for a good twenty minutes. I was able to do that because the boys were still at my brother's house with my parents looking after them. They practically refused to bring them back to the house given the mess and drama. To relax I was counting all the imperfections on the white ceiling like bits of bad painting or small cracks caused by the house still settling down. I was actually surprised how many flaws you could find on a seemingly perfectly white and smooth ceiling. *If you look long enough you always find something,* I thought and jumped out of the bed. I just couldn't wait for Alistair to tell me what to do.

"Of course, I'll help you," Hannah said enthusiastically when I called her, although she didn't know what I would ask her to do. A few hours later when she was standing next to Henry's door looking through its peephole her enthusiasm was fading away with every passing minute.

"Olivia!" she shouted pointing at me.

"What? Is there a spider or somebody in the corridor?" I asked full of worry.

"Put the blanket exactly where it was on the right side of the sofa. You said Henry was pedantic, he would definitely notice that."

"Fine but stop freaking me out. It's just a blanket. Besides I don't give a damn whether he notices or not... I would be truly fucking delighted if I could throw the whole flat upside down to leave it in a worse state than my house is now, particularly after I had just paid for it to be cleaned professionally for you to move in!"

"Take a breath," she said like a yoga instructor demonstrating to me how to inhale and exhale. "Don't get carried away with your emotions. It's not the right time. Now we need to be calm and clever," she drawled her words. "Put the blanket where it was," she nearly whispered.

I leant down to pick up a fluffy brown blanket from the floor, which I'd chosen over a year ago in a supermarket during our big weekly shopping event. I rolled it up and positioned it next to green cushions on the sofa.

Hannah nodded with approval, and I leant down again to see the place where Blanca's bullet made a hole in the couch. I knelt down putting my right cheek close to the floor.

"What are you doing?"

"Come and have a look," I encouraged her with a waving hand but she only opened her eyes wider.

"Somebody needs to guard the door."

"Nobody needs to guard anything. Come here and help me," I demanded. "We need to lift the sofa."

"We can't lift anything so soon after giving birth," she snapped but was still walking towards me.

"Get down on your knees and have a look," I said pointing with my finger at the hole through which I'd just seen a pile of books squeezed inside the couch.

"Jeeze, we need to turn the sofa on its back and get inside it. It looks like he put some stuff there and sewed it all up. We might need a knife or scissors. They must be the tests!" she was jumping from one leg to another while putting her white gloves on. "But shouldn't we now call the police?"

"Take the left side, I'll take the right," I said bending my knees and tensing the muscles in my arms, but the sofa turned out to be surprisingly light – as if Henry had disembowelled it to use it as a frame for extra storage.

"Maybe we could sell it as a patent – not a sofa bed but sofa storage," Hannah said and suddenly let the couch go and loudly drop on the floor.

"Can you just focus?" I asked irritated.

"Maybe we should go now. Somebody might've heard the noise and called the cops."

"No way. Not now when we're so close. Pass me a knife."

Hannah trod through to the kitchen annex and opened three different drawers before she found a large steak knife that she brought to me with her shaking hands. I put the knife into the black fabric and tore it apart to let a pile of books fall down on the floor. I shook them a couple of times and flicked through them but there was nothing that attracted my attention, although the titles were interesting: *The good boys go to heaven, the bad boys go to bed with beautiful women; Women love selfish bastards:* and *Men come from Earth, women arrive from a different galaxy.*"

"I would've never thought Henry likes self-help books! He would've never admitted it!"

"Would he have really made so much effort to hide these books?" Hannah was sitting next to me with her legs crossed. "Look there, something else is inside," she pointed at something bulky under the sofa fabric."

Once again I put my hand inside the sofa, feeling like a surgeon, to discover, "A photo album? You've got to be kidding me. I'm not in the mood to see his childhood photos, although I heard that he had an ugly face when he was a teenager. That would explain why he put…" I paused looking at the first page of the album. "What the hell is this? A memoire of his sexual conquests?"

"What?" Hannah sat next to me putting her elbow in my ribs. "Who's the girl?" she put her white-gloved indicator finger on a pretty petite girl with blond wavy hair sitting next to Henry on a beach towel.

"It's Isabella, his ex-girlfriend and childhood sweetheart, who lived on the same street in Cambridge… I can't believe he put us in chronological order… Tiggy?" I couldn't believe my eyes looking at a red-eyed Tiggy and Henry in a nightclub. Under the photo there was a handwritten note on self-adhesive yellowish page with information on how long they were dating. "He was going out with her for three months. I thought she had never been his *official* girlfriend, that they were just lovers."

"I think it's the least of your worries now. All due respect Olivia – I know you were going to marry him – but he looks like a proper weirdo."

"You don't have to tell me about it," I murmured while reading the size of Tiggy's boobs, her height and weight. "I didn't know she's five years older than me, she always inferred it's just a year... Her job, a senior manager... yeah, not anymore... I would never guess she likes dog racing and opera."

"Henry probably meant Oprah," Hannah giggled. "Let's find you," her enthusiasm was back.

"Kitty is twenty-four this year! He met her over two years ago in Miami! I wasn't even thirty and he was already looking for somebody younger!"

"She looks older."

"You think?" I asked looking for some comfort. "How old do I look?"

"Twenty-five," she said without hesitation. "Or twenty-five and a half... Hmm... maybe twenty... "

"Okay stop."

"But Kitty looks well over thirty," she said in a way that wouldn't even convince a three-year-old. I snapped close the album on my knees right in front of her eyes and shovelled it into my Hermes bag wondering whether detective Murray had already accounted for my expensive handbag, an almost impossible bag on my wage.

"I've got it," Hannah's cry stopped me from opening the front door.

"What?" I asked impatiently.

"Your page. It was lying loose on the floor."

I rushed back to the sofa which was still on its back, "Give it to me."

"It's says you're his current girlfriend."

"It says exactly the same about Kitty."

"Olivia, you need to be careful. He seems to be…"

"On the bright side all the girls from the album are still alive and seem to be fine, at least except me…"

"I'm not sure how *fine* they all are," she handed me another two loose pages from the album.

"Who else?" I asked in a crying voice and butterflies in my stomach.

"Joanna," I read with relief. "A lecturer from his work. I always knew she fancied him, and… Blanca?" I looked at Hannah and swallowed hard to get rid of a lump in my throat. "I'll need to see her."

"Are you sure it's necessary? You've only just recovered from that terrible event."

* * *

I'd assumed that getting in touch with anybody who could have information on Henry's shady businesses would be a miracle. Henry's parents weren't at home or had decided not to pick up the phone. It was weird because his mother was the kind of person who always had something to say, you would literally have to put a gag over her mouth to stop her from expressing her opinion, no matter what the topic was. Each time I called Meg I heard it ring for a few seconds before she clearly pressed ignore. Gatsby wasn't picking up either and his PI company website was closed down. Also, the photos that Gatsby had sent me, showing Henry passing some files to a young guy in a park, had mysteriously disappeared from my bedside drawer. When I called Gatsby's IT company pretending I was his relative, a nice but very suspicious secretary told me that he had taken a year's sabbatical to explore the world. My last hope were business cards, which I was practically forced to take from some incredibly pushy Shakespeare University students, who met me during *Don't Die for a Selfie* as they were desperate for a free internship at I-Heart-Travelling. I called each and every one of them, in total eighteen people, and I introduced myself as a policewoman investigating buying education at their university. I tried to convince them that any useful information on professor Henry Thyme would give them immunity and they would be allowed to continue studying at the university. One guy pretended he was climbing Machu Pichu and was losing reception. Another claimed he was just giving first aid to a victim of a selfie accident, and a girl called Stacey was apparently lying on a floor in a shop during a robbery somewhere in Texas. Fourteen people didn't agree to say anything without their lawyer, but there was one man – Dylan P. Weston, student and business communications specialist – who agreed to see me. He told me that he had never used exam dealers himself and that was why he was the only one who had failed some exams at his faculty a couple of weeks ago. Dylan, speaking in a very posh British accent, told me how angry he was with the Cheaters Gang and the whole situation, which forced him to choose between being dishonest or being the only failure of his year. I was literally rubbing my hands when I put my phone down. I quickly grabbed my coat and left the house to meet him at a café fifteen minutes' walk from Henry's flat.

Dylan and I were both so impatient to know each other that we didn't even think how silly it was to plan our meeting at lunch time in one of the busiest parts of London. When I opened the door to the café, which once used to be my favourite orange latte and blueberry muffin place, I almost immediately recognised Dylan. A tall and thin ginger guy, who with his hunched back looked like a teenager, was sitting in the corner nervously hoovering up a large sandwich – mayo was dripping on the table and salad falling on the floor. I thought he was one of those lucky people who could eat a lot and stay slim. He was the same man, who had insisted on telling me how he almost lost a part of his ear when he was trying to take a selfie with a lion in a zoo.

The queue to the counter was so long that I was afraid I would have to choose between no-coffee or no-Dylan… – unless I could save some time by asking a young girl, who had just picked up her takeaway latte, whether she would sell it to me. She agreed for a price four times what she had paid. Well, time is money.

"I'm detective Murray," I said putting my heavy and bulky handbag with Henry's album inside on an empty chair next to Dylan, which I presumed he had thoughtfully thrown his coat on to reserve for me.

"Hi, I'm Dylan," he stood up. "I won't shake your hand because as you can see," he gestured at the mayo dripping down his hands, "they put way too much stuff in these sandwiches now." I smiled thinking that the *too much* wasn't really *too much* for him as he was clearly enjoying it all. I sat down sharing my seat with my Birkin bag. I didn't want any mayo to drop on its madly over-priced leather. "Have we met before?" he asked as he sat down, eyeing me up and down like a race horse. "I would swear I've seen you before," he was frowning his eyebrows and enhancing a wrinkle at the top of his nose.

"I've been involved in the investigation for a while now. I'm sure you've seen me somewhere at the university. Let's say that I had to undertake various different roles to become more effective."

"Oh, I see," he said, clapped his hands and pointed his finger at me with a smile.

"Dylan, tell me everything you know about professor Thyme. When was the first time you found out he was selling exam questions? Do you know who've been buying them and how it works?"

"I'm actually not a hundred percent sure who the buyers are. I only have my suspicions," he said and I knew he had changed his mind at the last minute. Had he just recognised me as Henry's angry ex-fiancée?"

"Only a couple of hours ago you sounded very sure," I said categorically. I felt more confident as detective Murray than Olivia Eliot. "What has changed in the last two hours?"

"I don't want to destroy their lives and most importantly I don't feel like being sued for slander. I don't know whether you've realised it by now, detective Murray, but there're some pretty powerful people involved in this."

Dylan's phone buzzed a few times with a phone call and then flashed with a message which he appeared not to notice, although the mobile was placed just next to his left hand the café noise drowned it out. "Oh no!" I screamed throwing my hands up in the air. "An old lady has almost slipped on your lettuce that's on the floor. You need to clean it," I passed him a napkin.

"Where?" he turned back to his left.

I threw a slice of lettuce from the table on the floor to his right side, "There."

"Oh, right," he leant down exposing the top of his arse, while I quickly reached across the table for sugar and turned his phone to read the message: Don't tell! Will pay £5000! I held my breath while throwing sugar lumps into my coffee and trying to pretend that nothing had happened. I took a sip and immediately felt sick realising that the girl who sold me the ginger latte must have already put several spoons of sugar in it. For somebody who didn't add sugar at all it was virtually undrinkable. The only advantage of forcing myself to drink the oversweet elixir was to get more energy to get through the day after another sleepless night.

"Let's talk about Henry then... professor Henry Thyme."

"I've always liked him. He's good lecturer..." as he was listing Henry's virtues I reached into my bag for my phone, put it on the table and started recording. It was a bad move because it reminded him about his own phone. He read his message and smiled forcefully saying that it was his girlfriend asking him to come back home.

"I won't keep you long."

"Do we need to record this?"

"I prefer that to making notes," I said nonchalantly.

"You should've asked me first whether I would mind..." his face flushed with anger. "I think I should call my lawyer first."

"I understand. If you prefer to talk at the police station that's fine with me. I thought we could have a casual chat here and it wouldn't be necessary to drag you all the way to the station. People, even the innocent ones, feel very uncomfortable when they're being interrogated. When they're stressed, they say something stupid that can be used against them later."

Dylan took a sip from his paper mug, "I'm sorry. I'll see you at the station if necessary."

"But—"

"Are you leaving?" I heard a female voice from behind me and I turned around. Two middle-aged women were waiting for our table with a tray full of different salads.

"No," I snapped and suddenly noticed the girl who had sold me her coffee going towards the toilet. I waved to her and asked whether she would buy me a soy latte with no sugar.

"It will be twenty pounds," she grinned.

"Sure," I said but she didn't move an inch looking at me in anticipation. "When you bring me the coffee."

"Sure. And if you ever need an assistant, I charge less than twenty quid per hour."

I looked towards the entrance and to my despair I saw Hannah walking straight into Dylan and spilling his take-away coffee. Although it was her fault I could see him vividly apologising and rapidly running to the counter to bring her a whole pile of napkins. Hannah brushed him off, waved to me and started walking to the table that I was stubbornly occupying. Dylan obviously stunned by her rudeness was watching us with his mouth wide open. I was looking straight at him and waving but Hannah destroyed everything by waving back to me.

"Don't sit next to me," I murmured to her. "Pass the table and go to the loo."

"Sorry I can't hear you... No, I don't need the loo. Do I look like I do?" she leant over the table taking off her stained coat. In the corner of my eye I saw Dylan opening his green fabric bag and taking out his phone. Before I managed to cover my face he had taken a couple of photos and disappeared behind the door.

"You won't believe what I've found out."

"Oh no," I squeaked pressing my hands to my cheeks.

"What oh no? Oh yes!"

"No, Dylan, the student, he's just taken our photo. I've told him—"

"Never mind, I've got some more important news right now."

"Twenty quid," said the coffee girl with a cheeky smug face.

Hannah was outraged by the girl's boldness, "What charity are you from?"

"Lazy rich people," she snapped holding my coffee in her left hand and holding open her right hand expectantly.

I reached reluctantly into my bag. I knew I had twenty pounds but I unzipped only the part of my purse where I kept coins. I put ten pounds on her greedy hand and took my coffee.

"Hey, that wasn't the deal."

"Do you like soy latte?"

"No."

"So, do you prefer to lose two fifty or earn seven fifty?" I asked, and the girl took her money and walked away.

"Interesting," Hannah nodded. "Anyway, I've found Blanca."

"I didn't know you were looking for her."

"You said we needed to see her," she said sullenly. "I accept your apology for your initial reaction and you're very welcome," Hannah sat down and took a sip of my coffee. "Bleh... I visited Shakespeare University. I didn't know Henry lived so close to his job."

"How did you get in there without any ID? Jumped over their gates, bribed a guard?"

"I took Henry's ID card from his flat. I was worried they might have blocked it by now so I had a story ready if they caught me red-handed trying to swipe his card but it worked fine," she smiled proudly.

"I'm impressed. It hadn't even crossed my mind."

"When we finish with Henry, we're opening our own PI business," she said full of enthusiasm with dreamy eyes.

"Get real Hannah!" I rubbed my tired eyes. How did you manage to find Blanca?"

"You get real. Do you really think that they would just let her go like that..." she snapped her fingers, "after everything she's done?"

"True," I yawned feeling exhausted but Hannah interpreted it that I was bored and chastised me with her eyes.

"I can't believe that you didn't make sure she was still in jail. I wouldn't be able to sleep at night thinking that she could be some-where out there instead of being locked up."

"Good, so she's—"

"Excuse me, I can see you've only got one coffee between you both, so I thought you might be leaving soon and I'd like to have lunch here with my husband," I heard an irritating posh female voice and looked up to see a woman in her sixties dressed in a gigantic furry coat with too much rose blush on her cheeks. Next to her stood a man wearing military green clothes and struggling to hold a heavily loaded tray with tea, muffins and paninis.

"I'm sorry but we won't be leaving anytime soon," I snapped.

"But we've got so much to eat and there's no place—"

"Tough luck or rather you shouldn't have bought so much. We can offer you a favour and buy the lunch off you. Obviously at a discount because it's getting cold," Hannah smiled clearly amused by herself.

"No, thank you," said the woman.

"Wow, they were like a forest ranger and his fox... Since when have people become so rude? We'll need to order something though to avoid more angry people constantly bothering us."

"It's a coffee shop, not a restaurant," Hannah snapped. "I was pretending to be Blanca's cousin from Italy. I speak a bit of Italian, enough to trick an English person. I put some words *en Italiano* here and there and ta-da!"

"Italian with a London accent?"

Hannah took a breath and said a few sentences mispronouncing almost every word in English, adding some simple words in Italian and making her accent way sharper than it needed to be.

"I've never heard any Italian person speaking such bad English," I laughed. "Where is she?"

"A mental hospital," Hannah clasped her hands.

"Why does it make you so happy?"

"A – we know where to look for her and she can't avoid us. B – visits are less regulated than in a prison."

"Maybe we shouldn't disturb her treatment."

"Yeah right," she nodded. "She's only there to avoid going to a normal jail! I've already called the hospital. I'm Blanca's cousin Lucinda and you're my English wife. I asked them not to tell her we

417

were coming because we want to give her a pleasant surprise. Now repeat my story."

* * *

Blanca was placed on the ward for people suffering from depression. "What? She tried to shoot me!" I said to Hannah but she elbowed me and put a finger to her lips covered with strong red lipstick. We were following a nurse walking through a wide corridor with people slouching about and shuffling their feet – their faces expressionless like they had no care in the world, while in reality they were over-whelmed by the pain they were carrying deep inside them. I felt the sadness in the air – it was stuffy, sticky and impossible to brush off.

We entered a long room with pastel orange walls and six single beds – three on both sides of the room, all covered with well-used beigey blankets. Four of the beds were empty. On the one positioned closest to the window at the back of the room there was a middle-aged woman lying motionless on her back, arms along her trunk, and staring at the ceiling. On the bed just next to her was a young girl, maybe eighteen-years old – she was lying on her side with one hand holding her head, and another flipping through pages in a colourful magazine. Blanca was sitting on the wide windowsill and looking out of the window through black heavy bars. She was wearing light blue jeans with a hole at her knee and a tight black top. She glanced at us with no expression on her pale face and went back to staring out of the window. She had clearly been deprived of the sun for a while, one leg stretched out straight on the windowsill, the other dangling a few inches above the floor. Her arms were crossed with fingers clenching her elbows. She looked like she had been waiting for somebody to come and save her.

"Surprise," said our short plump nurse with a sweet baby face and the longest natural eyelashes I had ever seen. "Your cousin and her wife came to visit you."

"With a wife? Is it even legal?" the woman in her mid-forties stopped reflecting on the hospital ceiling and suddenly sat up to eye

Hannah and me with disgust painted all over her face. Then she snorted a couple of times and left when the nurse asked her to behave and be nice.

"Let me know if you need anything," said the nurse and walked away.

Hannah made a few steps towards the window, and I followed, uncertain whether we should put an end to the masquerade and just go home. I put my right hand on Hannah's shoulder when Blanca jumped off the windowsill, her arms still crossed, "You broke my leg, bitch."

"You almost killed her," Hannah went to my rescue like a good wife should.

"I warned you my dear *cousin* to leave but you insisted on—"

"I'm your cousin," Hannah murmured through her gritted teeth. "I'm Lucinda, your Italian cousin, and Olivia is my English wife. We need your help and you need us if you ever want to see the sun again," I chortled seeing Hannah saying this with her hands on her hips.

"That's a surprise," Blanca gave us a wry smile.

"I know Henry was your lover. I know he also sold you some exam questions and then gave you away to the cops," I said.

"If you know everything, why have you bothered to come here?"

"Henry has been trying to frame me in his shady business."

"I'm sorry to hear that. It looks like we're both equally naïve, if not stupid."

"You can make him pay for what he's done to you," Hannah said with an unusually deep voice."

"No," Blanca shook her head. "I've just changed my mind," she drawled. "You are tenfold more stupid and naïve than me."

"How come?" Hannah frowned her eyebrows and made a couple of steps forward to look straight into Blanca's eyes.

"He's got plenty of people to help him. It's in their common interest. Not only the Cheaters Gang but also thousands of wealthy students and their parents, who will pay anything to protect their lazy arses."

"Aren't you one of them?" Hannah smirked and this time I couldn't stop myself from elbowing her. Why would you tease a tiger?

"I was his girlfriend and that's all."

"He already had a girlfriend," Hannah snapped.

"Who said that you can only have one? We weren't married."

My jaw dropped and I needed a couple of seconds to pull myself together, "And you were okay with that?"

Blanca took a deep breath, "No, he said I was the one and only..." she rolled her eyes, "but it sounds so pathetic now. He told me he needed you for the university events so as not to instil any suspicions. We were hiding our relationship because it was theoretically legal but unprofessional and—"

"I was just a girl to show up with?"

Blanca nodded, "He convinced me he didn't sleep with you and you were the kind of woman who wanted to keep her virginity till the wedding night. You sort of looked like that in the photos I've seen."

Hannah burst out laughing, "Did you know that she didn't even know—" I elbowed her gently in her ribs and she stopped.

The girl with the magazine laughed too but when I looked at her she was pretending to be coughing and quickly put her nose into the magazine and turned a page.

"I'm sorry, could you leave us alone?" I asked the girl, who pretended not to hear me.

"Could you leave?" Blanca said impatiently and the girl reluctantly closed the magazine, rolled it under her armpit and walked out of the room looking insulted.

"How long were you together?"

"Olivia that's not important at the moment," Hannah said matter-of-factly and turned to Blanca, "When was the first time Henry sold you... or rather gave you an essay or exam?"

"We were dating for almost a year."

"A year? In his album—" I whispered and Hannah started hushing me.

"What album?"

"Never mind. When did you buy—"

"She slept with him so she didn't have to buy anything… unless it was a trade," Hannah was teasing our tiger again.

"I was studying two completely different subjects so in theory I was very busy, which by the way was a good excuse not to see many people from uni and hide away with Henry. In reality, he used to buy me essays so I had more time for him. It made me more flexible," she grinned.

"I told him once I would go out with him for dinner if he helped me clean the flat."

"He paid for a cleaner?" asked Blanca. "See? Very similar situation. He was just trying to be helpful," she said nonchalantly and it almost sounded honest.

"He booked the restaurant for another night."

"Let's focus on what is most important here," Hannah was like a judge constantly trying to make us focus on the case, and avoid any digressions.

"I thought he was spending a lot of time with his students…"

"We normally went to a pub and then finished the night at mine. After his flatmate moved out, we sometimes went to his."

"I was the flatmate."

"What a jerk," Blanca said unemotionally and yawned. As she continued talking on and on about her love rendezvous with my ex-fiancé I was struggling not to puke. Finally, I managed to switch off my emotions and switch on my phone recording. I pretended that I received an important text to do so but she didn't look convinced.

"What can you tell us about Henry's business with the Cheaters Gang?" Hannah asked.

"Nothing more beyond the fact that he bought exams a few times for me," this time she was speaking loud and clear with the exaggeration British people normally use for foreigners who don't understand English.

"If I go to jail because of Henry, the criminal will take custody of my two small children. You might hate me but have mercy for my children," I begged.

Blanca bit her nails and shook her head, "I'm sorry I can't help you.

I would like to leave this place soon, study again and not be afraid that one day somebody grabs me from the street, gives me a shovel and makes me dig in the woods..." she swallowed loudly.

"Her children will lose their mother," Hannah said completely unmoved by Blanca own problems. "She'll go to jail for something she didn't do. You owe her. You almost killed her. You can make up for it now... well, sort of... Trust me. We can beat the bastard."

"It's funny," Blanca sat on the windowsill and kept talking while looking out of the window, "those who ask me to trust them, generally let me down the most."

"You don't really suffer from depression?" Hannah said. "You only hide here from prison."

"You have no idea about anything," she hissed. "I had a breakdown."

"If you don't help us, I'll personally make sure you spend your twenties in jail. I'm a lawyer."

"You're not the first person to threaten me."

"Nobody has come here to threaten you Blanca," I said softly. "If you change your mind, this is my number," I passed her my business card from I-Heart-Travelling that I'd made and paid for myself. "Call the mobile."

She took the card reluctantly and put it in the back pocket of her jeans, "It's time for you to go. It was nice to see you, cousin – you and your beautiful wife."

"We'll see you soon," said Hannah.

"Olivia," Blanca said as my right leg was hanging over the doorstep, "You should take your sentence, it will be better than fighting and losing even more." I couldn't see her face because I was still standing with my back to her, but her words and the tone of her voice alone were enough to give me multiple shivers down my spine.

I turned to her slowly, "What do mean?"

"Just trust me on that."

36

THURSDAY, 24 MARCH
LONDON

Before I met Henry or Billy, who was my first serious pre-Henry boyfriend, I went out for scores of first dates, tens of second dates and only a few third ones. One of the very few third dates that I had was with *a* Steven-Something – he had a double-barrelled surname with long French and English components and three dates weren't enough to memorize it. He booked us a dinner in a Mexican restaurant and probably – if not for the fact that sometime between our mains and desserts we met his ex-girlfriend – we would have gone out for a fourth and possibly more. The problem was that the girl claimed she became his ex the moment she saw us together. Apparently, Steven struggled to break up with women if he wasn't sure that there was another one already waiting for him – the Ex-Girlfriend explained to me. Before she appeared, Steven had also tried to explain many things to me over dinner but I wasn't in the mood – partly because of what he was saying and partly because I couldn't stop staring at the bits of nachos between his teeth. I didn't remember him, however, as the guy who fooled me or broke my heart. I got over him pretty quickly by having many other first dates. I remember something else about him though – it was his love theory that we can love anybody – we just need to want it. He compared two people to two halves of different pieces of fabric needed for an outfit. His dad was a tailor, which explained his source of inspiration. According to Steven's Little Love Theory all relationships start from choosing the best material we can get in terms of its look, feel and general quality. After careful selection we check whether the chosen fabric fits us and matches what we've already got. When for some reason it doesn't, we leave it for somebody else. When it does, all that's left is some sewing and then looking after it, those steps require the most time, energy and cooperation. The final result depends mainly on whether we consider the result worth so much effort and we *want to* continue. "I've also noticed..." said Steven on our second date in a wine bar, "that the better the fabric we get, the more difficult the sewing seems to be. It's not that rare that the very intelligent, stunningly beautiful with fantastic wit and future prospects are dumped for those who are a little bit less than perfect, but just temporarily easier to manage..."

Steven's theory wasn't as romantic as I would have liked it to be, but it had so much common sense that it got into my head and some-how, more or less consciously, influenced me in the way I perceived love and future relationships. I *wanted* to love the kind, well-behaved Henry with great future prospects and an eagerness to settle down, the Henry who was adored by my friends, family and his students. I *wanted* to love him because he told me he loved me and I *wanted* to be loved by somebody who was so truly exceptional. I *wanted* to love him because he was likely to be the father of my children and then even more when he turned out to be one. I kept believing that every time the two materials tore, I could sew them again, again and again... until it worked. The problem was that the other material turned out to be a cheap imitation that kept failing and letting me down. It was falling apart – at the same time pulling all my stitches out and hurting me. I wondered whether I would have left Henry earlier, at least a few months before we were planning to go to Madrid if I was younger than twenty-nine and a half. In theory, surely it was better to be left with a piece of fabric for an average dress than be left with nothing. Damn you Steven, and your stupid theories!

I never wanted to love Hugo, it happened against all of my wishes.

It was actually the last thing I needed in my life that suddenly seemed to take the most unexpected course without asking my permission. I would happily have killed the love if I could, but Hugo never let me. When I finally decided to tell him about all my troubles he suggested sending me his lawyer and covering his costs. "Don't worry, he does a lot of work for my company and I can take his payment off my tax later," he insisted, and I agreed because I simply couldn't afford to be too proud and reject help when it was linked to the future of my children.

"He loves you, how can you not see that?" asked Hannah when I called her, causing me to immediately regret making the phone call. I wasn't in the mood to listen that we were meant for each other.

"I know, I know... men love a good challenge but how motivating is climbing the same mountain every single day to never reach the peak."

"What are you talking about?" she giggled. "You said sex with him was amazing."

I gasped heavily, "Will he ever look at my boys without regret that they aren't his biological children? Do you think that he'll never regret not having a chance to start everything from the beginning... first meeting a girl, proposing to her, getting married, having children... And there's also me – I don't know whether I would be able to stop applying pressure on the relationship to make it work?"

"Mmmm... you know... I think..."

"I hope I find somebody one day in a similar situation."

"Never-married father of baby twins, who..." she paused, "who didn't know for nine months who the mother of his children was so you've got something to bond over?" she laughed.

"It would be difficult. I don't mean it that specifically. Maybe a handsome father of two adult children... or at least of school age, who are obviously in a boarding school on the west coast of Canada or in Australia," I said seriously mulling over such a prospect.

"So, do you want him to be much older than you? I guess it makes him more mature. Would you consider up to ten years or is twenty still okay? I think the older he is, the more likely he'll settle with you.

You know, he'll be more motivated when he's got the prospect of having a much younger wife. It doesn't happen every day, unless… Unless he's got a beach house in California."

"Hannah!"

"I just follow your thinking!"

Hannah, Freya, Atlanta and even my never-meddling brother with his never-meddling wife all tried to push me into Hugo's arms. "Just give him a chance," said Philip once out of the blue. I had the feeling that they were all worried I couldn't face reality on my own. Let's face the truth, they weren't so wrong – I couldn't even prove I was innocent of a crime I hadn't committed.

"Maybe I could spend some more time debating the future of my love life if not for the fact that I'm in danger of ending up in a women's prison. Besides I need to finish in a minute because I'm going to the office to talk about my new role."

"Oh yeah sure," Hannah sounded like I let her down. "Congratulations on your promotion."

"Yeah, thanks," I said with no enthusiasm. "Not so long ago I would be jumping to the ceiling, but now I'm just gutted I can't accept the offer from *Travel the World.*"

* * *

Tiggy was gone, which I found out before I even entered Cecelia's office. Good old Polly couldn't miss out on telling me all the latest news just to see my reaction. She loved to spy behind every door, especially the executive ones, to later have the pleasure of going and spreading gossip.

"Are you sure she's gone?"

"She was here a couple of days ago only to pack her things," Polly said but I was afraid to get happy too soon. Tiggy might've changed her desk or got promoted, and Polly – who sometimes only listened to a small bit of a conversation and quickly drew her conclusions – might've misunderstood the situation.

I didn't have to knock on Cecelia's door because when I arrived, she was just opening the door for a grey-suited man to leave. They said their goodbyes, wished each other a good day, and then he turned towards me – Arthur MacArthur. I'd never had any particularly warm feeling towards him but I thought it was rude of him not to even reply *good morning* to me, when we were standing so close to each other that we could have practically rubbed noses. Unlike him, Cecelia was very kind, friendly and for the first time in ages she had some time for me. She asked about Patrick and Dominic and wasn't rushing or inter-rupting me when I kept telling her stories that were probably only interesting to the children's parents and grandparents. She talked about her kids, mentioning the first months of their lives and telling me how the twelve years gap between her sons affected their relation-ship. It was me who finally changed the topic. I looked at my watch and suddenly realised we had been talking for over an hour.

"Well, I must admit I've missed my job," I lied thinking I sounded pretty genuine. "I initially rejected your offer of promotion only because I didn't believe Tiggy would really leave I-Heart-Travelling, and as you can imagine after what has recently happened... I don't think we could work together anymore... Then I got an offer from Travel the World—" Cecelia opened her eyes wide hearing the name of the magazine.

"Wow, that's wonderful," she leant over her desk and rested her chin on her crossed palms. "Tell me more about that."

"Well actually, I think together we can make I-Heart-Travelling a better magazine than *Travel the World*," I said and she frowned her eyebrows. "I mean a better selling magazine... because obviously we're a better magazine," I corrected myself with a confident smile.

"I'm glad you've got so much faith in us and it's wonderful you're so enthusiastic. That means we achieved something here and Tiggy hasn't totally failed in that field."

What? Nooo... You're twisting everything I'm saying.

"Is there a chance Tiggy comes back?" I asked with a fear that I couldn't manage to hide.

"No," she said categorically. "Tiggy plans to use her maternity leave to requalify and start a completely new career but I'm sorry to say her position is not available anymore. Polly is going to take her job," Cecilia's face suddenly took a cold and ambivalent expression.

My fault and only my fault, I was beating myself up. I shouldn't have rushed into rejecting such an offer. How could I be so thoughtless and stupid in my current life situation? I'm more qualified and have worked longer at I-Heart-Travelling than Polly, but tough luck – it's too late to be sorry. On the other hand, if I was promoted to the managerial role I'd have to do longer hours and have more responsibilities which would mean less time with my boys and more money for nanny – mum couldn't become a full-time nanny for another couple of years. I decided to go back to the company to be able to keep the house and have enough money for the three of us, not to run away from my children. Besides working for Polly should make my situation completely different. She was one of the friendliest people in the firm. I couldn't reflect on a lost opportunity for business travel anyway. I wasn't permitted to leave the country while I was a prime suspect in the Cheater's Gang investigation."

"Olivia, can you hear me? I'm sorry. I know it might come as a bit of a shock for you. Would you like to have a glass of water?"

"I understand," I nodded.

"I also understand that working for Travel the World is tempting. Well, we both know you deserve better than your current position, and I'm sorry I can't do anything more about that now," she rolled her lips and got up to get me a glass of water, although I hadn't asked for one.

"Thank you for saying that. It means a lot to me," I took a big sip of overpriced sparkling water that Cecilia bought on a regular basis from the company account. I felt the bubbles coming up my nose and coughed.

"But we all know you won't feed your children with my compliments, and Travel the World can pay you significantly more."

"They do but I'd have to travel more, which of course I will if I have to... but I'd prefer to have a more stable job while the boys are still so small... and I've always enjoyed working with Polly."

"You've never worked on the same team," Cecilia snapped as if she had caught me lying.

"Oh… well… But I'm sure we can make a good team," I forced myself to smile. I started getting tired with the conversation. All I wanted was to come back to my old job and never see Tiggy ever again.

"I've already got somebody for her deputy role, if that's what you're inferring"

"No, no… That's not what I'm thinking. I'm happy to just stay where I was with my old job."

"I find that hard to believe," she said slowly while staring at me as if she wanted to read the answer from my body language because she couldn't trust my words. "You'll drop us like a stone as soon as you find a better job."

"I rejected the offer from Travel the World to work here," I almost screamed.

"Because you preferred to be a senior manager here than start from the bottom somewhere else," Cecilia also raised her voice. "I bet they didn't ask you to be one of their senior managers."

"How can you know that?" I asked slightly offended.

"I know what I'll do," she suddenly livened up, jumped to her feet and walking behind her desk with her forefinger waving in the air. "I'll call them today and offer them a referee to strengthen your hand for a more senior position."

"I don't understand why you're so insistent on me taking their offer," I said suspiciously. "Especially after you've just said I'm such a precious employee."

"I know from my own experience how difficult it is to be a single working mother. Every little pay increase helps and we won't be able to give you any pay rise for a while."

Of course, you don't know what it's like – it's all about the money, but I don't have other job offers to accept, so any port in a storm!

"Fine as long as I'm not paid below minimum wage," I giggled nervously.

"Listen…" she hesitated. "I've spoken to Sir Arthur MacArthur. He agreed to a generous severance payment if you resign. It's actually very generous… and you'll get good references."

"But why?" I asked flabbergasted.

"We need to further cut costs."

What about drinking tap water in the office or at least bottled water that doesn't cost more than two bottles of a good wine?

"Go on and fire me then. I'm paying for a lawyer anyway and I'm sure… oh I'm sure I can get more than a couple of thousand for you effectively sacking me while I'm on my maternity leave."

"Olivia listen…" she said calmly. Cecilia had done a course on firing people from work, Polly had told me, so I didn't believe any word of compassion coming from her mouth.

"You listen," I stood up and pointed my finger at her in such an aggressive gesture that she leant back on her chair. For a minute I was afraid she was about to press an emergency button to call a bodyguard who would walk me out of her office, but she only put both hands on the armrests and stared at me. "Don't bullshit me about me being such an exceptional employee because even if I was one you would never care or notice. You don't need good employees, you need obedient ones. And how do you even know about me being a single mother? Have you read about it on a billboard on your way to work or had a chat with Tiggy? You were forced to fire her after she got drunk at work alongside all those complaints about her abusing us for the last god-knows-how-many years – but I bet you're still best pals! I haven't talked to anybody at work about my personal life, and I'm not a celebrity for who you find out all the juicy details on the Internet!" As I finished I was breathing rapidly, my heart racing in my chest, hands getting sweaty and tears coming to my angry eyes.

She swallowed hard and said through a tight throat, "No news has mentioned you yet but we both know it's just a matter of time, and we can't afford bad publicity at this moment."

"What?" I asked in terror, feeling like all organs were slowing down in my body, Cecilia's voice was echoing in my head, *just a matter of time, a matter of time, time…*

"Detective Murray paid us a visit. We're aware of the ongoing investigation concerning the selling of essays and the Cheaters Gang, and the fact you're a suspect."

"I'm innocent!"

"Of course, you are," she said like a mother to a child. "But—"

"At least I'm innocent until proven guilty!"

"Look, I'm not here to judge you, I know in your situation you needed money, we don't pay you that well, you're a single mother of two children..." she was speaking quickly, words firing out of her mouth, not letting me interrupt, "you're a good writer, you thought why not use it... who knows if I was desperate maybe I would do exactly the same... I'm not judging you at all... we won't fire you for now but Arthur MacArthur would insist on suspending you which would mean that we would have to stop your salary until you're proven innocent... That's why I begged Arthur to give you the four thousand so you're not left with nothing... I'm sorry I can't do any more for you."

"I'm not any threat for the company..." I said tearily.

"I know that but some wouldn't agree. If you've been selling exam questions, what would stop you from selling our company information to the competition?"

"It's ridiculous and—"

"Besides, we've checked your computer and a few sets of exams were sent from your work email address."

"Do you really think I would be so stupid? Of course, Tiggy! Tiggy Brown the bloody—"

"You can't blame Tiggy for every problem in your life."

"I can for at least half of them!" I yelled and again imagined a bodyguard taking me out and Polly eavesdropping. I lowered my voice and nearly whispered, "Do you know she slept with my fiancé?"

"Aha," she nodded. "Well now I know why you were so hostile towards each other."

I gave up trying to explain anything. She would have twisted every word I said convinced that she knew it all. "No, that's not true."

"Let's hope everything goes well," she clasped her hands and smiled. "I wish you all the best. I'm sure the sun will shine for you again..." I felt I was getting sick with her fake niceties. "I've prepared all necessary papers for you to sign, and you don't have to worry about anything. You just have to sign that you resign and you won't sue us, and on our side we promise you the four thousand pounds."

"What if I don't sign anything?"

"Olivia, it's not the right time to be proud. You need to think about your children now," Cecilia put her hand on a pile of papers and slowly slid them across the whole width of her wooden desk while looking straight into my eyes. I only glanced through them counting fifteen pages written in small font. "Four thousand is better than nothing."

"I don't have time to read it all today. You also must be in a rush."

"Take as much time as you need," she said but I knew she was counting on me not being able to stand the pressure of her piercing, wide-open eyes that were completely fixed on me.

"Thanks, but no thanks. I'm seeing my lawyer today and I've just found out I'm going to have one more issue to talk through with him," I said matter-of-factly.

I raised myself up, my hands pushing against the arms of the chair, then froze as Cecilia started threatening me, "You're going to regret it. You're suspended… Your severance payment is gone." She grabbed the papers violently and tossed them on a shelf behind her desk, then stood up, picked them up again and put them into a black shredder under her desk. "I didn't know you're in a position to dismiss such a good offer."

"I didn't know that in your financial situation you can so easily discard so much good paper. Wasn't it you and Tiggy who always asked us to use the other side of the paper for printing or at least for notes?"

That was the end of my adventure with I-Heart-Travelling. I headed to the lift on shaky legs. I didn't know whether everybody was staring at me discreetly from behind the screens of their computers as I walked through the whole length of the open space office or it was only my imagination. The voices around me were melting into one loud mass – I found the sound unbearable – it was like listening to a hammer drill. I felt some relief in the lift but not for long because I was afraid somebody could suddenly stop it, walk inside and ask me a question about why I looked so pale. I got out two floors below and walked the rest of the way down by the stairs. I took a few deep breaths outside feeling like the cold March air was filling my lungs and freezing my fear about the future. I slapped myself energetically on both cheeks, shook my head, squeezed the tears back and decided to waste a few quid on an overpriced coffee, sold from a silver truck just outside the glass building where once I hated working.

I was walking through Regent's Park when I started shivering again. I squeezed tight a woolly scarf around my neck, pulled out an orange-cocoa energy bar from my bag and munched it within seconds. I thought about wearing gloves but first I needed to make a call. I didn't expect him to answer, I just didn't know what to do with myself and it seemed to be the most logical step as he was the source of all my misery.

* * *

"Olivia?" he asked feigning surprise, like it hadn't been him not answering my calls for all those days since detective Murray found the exam papers in my garden.

"Are you kidding me?" I yelled attracting the attention of tens of small kids marching in the opposite direction in bright yellow vests looking like they had been doing some road work. "Were your hands tied that you couldn't press one bloody button on your mobile to answer my call?" I imagined him sitting in a basement with his legs and hands tied and his mouth taped shut, which actually filled my heart with a disturbing kind of joy.

"My phone was blocked because I didn't pay the bills."

I laughed, "Henry darling, I don't know whether you're getting better at lying or I'm getting better at seeing right through you. But down to the point – are you really going to let me go to jail for the crimes that you committed? Clearly all that stuff you told me about children having one of their parents in prison is no longer relevant?"

"Relax," he said confidently and I imagined him smiling. "I think you'll be able to prove you're innocent... he paused for a few seconds, "provided you're innocent," he said questioningly. I could not make a sound with the anger and stupor filling my body from the tip of my toes to the top of my head. I was walking straight ahead with my mouth wide open, while he started talking again assuming I was still there to listen. "If it comes to the worst, you've got my word that we'll look after the boys."

"WE?" I squeaked. "How can you even sleep at night?"

"I don't sleep well at all, I worry about you and my children. Kitty bought me some herbal pills but they don't really work…" Suddenly everything became clear to me, he was thinking I was recording him. It would have been a great idea but in my current desperate state I was short on good ideas. "Kitty loves children and she's ready to adopt them. The only thing is she's got a job in Miami in one of the best estate agencies in America and she's going to be our breadwinner so we'll need to move there with her… but don't worry. We'll come to visit, or you can come when you… when you, you know…"

"No, I don't know," I screamed.

"I'm sorry Kitty's job is just not as mobile as mine or yours."

"When I finish with you – you little lying shit – your mobility will be limited to a walk from a prison bunk to a communal loo in the middle of your cell. You're not going to frame me for your crimes."

"Does every discussion have to end up with you threatening me?" he said with satisfaction. "We've got our differences but I would have never tried to frame the mother of my children with anything. I don't know how you can think so low of me. I've even forgiven you about the affair with Hue."

"Nobody is listening to us so you're just wasting your time on your bullshit."

"I'm starting to think that I ought to record our phone calls. I must admit I've got my doubts when it comes to your innocence. There's an aggressive side to you that I hadn't known until recently."

"Okay, now I'm wasting my time," I was about to disconnect but for Henry it wasn't enough just to threaten me with taking my children away.

"The kids will be safer in the US when nobody knows about their mother being in jail – just once, think about what's best for them not you. We need to sell the house and SHARE the profit so I can afford the move. We can't entirely rely on Kitty for money, it's not fair. It's enough she—"

"I swear to god that if you don't stop I'll cut you into thousands of little pieces and throw you to vultures so they can SHARE you for a fine dining supper!" I yelled and pressed disconnect. I felt like tossing the phone against the tarmac path in the park but I couldn't afford a replacement so I stamped my feet a few times and punched the air with my clenched fist wondering why I hadn't left Henry and quit my job ages ago – before he tried to put me into prison and before Cecilia kicked me out on the street as a single mother of baby twins.

37

FRIDAY, 25 MARCH

CAMBRIDGE

I decided to give myself one more week before telling my family how bad my situation was. I hoped that by that time I would at least be able to get some money for the lawyers. "I want to sell aunt Zelda's sideboard," I said calling my brother. "Are you interested?" I knew he was – firstly because he loved the old chunky piece of furniture and was jealous that aunt Zelda had given it to me in her will, secondly because he was convinced it was worth a lot of money, and its value was increasing every year.

"Yeah," he said hesitantly. "But I don't think I can afford it right now."

"I'm thinking about selling it. I could use some cash and I don't really have that much space for it in my lounge. Having split up with Henry I don't think I'll move to a bigger house any time soon."

"I understand but it looks good in your living room… although I know…" he sighed, "kids' stuff takes loads of space. You probably need an extension," he laughed.

"Exactly, I'll need more space," I tried my best to sound cheerful. "How much do you think it's going to be worth?"

"Sis, if you need some cash, you can borrow some… but can I

know why? You've got a job. Henry agreed to pay you child support, you don't need to hire a divorce lawyer – thanks god!"

"I don't have any savings. I want to sell it now, not when I desperately need some money."

"Okay. I think... I mean from what I heard from our parents it might be worth about thirty thousand. Just don't tell them you're going to sell it because they will kick off. You know how sentimental they are, despite the fact they never liked Zelda."

"Can I ask you for something?"

"Go on!"

"Have you watched the TV show where they price up your antiques? I would like to make sure I'm getting a fair price for it."

"Oh my god, you want me to take part in it?"

"You're better than me on camera," I said, which was true but it wasn't the reason why I wanted to avoid being on a TV show – I would do anything for my children! I was nervous though it would only confirm the police's theory I desperately needed money and was ready to do anything to get it, including selling family heirlooms or exam questions.

"I haven't done that much on TV," he laughed but I knew he was flattered and keen like mustard to do it. "Just the one interview at work and ten minutes on breakfast TV."

"I think it's enough experience. Besides I feel fat after being pregnant, and the camera only gives you extra weight!"

"I'll do it!"

"The show is being filmed today in the afternoon," I said and gave him the location of a park located in the suburbs of London.

"You knew I would agree! But how am I going to take it there?"

"I've hired a van and a small moving platform to use around the park. Atlanta's and Freya's husbands will go with you to help... you're the best! Thank you!"

While Philip was getting ready for the antiques show I was driving with Hannah to Cambridge. No matter how much she believed in Alistair, she insisted on carrying out on our own investigation, and I was ready to do anything that could improve my situation. Our first stop was Cambridge – the city where Henry the Pure Evil was born, spent his childhood and early adolescence. We drove my car, while I still could because I was going to have to sell it soon. We couldn't use the train anyway because of work on the line – it looked like not only Alistair was having to work over the Easter weekend. After three and a half hours of driving in terrible traffic I finally parked in front of the mansion belonging to Henry's parents. I still remembered how impressed but also intimidated I felt when I saw the house for the very first time.

I didn't have to press the intercom to drive through the gold and black gate – an entrance a la Buckingham Palace. Today it was open and there were no cars parked on the yellow tarmac drive, which easily could have taken the two Range Rovers belonging to Mr and Mrs Thyme, and probably four other large vehicles along with his and her campervans with boat trailers should they so wish.

I switched off the engine and turned to Hannah full of doubt, "It's not a great idea. Alistair is right, I shouldn't do anything on my own."

"What? Seeing his parents? Don't be ridiculous."

"Yes… I don't know but…"

From what I googled the night before, Alistair was the best lawyer I could afford, although barely and not without making sacrifices like selling Zelda's furniture as well as the SUV and the handbag from Henry. Alistair appeared to be a good, respectable lawyer with six years' experience in both criminal and divorce law – apparently the two specialisations were often linked together. As one anonymous woman put in her review of Alistair: "When your divorce case lasts for months, one of you will eventually commit a crime. It is just a matter of time before it get ugly. But on the bright side, we didn't go as far as poisoning the other party after the divorce took more than a year – even when I really felt it would solve most of my problems… Alistair takes it all in his stride, he's seen it all before."

I had only four days before my interview accompanied by my attorney – or rather attorneys because on Tuesday morning Hugo was flying to London with Enrique Jose Gonzales del Toro, one of the best criminal lawyers in Europe. Hugo had convinced me that Enrique's arrival had to remain secret. "Alistair is well-known in London. How can you be sure he hasn't been bribed by Henry or the Cheaters Gang?" he said in a begging voice on the phone. "What if they've already threatened him?" I had to admit there was a lot of sense in what Hugo was saying so I didn't even tell Hannah that I had a second lawyer working on my case. I was only afraid that innocent people don't normally employ two lawyers to defend them; and that Alistair, working through the whole of Easter, might drop me like a stone as soon as he finds out about Enrique or me trying to run a separate investigation behind his back.

"Take a breath we're getting out," Hannah said matter-of-factly.

"But…"

"Yes, move your butt! Move it! Move it! move it!" Hannah was throwing her hands in the air, and for a moment I had a feeling that I would be kicked out of my own car. "We're going to say *hi* to Mr and Mrs Thyme."

I reluctantly got out of the car, my legs were soft like they were made of cotton, my head pulsating and my ears could hear my thumping heart. "What if Henry is here?"

"Then we see how well he lies in front of his family. Trust me, it's not the same to bluff your partner and some perfect strangers, compared to faking it to your parents." I did trust her but decided not to verbalise my thoughts about her becoming a professional liar. "Are you going to press their fancy doorbell or do you want me to do it?" She said when we were standing just before two small steps with two large Roman pillars on both sides.

The Thyme's home could be best described as an estate or residence. It was a classic Gregorian style house, made of brick, with a simple black tiled roof. The nine long rectangular windows at the front were ornamented with open green wooden shutters. On the left side of the house stood a massive oak over a hundred years old, and on the right two double garages with guest and staff flats at the top. I took a breath and turned back to glance at the driveway roundabout with a grassed area in the middle. At its centre was a fountain and two

Christmas trees, which the Thymes always decorated on the first weekend of December with flashing golden lights. Actually, it was their handy man, who decorated them while they stood on their drive with glasses full of champagne, dressed in furry coats and designer slippers with outdoor soles, instructing him where to put the lights. I suddenly remembered vividly the evening when I visited Henry's parents for the first time. It was a cold Saturday in December – for the entire journey it had been snowing so heavily that we were glad to get there safe and sound all the way from London. Henry was grateful I had talked him into getting winter tyres. The house looked magical with the golden trees and lights spread across the whole length of the house. I was enchanted both by Henry and the palatial setting, and I started thinking how wonderful it would be to have one day a mini version of such a house with Henry.

"If we've got a house like that one day, we could put the Christmas decorations up at the beginning of December and take them down at the end of January or even the beginning of February like in Poland," I said with dreamy eyes. "The longer we can justify, the better."

"You can't be serious," he snapped. "Christmas lights for the whole of January? It would be just weird. Our neighbours would probably think that we couldn't afford a handy man anymore," he said and stormed to the main door to kiss his mother on her cheek. It was the end of the romantic atmosphere that evening but it was long after that event I realised that Henry was like a Christmas decoration himself – nice and shiny only when he was put on display for a certain time, any longer would just be weird.

Both Mr and Mrs Thyme were scientists, who regularly gave lectures at Cambridge University. Rosamunde Thyme was focused mainly on creating new creams for acne and psoriasis, while Edward Thyme was most interested in global warming and carried out a lot of research in the Antarctic Circle. Each time we came to visit them, Henry turned into a stiff toff who I barely recognised. His language suddenly became full of words and expressions that many British people would have to check in the dictionary, and his accent became way posher than the Queen's – he was like somebody in an American movie pretending to be part of British royalty or at least belong to a European, unknown before, kingdom that uses the poshest of the poshest English. I often found myself surprised that Henry still referred to his parents as mum and dad, I had expected to hear *my dear mother and father*. I also thought that given the formality in their house they should've answered their phone starting, "Thyme's residence, lady of the house speaking."

Rosamunde and Edward were friendly towards me but our whole relationship was primarily based on sufficient distance and a regular exchange of niceties. I had expected I wasn't their perfect match for their only child, who himself had been struggling to meet their expectations. Henry was a PhD professor at one of the best universities in the country but for his parents somehow it wasn't enough. In the whole United Kingdom they recognised only Cambridge and Oxford universities as the ones worthy of their prodigal son. When Henry announced to them once during a Sunday roast dinner that he was going to give guest lectures at Oxford University, his mother nodded and said sternly, "I pray every day to live long enough to see my son working full time at a decent university."

His father wiped his mouth with a white starched napkin, raised his chin up and said practically to the dark wooden ceiling in his dining room, "It would've helped if you graduated from a decent university yourself. I still cannot believe you compromised on your education by deciding not to retake your exams to Oxbridge and Harvard."

We drove home the same night although the next day was a Bank Holiday – all because Henry suddenly insisted he needed to check some exam papers that he had completely forgotten about. Half way to London I finally broke the silence hanging heavily in the air as if his parents were with us in the car, "Why didn't you retake the exams if you care so much about their opinion?"

"I respect their opinion but I don't let it get to me."

"Oh, that's such bullshit! So why have we left tonight? Do you really want me to believe that you had to—"

"I didn't retake the exams because I was terrified I could've failed again and I'd disappoint them even further." It was then I released his parents' opinion was constantly looming over his head. It was like a curse that he didn't want to believe in but he was still terrified of.

I pressed the doorbell. It was the first time I was doing it without Henry on my side. "See? They aren't at home."

"Press it again harder, or I'll do it," to my horror Hannah started repeatedly pressing the doorbell like an impatient child or an always-in-a-rush delivery driver. I'd just grabbed her hand, when we heard somebody's footsteps on Thyme's marble hallway floor, and I held my breath.

"Good morning Miss Eliot," said the Thyme's housekeeper, who as usual was wearing a simple black dress, cut just below her skinny knees.

"Good morning Camila," I forced myself to smile. "You're looking well. I wish I could chat, but I really don't have much time and I need to see Rosamunde and Edward."

"I'm afraid it's impossible," she replied with a stone-cold face.

"He killed them," Hannah whispered to me. "He couldn't stand their pressure so he shot them."

"You've got such a dark mind," I murmured.

"Nobody killed anybody. I'm only sixty and I'm not deaf yet," Camila was standing with her hands on her tiny hips.

"So, where are they?" Hannah raised her voice.

"Don't speak to me with that tone young lady."

"I'm sorry Camila. She didn't mean to, we're just both really nervous and we're worried about Henry and… we hoped Mrs and Ms Thyme could help us."

"Yeah, pronto," Hannah acted like she had suddenly forgotten all her manners but in reality, she had convinced herself that the only way to achieve anything was by being tough, rough and intimidating.

"How pronto?" Camila smirked.

"How about now?" I said meekly.

"Now ain't gonna happen," she said in a singing voice. "But if you hire a helicopter it could be reasonably *pronto*. I can call their friends from Surrey, they've got two, maybe you could borrow one."

"Great, call them," snapped Hannah and I chastised her with my eyes. "Would you be so kind to call them Camila? We would be ever so grateful."

"But where are they?" I asked.

"Henry bought them a cruise around the world. It's going to last over eighty days and they went away only a week ago."

"Why?" I screamed. "God, it can't be happening to me."

"Pull yourself together woman!" Hannah shouted at me. "We won't achieve anything if you fall apart."

"Why? Because they're his parents and he loves them," snapped Camila. "He's recently been doing extremely well at his job. He even got a reward for catching some members of a Cheating Gang, or whatever it's called. Mr and Mrs Thyme have been so proud of him. They've suggested he has a break, move back home and prepare himself for a PhD at Cambridge."

"See?" Hannah turned to me speaking as if Camila hadn't been there. "And I bet he paid some pirates of the Caribbean to get on that boat and scare the shit out of them so once and for all they stop pestering him with their ideas!" and before Camila managed to say something to her, Hannah continued, "and if not Cambridge, Oxford or maybe Harvard, yeah?"

"How do you know?" Camila asked surprised.

"I'm a fortune teller."

"Well, I'm sorry I can't help you," Camila said with the exact tone and words that I always thought she reserved only for the Friends of the Family sect.

"Actually, you could help us," said Hannah, and I looked at her terrified thinking she was actually going to ask for the helicopter after all. I didn't want to fly in anything that didn't have wings, it's just common sense. "You know how hard it is to park in the centre..." Camila nodded, "could we leave the car here for a couple of hours?"

"Yes. Something else?"

"No, that would be lovely. Thank you," I said and she practically slammed the door in our faces while we were still whispering our goodbyes.

The Thyme's estate was located twenty minutes away from the vibrant centre of Cambridge. I loved Oxford's historic landscape and its mysterious vibe, the feeling of being dropped in the middle of a detective movie. Cambridge was like Oxford but with wider streets and more space in the centre. The only downside of the city were the omnipresent cyclists, who often didn't want to recognise the presence of other people using their legs as a means of transport.

"Be careful how you drive, you bloody psycho-cycle-path!" Hannah was shouting after a guy who almost ran us over, but he was already too far to hear. "Bicycles can be a great thing, you know? But only when you know how to ride them!"

I took Hannah to an Italian café that I used to go to with Henry each time we went to visit Rosamunde and Edward. Neither of his parents were good cooks, and Camila's fine dining meals were too sophisticated for my palate, or too small to stay full. Hannah quickly walked away completely discouraged by the lack of a place to sit down. She began whinging that she was too tired to look for a bench to sit on and it was too cold outside. Since I'd been under threat of dining in jail, a cold bench wasn't a problem for me anymore. I got two bags of takeaway goodies: pita bread with roasted vegetables, focaccia with olives and biscuits filled with chocolate and pistachio cream. I was walking fast at the front, waving two paper bags while Hannah was tiptoeing after me in her high heels that had given her some blisters. She would never learn to at least pack an emergency pair of trainers and let herself look a little bit less than glamorous. I found a place to sit on a long wall separating the street from the wide strip of grass surrounding King's College. Hannah joined me after five long minutes looking anything but happy and chatty, but I tried to ignore her being moody.

"Do you know what would look great next to such an impressive building like King's College?"

"What?" she snapped taking off her shoes and I knew immediately we would have to call a taxi to get back to our car.

"Try the food first," I passed her one of the paper bags. She took a bit of focaccia and hummed like Sebastian's cat when he was happy or just after he ate the bird. "I'm thinking of a square!"

"A square like a Times Square or like a Market Square?" she asked licking her fingers.

"Like the Krakow one. It's a shame we don't have big town squares, I think they really add some spirit to cities."

"Do you miss Krakow? Why don't you go—" she stopped suddenly realising I wasn't allowed to leave the country. "I'm sorry, silly question."

"I'd love to take the job offer from Travel the World. They wanted me to work on their Krakow travel guide. I'm afraid I won't ever have another chance like that."

"How much time have they given you to make the decision?"

"If I don't call by Tuesday six o'clock they'll assume that I'm not interested. The meeting with the lawyers is at four."

"Right," she cleared crumbs from her black leather skirt, "we need to go. There's no time to lose. I want you to have that job."

When we got back to the Thyme's mansion it was dark and the gate was closed. I pressed on the intercom, again and again and again but nobody was answering.

"Where is your car?" Hannah shouted.

"Just there—" I realised I was pointing at a place which only a couple of hours earlier was occupied by my car but now was taken by a red mini cooper belonging to Camila. "There's no way she could move it, she didn't have a key. What the hell?" I asked and looked at Hannah staring at one of the top floor windows. Through a thick voile I saw a massive chandelier and a tall wide-shouldered man. "Henry?"

"What game is he playing?"

My phone beeped.

Sorry, Zelda's sideboard was mass-produced. Worth max £1000. The only thing I got was sunburn! Speak to u later!

"Is it him? Is Henry texting you?"

"Just my brother," I sighed and my phone beeped again. "Don't stalk me and my family. I'm sorry but your car has been towed away.

445

It's going to be pricey for you. To get it back call the number..." I read aloud.

"Your brother towed your car away?"

I looked at the window. Henry was waving to us with his phone and sending us kisses.

38

SATURDAY, 26 MARCH

CARDIFF

"I feel so guilty leaving my kids again. If you could've seen Veronica's face when I was telling Philip I wanted to go and see a concert in Wales this weekend!"

"Why didn't you just make something up?" Hannah asked loudly and a man in front of us in the queue turned back to eye us up. I felt significantly overdressed in my red outfit borrowed from Hannah, although other girls, including my friend, were even more dolled up. Most seemed to be in twenty-centimetre heels with strong lipstick and they looked like they were going to perform on stage themselves. "You do it for your children," she said looking into a pocket mirror and powdering her nose.

"Yeah, a relaxed mother is a happy mother, and a happy mother means happy children," said a guy enthusiastically before smiling flirtatiously to Hannah. I couldn't have blamed him – she looked stunning in her short silver sparkling dress showing her entire cleavage. The man also didn't look that bad himself in his sleek blue shirt and beige trousers. Hannah and I didn't say a word to each other until we reached the office to pick up our tickets and the guy was gone with another pretty girl, who he met in the same queue, just in front of us.

"I don't understand why you can't tell me why we're here," I whispered as a handsome cashier in his late twenties was printing our tickets. "How does an Olympia White concert help my situation?"

"You'll find out at the right time, trust me. Just enjoy the concert. Do you know how hard it was for me to get the tickets?"

"I can only imagine. Fifteen years ago I'd have given anything to listen to her live."

"Here you are," the man passed us freshly printed tickets that stained my fingers with black ink, he smiled exposing his white teeth with transparent braces. "Olympia will be on stage about nine. She's always late."

We moved towards the entrance surrounded by masses of people who had clearly spent a lot of time styling their hair, putting on stage make-up and choosing suitably fashionable outfits.

"I don't get it. On the internet it says that the concert starts at six, on the tickets it says seven, and the guy has just said nine!"

She gave me a merciful look, "Artists never show up on stage at the time you've got written on your ticket. First there's at least one supporting act and then they give you a chance to get a drink and spend money on tat…"

"Of course," I said embarrassed.

"When did you last see a concert?"

"I don't remember but I can tell you for sure it wasn't during the whole time I was going out with Henry," I shouted in Hannah's ear as we finally got inside the Cardiff Arena and started walking in zigzags to avoid somebody spilling beer on us. "He didn't like such big events. You know the standard Henry's excuses – too many people too close to you, too hot, too loud and too expensive."

"And it never crossed his mind he could just once *sacrifice* himself for you?"

"Nope. When the Backstreet Boys were last in London I had to do one of the stiff university events instead. To be honest, maybe it wouldn't have been so stiff if I wasn't there with Henry," I laughed.

"Hundred percent agree, and now we know the stiff Henry is just a charade to hide his true colours," Hannah was shouting into my left ear but I still had to focus to hear her. We stood in another queue to get some overpriced drinks. "Anyway, we need to pace ourselves and not drink too much too quickly because I bet Olympia will be on stage even later than nine."

"Ohmygod, I hope I don't fall asleep waiting."

"She's one of the biggest divas in the world so she needs to act like one when she is back on stage after more than ten years," Hannah said excited, and I suddenly thought that us seeing the concert had nothing to do with Henry, she just used the excuse to drag me out of the house.

I hadn't listened much to Olympia White for the last five years (Henry preferred jazz) but I had a chance to read some parts of her book, *Olympia White, Fifty-Five Years of My Life*, when Tiggy left her hardback copy in the I-Heart-Travelling kitchen and went on a four-day business trip. Over the last decade Olympia had mostly worked in her private music studio and stayed away from the limelight. No wonder – she began her career at the age of twelve taking part in beauty pageants all over the United States and then performing on various children's TV shows. By the age of sixteen she had her first music record and her first number one in the US and UK charts. Sadly, during the last decade she spent months in six luxurious rehab centres for people addicted to: (1) sex, (2) gambling, (3) alcohol, (4) smoking, (5) drugs and (6) chocolate. On the bright side, it was also the decade when she finally found the time to pass her high-school exams and graduate from a marketing and business management degree – something she had wanted to do for years but found impossible due to her overloaded schedule. She also put an end to her twenty-five year marriage with her cheating husband, a millionaire who owned a chain of hotels in the Caribbean. After a few months of passionate dating she got hitched with a Californian billionaire hotelier who was thirteen years younger than her. She divorced him six months later but kept half of his fortune. The last thing that I read was that Olympia had come out as a lesbian and was dating a famous artist and painter Tatiana O'Neil.

Her current tour around Europe, called Olympia White Comes Back, was the first one in ten years. She was visiting two other cities in the UK, London and Manchester, but Hannah dug her designer heels into going to Cardiff, which has the smallest but also the most personal arena. Initially I did not share her enthusiasm but I started understanding her point when we easily found a place to park only five minutes' walk from the arena and when I took my not-so-expensive seat that was only a few rows from the stage.

"Fancy some souvenirs?" Hannah asked suddenly as we finished our glasses of wine.

I shook my head, "I'm too comfy on my plastic chair," As soon as I said it she grabbed my right hand and dragged me outside into the corridor, surrounding the main part of the arena, to walk around the stalls with everything-Olympia: from mugs, key rings and phone cases to beach towels and candles. There was also a stand with her book, but that one was the least surrounded – I suspected her biggest fans had already read it at least once.

"Two hardbacks please," I saw Hannah taking out two twenty pound banknotes from her sparkling silver purse.

"Why are you buying two?"

"One for me, one for you darling," she smiled.

"We live under one roof, we don't need two."

"Can't you just say thank you?"

"Thank you," I smiled when I heard a male voice asking, "what have you got there?" and I turned round because for a minute I thought he was speaking to me. I saw three men in tights – or the tightest jeggings in the world. It immediately reminded me of Stefano saying, "Do you know the only thing worse than a fat woman in leggings? A gay man in leggings!"

"I just couldn't help myself," a thin thirty-something man was saying while jumping from one leg to another, he was holding two plastic transparent bags full of colourful fabrics.

"Holy cats, you're such a shopaholic. What have you got this time?" asked a man with fat calves squeezed in shiny leather leggings.

"Four T-shirts with Olympia for us and one for my mum," he was saying excitedly as if he had managed to buy Versace at a ninety percent discount. "Then...hmmm..." as he looked inside the bag, "an apron with Olympia in her twenties for my new kitchen and a gold jacket with an Olympia logo for my Frenchie. Then..." I kept listening but Hannah once again grabbed my elbow and dragged me this time inside the arena.

The whole place was in complete darkness except the stage, which was lit with twinkling lights. My eyes had to adjust to the new lighting, or rather lack thereof, and I had to focus to see a guy on the stage wearing a baseball cap and plunking something on a keyboard. When we finally found our seats with the help of a man in a bright yellow vest, the plunking guy was replaced by a muscular, wide-shouldered man in a white tank top who was energetically dancing. Then we had to listen to a couple of songs of a boyband I hadn't heard of, before the lights went on again with such an intensity that I got temporarily blind. "This is it?" I asked keeping my left hand on my forehand and narrowing my eyes. "Are you sure you bought us tickets for Olympia White?"

Hanna looked at me with pity, "I can tell you haven't been out for a while."

"You don't have to be so harsh on me."

"Am I being harsh? I got them for you but you can't appreciate anything."

Fair enough, she had taken me out to see a concert but I had no idea how it would aid in preventing me from going to jail for Henry's crimes. I decided that the best thing to do was to shut up and fix my eyes on the stage. It went dark again but nothing happened except I began to get a headache from the intense light changes. The audience started shouting *Olympia* but it wasn't until fifteen minutes later that she eventually appeared above the stage, dangling on a rope squeezed around her waist. She was wearing a sparkling red corset with long sleeves that was fully exposing her large breasts and the full-length of her legs. My pre-pre-pregnancy swimsuit had larger pants and I was twenty-five years younger than her. Olympia swayed lightly on her matching red high heels when she landed on the stage and immediately fired off the show with a very well-known hit. It was striking that she was such a good singer when performing live. It was six years since I saw my last concert in London – in my pre-Henry life I'd been a regular guest at Wembley Arena, and I'd never heard anybody sing so well live to a large audience.

I was singingly loudly, feeling like a teenager again, and enjoying the fact nobody could hear me. The whole time I couldn't take my eyes away from Olympia – I was hypnotized by her energetic bouncing, bending her body in all possible directions in a costume, which must've been digging into her bum and *lady bits*. It was impossible to stay unmoved by the confidence with which she was wearing the skimpy outfit at her age and with a far-from-perfect body. In fact, the confidence emanating from her was so strong that by the end of a third song I was looking at a sexy, beautiful woman who everybody surely admired.

What was happening around us was almost as interesting as the performance on stage – it was just less admirable. In the middle of a song, which once inspired Charles from year ten to kiss me at a school disco, I had to bend towards Hannah to avoid a girl who was puking up like the Trevi Fountain, while climbing the stairs on my right with the effort of a nine-month-old baby. The sick landed on a man in the next aisle up. He took a bottle of water from his girlfriend and poured it straight over his legs in disgust.

"You're such an amazing audience. You're giving me so much positive energy. You're the best! I love you all!" Olympia was shouting in ecstasy standing on a gold box on the stage, while I was staring at a woman in front of me who was angrily taking off her blouse soaked with beer that somebody had dropped down her back.

The show was incredible, the audience interesting, with many probably waking up the next day remembering nothing from the event they paid hundreds of pounds for. It was when Olympia finished singing her last song of the encore that I realised we were also there for another but only-known-to Hannah reason. As we got outside the crowd quickly dispersed with some heading to car parks and some going into pubs and clubs in the centre of Cardiff. Once again I appreciated the location and the size of the arena – I didn't have to spend hours squeezed in a crowd guided by the police on their horses to finally reach an equally packed underground.

"No, this way" Hannah pushed me with her hips towards a frozen mud path with a wide metal gate at the end. I was impressed with her running around in high-heels on frosty surfaces just a few months after giving birth. I kept saying she was born in stilettoes.

"Where are we going?" I was following her obediently while looking with curiosity at a small group of women gathered in front of the gate, holding in their red shaking hands Olympia's biography and small colourful notebooks. All I could see behind the gate were a few black coaches with privacy windows and bodyguards standing outside. "I think I've passed the age when I get excited about auto-graphs," I said and Hannah frowned her eyebrows probably thinking that I was being ungrateful again. "Don't tell me you also paid to have five minutes and a photo shoot with Olympia."

"That's exactly what I did," she snapped.

"I hope it wasn't too expensive... Thank you," I started feeling guilty that I didn't really appreciate her gesture.

The women around us were in their thirties, which would make sense considering when Olympia was at the peak of her fame. One woman had brought her two teenage daughters and neither of them shared her enthusiasm to wait at night in the cold air for a diva who clearly wasn't in any rush. The girls spent the whole-time whinging about being tired, cold and not having good reception. Suddenly Hannah took out of her handbag two identity badges and passed them to me. Before I got my voice back and was ready to say something the men in jeggings walked up just next to us breathing heavily. I bet their trousers at least were keeping them warm. Now I could see some sense in dressing into such tight outfits for a night out.

"Blimey, so glad we've made it on time!" said the slimmest man holding a massive cloth bag stamped with a black logo of OW and packed full of Olympia branded tat.

"You haven't sold everything?" Hannah asked innocently but I saw her smirking. I was getting irritated with her for dragging out the evening for no obvious benefit, and also for taking the piss out of somebody who seemed to be a nice guy.

"Oh no," he giggled. "I bought everything," he said proudly, and I was relieved he didn't notice Hannah's sarcasm.

"Aaaa…" she nodded. "To sell later?" she asked and I could barely hold myself back from not elbowing her.

The man in jeggings didn't reply but suddenly screamed like everyone else standing next to us. Olympia White was walking out of the arena through the back entrance. I took out my copy of the book feeling relief at how light my handbag became and that it stopped digging into my arm. I opened the book on the title page to be signed but when I looked up Olympia was already gone.

"What a bitch! I can't believe it," one of the two daughters was saying. "How much time would it take her to wave to us and scribble a few autographs?"

"Exactly!" shouted her sister. "I'm going to write something on her Instagram as soon as my reception is back!"

I turned to Hannah who looked totally ambivalent to the whole situation, which was clearly so upsetting and emotional for those around us. "I'm sorry. Would you like to go for a drink?" I said not feeling like going anywhere but to our hotel.

"It's not her best day," a bodyguard told us through the gate. "I'm sure you'll get your money back at the box office tomorrow."

Everybody walked away until it was only me and Hannah still standing next to the gate like two women waiting for their lovers to be released from prison. "Show him our badges Olivia," she said matter-of-factly.

"We better go," I said but I passed the badges reluctantly to the bodyguard.

The man, dressed in a black bomber jacket and black trousers with large pockets on the sides, opened the gate, "Please, this way ladies."

"Can somebody tell me what's going on?" I asked quietly but nobody replied. Hannah was walking quickly beside the bodyguard and I was following them until we reached our final destination – coach number three. When the man left us to have a smoke a few meters away, Hannah knocked on the door. "Just like that? He's not even going to search us for a gun or nail file?"

"Just like that," she said and the doors swung open, and we both jumped back not to be hit.

* * *

"Sorry, I didn't know you were standing so close," said Olympia White herself. She was wearing a red silk dressing gown so thin I could see one of her stage outfits underneath, a skimpy black shiny corset.

"This is a close friend of mine, Olivia Eliot," Hannah introduced me when we got inside. Olympia gave me a wide smile and tightly squeezed my hand.

"And this is my close friend Hannah Kendal," I said proud of myself that I reacted so quickly in such a stressful moment.

"You really didn't tell her anything," Olympia said looking at *my close friend.*

Hannah shook her head and sat on a white moon leather sofa, which Olympia had pointed us to with her hand holding a full glass of something pink. Cosmopolitan? I felt like I'd won a competition in which the reward was a private audience with a diva.

"Have a sip," said my childhood goddess and passed us glasses of something that now looked more red than pink, if not even brownish. My head was already spinning and I didn't need any alcohol to feel any dizzier but I took a sip and gulped. I hadn't expected it to be so strong. "It's a Manhattan, in case you're wondering," said Olympia while getting herself comfy in her fluffy white armchair with a leopard blanket draped down its back. "Currently it's my favourite drink but it has nothing to do with the fact I live in New York and just looove Manhattan."

"Delicious," said Hannah and took another sip, while my eyes were looking around for a plant that could save me. I spotted one next to Olympia's chair but it was too far to water with my complimentary drink from this world class star.

"Oh, the leopard skin is fake, just in case you're wondering," Olympia giggled.

"It's beautiful," I said elbowed by Hannah.

If I'd seen the interior of the coach in a magazine, I would have thought it was the living room of a suite in a five-star hotel. The walls were decorated with silver wallpaper and oil paintings framed in heavy carved dark wood. Olympia pressed a button on a tiny remote and the lights around us dimmed. She took off her slippers with white feathers and put her bare feet on a thick soft carpet in the middle of the room. I resisted the temptation to do the same with my pumps. My face was warming up from the heat coming from a chimney in the corner and a slowly sipped Manhattan. When Hannah had run out of ideas on superlative adjectives to describe the concert, she suddenly turned to me and said, "Olympia and I," she cleared her throat, "we've known each other for a little while."

"Her husband—" started the diva but Hannah immediately corrected her saying ex-husband. "Of course, ex-husband... I'm so sorry your marriage hasn't worked out but I can tell you every next marriage is better than the previous one!" she laughed. "You need to keep trying girl until you're truly happy." Hannah wasn't in the mood to laugh but she forced a faint smile. "Recently I met an amazing guy, and god, he's so well equipped!"

"What about Tatiana?" Hannah saved us listening to the story about a guy's equipment.

Olympia waved her hand, "It was just an experiment – a phase in my life. I wish I was a lesbian but sadly I'm not. I think my life would be so much easier and maybe I would finally settle down."

"I know what you mean," I nodded. "But how did you two first meet?"

"Oscar used to be my lawyer... Oh, I'm so thirsty today," she stopped to take a gulp of a fresh Manhattan that she had been making while talking. She prepared it with such an accuracy and easiness that I strongly suspected she was used to making herself a lot of drinks, even if she had a house full of staff. In my world alcohol was a diuretic that dehydrated you, in hers it was a primary means of hydration.

"Once I was accused of buying exams," she finally continued. I felt my blood flowing quicker in my veins, too quickly for my brain and making it spin. I bent back on the sofa, it was softer than I had expected.

"Olympia was studying part-time in London," Hannah said.

"Hannah knows everything. Once I drunk a little bit too much, a little bit…" she pressed her right forefinger against her thumb, "and I told Hannah a little bit too much, a little bit. I forgot her husband hadn't told her about my case before. I used to tell my exes absolutely everything and now I regret – god," she gasped, "God how much I regret telling them so much."

I switched on a Dictaphone in my handbag, which I'd bought a few days earlier. It was more effective than my phone and I'd already checked it worked, even in my handbag. "So, you bought exams?" I asked loudly and she nodded. "Who did you buy them from?"

"Just don't think I was cheating for my whole degree, oh no," she waved her forefinger in front of her red nose and red-hot cheeks. "I only paid for two, maybe three essays and a couple of sets of exam questions and I did it only because I found myself at rehab half way through my studies."

"But who sold you the essays?"

"And I didn't really buy them because I was afraid to fail, oh no! I bought them because I wanted to have the best possible grades – I knew the media would want to write about my grades later, mhhh… They were just dying to say I was rich, successful and beautiful but all I could do was scream into a microphone. You can't imagine the pressure I was under, my darling… My agent wanted me to study to prove I did something useful during the last ten years… that I didn't just fly from one rehab to another but I really, really wanted to become a better person—"

"You said Henry Thyme didn't sell you the exams personally but you were sure he was involved in the business and you heard his name on occasion," Hannah raised her voice to interrupt Olympia, who was getting more and more drunk and soon would clearly be totally useless for our investigation.

"He didn't sell me anything personally but I met him later, he seemed to be a nice guy actually. I sent a few friends to him."

"I had nothing to do with the Cheaters Gang but Henry's been trying to frame me with his illegal business."

"Hannah told me," she said rolling her lips in compassion.

"It's wonderful you agreed to help us," Hannah said.

"I'm sorry my sweetie but I won't be able to. I talked to my new lawyer and I can't do anything. I would have to admit to the public I cheated and that your husband... your ex-husband saved my arse in court."

"I thought it was what you wanted – to warn all students out there, to be the good example for others. You said it would be heroic."

"Nah, I was a little bit too drunk, a little bit too much... you know how it is sometimes. We've got all these heroic ideas but life... the public is a bitch and I can't afford to throw myself out there to be ripped apart... so I'm sorry I gave you so much hope."

"My best friend might go to jail. She's got two small children at home," Hannah was begging. "Don't abandon us."

"I understand but I can't help you. It would also destroy your life Hannah."

I looked questioningly at Hannah who seemed to be equally surprised as me.

"Oh, he didn't tell you everything in the end. Oscar went as far as faking evidence to save me. If somebody finds out, he'll lose his licence and go to jail. If you want to keep getting money from him every month, you need to accept this sweetie."

Hannah was staring blankly at one of the paintings on the wall. I could not tell what it was portraying except that it was modern art. Then, all of a sudden she grabbed her handbag and me, before heading towards the door saying, "Goodbye Olympia, thank you for the drinks, it was nice seeing you."

"I'm sorry sweetie," I heard Olympia shouting as her voice faded away behind my back.

Hannah slammed the door so hard I felt like the whole coach shook. For a moment I was waiting for the bodyguard to come and start shouting at us but he was quietly standing in the exact place where we had left him, smoking and typing on his phone.

"I'm sorry I dragged you all the way here for that."

"Don't be silly, I know how much you've tried and I'm really grateful to you for it."

"Stupid me! I believed in her. We were at so many parties together," Hannah was almost crying.

"I recorded the whole discussion," I said. "What about if we cut the part about Oscar?"

Hannah looked at me terrified. "Olivia, you don't get it. She's right. If Oscar goes to jail, I'm left with no money and two children. I have no work experience!"

"Okay, okay. I'm not going to use it. Let's hope Alistair will be able to get me out of the shit on Tuesday."

"I'll help you! We'll make something up, just promise me you'll destroy the recording!"

"I promise," I said thinking I would only use it as a last resort. Why would I go to jail for one bastard, who decided to become a gangster to enhance his self-esteem, and another one who thought it was a good idea to defend a spoiled diva by faking some evidence and risking his whole career and family life?

39

TUESDAY, 29 MARCH

LONDON

When a black limousine parked in front of one of the biggest police stations in the city the three of us stopped talking and our eyes wandered almost involuntarily towards the limo's wide polished door. We were waiting in silence for a long couple of minutes for somebody to finally open it. My whole body had been sensing some bad energy steaming from the car. Just when I thought I couldn't endure the tension any longer the back door opened wide and I saw Henry's confident smug face. He was closely followed by his lawyer – jumping swiftly out of the limo, wearing dark sunglasses and a tailored shiny suit – he looked young despite having grey hair. They both looked like high calibre pop stars. Henry gave me one of his practised smiles a la Avenger. He covered the short distance – max twenty meters – between the curb of the road and the door to the police station in slow motion, not taking his eyes from me for even a second. I couldn't believe what I saw – he was there right in front of me and was looking so fresh, confident and content.

"I can't believe it. I can't believe that they hadn't told me about him coming here," I was shaking like jelly outside the police station building – the same building I'd passed many times on my way to Shakespeare University to see Henry.

Hugo put his arms on my shoulders, lowered his head, looked straight into my eyes and said softly, "Pretend he's not here. I know it must be difficult for you but please, please just try."

I didn't know anymore how I could've ever thought that it was Hugo who made my life complicated – he was actually the only person who was making everything easier.

"Miss Eliot," Alistair gave me his stern look, "nobody had to inform you about anything. It's an exploratory interview and the police can invite anybody they wish without telling you about it beforehand. You also decided not to tell… anyway we don't have time for irrelevant matters," Alistair suddenly decided to hold himself back from reminding me again I'd employed a second attorney without letting him know. I understood he could have been offended and I was grateful he didn't drop me like a stone after I said I wanted to introduce him to my Spanish lawyer – only ten minutes before the two attorneys met in person.

"Señora, please don't be preoccupied by such details. It's just an interview and we're well prepared," said Enrique in a strong Spanish accent and a smile that could easily seduce many women, even the most resilient ones. He was also the most gesticulating lawyer I'd ever met – he was constantly throwing his hands in the air and making invisible circles around himself which reminded me of a life coach on stage or a magician, certainly not a lawyer. I wondered whether being so expressive would be well received in England, where people were rather proud of staying reserved and aloof.

In the corner of my right eye I saw Alistair, who thinking nobody was looking, was mimicking every smile and gesture made by his strongly UNdesired helper. Alistair had claimed as I thought he would that the presence of the second attorney could only work to my disadvantage by making me look guilty in the police's and the court's eyes. However, when he shook Enrique's hand when they met he stopped acting for a moment like a sulky teenage girl and made a great impression of a man who didn't give a damn. I couldn't, however, count on his emotional support after something he clearly took as a betrayal.

* * *

The moment had come – the moment that had been regularly preventing me from a good night's sleep and for the first time in my life made me take some Xanax. I took two pills, but I would have taken more if not for the fact I was not Olympia White and I couldn't afford a luxurious rehab centre.

I felt dizzy stepping into the interrogation room off the back corridor on the first floor of the five-storey building. My right foot suddenly froze above a wooden doorstep but Enrique and Alistair gave me a gentle push to encourage me on. We were welcomed by two detectives, Henry, and his lawyer who without his sunglasses now looked mid-fifties. Detective Murray pointed us to three seats on the right side of a long oval table. I sat in the middle, Alistair fell heavily into the black leather chair on my right while Enrique sat down gently on my left and leant back with both hands resting on the wide armrests. I had a feeling that the chairs were designed to accommodate longer meetings.

"As most of you already know I'm detective Mark Murray. Together with detective Simon Hoffman..." he stretched his right hand towards a stumpy man sitting on the opposite side of the table, with a black tie squeezed tight around his flabby neck as if it was suffocating him, "we've been investigating this case of trading exam papers. On my left, we've got Mr Henry Thyme with his attorney Mr Richard Fitzgerald-Spencer..." he continued with the same flat voice naming our side of the table. Alistair's surname brought a little smirk to Henry's face, but when he heard Murray saying 'Enrique Jose Gonzales del Toro', he started fidgeting nervously in his chair. He kept adjusting the tie I gave him a couple of years ago, but as far as I knew had never worn before. I expect Henry had seen the name at least once in The Times, his favourite newspaper of all time. Except for Spanish and English, Enrique also spoke Mandarin and took many significant international cases.

"Mr Henry Thyme isn't currently accused of working for the Cheaters Gang," said Hoffman impatiently, as if Murray's introductions were wasting his time and he wanted to move on to the point of why we all were gathered in the small stuffy room without any windows and air conditioning. "Mr Thyme has been invited here because he was in a long-term relationship with Miss Eliot," he said staring at me and sending a tingle down my spine. "Miss Eliot stubbornly claims that Mr Thyme is guilty of all crimes that she has been accused of and that he has been trying to frame her." Hoffman paused for a moment to look around the table like he was looking for the answers in our eyes.

Henry gave me a merciful look, which looked bizarrely genuine before smiling first at Hoffman and then at Murray.

"The whole interview is being recorded," Murray said out of the blue.

Henry again adjusted his tie and reached for a glass of water, which he placed in front of him without a coaster forming a wet mark on the wooden oval table.

"Miss Eliot, do you confess that you've been involved in trading education?" asked Murray, although being focused on the glass I initially missed that he was speaking to me.

"I'm innocent," I said after a water-mark induced pause that was long enough for somebody to think I was hesitating.

"Have you ever worked for the Cheaters Gang?" he continued.

"I said I'm innocent," I repeated but this time with a glimmer of the confidence I'd been practising in front of my bathroom mirror.

"Miss Eliot, please answer my question."

"No, I haven't," I said feeling humiliated, trying to somehow stop my cheeks from flushing and my head from spinning.

"Okay, let's start again," Murray leant back on his chair, bit his pencil with his large teeth exposing his high gums, before quickly pointing the black chewed pencil at me, "If you confess today and help us identify other people involved in trading education, we'll consider all mitigating circumstances."

"That's a rather vague statement," said Alistair.

Murray smirked as though he had just made a deal, "To put it simple miss Eliot will avoid going to jail."

"My client said that she was innocent. She doesn't need to be afraid about going to prison," said Enrique.

"You can take a fifteen-minute break to consider my offer."

"No, thank you," I said irritated that Murray was so convinced of me being guilty.

"Do you still claim that Mr Henry Thyme has been trying to frame you?" Murray was asking the questions while Hoffman opened a dark blue cheap notebook and started making some notes.

"I do."

"I personally took part in searching your house in Dream Fields. How do you explain that in your back garden we dug out several sets of exam questions dated in the future?"

"I don't know where you found them. I didn't witness this and I didn't bury anything in my back garden. I didn't even plant a single tree. Henry landscaped my whole garden. It was a gift from him for my thirtieth birthday. I've got more than twenty witnesses who can confirm it," I carefully repeated everything that Alistair had told me to say.

"I'm going to refresh your memory and tell you where we found it," Murray raised his voice sounding like a teacher chastening a child for running too fast in a school corridor. I was regretting not taking the extra Xanax. Any kind of rehab centre sounded like a much better prospect than a prison cell shared with a drug addict taking smuggled heroine. "It was at the very back of your garden, next to your little funky bin store, buried under your pavement slabs and packed into plastic folders wrapped in tons of cling film, which—"

"We all already know what the plastic files contained," Enrique interrupted Murray which took the grin away from his face. "We also know that anybody could have done it, including Mr Henry Thyme who had the keys to Miss Eliot's house and the gardens' gate. The garden was the best place to hide anything as there's a camera in the downstairs hallway and the house itself is secured with an alarm."

Murray didn't even twitch, "Miss Eliot, have you touched any of the documents that were buried in your garden?"

"No," I said without any hesitation, but I immediately regretted it. *What if...?*

"Did I warn you not to touch anything that I was showing you from that discovered file?"

"You did."

"Every page that we found has your fingerprints on them."

"Every?" I squeaked through a tightened throat. "That's impo—"

"My client knows she didn't touch the specific papers therefore..." Enrique was saying, now sitting on the end of his chair with his back straight and elbows resting on the table, "it's highly likely Mr Thyme deliberately placed her fingerprints on the exams. They were a couple, they have children together, and Mr Thyme lived in Miss Eliot's house. How difficult would it be for him to get her fingerprints?"

"From a legal point of view the house also belongs to my client," said Richard Fitzgerald-Spencer just as I'd managed to forget about him being in the same room.

"We're not here to discuss the ownership of the house in Dream Fields," snapped Hoffman taking his eyes away from his notebook. "What do you imply Mr Gonzales?"

"Miss Eliot could have touched the papers without knowing what they really were. She might have arranged them on a desk, moved them while cleaning a table—"

"It's nonsense, if I wanted to trade education, I would have never brought the exams home," said Henry.

"Unless you wanted them to have Miss Eliot's fingerprints on," said Alistair. "The exams found in the garden are as incriminating for Mr Thyme as for my client. Are you able to provide any other evidence that could prove my client is guilty? If not, I would like to save us all a lot of time and present some *re-liable* evidence that confirms it's Mr Thyme who is the one who has been working with the Cheaters Gang for the last couple of years."

I glanced at Henry, he was sitting comfortably with his elbows resting on the wide armrests and yawning without even trying to hide his open mouth. I prayed for the little annoying fly that had been making circles around us to go straight into his mouth, but she chose to land on the top of a floor lamp standing in the corner of the room – the decision cost her life.

"Then I'm really curious Mr Dragon," said Hoffman going through some pages in his notebook. "Hmmm… yes, Mr Alistair Dragon, please explain," he said with a smirk and folded his arms.

Alistair cleared his throat before saying loudly and confidently, "Mr Thyme's London flat has also been searched, which for some reason detective Murray and detective Hoffman have decided not to share with all of us yet. What's also interesting—"

"That should've never happened," Fitzgerald-Spencer instantly cut him off with his red angry eyes and frowny nose, which looked rather comical. "You…" he pointed at Alistair, who sat totally unmoved, "you manipulated the facts, provided – known only to you – information to MI5 which got them involved and resulted in the search warrant of my client's flat. There will be consequences as nobody had the right to search that flat."

Alistair, MI5? How? Why didn't he tell me? I was thinking stunned, looking around the room to see whether everybody was as surprised as me.

"Mr Thyme drew MI5 attention to himself," snapped Alistair.

Murray didn't let Fitzgerald-Spencer comment on that. He stopped him with his open palm while his eyes were set on Alistair, "We cannot consider that evidence at present because we still don't have the information, which justified the search warrant, it remains classified."

"Obviously it was justified as they found evidence incriminating Mr Thyme," said Alistair who only continued louder when Murray tried to interrupt him. "We can't pretend nothing has been found."

"There's also another problem with the evidence in that flat," Murray looked at Hoffman who gave him a nod to continue, "We've got reason to believe that Miss Eliot planted the evidence there—"

"Excuse me, can you at least tell me what I was supposed to have planted according to you?" I shouted and then whispered to Alistair, "it's just ridiculous."

"We've got records from the CCTV in the hallway of the building where Mr Thyme lives, "said Murray. "It shows Miss Eliot, accompanied by another woman in her thirties, going into the flat at a time when Mr Thyme was overseas. It also happened when he and Miss Eliot weren't together anymore. It could be classified as a break-in."

"I had his key that he personally gave me."

"He gave them to you Miss Eliot when you were in a relationship. The fact that my client had trusted you and hadn't changed the lock doesn't make it legal," said Fitzgerald-Spencer, who then reached for a glass of water and brought it slowly to his smug face.

Murray asked Hoffman to pass him the blue notebook and took a few seconds to find a page, "We've got records of Miss Eliot after leaving the flat saying to her friend…" he paused to read something in the notebook, "I quote, *I wonder how he'll be able to explain that. He will be fucked.*"

Alistair and Enrique both looked at me simultaneously.

"I was referring to the photo album I'd found under Henry's sofa. It contained a whole collection of pictures of both his exes and current lovers. I discovered that day that he had cheated on many women, not just me."

"I'd like to point out that taking anything from my client's flat was theft."

"My client was devastated. She had just found out the father of her children had been notoriously cheating on her. At the time she was still considering rebuilding the relationship," Alistair saved me a sad explanation.

"Except she took the album and in revenge left something that was aimed to incriminate my client."

"Miss Eliot wasn't entering her ex's flat knowing that he was a notorious cheater. She discovered it when already inside. Are you trying to tell me she had been carrying in her bag some incriminating evidence just in case he turned out to be unfaithful?"

"She must've had a serious reason to go there, more than feeding his fish."

"I don't have fish," Henry mumbled but nobody except me paid any attention to him.

"What we should really be discussing right now is the contents of Mr Thyme's freezer," said Alistair which made Hoffman and Enrique burst out laughing. "Yes, his freezer – that was where the police found a pile of future exam questions as well as a list of phone numbers for dealers. Everything was packed in thick layers of cling film. MI5 ordered ice analysis on the cling film so soon we should find out how long the papers spent in the freezer."

"I'll be impressed if such analysis is possible," Fitzgerald-Spencer laughed.

"It will be my pleasure to impress you Mr Fitzgerald," said Alistair and I could see doubt slowly building up on his opponent's face.

"Fitzgerald-Spencer please," he corrected Alistair as if using his full surname could have had a magical influence on the whole case.

"Mr Spencer-Fitzgerald..." started Alistair not letting Henry's lawyer interrupt him and once again correct his surname. I had a feeling he was doing it deliberately only to irritate him. "Because of the lifestyle Mr Thyme has been living we can certainly suspect that many other women had a key to his flat and there is no basis to claim that my client left anything in Mr Thyme's flat except a few years of her life. As we're on the subject of the apartment I think it's more important to consider the event when Blanca Spaggiato tried to kill my client."

"It's irrelevant now," Fitzgerald-Spencer protested.

"I think that many will agree that it's crucial for the case. It was a direct consequence of Mr Thyme being involved in illegal activities and selling Miss Spaggiato exam papers and essays. When she left him, he exposed her, threatened her and soon after had her expelled from university."

"I must admit I've got a problem with staying faithful," Henry suddenly spoke. "I also admit that I was unfaithful during the five years of my relationship with Olivia. We can question my morality here but nothing that I've done has been illegal, I'm not even married. I'm only sorry now that my unfaithfulness has caused so much trouble. I never expected that I would have such an influence on women, you know... that they would always react so..." he looked into the distance, "so aggressively, you know... and so emotionally and so—."

"Are these reflections heading somewhere Mr Thyme?" asked Hoffman.

"In my wildest dreams I never suspected Blanca would try to kill me and Olivia, and intend to commit suicide. It never crossed my mind that Olivia would try to take revenge on me and frame me in a crime that she herself committed." Henry was a good speaker and lecturer but I hadn't realised before that he was able to lie so well in public. If I hadn't known him, he would have probably convinced me. "I trusted her with all my heart. I was the unfaithful bastard, while she was an angel. I was surprised when she asked me to pretend in front of her whole family that I'd bought her the car for her birthday but—"

"Oh please, save this nonsense for your autobiography. You could call it, *A man hated by women.*"

Enrique choked but Fitzgerald-Spencer frowned his eyebrows and spoke to Murray through clenched teeth, "We've got witnesses who can say how vengeful Miss Eliot becomes when somebody steps on her feet."

"What are you talking about?" I exploded. "With all due respect you and Henry are creating fiction!"

Fitzgerald-Spencer leant across the table with his hands stretched in front of him, "Really? Have you already forgotten about your revenge on Mrs Tiggy Brown. You sabotaged her job. You were the reason why she lost her husband and most of her friends. Are you still going to deny that? We've done our research," he straightened his back and adjusted his tie.

"Tiggy has never had any friends," I didn't mean to say it but it just slipped out and it was immediately too late – here I was, the vengeful woman they were talking about.

"Tiggy Brown was fired for excessive drinking during working hours and offending her subordinates. She was lucky because she should have also been accused of abuse," said Enrique who must have received the information from Hugo as I hadn't told him much about

Tiggy beyond the fact she slept with my ex-fiancé and we used to work together.

"Miss Eliot not only successfully took revenge on Mrs Tiggy Brown and has been trying to do the same to my client but she's also been stalking and threatening potential witnesses. I'll begin from Miss Eliot appearing unexpectedly at Mr Thyme's parents' house in Cambridge," Richard obviously considered attack was the best line of defence for Henry.

"If every unexpected visit was considered to be stalking, the door of the police station would be wide open twenty-four hours a day," Alistair said.

"I've got a witness who can confirm that Miss Eliot forced her way into Mr and Mrs Thyme's estate and threatened that she would not leave until somebody invited her in the house. She arrived accompanied by the same woman who helped her to break into my client's flat."

"There's nothing weird about wanting to speak to the grandparents of my children and parents of my ex-fiancé. I hoped they could have reasoned with Henry but their housekeeper informed me that they had gone for a cruise around the world. What a coincidence, right? Then I asked her whether I could leave my car in their driveway for a few hours. I think everybody agrees Cambridge is a pig when it comes to finding a free parking spot."

"Good story and perfectly logical if not for the fact that we've got recording from Mr and Mrs Thyme's CCTV," said Murray.

"I don't understand."

"We watched how you talked to the housekeeper, Rita, right?"

"Correct," I said completely baffled.

"Then your friend shouts aggressively at her, Rita slammed the door, you get into your car and remain there for several hours before leaving on foot. The video supports Mr Thyme's version in which you refused to leave unless you saw him or his parents."

"When she finally left, I just called the police to tow away her car. I didn't know what else to do," Henry kept pretending to be the victim of the whole world.

I knew immediately what he had done. The son of a bitch must've changed timings on his CCTV! He told me once when we were watching a thriller that a good IT specialist could do it.

"Can I see the recording? I'm sure it's a fraud," I snapped.

"Of course, but it will take us a couple of days. At present it's being checked by our experts."

"Even if Miss Eliot was insistent on seeing the people, who for a period of time were to become her in-laws, it's perfectly understandable. She has been fighting not only for her own sake but also for her children," Alistair spoke gently more like my friend than a lawyer but I knew once we were alone he would be disappointed and probably furious with me for hiding my trip to Cambridge from him.

"Except miss Eliot has been trying to force my client to take the blame for the crimes that she committed. She blackmailed him threatening to take the children away. Most of the threats were verbal but I've got one text here that I can read you now," Fitzgerald-Spencer reached for his phone in an internal pocket of his suit, he scrolled down the screen of his smartphone with his finger before turning to Henry, "I can't find it, could you please—"

"Of course," Henry rapidly took his phone out of the same leather suitcase, in which I'd found the letter addressed to me from Gatsby. "Keep doing what you're doing and you won't see your children again," he read.

"I've got that message," Enrique bluffed. "It's completely out of context. "Mr Thyme deliberately antagonised my client to get that exact message."

"Olivia was threatening me, saying that if I didn't take the blame she and her lover, Hue the Spaniard, would take my children away."

"Do you have a problem with Spanish people Mr Thyme?" Enrique asked.

"Of course not. My client is just very upset with the current situation," Richard tried to rescue Henry before he responded with something equally or even more stupid than using the word *Spaniard* in a particularly negative tone.

"Miss Eliot, all evidence indicates that you've been trying to manipulate witnesses and you've been threatening—"

"As far as I'm concerned this is an interview, it's not throwing unjustified accusations at my client," Alistair interrupted Murray.

"Then can you tell me miss Eliot…" Murray started and I felt a squeeze in my stomach, "why did you arrange a meeting with one of Mr Thyme's students pretending to be me? Why did you go to the psychiatric hospital to see Blanca Spaggiato pretending you were her family? Wasn't it because you wanted to persuade those people to make false accusations against Mr Thyme?" Murray set his angry eyes on me.

"Miss Eliot was looking for partners in crime, who could help her take revenge on my client."

"Blanca Spaggiato's condition got worse after seeing Miss Eliot," Hoffman looked up from his notes, he seemed tired but it didn't seem to make him less attentive.

"I'd like to remind you that my client is the victim here. Blanca tried to kill her," said Enrique.

"Of course, a victim," Fitzgerald-Spencer said ironically. "I can prove that Miss Eliot was making money writing dissertations herself just after she graduated. I've got a login to a page where we can still find her advert. Our IT specialist can easily reveal that it was her. We've done our research," he said with a smug face.

Research, that's good! Henry knows my login! I used to write a lot on his laptop but I never thought he would use that against me. The money that I made from that job bought us the expensive sofa he now had in his flat!

"Miss Eliot, it's your last chance to tell us the truth," Murray was putting a strong accent on every word he was saying. "Give us some names of Cheaters Gang's members and you'll avoid prison. You won't have the chance to make this deal later when we're in court."

"My client can't give you information she simply doesn't have," said Alistair. "Shall we have a break now?"

Henry smirked to his lawyer. What was Alistar doing? He must have known that the sudden break would look like we needed some time to discuss the deal.

"Of course," said Murray clearly content he would probably solve the case before the day's end and go home early. "Half an hour," he said rising to stand.

* * *

"Before we all head for some lunch I'd like to present further evidence of my client's innocence," said Enrique.

"Is it really so good it can't wait thirty minutes?" asked Hoffman putting a hand on his rumbling belly.

"It is," Enrique said decisively.

Alistair looked at me questioningly but I only shrugged. I had no idea what Enrique was talking about and I had very mixed feelings about it. One second I was full of hope he had something that could rescue me, but in the next I was full of doubt and praying that whatever he was about to say wouldn't incriminate me even further.

"Mr Thyme, do you go to the supermarket a lot?" asked Enrique not waiting for the detectives' decision to continue. Murray sat down and everybody did likewise.

Fitzgerald-Spencer arched his eyebrows, "How is that relevant to anything?" Hoffman waved his hand in front of his face so he stopped talking.

"Yes," Henry sighed.

"How often?"

"I like doing my own shopping, I rarely shop online so at least a couple of times a week, sometimes more. Generally, I don't stock my fridge unless we're going to have a snowstorm. I prefer fresh produce."

"Is that answer exhausting enough?" Fitzgerald was rushing Enrique. I wasn't sure whether he was just hungry or he was worried about a potential grenade that my lawyer was going to throw at him.

"I do enjoy shopping for food," Henry said with a weak smile. He was sitting still on his chair as though he was a stuffed animal. He made a good impression of being confident but when he finished talking I noticed how much his jaw was clenched.

"Do you have a favourite supermarket?"

"I don't understand the question," he snapped irritated.

"Mr Gonzales please get to the point, we don't have all day," Murray said trying to prevent himself from yawning.

"Gonzales del Toro," Fitzgerald-Spencer corrected him.

"I can assure you it's all relevant. Mr Thyme, can you answer my question?"

"I don't have a favourite one. I use a few local ones."

"Do you walk there or drive?" Enrique was dwelling on the subject and it crossed my mind he had mixed his cases. He had arrived in London straight from Mexico, he must've been jetlagged.

"I normally drive and to speed this up anticipating your next questions," he hesitated while rubbing his temples, "I try not to use plastic bags whenever possible, I take fabric bags made of pure cotton that are fair-trade from Africa. Currently I choose to travel to the supermarket by a car fuelled by diesel but at some point in the future I'm going to get an electric one. I normally don't jump in the queue but—"

"I'm glad you still find it funny," said Enrique with a beaming smile. "You sound like you go to the supermarket so often that I suggest you start making shopping lists or... I have a better idea, I'm going to send you an invite to my online shopping provider – in this way we both get a twenty percent discount."

Henry glanced at me like he didn't want me to listen to what he was about to say but he had no choice after my lawyer had pressed him to the wall. "Fine," he snapped spreading his hands, his elbows still resting on the table as if they had been glued to it, "I often spontaneously invite women to my flat and then I need to get a take-away meal for two, bottle of wine and some con—"

Enrique interrupted Henry with a loud burst of laughter. "And then you call somebody to pick up all these emergency items and bring them to you in the supermarket car park?"

"Mr Gonzales del Toro is this discussion heading anywhere?" asked Murray looking bored.

Hoffman put his pen down and yawned ostentatiously, he was quickly copied by everybody in the room.

"You've got an annual membership for online shopping. You don't go to any supermarkets. You're only interested in their car parks," said Enrique. Henry straightened his posture like a guitar cord. "You look for spots where there are no cameras to swap essays for money."

Fitzgerald-Spencer crossed his arms exposing a little hole on his elbow. "If there're no cameras, how are we going to believe you?"

"Do you know that in Russia people drive with cameras in their windscreens? It's also started to cotton on here." Murray wanted to interrupt Enrique but it only made him speak louder. "Mr Thyme lives in an affluent part of London. Some of his neighbours come from Moscow, among them there're many who just out of habit have installed cameras in their cars. As luck would have it, one Russian family fully recorded what Mr Thyme was doing during one of his evening escapades at a supermarket car park."

"I presume you're in possession of such a recording, Mr Gonzales del Toro," said Murray.

"Of course," Enrique reached into his leather bag under the table to get a CD packed in a transparent plastic envelope.

Murray immediately stood up and took the CD from him, then looked around sighing heavily. "I guess none of you has a laptop that you would let me use." Nobody even twitched. "Right, you think I would copy the contents of your whole computer to the CD or scan your laptop with a blink of my eyes… Well, you're probably right," he smirked. "Give me a minute," he said walking out of the room to come back in less than a minute with an old chunky laptop. He put the CD in the computer, which made a loud noise and made us wait for a few long minutes to do its job. "Everybody has to stand behind me if you want to see anything," he said impatiently and we surrounded him trying hard not to step and breathe on each other.

When Murray pressed a button to play we immediately saw two hooded figures standing between cars in the rain. One of them turned back to look at a man making a loud noise by trying to take a trolley without putting a coin in it – and that was when we saw the hooded figure who turned was Henry. He was talking to a slim woman in dark tight jeans and short shiny wellies. The discussion didn't last very long – they clearly knew what they were there for. Henry passed her a large file, she said a few words and both disappeared in their cars to quickly drive away.

"Undoubtedly, it looks suspicious," Murray broke the silence and set his eyes on Henry, "What was in the file?"

"Oh god, again I've tried to avoid this so as not to hurt Olivia but I see I've got no choice," he sighed with theatrical exaggeration. I knew he was about to start spitting out some new lies but I couldn't stop my heart from pounding. "Olivia had always been very possessive, I did love her and I tried to justify her behaviour but sometimes it was so wearing," he sighed again and I barely managed to keep myself from screaming. Enrique helped by distracting me – he nodded towards my seat with his head and then everybody noticing his gesture followed and went back to their comfy armchairs. Henry continued, the few seconds probably enabled him to improve his story. "So, where was I? Oh, Olivia had been very possessive. She used to check my emails, read my texts and letters. Without telling me she also installed and switched on an app on my phone that let her spy on my location. Her possessiveness was actually the main reason why I had so many affairs, the pressure—"

"Mr Thyme, we're not interested in your digressions or psycho-analysing your relationship with Miss Eliot," said Murray.

"I knew she could've seen me on her phone so I decided to go to the supermarkets – you know not to instil her suspicions..." he glanced at his lawyer and Fitzgerald-Spencer nodded encouragingly. "Sometimes we had sex, sometimes we just talked. Most women found it very exciting," he smirked. "Some wrote love letters, which we hid in plastic files—"

"Very peculiar," Hoffman murmured without stopping scribbling in his notebook. "None of the women who slept with you found it weird?"

"Many of them also wanted to keep the relationship a secret. They had their... husbands or boyfriends... you know."

"No, we don't," snapped Enrique. "How many women are we talking about?"

"I've never counted."

"No, you kept their records in your freaky little photo album," I suddenly exploded.

"How many?" Enrique was not going to give up.

"I don't understand why that would be relevant for the case," Fitzgerald-Spencer was trying to rescue his client who now looked baffled.

"Please, answer the question Mr Thyme," said Murray.

Henry looked in the corner of the room and pretended to count them by whispering to himself. I wondered whether Murray insisted on him answering the question because he really thought it was relevant or he was just curious about how many women somebody like Henry could have slept with.

"Approximately fifteen during the time I was going out with Olivia."

Enrique read something in his notebook and frowned his eyebrows. It looked like it wasn't the answer he had been expecting. "And how many men have you slept with?"

"Excuse me?" Henry was blushing and clearly couldn't believe what he had just heard.

Henry was bisexual? He used to compliment well-dressed and good-looking men on many occasions but I'd never suspected he actually fancied them!

The room went silent, all eyes on my potentially bisexual ex. "Several," he said through a tight throat.

I felt a few flushes of heat. *Menopause?* I thought. *Well, convenient as I'd already given birth to two children!*

"That would explain why you passed so many mysterious files to men of student-age," said Enrique.

"Have you got other recordings?" asked Fitzgerald-Spencer.

Enrique couldn't stop himself from displaying a wide grin. At this point we probably all knew my lawyer had been bluffing and pushed Henry to make a false confession about sleeping with *several men.*

"I'm genuinely surprised about what we've managed to find out today…" Murray stood up like he was going to make a speech. Everybody except Henry smirked. "I see many of you have played detective in this case…" I felt another wave of heat, my head spun and made me miss a couple of sentences before I zoned back to Murray's summation. "I hadn't expected such an outcome. Mr Thyme is a new suspect in this case of the Cheaters Gang," Enrique smiled to Alistair but he pretended not to see it. "It doesn't mean however that Miss Eliot is innocent. Ultimately I'm sure this case will go to court. Please try to avoid speaking to the media – anything that you say may be used against you."

Hoffman stood up rubbing his lower back and panting. I was convinced I could hear his bones cracking. He had needed the break more than anybody else in the room.

"That's it?" I looked at Enrique in disbelief. "So, we're going to court."

Enrique put his hand on my right shoulder, "We're going to win this."

I wasn't so sure anymore. My lawyers managed to raise enough doubt around Henry to make him a new suspect but I remained one too. I bent down to pick up my handbag when the door opened with a swing, and a woman walked inside nearly hitting Murray in his stomach with the doorknob.

"Nina, why the hell haven't you knocked?" Murray got angry. A long interrogation and an empty belly probably didn't help him to be nice.

"Because you'd finished and were going to leave anyway," she said confidently as if she was his boss.

"Have you been eavesdropping again?" he said in a tone of clear disapproval and sighed.

She ignored his question or considered it purely rhetorical. "There's a woman here who says she needs to see you right now."

* * *

"I'm going out on my break. Tell her to call tomorrow."

Nina didn't move even an inch, obstructing the door.

"Excuse me, excuse me," I heard Fitzgerald-Spencer shouting from behind my back. "It's really stuffy in here, we need to get some air before somebody faints and we have the first casualty of this interview."

"Sorry Mr Spencer, I'll bring you some water and a mini fan in a minute," Nina said flatly and turned again to Murray, "She says it can't wait. She's got some information about the Cheaters Gang."

"Fine," shouted Murray. "Everybody back to their seats, and... Nina, please bring us more water, coffee for everybody and something to eat."

"Where do you want me to get the food from?" she whispered to him through gritted teeth.

"Send our intern to Tesco... whatever, make something up, it's your job for god's sake... Oh, and bring the woman here."

"Mark, we need at least a toilet break," Hoffman was still standing ready to leave, he was all pale and looking like he was about to start chewing on one of his chubby fingers. His belly, squeezed under a blue shirt with some hairs pushing out next to the buttons, couldn't wait a moment longer.

"Ten minutes then," Murray announced.

Henry and Fitzgerald-Spencer disappeared somewhere down the narrow magnolia-painted corridors of the police station. They didn't say a word to each other while still in our sight. I ran outside without looking back or waiting for either of my lawyers. I pushed a heavy, green double-door to get outside. As soon as I ran down the entrance stairs and stood on the little square dividing the police station from a busy road I bent half way, put my hand on my stomach and started breathing heavily. I raised my eyes to glance at the pavement – through a thick mist I saw people passing by. All voices were melting into one loud sound that was making my head spin. I didn't know what would happen if not... for Hugo who put his warm hand on my cheek. He bent down, put my head into his hands and whispered to me, "Have you been practicing again holding your breath under water? Inhale and exhale..." he was forcing himself to smile but all I saw in his eyes was sadness. I straightened my back and fell into his arms weeping like a baby.

"I've asked Murray for ten minutes longer. If necessary I can go back and ask for another ten minutes," said Enrique before I realised he and Alistair were standing just next to me and witnessing my breakdown in the arms of my ex-lover.

"Can you postpone it till... let's say tomorrow?" Hugo suggested, completely unaware that the interview was practically over and I would most likely be one of the primary suspects in court.

"The only reason why we're going back to the interview room is a mysterious woman who's apparently got something urgent to say about the Cheaters Gang," said Alistair coldly. "If not for her—"

"Let's go inside," I said briskly to save providing Hugo any explanation before I really knew where I stood. "Anybody have a mirror?" I hadn't expected any of the three men surrounding me to suddenly pull a mirror from their pocket but...

"Here you are," Alistair passed me a compact black mirror. "What?" he said replying to Hugo's and Enrique's highly arched eyebrows.

I was relieved that my waterproof make-up had persevered but I had eyes like an albino rabbit. "Never mind, Henry will look worse when we're done with him."

"I'd like to share your optimism but..." Alistair paused for a second as both Enrique and Hugo chastised him with their eyes, "okay, have you done something else that I'm not aware of? If you have I need to know as your lawyer. I don't want to keep being surprised by those people," he pointed his right hand at the building. "Have you pretended to be a detective with anybody else because—?"

"No, just one guy and I swear there's nothing more out there that could surprise you. I'm sorry, I'm sorry I didn't tell you."

"Don't apologise to me – I'm not the one who is in danger of seeing the world behind bars. A very good lawyer can do a lot but I can't make them believe the sun goes around the earth, so if you've got anything else to hide—"

"The break is almost over," Enrique said and we started walking slowly back, my legs already felt as heavy as if they were dragging a ball and chain.

"And I'm sorry you worked the whole of Easter on my case and… and I just keep ruining everything for everybody." I was going through a mental rollercoaster – one minute I was confident we were going to win because I was innocent and the good always wins, but the next moment I felt guilty of running my own investigation behind Alistair's back and I was convinced my own stupidity would destroy me.

"If it makes you feel any better, I'll celebrate Easter on the first of May this year like the rest of my orthodox catholic family in Greece."

"Wonderful…" snapped Enrique, "but I worked my whole Easter on your case and I don't want my work to be wasted so get moving."

Hugo accompanied us right to the door of the interrogation room, where inside Henry was whispering something to Fitzgerald-Spencer. Hugo wasn't just looking at my husband-not-to-be, he was sizing him up like a hungry wolf does a rabbit. Hugo the Wolf was saying, *'Wait until I get you, I'm going to tear you to pieces, turn you into a shashlik, and grill you until you're crusty'*. Henry the Rabbit was smirking, *'You're not going to get me, I'm quicker than you'*. Hugo the Wolf only laughed while glancing at Enrique, *'That's why I'm going after you with my pack, there won't be a bone to find after we've finished'*.

She marched into the room in her high heels like a model on a catwalk, head up, back straight and with a confidence far higher than her stilettoes. There was a brief moment I expected her to spin around and just leave – it was when she put her right hand on her hip and looked down on all of us sitting around the oval table with many hands nervously tapping its surface. Murray asked her to take a seat between Henry and his lawyer, who suddenly started blushing like a teenage boy asked to dance by a girl at a school disco.

"Ms Kitty Allen would like to give a statement in the presence of all of you here today," said Murray looking like he wasn't sure himself whether her statement would only complicate the case even more or solve the whole mystery. Kitty was dressed up in fifty shades of pink. She was wearing a light pink blouse through which we could admire her dark pink lacy bra and massive boobs that seemed to want to jump out and show themselves free and unrestrained by anything. She scanned me with curiosity like she was wondering what Henry saw in me. *Vice versa*, I thought.

'*Don't worry, Kitty will look after the boys*', Henry's words were drumming in my head.

"Take him to the end of the world and please, please never come back here, but hands off my children! Hands off! Have you heard me?" I said while instinctively rising up from my seat.

"Miss Eliot, calm down if you don't want me to make you leave," said Murray.

"Objection!" Alistair also let himself be carried away by emotions.

Only Henry seemed to be amused with the whole situation, "Maybe now you understand why I've been struggling to find the right woman. At the beginning they all act normal but give them a bit of time or god forbid do something they don't agree with and—"

"Mr Thyme, we're not interested in your philosophical divagation," snapped Hoffman and licked a crumb from the right corner of his lips. "Ms Allen, tell us please why you're here?"

Kitty put her elbows on the table and started fiddling with the ring that had been supposed to be mine. "Yes, Henry makes women crazy…" she started slowly while flapping eyelashes that were heavily coated in black mascara. Henry smiled at her but he was definitely giving significantly more attention to her boobs than to her face. "Luckily there are women who get their reasoning back just in time," she kept playing with my ring. Hoffman and Murray were drinking their coffees and yawning, which made Kitty irritated – she suddenly went quiet, which brought some inconvenient silence to the room before starting again louder, "Henry used to be my lover. Yes, we had an affair and please don't judge me because you don't know the whole story. He convinced me I was the one and only, he claimed Olivia just wouldn't let him go. Long story short, he made her into a villain and asked me to help him frame her with a crime he had committed. I thought she was evil so she deserved punishment... not that it would have justified it but I was crazy in love and... well you should understand... it's not like I'm the only one who's had an affair in this room, "she looked at Fitzgerald-Spencer who almost choked on his mini biscuit that Nina had brought with his coffee.

"What did he tell you about me?"

"It's not relevant," snapped Hoffman.

"No, please continue," said Murray.

"As I've already told you we had an affair that lasted a few years with some breaks. Henry claimed he wanted to leave Olivia but each time he told her it was over she ended up in hospital having tried to commit suicide. He also inferred that she only got pregnant to trap him for good. He wasn't even sure whether the children could be his because they rarely slept together, although he said she once made him a drink, which was the last thing he remembered before waking up completely naked and lying next to her. She had her legs up resting on the headboard. Of course, I had some doubts, men are lying pigs so I hired a private investigator who confirmed that Olivia did do a DNA test but it wasn't because Henry asked her to—"

"But finally, the children turned out to be Mr Thyme's," Murray interrupted her.

"Yes and I assumed that's why he was so devastated... I mean not because the sweet little boys were his but because he never wanted kids with her. Then he also found out that he was of interest to the police and the children could end up with his crazy ex-girlfriend and without a father..."

"So you had already known he was involved in trading education," said Murray.

"Not exactly. At least not at such scale... I thought he was writing and selling dissertations to recover some money he lost when he had invested in the house with Olivia and... he was simply too good to try to take it away from her and his two children."

"And you thought that helping him to frame Olivia and put her in jail was the most logical option?"

"No detective Murray, it wasn't that simple... But if you had seen him crying on my shoulder, going down on his knees and kissing my hands, begging me to save him from going to prison and missing the first years of his children growing up..."

"Then I would understand?" he asked and she nodded. "No, I wouldn't."

"Naturally I was scared, but I'd have never done anything like that!" Henry protested. "Olivia committed the crime and when I discovered it and told Kitty she wanted me to report her. She thought it was the best way of getting rid of her, that's all."

"Bullshit!" Kitty hit the table with her fist which made both Henry and me jump. "I did it because he wouldn't have to go to prison, Olivia would finally disappear from our life and we could get married because my divorce was also finalised. I agreed to adopt his children provided he didn't want any more babies. I love kids but I also love my body and I'm not prepared to ruin it... at least not without considerable planning and plastic surgery lined-up."

Henry took a deep breath and sighed, "I haven't been lucky when it comes to women."

"You were very lucky Henry!" snapped Kitty.

"How can we believe that what you've been saying is the truth?" Fitzgerald-Spencer asked.

"I can show you emails and messages from Henry in which we're plotting to frame Olivia."

"Why would you incriminate yourself to save Miss Eliot? You've just alleged that you were involved in a crime."

"Mr Spencer—"

"Fitzgerald-Spencer," he corrected her.

"Mr Fitzgerald-Whatever, I've been given immunity in exchange for information regarding the Cheaters Gang."

"That's correct," said Murray.

"Both women were rejected by my client, that's why they've decided to collaborate against him."

"One more thing, and sorry to interrupt you Mr Spencer, Henry bought an apartment in Miami with me but I paid the entire deposit."

"The inheritance from his aunt was held up?" I asked and she nodded. "You should check how many other properties Mr Thyme owns."

Hoffman was frantically writing in his diary while his eyebrows were getting higher and higher.

"Do you know who put the exams in Miss Eliot's garden?" asked Murray.

"Oh, it was poor Meghan. Henry blackmailed her. I felt bad about it but I convinced myself that sometimes the ends justify the means."

"Can you provide us with some details?"

Kitty repeated everything that I'd already heard from Meg, only adding that Henry had promised to leave Meghan alone if she swapped her money in the garden for Henry's tests. "I felt bad for her so I gave Henry a couple of thousand dollars to pass to Meghan but now I'm sure he just kept it for himself."

"How do you explain her fingerprints on the papers?" Fitzgerald-Spencer asked and I could see on Henry's face he wasn't happy about the question. Clearly, he hadn't told his lawyer everything.

"It was my genius idea!" she exclaimed happy she had a chance to intellectually shine. "Henry asked her to count some white sheets of papers, which he then printed the exams on. Clever, isn't it?"

"Ms Allen..." Hoffman stopped noting and fixed his eyes on Kitty's face, unlike the other men in the room who were admiring her boobs, "Why are you helping Miss Eliot? Is it simply revenge on Mr Thyme because you weren't the-one-and-only after all?"

"I received an email from a woman explaining to me how badly Henry had treated her... apparently he also promised to marry her and kept assuring her she was the only one. She said that it was Henry who didn't want to let Olivia go, not the other way around."

"Do you remember her name?"

Kitty frowned her eyebrows, "Very catchy name... Ah, yes, it was Tiggy Brown... Well, two heads... two lovers are better than one, isn't that what they say?" she giggled.i

40

WEDNESDAY, 13 APRIL

DREAM FIELDS

"Are you ready to find out the latest update on what your life would have been like if you didn't do the DNA test, but instead chose the father of your children according to what you want and need," Hannah sounded cheerful but I knew she was sugar coating the whole thing. The truth was that every night after seeing Tony she cried into her pillow.

"Hannah, you've got to give him some more time to forgive you," I said wondering whether I could've ever forgiven something like that, and concluding that it was a big fat *no*. "On the bright side he's happy that he's got a little daughter and Zoe likes him."

"The fact that he cares so much about her makes him even more angry because he missed the first years of her life and he'll never be able to get them back. Oh god, he'll never forgive me."

"Never is a really long time. Let's focus on the near future."

"That's even worse because I see the near future as a black hole," she hid her face in her palms, her legs dangling on the bench in my garden not far away from the place, which had been dug up by detective Murray and his boys. She sighed and looked at me sitting right next to her. I wondered about holding her hand but I'd tried it in the past and it only made her cry.

486

"I'm sorry if I ever advised you not to do the paternity tests."

"You only wanted to help."

"Hell is paved with good intentions..." she said it so gloomily I felt like a layer of heavy clouds were building over my head and trying to press me to the ground – in spite of the fact I could see the sky was brightly illuminated by the moon and billions of stars. "But have you ever regretted it?"

"Sometimes. But I know it wouldn't necessarily mean I would be with Hugo and I didn't know Henry was such a monster. If he didn't find out he was the father maybe I would have never had a chance to see the dark side of him..." I said and we both went silent for a while leaning back on the bench and looking up at the sky. "Thank god for the tests anyway," I said all of a sudden and sighed.

"I don't understand," she said puzzled.

"At the time I wouldn't have known who to pick and I couldn't stand the responsibility and god... all the consequences of that decision. The test was right there to help me to decide." Hannah frowned her eyebrows. "If I had to make the decision completely by myself then my brain would probably have made me go for Henry and I would have regretted it for the rest of my life."

"Nah, if you started to regret it you would have suddenly reminded yourself that you should probably do the DNA tests!"

"Hannah, you're awful," I screamed and she smiled bitterly.

"Yeah, and literally everybody would hate you like me now. Both Oscar and Tony would be very happy not to see me ever again but we're destined to see each other for a really long while. Have I already told you that Oscar found out I'd hired a PI to follow him?" I shook my head. "He was furious that – as he said it quite rightly – his wife was spending his hard-earned money to spy on him, while she was the unfaithful and lying..." she paused, "you know what," Hannah hung her head and started fiddling with her newly done burgundy nails. "I didn't even argue with that."

"It's not like he can exactly play the good one here. All the scams with Olympia White."

"I know... I wish I could have turned back time but then there wouldn't be Nicolas or he wouldn't be the same – and he's just the most perfect man I've ever met," her whole face was beaming now. "It's not like I planned on lying to Oscar for the rest of our lives… I tried to love him but I failed."

"You shouldn't have to try so hard."

"Probably… I guess the biggest obstacle was that I'd never stopped thinking about Tony. Each time I get to see him, all my memories return and I feel so helpless, stupid and not worthy of him. I'm never going to get him back."

"Never is a very long time," I muttered.

"Wasn't it you who said last night that you had been regretting that you would *never* have another chance for a life with Hugo?"

"Oh, you know it's totally different," I snapped not being able to hide my irritation. "Tony at least is a part of the chaos, your chaos. Hugo can log himself out from my life, leave without a trace and I can't even blame him for it."

"Honestly Olivia he doesn't look like he's going anywhere. I saw the way he looks at you. Besides Henry is going to be out of the picture for at least half of the next decade. You could start all over again."

"The whole point of defining every *beginning* is that there can only be one point in time when we really start. You can't start again with the same person. You've already started. Done. You can only pretend."

"So Tony and I – we are done? No chance for us?"

Women! She just said they had no chance!

"Completely not what I meant."

"Chill, I was kidding," she smiled. "How long is Henry going to prison for?"

"He might get three years instead of five because he agreed to testify against the Cheaters Gang."

"Is that good or bad?" she asked meekly.

"Not long enough after what he's done but I don't want Dominic and Patrick to have their father behind bars."

"God, I wish he mentioned the singing pig when he testified, it's the least Olympia White deserves after backing away from us at the very last minute."

"It wouldn't be good for Oscar and—"

"And me. I know," she sighed heavily. "I just don't like the fact she'll get away with it. By the way thank you for not using the information," she put her arm around my shoulders.

"I couldn't do it," I gave her a faint smile. The truth was I'd have used the recording if I ran out of options, and Hannah knew it. "Do you know that Henry attempted to justify working with the Cheaters Gang?"

"Let me guess," she took her arm away from my shoulders and clapped her hands energetically, "Has he got a stinky-liar gene? Or better, was he born with an overdeveloped part of the brain that is responsible for being an arse and a cheater of every kind. His argument in court will be that it's not his fault!"

I chuckled, "Not quite but that sounds very much like him." Hannah was waiting with anticipation but my brain suddenly paused as I looked around my garden. No matter what his intentions, one thing that Henry did do for me was create a mesmerising private space, the one I'd always dreamed of while living in the city. Twinkling stars were perfectly completing the light show in the garden – the little lights hanging on the fence, smart sleek lamps on both sides of the path going down the whole length of the garden, and last but not least the illuminated fountain. Lights, fountain, music... the light show at Montjuïc in Barcelona... Hugo. Hugo and me... I wondered what he was thinking while on his flight back to Madrid."

"So?"

"Henry said that the whole problem was his environment. Apparently, he didn't do it purely for money," I said and Hannah chortled. "He wanted to help those who for one reason or another couldn't meet the expectations of their families and their closest environment. Just like him."

"I don't know about you but I find him pretty convincing," she laughed. "And while he was helping all the little lost souls like

Olympia and Blanca, he had to try to put the mother of his children behind bars so he could continue on his noble journey. You were just collateral damage. Let's have a glass of wine for Henry, our saviour!"

"Oh, I need a glass of red," I stood up to go inside. "I just don't understand how I didn't realise what sort of person he was."

"Give yourself a break darling, he's an exceptionally great liar."

"I spent almost five years with him. We lived together."

"Don't blame yourself. You couldn't have done anything and—"

"I'm not so convinced. I thought we had similar goals. We wanted a four-bedroom house in the countryside with train links to London, a couple of children..." I was counting on my fingers, "a dog when the kids were big enough to walk him... maybe we focused too much on what we wanted *to have* instead of what we wanted *to be*. Maybe we didn't listen to each other enough, but I suppose how can you have a real conversion when you both talk and neither are really listening?"

"Well, it could've been much worse. You've got two beautiful children; the house is now all yours after Henry signed over his share."

"He claimed he didn't have to do it and it has nothing to do with Enrique threatening him with another lawsuit for seducing women for money," I laughed. "He also gave up his rights to Kitty's and Tiggy's apartments, only because he's afraid of doing more time in prison."

"Who would think that Kitty and... and Tiggy Brow... that the Tiggy Brown would help you when you needed her the most! I think she wanted to redeem herself," Hannah said nodding her head convinced she had worked Tiggy out so quickly.

"I'm going to disappoint you—"

"You are if you don't bring us the wine," she smiled.

"Well, with wine the older the better so with every minute of me standing here I'm making us a better vintage... It's not going to have long though because the story is simply it was Polly who helped me out and Tiggy had nothing to do with it. Polly got Tiggy's job and for a while was able to keep the original email address, *tiggy.brown@ihearttraveling.co.uk*. They lost their IT guy and it took them a while to hire another one. It was all my idea to write to Kitty from the address and Polly agreed – reluctantly, but she agreed. I also scanned and sent her Henry's photo album to add a bit more colour."

"That's genius! But why didn't you tell me about it before?"

"I didn't count on Kitty helping me. I did it only to know I'd done everything I could to save myself... Right, the wine must be good enough now and it's getting chilly," Hannah stood up quickly and we both walked towards the house.

We went through the lounge and hallway to the kitchen, where on the table was my phone that I had left to charge. Hannah poured us two glasses of wine and started slicing some cheddar, washing grapes and buttering wholemeal organic crackers. I had a few messages, including one from my parents saying that the boys were sleeping very well and one from Freya asking when we could see each other. I also had several missed calls from an unknown number and one voicemail. I wasn't in the mood to listen but suddenly in my imagination I saw Hugo sitting somewhere in the back of beyond and looking for help after his plane crashed into some wild woods. I must've started projecting some of Henry's fears! I pressed play expecting Hugo to start shouting for me to get him some help, then telling me he loved me, that he had always loved me and always would... but it wasn't him. I'd already flushed all my Xanax down the loo but after what I heard I thought it was a very premature decision.

"What just happened?"

I wasn't able to say a word, and where would I start anyway.

"Was it Henry?"

I shook my head, "It was the hospital."

"Henry tried to kill himself?"

"No."

"Henry killed somebody?

I shook my head again.

"Somebody had an accident?"

"Yes," I whispered.

Hannah put her right hand to her open mouth, "Who? Olivia for god's sake who had an accident?"

"I had one!"

"What?"

"I had an accident getting pregnant and since then my world has been spinning quicker than I can handle."

41

THURSDAY, 14 APRIL
OXFORD

Doctor Julius Hammer's office, once probably spacious and full of light with its large bay window and high ceiling, was now jammed with books, plastic skeletons, colourful frames and pictures painted by children.

"Sit down please," the doctor pointed out three wooden chairs standing in a perfect line in front of his heavy oak desk buried under piles of papers.

Is he one of those people who like to have everything printed out in case all computers and memory sticks suddenly stop working? I thought taking the chair in the middle. Hugo sat down on my right side while still sipping his coffee from a brown plastic cup. It was his third expresso from one of the hospital's machines – which he had to kick hard to get his change back – and god only knows how many he had drunk before arriving from Heathrow. Having only just landed and receiving the same message from doctor Hammer that I had, poor Hugo spent the whole night trying to fly out from Madrid-Barajas to get back to London.

"Right, we can start now," said doctor Julius rubbing a bushy moustache that looked almost comical on his round and boyish face. He wasn't more than forty but the facial hair added at least another five years to him. "We don't have to wait for Mr Henry Thyme. He insisted on seeing me on his own so we've already met this morning." He must have seen Henry very early because it was only eight o'clock and we'd spent at least twenty minutes waiting for him outside of the office while there was nobody but him inside. "Have either of you had a chance to speak to Mr Thyme?"

"No," Hugo and I said simultaneously.

"Oh, right," doctor Hammer sounded disappointed. "So," he started fiddling with one of a dozen pens that were thrown around the desk. "Would you like some coffee or tea?"

"No," Hugo said decisively as if the question had been offensive.

"No, thank you."

"Sure?"

"Unless you mean Irish coffee," Hugo laughed nervously, but as soon as he had said it doctor Hammer disappeared under his desk. Hugo and I looked at each other surprised when we heard Hammer loudly turning a key, the sound of glasses knocking against each other and the shutting of a cupboard with a bang. A bottle of whisky materialised in front of us, along with three tumblers and a pack of new and still packed whisky stones. "Here you are. It's twenty years old. I got it from one of my patients. Would you like me to pour it straight into your plastic cup or would you prefer it neat?"

"If you insist I'll pour myself some in a minute..." Hugo said calmly, "but could you tell us first why we are here so I can estimate how much I really need to drink."

Hammer giggled nervously. "My secretary left you a message last night, right?"

We nodded.

"And she said she was calling you regarding the paternity tests?"

"Yes," I said while Hugo sighed impatiently.

"Did she say something more?" Hammer's voice was getting thinner and thinner.

"Nada."

"Oh, I've forgotten you're Spanish. You don't have an accent. You

494

speak very good English. Did you fly here specially to see me or do you—"

"I'm not going to ask you to refund me the tickets if that's what you're afraid of," Hugo snapped. "Can you tell us finally why we're here?"

Hammer took a deep breath. "The DNA sample taken from Patrick proved he's your son." None of us said a word, and our doctor found the silence deeply uncomfortable. He gulped a whole glass of water in one go and then poured himself a generous amount of whisky into the same glass. "I'm not at work today," he explained seeing disapproval painted all over Hugo's face. "I've only got this meeting with you... and Mr Thyme before you, of course."

"Is this a joke?" Hugo looked around the room, "Is there a hidden camera somewhere here? I thought you wanted to talk about repeating the tests."

"Is that what Inga told you?"

"Who is Inga?" Hugo asked angrily.

"My secretary," he said meekly. "I'll have to have a word with her... Anyway..." he cleared his voice, took a sip of whisky and breathed out an unpleasant smell of petrol, "We've already repeated the tests using the old samples, which we normally store for a period of one year."

"Can you explain to us how you can make so many mistakes doing one, just one DNA test?" I could see Hugo was trying not to shout, but he couldn't help raising his voice, his fists clenched, face reddening. "First the boys were mine, then Henry's, now they're mine again. Mr Hammer..." he pointed his right forefinger at the doctor like a gun, "be ready for a lawsuit for punitive damages. I can also assure you that some people in this hospital are going to lose their licence!" Hugo stood up so abruptly that his chair almost fell over.

"Before you do anything Mr Tortilla, there's something—"

"Torilla for god's sake. It's like me calling you Mr Hamster."

Doctor Hammer put his hands into a pyramid shape and pressed them against his lips. "Please sit down, Mr Torilla. Trust me, it's better that you sit when you hear what I'm going to tell you right now." Hugo felt the seriousness in the doctor's voice and sat down obediently like a misbehaving student. "Patrick is your son, but Dominic is Mr Thyme's child."

Hugo bust out laughing and quickly hid his face in his hands, "Oh my god, and you've been ranked one of the best hospitals in the country…" Doctor Hammer listened patiently to Hugo telling him how his clinic must have bribed the right people to be considered the best in the UK. He understood that Hugo needed to shout his anger out. "So you still haven't worked out that the boys are twins? They were born at the same time and they came from the same mother… Jeez, it's not rocket science!"

"It's a rare case but not as rare as it seems to be… sometimes people never know about it because they don't do the paternity tests—"

"We did it and you still can't agree on who the father is. You seem to be so confused as if the choice is yours," Hugo interrupted him angrily.

"Patrick and Dominic are non-identical twins and they have different fathers."

"Is that possible?" Hugo rubbed his forehead and reached for the bottle of whisky, poured himself a full glass but didn't take even a sip.

I had no idea it was possible either! Was Dr Hammer about to make it official now that I was *a promiscuous lost* woman – because let's face the truth how many women sleep with more than one man during one cycle.

Doctor Hammer looked much more relaxed, "It can happen when during the same cycle two separate eggs get fertilized."

Hugo raised his eyebrows, "I don't understand. I mean…"

"For this to happen a woman has to have intercourse twice with two different men during one cycle and—"

Hugo laughed loudly looking relieved, "No, that's impossible. There was no threesome!" his whole body shook. I wasn't involved in anything like that with Henry. Even if I wanted to have… I wouldn't have chosen him…" he glanced at me looking terrified but also slightly offended… "I mean I understand that women can like him but what I'm trying to say is—"

"Mr Torilla, would you like to talk to Miss Eliot in private? I can leave you in my office for quarter of an hour and come back later."

"No," we shouted over Hammer's despair. He wanted to leave, he had had enough of explaining *the rare case scenario.*

"I wasn't even suggesting any... you know..." he threw his hands in the air and waved them in front of us. "For this to happen a woman normally has two separate sexual intercourses with two different men normally not more than six hours apart, very rarely more than twenty-four hours."

"You said Henry left you at the airport in London," Hugo's tone was now accusing.

"Would you like to talk in private," doctor Hammer repeated his offer and once again we rejected it with no hesitation.

"Friday morning and Saturday night, is it possible?"

"It's an even rarer case than I thought but yes it's absolutely possible. Patrick and Dominic don't have the same father."

"Unless..." Hugo looked at me with terror.

"Unless they switched one of my boys at birth?" I screamed covering my mouth with my trembling palm. "

Doctor Hammer hesitated for a moment, obviously he hadn't thought about that equally rare scenario. "Dominic is Henry's son and as you just admitted you had mhhh..."

"I slept with Henry, so have hundreds of other women as we recently found out," I shouted, and Hammer arched his eyebrows like he was trying to smooth his wrinkles while scrutinizing some notes.

"First of all, we never separate new-borns from their mothers, and secondly both Patrick and Dominic have your blood group Miss Eliot, A negative like you and Mr Torilla. Henry is A positive so the other woman would have had to give birth in the same hospital at the same time and have the same blood group as yours and then the children are switched by mistake. What's the chances?"

"What's the chances twins have different fathers? You told us that you made the first mistake because Henry and I have the same initials."

"Our staff took DNA samples from both twins but checked the

DNA of only one of them, and it was Patrick. That was the result that Miss Eliot received in the hospital. The problem occurred when we discovered that we hadn't recorded the results on our system. It would have been embarrassing for our clinic to call you later to ask *you* who the father was so we repeated the test but this time using Dominic's sample, which determined Henry to be the father. However, one of our nurses was adamant that we've told you Hugo was the father. Yes, I know Gretchen is a bit too nosy, but it turns out it can be useful sometimes," he giggled nervously. "She insisted on calling you all as soon as possible to tell you about the misunderstanding."

"So, the confusion over our initials was just an excuse?" Hugo took his first sip of whisky and screwed his face, he didn't like most spirits – they were too intense for his taste buds.

"Somebody genuinely thought that the same initials caused the confusion."

"If our case is not the first in the world, why didn't you check the DNA of both twins?" I got a feeling Hugo wasn't that happy after all to have a son with me.

"Our cleaning lady recently found the first paternity result behind the desk in our lab. When we went to file the result, an administrator picked up the discrepancy between the first and second tests. We then sent the DNA samples to three other clinics in the country and all the results came back the same. You've got a son Mr Torilla, my congratulations," Hammer passed us a thin paper file.

"I've got a son whose twin brother is not my son," Hugo glanced quickly on the papers in the file but I wasn't sure he was able to absorb any more information at that very moment.

"That's correct, but on the bright side the mother is still the same," Hammer said cheerfully but his smile quickly made space for embarrassment.

42

SATURDAY, 14 MAY
KRAKÓW

I peeled four large carrots, half a celery, two parsnips, three medium sized beetroots and a kilo of apples – everything that I'd bought on the sunny morning at a local market, located five minutes' walk from my new apartment. I threw some of the fruit and vegetables into an extractor that instantly separated juice from pulp and filled a transparent plastic jar with a colourful drink. It had been a while since I felt so full of energy – ready to squeeze from my life what was best, and discard everything else, which didn't live up to my new standards.

My happiness was only slightly disturbed by a malicious comment that I'd heard at the market. I was in Poland, once my second home, but as I was walking between some fruit stalls immersed in a language I hadn't heard for over a year, I felt I was in some exotic country. *I really needed to change my environment*, I thought smiling back to an elderly lady wearing a flowery headscarf and holding one bag full of oranges and one full of onions.

"How old are they?" asked the lady encouraged by my smile.

I looked at my sweet little boys in their red pram with a large new scratch on its handle, which was the result of an uncaring baggage handler at one of the airports. "They're three months but they grow so fast."

"Are they both three months? Are they twins?" the woman asked in utter disbelief.

"They're non-identical twins," I explained unmoved by the exaggerated astonishment painted all over her face.

"The dark-haired boy looks older. Does he eat more?" she gave me a friendly laugh.

"Possibly."

"Come on Helena…" an old woman with all grey hair pulled into a bun whispered to my old lady, "she must have adopted them. You know… just like Angelina Jolie she also wants to have kids from different parts of the world."

Patrick and Dominic didn't look like twins but they weren't strikingly not alike. The malicious cow obviously had some problems with her eyesight; although it wasn't stopping her from enjoying gossip magazines.

The boys were now dozing in their pram, which was standing on an ivory tiled floor in my new open-plan kitchen. Bright rays of afternoon sunshine were breaking through two wide floor-to-ceiling windows and dancing on the white gloss cupboards, shiny kitchen floor and wooden boards in the lounge. I switched the juicer on again waiting for the last drops of my drink to fill the plastic jar. I was making homemade juice every day to cleanse my body, boost my energy and mark this new chapter in my life with healthy and good living. When the machine stopped, the flat was filled with a peaceful silence. That was when I realised that the twins had completely ignored the sound of the juicer – a good dose of outside air and probably a bit of baby jetlag turned out to be very helpful.

I loved the apartment in Kraków, which *Travel the World* rented for me, and was about to become my new home for at least the next three months. The flat was located in a renovated townhouse ten minutes by tram from the very heart of the city, its magnificent Market

Square. There were only thirteen apartments in the whole building, and they were served by two wide and modern lifts. We had an underground car park, basement storage for every flat and a good-sized back garden, which I could see from my balcony – where I planned to do some of my writing. Since I'd moved in the day before I hadn't seen anybody in the garden except one ginger cat lying on perfectly mowed grass in the sun. I had three light double bedrooms with high ceilings and designer chandeliers. The smallest bedroom was waiting for all the guests who planned to visit me during my stay in Kraków: Hannah with her kids, Freya with her Peters, Atlanta with her husband, and of course my whole family. I couldn't wait to show them around Kraków – by doing that and writing a Kraków tourist guide I had a chance to perfectly mix business with pleasure – something I'd never done before but always wanted to. I was going to start my research as soon as I'd chosen a couple of baby-sitters from a group preselected by the magazine.

I sat down at a round glass table admiring a bunch of purple tulips, which along with a bottle of champagne and a box of locally made artisan chocolates were my welcome gift from *Travel the World*. I read again the note stuck into the flowers saying in gold font: *Welcome on board. We hope you enjoy your journey with us.* I smiled to myself and reached for a folded newspaper I'd bought at Heathrow, but I'd had no courage or desire to read any earlier. On its front page there was a photograph of Henry dressed in a dark suit and leaving a court in London with Fitzgerald-Spencer. The headline said: *Henry Thyme, one of the bosses of the Cheaters Gang sentenced to three years in prison.* I'd had no idea he was anybody's boss! At least he managed to make one of his dreams come true, being somebody important – being a boss – just a shame it was in the criminal world. He had his five minutes but he was about to pay a high price for it. Henry, however, was not going to waste any time. Provided he behaved well, the prison allowed him to use the Internet. My husband-not-to-be had some ambitious plans including writing a blog that he'd already named as *Henry from Cell.* Apparently, several companies had already agreed to pay for banners on his website. In the article Henry denied being bi-sexual but

admitted he was involved in numerous love affairs, often simultaneously. After some phone calls from English and American publishers
he was also considering writing a book about his adventurous love
life. I turned the page to a short article about Olympia White. She kept
claiming that she hadn't bought her university diplomas but nobody
believed her.

I closed the newspaper, rolled it and threw it into a bin fitted
within one of the kitchen cupboards. My parents were collecting all
articles about Henry, so I didn't have to store and read them just now,
I was desperate to have a Henry-break, but I knew they had them in
case I ever felt like knowing more about the man with whom I'd spent
five years of my life. I also tried not to reflect on the fact that one day I
would have to tell Dominic the truth about his father. It would be a
while until he could talk, read and comprehend the whole story so I
had some time to prepare myself for the inevitable.

I unplugged the juicer and dismantled it before giving it a wash.
The pulp from the fruit and vegetables covered the rolled newspaper.
I poured myself a whole glass and took a big sip to quickly absorb the
high dose of vitamins and new energy. *Yuck!* I poured the juice back
into the plastic jar and put it in the fridge. I wasn't ready yet for such
sacrifice in the name of health, youth and beauty – it had to wait. At
that particular moment I preferred to get some more energy from the
city buzz, and I suddenly felt like melting into the crowd and
becoming a tourist. I quickly put on some basic make-up and changed
my once-white T-shirt – now covered in fresh juice and baby milk –
for a light salmon blouse. The boys were still napping so I threw a
blanket over them and pushed the double pram into one of the two
wide elevators – something which was high on my list of priorities,
when looking for a flat. My enthusiasm to go and explore slightly
faded away when I had to fight with high pavement curbs but was
right back when I drove easily onto one of the modern trams.

"Welcome to Krakow's Market Square," I said to the boys bending
to the height of their smiley faces. They had woken up right in the
middle of the square to the still bright sun and a young guy playing on
a guitar while loudly singing some ballads in English, his eyes closed

and right foot tapping to the sound of his music. My sons didn't look particularly impressed by the scenery but they seemed to like the man singing his heart out. Before my first trip to Madrid I used to come to Krakow more regularly – or enough to take it for granted and not appreciate the city as much as it deserved. For the very first time I was really listening to the sound of carriages pulled by white horses riding through the square – their horses and drivers dressed up like for a parade, creating a bit of a fairy tale. I stopped next to the flower market to breathe in fresh scents and feel like I was in a French perfume factory. I bought a pretzel, not from a food truck but from a transparent plastic box on wheels – I'd never before enjoyed the sweet and salty taste so much. It wasn't high season so the square was busy with people choosing it as a shortcut and rushing through it, while others were strolling around with their big cameras on their necks or phones glued to their fingers. The vast space gave me an incredible sense of freedom to breathe using my whole chest. The boys were quiet – they were absorbing all the intense colours and sounds surrounding them. I sat down in one of the square's outdoor dining areas bordered by potted plants. I had time and a certain peace of mind enjoying watching people passing by – people who were totally ambivalent to my existence.

"Is the seat free?" a male voice interrupted my contemplation, speaking English.

"That really depends," I said not taking my eyes away from the market square.

"On what?" he asked gently.

"Depends on the purpose of you sitting down next to me, when there're so many other free seats."

"And if I said I would like to have a glass of wine with you and… and flirt with you for the rest of the afternoon?"

"Flirting, picking me up and the like – none of these are currently on the menu."

"Can I know why?"

My eyes wandered towards the pram parked just next to my rattan chair, "There are two reasons, one is currently dosing after being overwhelmed by this place, and the other one is trying to shamelessly chew his foot."

"I would like to get to know the two Reasons."

"Then take a seat Hugo," I looked at him intensely staring at me, feeling at the same time wonderfully safe and awfully threatened. He sat down next to us, his arm slightly touching mine.

* * *

"I'm glad to hear you know my name but well... I am quite famous. Not because of my looks, just in case you're wondering but—"

"I haven't been wondering actually."

"Oh," he said pretending to be deeply disappointed. "And what's your name?"

"Olivia," I sighed.

"Simply Olivia? I thought every Polish-English person has at least three names."

"I see you like stereotypes, and your flirting... well, I think you're a bit out of the game."

"I normally don't have any need to flirt... with my charm...I'm sure you understand," he smirked. "Besides my flirting might be amateurish but I'm afraid you would be disappointed if I stopped."

"Your modesty is killing me. I think I might fall in love," I laughed.

"I thought you'd already done so," he snapped which was like a glass of water on my over-sunned head. "Luckily for you, you're very pretty so I'm open for any offers you want to make me... I wouldn't sit next to you if you weren't pretty so I hope you're flattered."

"What about the two other Reasons that you're here for? I thought you being here had nothing to do with my looks."

"If you didn't have the looks I would contact you by phone. I wouldn't want to ruin my image."

"Yeah? And what currently is your image?"

"A local Casanova," he said without hesitation.

I chortled. "Since when did you become local?"

"Since last night and I'm going to stay here for a while..."

"How long?" I snapped abruptly.

"You never know how to express your happiness. Maybe a month, maybe two, three or even longer. It depends..."

"On what?"

"Would you like something to eat or do you just need the drinks menu?" we were interrupted by a young waitress in a tight blue dress.

"Can I have a double espresso?"

"And Russian *pierogi*?" I asked looking at him. "You should really try them."

He nodded.

"One latte, one double espresso and two Russian pierogi please," I said and the girl wrote quickly in her notebook then walked away.

"My step-father is Russian and I'm sure the pierogi have nothing to do with Russia."

"Who cares?" I smiled. "So, what does *how long* you stay here depend on?"

"I'm going to look around," he said mysteriously. "Who knows, maybe I'll open another Hugo TorTilla here."

"Fantastic," I said without enthusiasm.

"I told you," he said with a massive grin.

"I don't understand," I frowned my eyebrows.

"I told you that you would be disappointed when I suddenly stopped my amateurish flirting," Hugo said with a smug face. "You know the truth. You know it depends on nobody but you and whether you give us another chance."

"Hugo, please listen to me—"

"You don't have to ask me to listen to you, I always do," he snapped.

"Now is not a good moment for any more change. I need to focus on my boys and my new job. You need more time with Patrick but not with me... What if we're actually a bad match and... I just... I don't feel like I could cope with more drama in my life."

"Drama? Am I your drama, that's what I am for you?"

"You know that's not what I mean. The problem is that if we don't work together then—"

"Henry was your drama," he said sounding hurt. "What we've got together, I admit, it's been tough at times but it's not been a drama."

"Then let's say I'm currently enjoying living in a world where everything seems to be in the right place at the right time, instead of being surrounded by chaos. I'm not ready for a relationship."

"Right, like love is all about being ready," he said pulling his hand through his dark bushy hair. "You still haven't realised it, have you – life is constant chaos – and any attempt to put something that by definition is a constant change into an undisturbed order is going to end up as an utter fiasco. Should we happen to be together, I agree, it will never ever be straightforward, but it's no different if you decided to date somebody else. I'm not here to disturb the order in your life."

"But you could if—"

"To your despair you'll never be able to fast-forward your life to see what happens if you make certain decisions, and then go back where you started and change your choices."

"Hugo listen—"

"I wish you listened to me sometimes. You used to say that I could have logged out of your life at any time, but now when Patrick is my son, I can't do it anymore. And I also care about his brother and I care about you!"

"Hugo, the fact that Patrick is your biological son doesn't suddenly make us one big happy family." I shouted just as the waitress brought us pierogi. She tried to leave us alone so quickly that the two plates nearly crashed on the table, and some of their fat landed on my silky blouse. The girl apologised and walked away.

"The fact that Henry broke your heart and let you down doesn't mean you can treat me like this." I didn't answer that, I preferred to watch pigeons constantly landing and taking off from the square. I wondered how they never bumped into each other without any air traffic control. They knew exactly what to do and it was all intuitive. "I'm glad we haven't automatically become one big family because I want to have nothing to do with Mr Henry Thyme."

"You can avoid him but he will always be the father of your..." I laughed. "God it's so freaking complicated!"

"The father of my son's brother," he said as if it had been the most normal and logical thing in the whole world. "He is but you're not being given a family. You make a family and constantly work on the bonds within it so it can survive… Olivia, you and me, and the boys… it can work. The only thing stopping us now is you."

"For the very first time in a while – I feel I've got control over my life… and please don't give me a lecture on not being able to be truly in control of your life and don't say it's only an illusion. I'm not afraid of living on my own, without men in my life. I'm not afraid of facing the future all by myself."

"And that's why you're wrong – now when you're not afraid to be alone, this is exactly when you're ready for a relationship."

"But I don't want anybody to stop me from going in the right direction…"

"I'm not Henry. I'm not going to be in your way – whatever you want to do or wherever you want to go."

"It sounds wonderful and right now makes sense but it's not that easy in the position we're in…"

"And since when is *easy* the best choice?"

"Have you even had time to accustom yourself to this whole crazy situation? Hugo, I'm a mother of twin boys, who have got two different fathers – one of them is my ex currently in jail, and the other…"

"The other was a one-night stand."

I pretended not to hear what he had just said. "Have you thought about it? How will you feel telling people that only one of the twins is your son? Or maybe you want to lie in the name of our relationship? We don't have the luxury of starting something and seeing what happens. There will be difficult consequences…"

"There always will be," he snapped. "Why would I plan my life around what other people think? They normally don't know how to handle their own lives."

"I'm sorry Hugo but the only way for us to have a decent relationship that doesn't involve any drama is to become friends and focus on what's best for the boys."

Hugo didn't seem to be moved in the slightest by my dramatic statement. He finished his pierogi in silence and glanced at a bulky plastic bag that was lying next to his feet.

"Have you been shopping?" I asked only to change the topic.

"Not much," he said looking into the distance.

"So, what do you have in that bag?"

"Feather pillows."

"Have you rented a flat without pillows?"

"I'm staying in a hotel."

"Is there something wrong with their pillows," I asked intrigued thinking I really didn't know him that well, "or have you become one of those people with a germs phobia and—"

"I bought one for you too."

"Seriously, there's nothing wrong with Polish pillows, on the contrary they export many so if you brought some from Spain – you'll need to check because they might've been made here anyway."

"Today is International Pillow Fight Day. It starts in exactly…" he looked at his watch, "in ten minutes on the other side of the square, and you're going to celebrate it with me."

"And what about the boys? We don't even know if they're allergic to feathers or not." Hugo smiled and without a word reached into his pocket for his mobile. "What are you doing? I'm not going to leave my children with a stranger, with an unchecked nanny or—"

"What about their uncle?"

"Which uncle?" I arched my eyebrows and opened my mouth fossilizing like that for a moment.

"Stefano came with me to see his nephew and his little brother."

"The last time he saw me, he didn't seem to like me anymore," I said sounding like a sulky teenager.

"Well, I don't think he's going to be your BGFF but—"

"My what?"

Hugo rolled his eyes, "I can't believe I need to explain it to you, like that's not every woman's dream. BGFF is Best Gay Friend Forever… Anyway, you're not likely to be best buddies but there's still a chance that you two… will be just fine."

Stefano was with us within five minutes, it turned out he had been waiting in a coffee shop around a corner for a phone call from his brother. He gave me a warm hug and congratulated us on having two cute boys. Burying the hatchet with that guy was far easier than I'd expected.

I felt like I was trapped in a snow globe that had been shaken by a curious kid. The Market Square within a few seconds became a paradise for those who didn't mind feathers getting into their hair and noses or tickling them on their backs. For those allergic to feathers it was a vision of hell. I'd never seen a fight that made people laugh so loudly, making their bellies shake like jelly, even when they were the ones getting hit. White feathers were falling out of the sky and flying above people's heads like clouds tormented by wind, Hugo and I were covered in them from the soles of our shoes to the tip of our heads. I didn't know whether we were particularly aggressive fighters or whether Hugo had bought some particularly poor-quality pillows but they exploded quicker than anybody else's. Feathers appeared glued to our clothes like we were covered in butter or freshly painted.

"I don't remember when I had so much fun," I shouted into Hugo's ear. "But what's the purpose of it?"

"Does there have to be any purpose? Can't you just have fun without looking for meaning in it?"

"Is that your new motto now?"

"No," he said taking a strand of my hair along with a feather from my forehead. "Sometimes it's best to focus on what you feel instead of trying to form the surrounding world like some meaningful puzzle."

* * *

Hugo encouraged with my current good mood invited himself to my apartment for dinner. While I was putting the boys to bed he was shopping at the nearby market. He was soon back with a bottle of Spanish wine and a whole bag of vegetables.

"Here you go," he passed me a glass of white wine that he first tasted himself. "Now, sit and relax. I'm not an amazing cook but I've recently mastered a few vegetarian meals. I'm going to make courgette and feta soup, as well as stuffed peppers, any objections or allergies?" I shook my head thinking how nice it was to have somebody making dinner for me. "Have you got any butter?" he asked with his head in the fridge.

"I bought some this morning."

"And are you sure you haven't eaten it because I can't see any."

I moved reluctantly from my comfy chair. Hugo as usual was looking for something only with his eyes as though touching anything in the fridge was too much of an effort. I stood in front of the open fridge, moved the ketchup, a couple of yoghurts and my failure-juice to display a whole new block of butter.

"Oh, thank you," he said surprised as if I was a magician. "What's that in the plastic jar?"

"Vegetable juice. It doesn't taste as good as it looks."

"What's it made of?"

"Carrot, parsnip, apple, celery and beetroot. I know what you're thinking – it's easy to predict it would taste awful. I took me an hour to make it including washing the juicer, and now I have to force myself to drink it."

"Can I try?"

"If you insist," I said and passed him a glass. As I had expected he screwed his face in disgust.

"Do you have *jengibre*?"

"Ginger? I think so... Do you want to finally make your grandmother's ginger cake that you've always been talking about so much?" I found the ginger myself in the fridge, and Hugo without saying a word walked towards my juicer. From an entire ginger he managed to squeeze one fourth of a glass, which he poured into my juice mixture and stirred well with a metal spoon.

"Try now."

Initially I took a tiny little sip not believing that ginger would make any significant difference – but it did. "Weird, I can't taste the parsnip or beetroot at all. It's like a totally different juice. It tastes great but is still healthy – this morning I stopped believing it was even possible."

"Sometimes just the right ingredient can change everything," he said looking straight into my eyes. I felt shivers down my spine.

"And I don't have to change anything else," I said questioningly.

He nodded. "You add love... "he cleared his throat with a smile. "I mean ginger and everything suddenly changes and make sense," he was saying this while getting closer and closer to me, making my heart race a hundred miles an hour. "I love you Olivia Eliot."

"If it's true why haven't you said it earlier? Is it because you found out that Patrick—"

"I've told you many times in many different ways but you never listen."

When he kissed me, the apartment span like a carousel. It was so fresh and intense like our first kiss on the Plaza Mayor. I could swear I heard Spanish rock playing in the background.

"Hugo Torilla once again you just appear and rock my whole world."

"And you don't like it?" he asked with a beaming smile.

"I think I've learned to live with it," I laughed and he looked at me with anticipation. "I don't want anybody else to rock my world. You've got a certain and unique ability to sweep me off my feet so keep doing it because it feels amazing."

"I plan to do it for the rest of your life."

THE END

Printed in Great Britain
by Amazon